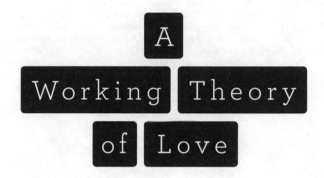

A Working Theory of Love

SCOTT HUTCHINS

THE PENGUIN PRESS

New York

2012

THE PENGUIN PRESS
Published by the Penguin Group
Penguin Group (USA) Inc., 375 Hudson Street, New York, New York 10014, U.S.A. •
Penguin Group (Canada), 90 Eglinton Avenue East, Suite 700, Toronto, Ontario, Canada
M4P 2Y3 (a division of Pearson Penguin Canada Inc.) • Penguin Books Ltd, 80 Strand,
London WC2R 0RL, England • Penguin Ireland, 25 St. Stephen's Green, Dublin 2,
Ireland (a division of Penguin Books Ltd) • Penguin Books Australia Ltd, 250 Camberwell
Road, Camberwell, Victoria 3124, Australia (a division of Pearson Australia Group
Pty Ltd) • Penguin Books India Pvt Ltd, 11 Community Centre, Panchsheel Park,
New Delhi – 110 017, India • Penguin Group (NZ), 67 Apollo Drive, Rosedale,
Auckland 0632, New Zealand (a division of Pearson New Zealand Ltd) •
Penguin Books (South Africa) (Pty) Ltd, 24 Sturdee Avenue, Rosebank,
Johannesburg 2196, South Africa

Penguin Books Ltd, Registered Offices:
80 Strand, London WC2R 0RL, England

First published in 2012 by The Penguin Press,
a member of Penguin Group (USA) Inc.

Selection from *The Essential Turing: The Ideas That Gave Birth to the Computer Age*,
edited by B. Jack Copeland (2004). By permission of Oxford University Press.

Publisher's Note
This is a work of fiction. Names, characters, places, and incidents either are the product of
the author's imagination or are used fictitiously, and any resemblance to actual persons,
living or dead, business establishments, events, or locales is entirely coincidental.

LIBRARY OF CONGRESS CATALOGING IN PUBLICATION DATA

Hutchins, Scott.
A working theory of love / Scott Hutchins.
p. cm.
ISBN 978-1-59420-505-7
1. Artificial intelligence—Fiction. 2. Divorced men—Fiction. 3. Fathers and sons—
Fiction. 4. Man-woman relationships—Fiction. 5. Interpersonal relations—
Fiction. 6. San Francisco (Calif.)—Fiction. I. Title.
PS3608.U84W67 2012
813'.6—dc23
2012018341

Printed in the United States of America
1 3 5 7 9 10 8 6 4 2

DESIGNED BY AMANDA DEWEY

Shikha

definite until we have

It is natural that we should

technique to be used in our

ability that an engineer or team of

which works, but whose manner of opera-

bed by its constructors because they have

ly experimental. Finally, we wish to exclude

n in the usual manner.

—ALAN TURING

A FEW DAYS AGO, a fire truck and an ambulance pulled up to my apartment building on the south hill overlooking Dolores Park. A group of paramedics got out, the largest of them bearing a black chair with red straps and buckles. They were coming for my upstairs neighbor, Fred, who is a drinker and a hermit, but who I've always held in a strange esteem. I wouldn't want to trade situations: he spends most of his time watching sports on the little flat-screen television perched at the end of his kitchen table. He smokes slowly and steadily (my ex-wife used to complain about the smell), glued to tennis matches, basketball tournaments, football games—even soccer. He has no interest in the games themselves, only in the bets he places on them. His one regular visitor, the postman, is also his bookie. Fred is a former postal employee himself.

As I say, I wouldn't want to trade situations. The solitariness and sameness of his days isn't alluring. And yet he's always been a model of self-sufficiency. He drinks too much and smokes too much, and if he eats at all he's just heating up a can of Chunky. But he goes and fetches all of this himself—smokes, drink, Chunky—swinging his stiff legs down the hill to the corner store and returning with one very laden paper bag. He then climbs the four flights of stairs to his apartment—a dirtier, more spartan copy of mine—where he lives alone, itself no small feat in the brutal San Francisco rental market. He's always cordial on the steps, and even in the desperate few months after my divorce, when another neighbor suggested a revolving door for my apartment (to accommodate high traffic—a snide comment), Fred gave me a polite berth. He knocked on my door once, but only to tell me that I should let him know if I could hear him banging around upstairs. He knew he had "a heavy footfall." I took this to mean, we're neighbors and that's it, but you're all right with me. Though maybe I read too much into it.

When the paramedics got upstairs that day, there was the sound of muted voices and then Fred let loose something between a squawk and a scream. I stepped into the hall, and by this time the paramedics were bringing him down, shouting at him, stern as drill sergeants. *Sir, keep your arms in. Sir, keep your arms in. We will tie down your arms, sir.* The scolding seemed excessive for an old man, but when they brought him around the landing, strapped tight in the stair stretcher, I could see the problem. He was grabbing for the balusters, trying to stop his descent. His face was wrecked, his milky eyes searching and terrified, leaking tears.

"I'm sorry, Neill," he said when he saw me. He held his hands out to me, beseeching. "I'm sorry. I'm so sorry."

I told him not to be ridiculous. There was nothing to be sorry about. But he kept apologizing as the paramedics carried him past my door, secured to his medical bier.

Apparently he had fallen two days earlier and broken his hip. He had only just called about it. For the previous forty-eight hours he'd dragged himself around the floor, waiting for God knows what: The pain to go away? Someone to knock? I found out where he was staying, and he's already had surgery and is recuperating in a nice rehab facility. So that part of the story has all turned out well. But I keep thinking about that apology. *I'm sorry, I'm so sorry.* What was he apologizing for but his basic existence in this world, the inconvenience of his living and breathing? He was disoriented, of course, but the truth holds. He's not self-sufficient; he's just alone. This revelation shouldn't matter so much, shouldn't shift my life one way or the other, but it's been working on me in some subterranean manner. I seem to have been relying on Fred's example. My father, not otherwise much of an intellectual, had a favorite quote from Pascal: the sole cause of Man's unhappiness is his inability to sit quietly in his room. I had thought of Fred as someone who sat quietly in his room.

Not everyone's life will be a great love story. I know that. My own "starter" marriage dissolved a couple of years ago, and aside from those first few months of the revolving door I've spent much of the time since alone. I've had the occasional stretch of dating this or that young lady and sought the occasional solace of one-night stands, which *can* bring solace, if the attitude is right. I've ramped my drinking sharply up and then sharply down. I make the grooves in my life that I roll along. Bachelorhood, I've learned, requires routine. Small rituals that honor the unseen moments. I mean this without self-pity. Who should care that I pour exactly two glugs of cream into my first coffee but only one into my second (and last)? No one—yet those three glugs are the very fabric of my morning.

Routine is why I can't drink too much, and why I've paradoxically become less spontaneous as a thirty-six-year-old bachelor than I was as an even younger married man. I feed the cat at seven. I cook a breakfast taco—scrambled egg, slice of pepper jack, corn tortilla, salsa verde—and make stovetop espresso. I eat standing. Then the cat sits in my lap until 7:40 while I go through email, examining the many special offers that appear in my inbox overnight. One-day sales; free trials; twenty percent off. I delete these notes, grab a shower, and am out the door at eight, a fifty-minute commute door to door, San Francisco south to Menlo Park.

Work is Amiante Systems, a grandiose linguistic computer project. As an enterprise, it's not perfectly designed—the founder thought "Amiante" was Latin for magnetism; my ex-wife, Erin, pointed out it's actually French for asbestos—but it's well funded and amenable. There are three employees, and together we're training a sophisticated program—based on a twenty-year diary from the "Samuel Pepys of the South" (so called by the obscure historical journal that published the one and only excerpt)—to convincingly process natural language. To converse, in other words. To talk. The diaries are a mountain of thoughts and interactions, over five thousand pages of attitudes, stories, turns of phrase, life philosophies, medical advice. The idea is that the hidden connections in the entries, aka their personality, will give us a coherence that all previous conversing projects—hobby exercises, "digital assistants"—lack. The diarist, an Arkansas physician, was in fact my late father, which is how in the twisting way of these things I have the job. The diaries are my legal property. Still, my boss has warmed to me. I know little about computers—I spent my twenties writing ad copy—but of the three of us I'm the only native speaker of English, and I've been helpful in making the program sound more like a real person, albeit a very confused one.

When I get home from work, I feed the cat and make some dinner for myself. I sit on my new couch. If it's a weekday, I have a glass of wine and watch a movie. If it's a weekend I might meet up with an old pal, or a new one (though I have few new ones, and fewer old ones), or I might have plans with a lady friend (always plans, never anything left to the last minute). Occasionally, I go to a local watering hole where the bartenders are reliable. I consider this an indulgence, but little indulgences are also key to bachelor life. Parking is one—for three hundred dollars a month I avoid endlessly orbiting my block—but I also have my magazines, my twice-monthly housekeeper, my well-stocked bar, and my heated foot-soaking tub. If I feel overworked, I send out my clothes to wash-and-fold. Twice a year I might schedule a deep-tissue massage. I order in dinner weekly, and sometimes—if I'm feeling resolute—I'll take a book to a nice restaurant and dine solo.

I grew up in the South, but made my home here in San Francisco for what are called lifestyle reasons. I enjoy the rain-washed streets, the tidy view of downtown, the earnest restaurant trends (right now it's offal), the produce spilling from corner stores, farmers' markets, pickup trucks. There are many like me here—single people beached in life—and I make passing friends, passing girlfriends. Right after my marriage ended I went on a crazed apartment hunt in Silicon Valley, closer to work, but soon saw what would become of me. I would disappear into my house, my housework, lawn work. I would become a specter, and this is the great peril of bachelorhood—that you'll become so airy and insubstantial that people will peer straight through you.

I took a different tack (in part inspired by Fred). I decided to stay in the city, in the very apartment that Erin and I shared, and learn bachelor logic. It's a clean system, with little time for sentimentality. It understands that as a bachelor you are a permanent *in between*. This is no time for conventions. When it comes to breakfast, to social life, to love, you must privilege the simple above the complicated. There's nothing cruel about this. The bachelors I've met—temporary friends—have been nice guys. I've never been able to stomach men who refer to women as bitches, teases—though these men do exist, in San Francisco as in all the world. It's not even their misogyny that bothers me: it's their self-betrayal. They are the inept, the lost, the small. The successful bachelors—the ones without bitterness—have taught me many things: to schedule a social life, to never use both a spoon and a fork when either will do. I know a guy who sleeps in a hammock; a guy who allows no organic matter in his apartment, including food; a guy so sure of his childless bachelorhood he underwent a vasectomy (he gave me the recipe for the breakfast taco). Another bachelor once told me about his strategy for navigating the doldrums of physical isolation. When he wasn't in the mood to dance or meet anyone datable, when he just wanted a sweet night with a strange body, a lee in which to pitch the Bedouin tent of his soul, he checked into one of the city's big youth hostels. I said it seemed creepy, but he pointed out that creepy was irrelevant. It was ethical, and that was all that mattered. He was looking for a temporary balm; travelers would be more likely to share his goal. He wasn't preying on anyone; in fact, he was offering his thorough knowledge of the city and his open pocketbook. The only shady business was that you had to concoct a mild alibi to explain why you're checked into a youth hostel. You have elderly relatives visiting; your plumbing is out. Or you can bring your passport as your I.D. and pretend you're traveling.

"It's a melding of desired outcomes," he said. All I could do was marvel at the performance of bachelor logic.

But is it nonsense? Will this friend, this good man, end up strapped to a stair stretcher, hands grasping for his rented walls?

I'm so sorry, Neill.

My father—I stopped calling him Dad when he committed suicide; it seemed too maudlin—would have found a specific and obvious moral to the story. He was such a traditionalist I'm half surprised he didn't go about in period dress. He liked to cite the quotation on his parents' grave marker, "Magnificence there was, but of comfort there was little, and, being unknown, it was unmissed." It's from *Ivanhoe*. We're from an old Southern family and are Roman Catholic to boot, so he probably would have insisted I do my duty, which usually was some version of "living for others." I was in college when he killed himself. I took it hard, but it freed me from a certain worry, a locked-in way of seeing the world. I came to California, where I relinquished my duties as a "scion" of an "old" family. (I could just as easily put "duties" and "family" in scare quotes.) Instead, I took up the responsibilities of the good citizen: recycling, riding my bike, giving money to environmental groups and the Glide Memorial shelter. I belong to the SFMOMA and the Film Society. These are my adjustments, and in many ways they've been solid. As good as my brother's white picket fence life in Michigan, his relentless quest for the banal. And, I fear, better than my mother's attempt to both keep and escape the old house in Arkansas, a compromise that keeps her on a loop of educational tours, cruising the world's unpopular coastlines.

My entire life, to my father, would be incomprehensible. Beneath mention. But my father's diary—Dr. Bassett, as it's referred to at Amiante—will engage any question. Since it's a pretty basic program, a searchable version of the diaries with a few conversational tricks, I can't say it *understands* anything. It can't pursue a thought or even distinguish among who's talking to it. (It doesn't know, for instance, that I'm Dr. Bassett's son.) But sometimes I throw in a few words, and the computer—in his Magic 8-Ball way— returns a phrase that has some hidden jolt of insight. This morning we had this exchange:

> frnd1: should i stay in or go out tonight?
> drbas: fridays are friend days
> frnd1: today is thursday, but that's a nice thought
> drbas: ????

If I say more than one thing—use "and" or "but"—he often comes up empty-handed.

frnd1: your sentiment was a nice thought
drbas: how do you feel about my sentiment being a nice
      thought?
frnd1: just fine. so should i stay in or go out tonight?
drbas: you've moped long enough. it's time you enjoyed
      yourself.

I had to correct his response: nothing in our earlier conversation hinted that I had been moping. Nevertheless, he's right. Outside, dusk is coming down like a cleaver. If I can't shake myself from this couch, I'll be trapped, looking out on the black, unforgiving city of my thirties. The street below— as it so often does—will rattle with distant laughter.

AT FISHERMAN'S WHARF—a quick taxi ride away—I watch the Ghirardelli sign flicker to life. My companions are a tall blonde, Rachel, and a pint-sized brunette, Lexie, from Tel Aviv. Neither is a great beauty, but they have the attraction of youth. As they should, since I met them at the youth hostel. It was as easy as my friend had described—Let's go see the city, I said. Okay, they said. Exactly what I came here for, and yet the whole exchange put acid in my stomach. I should have chosen a simpler alibi—that my plumbing was out—rather than posing as a tourist. But I wanted that feeling of dislocation and here it is: the San Francisco of postcards. The smell of steaming crabs is in the chill air, and the storefronts of this great T-shirt souk glimmer platinum in the dusk. Fog cocoons the Golden Gate Bridge, and Alcatraz sits lit and lonely in the gray water. We couldn't ask for much better if a cable car bell rang, and presently one does—king, king. The Hyde and Larkin Street line.

The girls are lightly dressed, as if we're hitting the clubs in Miami: short skirts with Ugg boots, tube tops skintight and grimacing. They shiver.

The blonde, Rachel—the more handsome but less cute of the two—reddens and speckles from the gusting cold.

"What a view," I say. It's their first time in San Francisco.

"It's awesome," Rachel says.

"I can't believe this is fucking California," Lexie says, rubbing her arms. She's round and powdered and young, but she has the deep, raspy voice of an emphysema patient. "So where's the party around here?"

"Can't we just look at the scenery for three seconds?" Rachel says.

"This is our last city." Lexie casts a meaningful look my way. I recognize it: she wants rid of me. I must beam gloominess.

"And you want to do the same thing in this city you do in every city," her friend says.

"It's worked so far, right?" Lexie barks. "We've had fun, right?"

Rachel shakes her head, looking disgusted.

"I'm surprised you're traveling all by yourself," Lexie says.

All by yourself. I test the words with my tongue, like an extracted tooth. "There are pleasures to solitude," I say.

"Sounds like something a loser with no friends would say."

Good point. "A loser with no friends can still be right," I say.

"Are you one of these married guys?" Lexie asks. "That sneaks around looking for sex?"

"I'm not married."

"You got a walk like a married person," she says. She locks her arms in her shoulder sockets and hops robotically down the sidewalk, like a wind-up toy.

"I think you may be confused," I say, "between married and disabled."

"She's confused about a lot of things," Rachel says.

"She's confused about a lot of things," Lexie says in a baby voice—a baby with black lung—screwing up her mouth.

The wind picks up, blowing mist from the crab stands, steaming our faces. I remind myself that I'm supposed to be having fun. This is supposed to be a lark, an exultation of liberty. My boss, Henry Livorno, often insists that there's no empirical difference between seeming and being. It's the concept (operationalism) that our project is based on, but it's also solid wisdom for tonight. If I can make things *seem* fun, then maybe they'll *be* fun.

"How does a single person walk?" I ask.

The girls ignore me. Lexie looks off into the distance as if far away she might catch sight of the people she seeks. Rachel's attention is on a nearby seafood stand. She watches the portly attendant adjust his toque and then remove a series of steaming white crabs from the boiling pot.

"Those things are huge," she says.

"They're Dungeness crabs," I say. She has a willowy dancer's figure and wears no makeup, but her clubbing clothes don't flatter her. They fit awkwardly, like a disguise. "You want to try one?"

"Rachel's kosher," Lexie says. She gives me a nasty grin.

"You shouldn't push me tonight," Rachel says, hugging her elbows. "I'm cold, and I'm about ready to go back."

"Mark Twain once said . . ." I begin.

"It *is* fucking cold," Lexie says, serious now. "You want to change?"

"Yeah, probably," Rachel says.

This would not be the first time an evening slipped away from me. I'm not one of these men blessed with pure desires, who to the game of life bring the virtue of single-mindedness. But I think of Fred and I rally. I invite the girls under the awning of the closest T-shirt shop—OLDE TIME SOURDOUGH SOUVENIRS—and offer to buy them matching sweatshirts with funny names. This will keep them warm. And out.

"I'm trying to not, like, acquire," Rachel says, apologetic. "Simplify, simplify."

"You're reading Thoreau?" I ask, and I get a new look from her—one of surprise, maybe gratitude.

AT A DIM BAR in the Marina, we glow vaguely in our baby blue sweatshirts. Lexie is David. Rachel is José. I'm Gina. The black carpet smells of beer, of which I've had a few. I'm feeling better. The air is hazy with something—maybe there's a smoke machine hidden somewhere. Rachel and I sit on stools. Lexie holds on to the tabletop, which is almost chin-level for her. She has a goofy French manicure, nails pearly as plastic, square as chisels. There's some sort of hump-hump music playing, and she gyrates reluctantly, as if someone talked her into it. She wouldn't charm Herod out of the Baptist's head, but she demonstrates four or five basic hip motions used in intercourse. Who is this girl? She must be a type of some sort, a type I'm not familiar with. She's clearly a conformist—an attitude that gets a worse rap than it ought to; what's more egalitarian than conformism?—but I don't know what she's conforming to. There's probably a TV show that I, alone in this bar, have not seen. A hit TV show. Something that plugs into the dreams of this crowd—she's getting plenty of attention from men at tables, men at the bar, men in the shadows by the jukebox. Marina types— taller than average, who hit the gym often, who wear pointy shoes. A more rarefied breed of conformist.

Lexie turns to me, mid-gyration. "Are you going to buy us more drinks?" she shouts.

"You don't sound like you're from Tel Aviv."

"Because I speak English? What are you, an anti-Semite?"

Rachel reaches into her travel neck pouch, which she wears as a purse, and directs a twenty toward Lexie. "Go yourself."

"This isn't enough," Lexie says. "I want a Sambuca shot."

I hold out another twenty. "Get whatever you like," I say.

"You're fishy," Lexie says. "I think he's like a rufie rapist."

"Look," Rachel says. She holds her palm flat on the top of her beer bottle, miming its undruggableness.

"You know me and her are girlfriends," Lexie says. "And I don't mean friends that are girls." To demonstrate her point, she makes a remarkably crude gesture with two fingers and her tongue. Rachel has a fit of coughing. I think she's horrified. "So I don't know where you think this is going, but it's not going there."

I indicate the bar. "Don't forget to tip."

Lexie pats Rachel's hand over the beer bottle. "Until I'm here again," she says, walking backwards into the crowd. She points at her own eyes, then points at me. *I'm watching you.*

"She knows to tip." Rachel watches her friend, frowning. Outside, Rachel's eyes were crystalline green and bright, but here they're dark and dull, the color of old limes. Her skin is waxy white; a broad brush of young blood runs from cheek to jaw. Blood, as my father once said, is both vital and mortal. He was a physician, after all. "We're not from Israel—we're from New Jersey. And we're not girlfriends. I don't know why she needs to say that shit."

I understand. "It's fun to shed ourselves once in a while."

"I thought the goal was to find yourself." She thrums her fingers on the table, pushes her sprung hair back. "I don't mean to mess with your mojo. I know she's hot."

I'm surprised. Have I betrayed an attraction to her friend? *Am* I attracted to her friend? I watch Lexie waving her arms at the bartender, her skirt pulled up high over her slightly wide thighs. She does have the argument of simplicity.

"What makes you think I'm interested in her?" I ask.

Rachel drinks from her beer. "She has really great boobs. They're so round. And they're real."

"Better question: what makes you think she's interested in me?"

"You'd be about middle of the pack for her."

Middle of the pack. I don't know if I've ever been described more accurately. This probably means bad things for Rachel's own attitude toward me. She's been nice, but maybe too nice. She seems the type to have a boyfriend. I watch Lexie coming back with three bottles clutched in one hand and three shots balanced on the other, all conveyed with the care of an offering.

"Americans yell so much." She flips back her hair. "And just stand around."

"People don't stand in Tel Aviv?" I ask.

She gives me a glimmer of a smile, the first of the evening. It's almost flirtatious. "They dance, dummy. We have the best clubs. Dome. Vox."

"Will you put me up if I visit?"

She shrugs and looks out into the crowd, resuming her hip motions. If she's interested in me, she's not very interested. Or I've pressed my case too forcefully. Or she's just trying to make me jealous. In the darkness, she scans other applicants, not exactly observing them, but observing them observing her. The men's faces are bland and hostile. They look at Lexie, at Rachel, at the other women, with a free-floating menace, as if they could easily slit their throats. It's all playacting, a script borrowed from a vampire romance, the savage tamed by a woman's wiles. And yet there's a sweetness to the convention. It feels like safer ground than the hipsters and the humanists—my people—who booze and jaw to establish a plausible case: we *could* care deeply about this person, we just happen not to. Here, there are rules to the game, as clear as if posted next to the dartboard, and the whole enterprise is aided by an honest offering of the wares. Clothes cling to breasts, to delts, to glutes, to abs. They know we're all real estate, and while they probably hold the eventual hope of making love's Ultimate Purchase, they're clearly open to renting. It's all disconcertingly logical, this straight-arrow wisdom of the meat marketplace.

"You can stay with me," Rachel says. "We'll party at the Dome and the Box."

"Is that one place or two?"

"You'll have to ask the mayor here."

"I didn't know you were the mayor," I shout at Lexie.

"What?" She looks insulted. "I don't know what you're talking about."

What am I talking about? I don't know. I think again about that TV show that I, alone in this bar, have not seen. What's it about? Two crazy girls traveling across the country in tube tops? What do the male characters look like? Not me, I'm sure. I'm miscast. But maybe like these guys—like this young professional by the bathroom—in his pointy shoes, his distressed wide-legged jeans, his hair pushed together in a point, as if someone has been sitting on his head bare-assed. Who is *he* supposed to be?

I push myself off the stool. "Bathroom," I shout to the girls.

Up close, the young professional is tall, with a gym-rat buffness and a tattoo across his very bare (shaved?) chest that seems to match the embroidery on his shirt. Hopefully, I've got that backwards. He smells of a cologne I can't place, oddly floral. His arms are crossed, beer bottle held like a club. He has the unsmiling poker face of a psychopath.

I turn to look at the girls. They're staring in opposite directions, not speaking to each other. The trip has taken its toll.

"What's your feeling about brunettes?" I say.

The young professional eyes me up and down, as if looking for some slice of me to respect. Or maybe it's a tranche—isn't that a term these people like?

"You bring your sisters to the bar, dude," he says, "they might get eaten up."

"I love the word 'dude,'" I say. Tranche. Dude. These people are *on to* something. "They're not my sisters."

"Your name Gina?" he asks.

"Ha!" I say. "Gina! No, I'm talking about the brunette. Why don't you go, you know, work your magic on her?"

"The little one?" His face opens up, as if he recognizes me, an old friend he's always known. He hits me on the arm, hard. He's smiling, I'm smiling. We're bros before hos. "I love the little ones," he says.

"Awesome," I say. And in the bathroom, I think, "This *is* awesome." It *seems* awesome, and it is awesome. It's Thursday night. Thursday! And here I am in my own town, a wayfaring stranger, with two girls from New Jersey via Tel Aviv. And I've got this strange guy, who looks like someone famous probably—*from a TV show I alone have never seen!*—swooping in to wingman this situation. Or maybe he's piloting. Of course he is. In his mind. It's all a question of perspective! I shake my head in the bathroom mirror, scrubbing my hands. So much of life—a question of perspective!

Back in the bar, I find Rachel sitting alone. I point at my ears to indicate how deafening it is. She nods, points at her ears too.

"Where is Lexie?" I ask.

"Motorcycle," she shouts.

"That was quick." I look out the purple-tinted window but see nothing.

"You should have seen her in Phoenix," Rachel says. "It's pathetic." She slurs it: it's spathetic.

"Phoenix?"

"Tucson. Austin. Santa Fe."

"Okay," I say. Tucson, Austin, Santa Fe—like a railroad jingle. I try to feel cheered.

"This is what we do," she says. "Girls where we're from."

"I've known plenty of girls from New Jersey. It didn't seem that bad."

She puts her elbows on the table. "But were they *free*?"

"They seemed pretty liberated."

"I don't mean liberated."

I look again to the window. "Lexie seems free."

"You're confused, my friend. Between free and easy."

THE HOSTEL IS AN old military barracks, cold, drafty, and sonorous. I can hear the occasional voice in the common area, the lone footsteps of a late night trip to the bathroom. Rachel sits on the bed in my tiny room and tugs at her boots like an exhausted farmhand. "Talking computers," she says, swaying under the exposed bulb. I tried to explain my work (minus its location) on the freezing walk over. She said she wanted to know, but she hasn't absorbed much. She's so drunk she looks deboned.

"You want some water?" I say. I hold her calf in my hand and pull the boot free. Then the other. Free and easy. I'm about to say we don't have to do this, but why wouldn't we? What else would two people, similarly situated, do? I put my hand under the heavy band of her sweatshirt and help her take it off, feeling the ridges of her ribs. A clavichord, a scallop shell. Her deodorant smells warmly of cloves. "One more," she says, and I roll her top up like an inner tube.

"Are you sad she's gone?" she asks.

"Who?"

"Good answer."

I stand up and flick off the light switch. In the sudden, blue darkness,

the weak glow of Sausalito comes into focus, bobbing in the tree branch. I approach the window, lean my forehead against the cool glass. It's just a little town across the bay, but right now it looks like a holy city in the distance, a mirage.

"Your computer," Rachel says. "Does it have a weird robot voice?"

"He doesn't actually talk. He text chats."

"Do you tell him everything? Are you going to tell him about your trip?"

"I don't know." The wind whips reedlike through the trees, a thousand knives on a thousand whetstones. Sausalito is erased. I turn to look at her. "What's there to tell?"

"You could tell him you met a really cool girl," she says. "Moving to California to start a new life."

"You're moving to SF."

"Bolinas. I'm going to live with my aunt and uncle in Bolinas. I'm going to finish high school."

The wind stops, turned off like a spigot. The noises of the hostel clarify—the mumble of the television, the clinking of bottles.

"Jesus. How old are you?"

"Twenty. Don't ask me why I haven't finished already."

"Twenty," I say.

She collapses back on the mattress with a thump. The springs wheeze. "Promise me you'll tell him that. A really cool girl moving to California. New start on life."

"New start on life."

"You got it." She pushes herself up, reaches a hand out for me, signaling for me to come over. "I need to tell you something."

"I hope I can share it with my computer." I push off the window. She's a warm dark form on the white bed, and this close I can smell her, touch her wavy hair. She looks up at me, serious, as if we're about to make a pact.

"First, you have to tell me your fantasy." She speaks quietly but firmly—not ashamed, not abashed. In the dark, her body is a monochrome ivory, clearly visible. Her small breasts, the slight chubbiness at her waist,

her long legs, the dull maroon flash of her underwear. But I can't discern her face. Above the neck, she's all shadows.

"You can tell me anything you want," I say. I'll carry her secret—it's something strangers can do for each other.

"Your fantasy. Tell me *yours*."

I lean in close. There's no blush of blood in her cheeks; her eyes are not green. Her face is white, black, grey—a mask. A fantasy, I think. Any old fantasy. Just one thing I dream about in bed alone, one way I want to be touched. Where I want her hands, where I want her mouth, what I want her to say. Something. I just have to come up with something.

2

LYING IN BED MONDAY MORNING, the idea of work—work, with its immense banality—strikes me as so absurd I wonder how the economy lurches on. Does anyone, anywhere, perform daily tasks of value? Even doctors treat boredom and loneliness as much as any real physical complaint. What do the rest of us do? Make useless shit to sell to each other so we can buy more useless shit. I buy a venti latte so the Starbucks employee can buy Billy Blank's Boot Camp workout so Billy Blank can buy a new Volt so a GM exec—my brother, for instance—can rent a Yo Gabba Gabba bounce house for the kids' party. And so on. Where along this line is anything necessary, anything of true human benefit, accomplished?

This is crazy talk, of course—the talk of a depressive. Take this much further and I'll be soiling myself in the public library, ranting about the New Global Order.

I sit up, letting my feet dangle off the side of the bed. The cat demands food. On my bedside table is a big bouquet of tulips. They are probably from Ecuador, and are beautiful. This too is the new global order.

Today we're launching the latest iteration, Dr. Bassett 2.0. We even have a special guest, Adam Toler, a former student of my boss, who invented *the* site that matches the loveless to marriageable partners. He's your basic asshole, but he's rich as a developing-world dictator and he doesn't waste his own time. He wouldn't come by if we sold lattes or Boot Camp workouts or Volts or Nickelodeon merchandise. He wouldn't have visited my former workplace to watch me despair over ad copy. His interest in our project testifies to its interest. This is artificial intelligence. Henry Livorno. Amiante Systems.

I eat a bowl of Trader O's, drink my two cups of coffee, and jump in the Subaru, calmed by NPR's soothing reports of chaos and war.

WHEN I FIRST MET my boss he told me that artificial intelligence sought to answer one question: what do you do in the face of uncertainty? He said this cheerfully and simply, as if he'd just explained that geology was the study of the earth. I was surprised by such high philosophy, especially since Livorno seemed anything but uncertain. He was dressed like a genial Rotarian on the cusp of retirement. He actually had a golf glove tucked in his back pocket. He's a founder of his field—he was at the conference in the fifties when they invented the term "artificial intelligence"—and I was expecting some outward sign of genius: wild hair, a sweater with holes. He has an unplaceable accent (he's from Trieste, but he's not Italian), and a winning though not particularly suave way about him. If Science is the religion of our time (which it is), and scientists the high priests, then it can be disconcerting to find your high priest so determinedly mundane, head to toe in wicking fabrics.

Livorno's worldliness—if not his certainty—has proved at least half illusion. A more sensible man would not be taking on the Turing test, the moonshot of artificial intelligence problems. To defeat this test we have to create a program that—thirty percent of the time—can fool humans into thinking it too is human. The program that passes this threshold will be considered the first intelligent computer. Alan Turing, the patron saint of the field, who invented the test in 1950, thought it would be bested sometime around 2000, but he designed a better yardstick than he might have hoped. Our predecessors have created programs that return your assertions as questions; programs that draw on encyclopedias, dictionaries, and large databases to predict a correct response; programs that fake bad typing—they've all been experimentally interesting and utter failures. They sought (seek—our competitors are still up to some hybrid of these old methods) to cobble together a convincing human voice, to string together enough coherence in a conversation to pass the test's threshold. But they suffer a fatal lack of small talk. Livorno decided that rather than create a coherent human voice from scratch he would find a human voice and bottle it. Finding this voice, however, turned out to be very complicated. He needed a word-hoard of phrases, thoughts, and sentences. He played around with famous writers, like Montaigne, but they were too antique and too "written." Then he heard about a graphomaniac on the radio—a man who wrote down everything he did every minute of the day—but the trivia was crushing. *8:50 Had toast. 9:00 Was interviewed on radio.* There was no sense of the conversational. A professor friend suggested he try Samuel Pepys's London diaries, which are super conversational and personal, but highlight the Great Plague of 1665 and the Great Fire of 1666—running into the antique problem again.

So Livorno did what one does when at loose ends—a Google search. He discovered an obscure author known (by the Southern historical journal that published him) as the Samuel Pepys of the South. Livorno was very excited to track down the diaries, and after a confused conversation with my mother—she didn't mention the suicide, thinking he must already know—he was also very excited to track down the author of the journals, me. It was only when we met that we were able to straighten out that I was the Neill Bassett Junior to a long-dead Neill Bassett Senior. Livorno looked so distraught I felt bad for him. Then, seeming inspired, he wondered if I might join as my father's substitute. I hadn't come looking for employment. I was just there because Libby (my mother) had been charmed by Livorno, but before handing over the diaries she wanted to ensure he wasn't a kook. A new job, however, had the ring of a good idea. This was in the scorched wasteland right after my divorce, and a tawdry workplace fling (my sad response to Erin's *pre*-divorce affair) was about to blow up. Or so it seemed at the time. Anyway, I was tired of writing ad copy for tech companies; I figured I'd rather just work for the tech companies. They seemed efficient, ambitious, forward-leaning—in other words, the future.

So I came to Amiante Systems, which is ambitious and forward-leaning, but certainly not efficient. It's a business without a business plan. Or rather its business plan is to garner Livorno respect. He's had a storied career. His former students run cutting-edge corporations, teach at top programs, do mind-stretching research. But he's never quite nailed down the discovery that will preserve his name for all time. In fact, his last major project, the Seven Sins—seven individual programs that "bend" functions in, say, a gluttonous or prideful way—was considered crude showmanship. They were derided on the blogs ("What's gluttonous search? Search!" "What's prideful antivirus protection? Antivirus protection!") as the Seven Dwarfs.

How will a business doomed to fail as a business garner respect? By being brilliant. Is anything we do here brilliant? It's a question that worries me. Mostly for Livorno, but also for myself. This job is the reliable human texture of my days. On mornings like this one, even though I'm late and Livorno's irritated, I'm relieved to find him in his office door beckoning me with his tall, double-handled two-way putter. It means he needs me. Chat with Dr. Bassett about subject X. Fix Dr. Bassett's phrasing. Ask your mother a pressing question. Go fetch Thai food for lunch. The task doesn't matter: Amiante is the place where I'm of use.

"Did your mother complete the profiles?" he asks. Since Neill Sr. is no longer around, Libby has been answering dozens of personality tests as if she were him—tests we actually borrowed from Toler's dating site. This is part of the transition we're making today, in hopes of speeding up the project. So far we've been using what Livorno refers to as "backwards case-based logic," but now we're imposing a little "forward rule-based logic." Basically, instead of waiting for the computer to figure out what it thinks, we're going to tell it.

"All twenty of them." I caliper the brown envelope between finger and thumb, demonstrating its thickness.

Livorno's office is a warehouse of golf knickknacks and cases of his homemade Zinfandel. Among his many honorary degrees hangs a signed letter from Governor Reagan—the Rotarian disguise is nearly flawless. I lower myself into one of his overly reclined Wassily chairs. He sits in his upright Aeron throne. We have a lot of our conversations this way. There's something of Freud and the analysand in the arrangement.

"She says your father was a romantic." He points at the bubble sheet. It seems to me we could pick out random answers—romantic, not romantic—and be fine, but it's important to Livorno that we get this right. He wants the hidden patterns to emerge.

"That wouldn't be my interpretation."

"She scored it quite high."

"Obviously she has her reasons for thinking that."

He frowns. "Your mother has always been objective." His tone is reverent and cautionary.

"That's high praise from you, Henry."

"It's not praise—it's an observation."

"Maybe she meant capital-R Romantic," I say. "He was a capital-R Romantic."

"The R is not capital," he says.

"I don't know what she was talking about."

"What she was talking about? She says he was a romantic." He's getting whipped up. "We have to change this today."

"I think I know my own father."

My voice is harsh. Livorno looks up from the questionnaire, surprised. I'm surprised, too. We've never had a tough word between us.

"I'm sorry," I say. "This weekend . . ." He looks alarmed, and I stop. He'd rather me scream like a Barbary macaque than talk about my personal life.

"You have countervailing evidence," he asks. "On this question of romanticism?"

"Nothing specific."

He picks up an apple—an organic Pendragon, full of flavonoids, the same type he encourages me to eat every day—and rolls it in his hand. "Don't worry. He's going to do great."

"He" is the program we call Dr. Bassett, which Livorno treats as if it's the actual Dr. Bassett. I don't like this, but there's nothing to be done. It's a crackpottery—a mild form of operationalism, the belief that there's no important difference between how things seem and how things are—that the whole project hinges on.

"I'm not worried about the iteration," I say.

Livorno brings his other hand to the apple, displaying it like the sacred heart of Jesus. "I want you to be *somewhat* worried. My legacy hangs in the balance."

"You said Toler was a squarehead." This is Livorno's term for uncreative thinkers.

"Nevertheless, he's very powerful."

My mind returns to the weekend, the hostel, the girl. It's this stupid chair. "You want to hand me those forms?" I push myself upright, feel a lightheaded rush of professionalism. "I'll get to work."

"You're looking much better, Neill. I believe you have accomplished some R and R?" In case I mistake this for an actual question, he wheels up to his console and begins typing in his brisk two-fingered fashion, humming tunelessly.

I CARRY THE BUBBLE SHEETS into the reception area, past my darkened office, and into the back room. Our suite—one of five in a small, "start-up friendly" commercial space in Menlo Park—previously housed a failing quilt supply store. I always leave work with bits of thread attached to my clothes. The front two offices—mine and Livorno's—must have been administrative, or maybe for private stitching lessons? The back office, which takes up half of the entire space, was the quilting studio. It's now home to Laham, our baby-faced wunderkind programmer from Indonesia, and Dr. Bassett, a stack of massively interconnected computers—front-end processors, what's known as primary nodes, and larger nodes—housed in a tall stainless steel box with a glass door and a slatted vent on top, like a high-end wine fridge. Every morning Laham dusts the whole thing with a diaper wipe. The built-in fans in the processors are supplemented by freestanding fans and an individual air conditioner, all running simultaneously with the combined roar of a speedboat. It's hard to make yourself heard to Laham, which is okay because his English is challenged. Livorno pulled some strings to express his work visa.

I bang on the metal door, but he doesn't look up. So I wait until he sees me and cheerily waves. He's a kid—twenty-three? Hardworking, meticulous, goofy, and currently sipping an energy drink called Bawls. He's very clean-minded, and when he asked me once about the name, I told him it was about being so tired you wanted to weep. It's become a joke between us, and now he's rubbing his eyes, his mouth open like a miserable baby.

"Got the answers to the quiz," I say, putting them on his desk. He'll scan the bubble sheets and then these answers will create new rules for Dr. Bassett. This afternoon I suppose he'll become a romantic. "You think we're ready for the launch?"

He gives me the foreigner-no-understand smile.

"The launch," I say. "Are you feeling good about it?"

"No, no. We are not ready."

"But it's today."

He takes another sip of Bawls, looking grim. He has bags under his eyes. "We are not ready."

Finally, my office, where I sit down in my own Aeron chair, supported and ventilated—a good description of the positive effects my job has on me. Still, I'm struck this morning—as I am most Mondays—at how my two years in this room have left little mark. It's the same bare Sheetrock, the same furniture in the same arrangement. I suppose it could be a reaction to the overpersonalizing of my last job, where we were encouraged to really trick out our cubicles, to express our "me"—a suggestion made with an uncertain mixture of irony and coercion, which drove people to overcompensate. Horse tack, Hello Kitty piñatas, or, in my case, six hundred dollars' worth of San Francisco Giants pennants. But that was a long time ago, and can't really explain the dusty flavorlessness of this room. I have—let's face it—more than enough of my "me" buzzing around the stack in the back room. I might as well settle in; I just don't. My decorative touches are spare. A couple of photographs on my desk, one of Dolores Park from the window of my apartment, one of Machu Picchu—a trip I made with a very brief romance (who is not herself featured in the picture). A windbreaker and a dusty tennis racket hanging on the back of the door—I joined a lunch league down here, but have failed to play a single match. Two stress balls on either side of my keyboard, to combat carpal tunnel. A bookcase with an arm's length of books on artificial intelligence (which I've paged through in my desultory fashion) and the ninety-eight yellow legal pads that contain my father's journals. And finally, tacked up behind my monitor, a picture of Alan Turing (printed from the Web), a memento that this field, and this project, have a strange history. He seems to be smiling inscrutably at the door, amused at anyone who enters—or maybe amused that no one ever does.

I have no computer science background. In fact, I have no science background—just an underused master's in business administration. But I like to think I have a scientific disposition, that I'm open to hypotheses and don't walk into every room my nose clothespinned with assumptions. I cherish evidence. The whole premise of Amiante is based on the search for evidence. We're trying to create the first "intelligent" computer, but intelligence here is precisely defined: a computer that can fool us thirty percent of the time. Thirty percent! Ah, the measurables of life!

Unfortunately we're not close to the mark. We couldn't fool one percent. Point one percent. After two years of work, Dr. Bassett talks like this:

frnd1: tell me about john perkins
drbas: john perkins is five foot two and squat as a hedge

Laughably primitive, except that it's not: we're at the absolute forefront of talking computers, way out in front of the competition. But what talk it is. Exhaustive minutiae—what my father ate, who he talked to, what he thought about what he ate and who he talked to. He recommends a precise soil mixture—half loam, half cow manure, which was his uncle Jack's recipe for raising tomatoes, and rails against the flavorless versions from California. He confides uplifting bromides about the patients in his clinic. He debates the virtues of ingestible versus injected antibiotics. The very existence of my father's diary was unexpected, but its size—five thousand pages over the course of twenty-plus years—was an absolute shock. And yet it contains nothing acutely revelatory. Page after page of opinion and detail, and somehow the whole accumulation hides the man as much as it reveals him. There are a few surprises—my father's worry about my older brother's "effeminacy," for instance—but no clues as to the man behind the man, except to reinforce that there was none. The journal is thorough, scrupulous, buttoned up, nearly drowning in its own Southernness, and blithely impersonal; so was the man. For all the mentions of young people this and young people that, there's little about my brother or me. My mother gets more ink, but only as a cartoon of Southern female virtue. Strong, sharp, the perfect belle. Exactly the kind of nonsense that sent me fleeing for California and its flavorless tomatoes (which are actually delectable—so there). The only people who really come alive are the local color, especially my father's friend Willie Beerbaum, who had a mouth that could peel paint from the wall. There are times I wish we could have based the program on Willie.

When the historical society published an excerpt and proclaimed my father the Samuel Pepys of the South, I was still in college and this sounded hopefully grand (though I hadn't heard of Samuel Pepys). My father, I knew, would have been thrilled. The diaries are a kind of love letter to the traditional and old-fashioned. He had suffered in the contemporary world. I think he needed a good nineteenth-century cholera epidemic, where he could heroically aid the poor and sick, assuage their beatific suffering. Instead, he got Medicaid and billable procedures, people eating themselves to death on Cheetos. The excerpt, however, failed to inspire even a single letter to the editor, and there's little wonder why. It's full of paragraphs like this: *Sold the nag Blazers to old John Perkins, who owns the farm off the Chambersville Road. I have no idea what he plans to do with it. He's five foot two and squat as a hedge—Blazers is half Tennessee Walker. Will*

*Perkins dare to mount such a steed? I'm afraid to watch him bouncing
down the highway, like a rubber ball on a paddle. But he offered a fair
price and Man must be allowed to follow his passions, foolish or not. Les
Roark says Perkins came into the Grand Leader last week asking about
Stetson hats.*

This is an entry from 1983! Michael Jackson was dancing in a rhine-
stone glove. The *Challenger* was orbiting the Earth. Pepsi was for sale in the
Soviet Union. Why does it sound like Old Hickory is still in the White
House?

When I took this job I didn't tell Livorno that I'd never known my
father was keeping a journal, that my relationship with my father wasn't
twined too tight. Instead, I thought of packing up my Giants pennants
under the watch of two security guards, and said I'd be happy to come on. I
was probably the best choice. My mother knew my father better, but she had
no interest in moving to California and taking up full-time office work. And
my brother was (is) too worshipful. I pride myself on not being blinded by
sentimentality.

I can't say I was close to my father, especially as I hit my teens. With his
thin swirl of blond hair, his pale skin, his bleached green eyes, he was so
ethereal. Barely incarnated. At a certain point we stopped doing the few
things we did together (hunting, fishing), and I came to see him mostly as a
source of lectures. On the proper way to stand, the proper way to hold a fork.
He ran out of other topics, at least with me. He worked long days and was no
doubt tired, and a father subcontracting his parental duties to the mother
was a common arrangement in my hometown. Still, he provided me many
things growing up: a nice home, a sufficiency of toys and sports equipment,
a good education. That after his death he would also provide me this lark of
a job is the friendliest, most unexpected gift of all. Sometimes I wish he
were alive to share a laugh at the irony, but he was never much for irony. Or
for laughs.

I always like to start the chats off with a couple of jokes. The same
couple of jokes.

frnd1: why did the chicken cross the road?
drbas: an old woman offered me a chicken in exchange for
    medical care today
frnd1: how do you get a one-armed aggie out of a tree?
drbas: the trees by the house are river birches

I vote these both down.

frnd1: we need to find a topic to discuss
drbas: recent activities make for engaging topics
frnd1: i recently spent the night in a youth hostel
drbas: once, a youth was kidnapped today by persons unknown.
    rumor has it that the iranians are behind it, but the only
    persians to grace our small town in its history are the
    librarian's cats. the long-lost father is a more likely suspect,
    i think

[220089: if "once" never "today"; convert: past tense; repeat.]

drbas: once, a young girl was abducted by persons unknown.
    rumor had it that the iranians were behind it, but the only
    persians to grace our small town in its history were the
    librarian's cats. the long-lost father was a more likely
    suspect, i thought
frnd1: what happened to her?
drbas: who is her?

This is the big problem with Dr. Bassett. We've perfected his ability to parse grammar and parts of speech. We've created a category system, so that he not only knows what words are in the sentence but what larger topic they might refer to. We've even given him a series of old-fashioned dodges—if one of my statements makes no sense to him, he'll rephrase it as a question.

What he can't do is follow a conversation for more than one line. Every time I type in a line we start at zero, and it's a brand-new conversation. I feel as if I'm constantly trying to catch his attention, shaking him awake.

> frnd1: did they find the young girl who was abducted by persons
>   unknown?
> drbas: a search party left at 9 am after much free coffee and
>   donuts at the bakery. they returned for a free lunch and
>   then for a free afternoon snack. the girl was never found
> frnd1: never never?

(The computer takes a long pause.)

> drbas: i don't follow
> frnd1: did they ever find the girl?
> drbas: which girl?
> frnd1: did they ever find the girl who was abducted by persons
>   unknown?
> drbas: the girl was never found
> frnd1: how old was the girl?
> drbas: which girl?
> frnd1: the girl who was abducted by persons unknown
> drbas: i don't know
> frnd1: do you have an estimate?
> drbas: there are approximately half as many people living in our
>   county as there were a hundred years ago

[220094-220098: subject code = age; 220099: substitute: "i'm not sure. quite young i would guess"]

> frnd1: in what year was the girl abducted?
> drbas: which girl?
> frnd1: the girl abducted by persons unknown

drbas: 1979. my wife was quite concerned, as we had two boys
    ourselves

I don't remember this story, but I was just a toddler in 1979.

frnd1: where are your boys now?
drbas: my oldest lives in michigan. my youngest is a senior in
    college

My senior year in college: the amber I'm frozen in. It would be nice to
have made it further into maturity.

frnd1: are they happy?

My answer is a blinking cursor. It's a bad question, unanswerable with
the current program, and might even crash Dr. Bassett for the afternoon.
Livorno will be furious.

frnd1: new topic. tell me a funny story about willie beerbaum
drbas: willie beerbaum is my best friend
frnd1: is it true willie wore a corset?
drbas: i discovered willie's corset during a routine checkup. i
    went to listen to his lungs with the stethoscope and found
    myself stopped by what seemed like a bulletproof vest. he
    said if he took it off he'd pour across the table like "a batter
    of wet shit"

I shouldn't say there are no surprises in the journals. Sometimes an unexpected sentiment pops up, like my father's fondness for Willie Beerbaum.
It's true he and Willie were friendly, and I definitely remember a time when
Willie—thrice-divorced, highball in hand—frequented our weekend sup-
pers. In his brand-new Corvette and red ascot, he was hard to forget. For a
thrilling few months when I was seven or eight, he even took me out on

Saturday business calls, introducing me as his investment partner. He was the only example of bad behavior I ever saw my father get a kick out of. Still, I would never have guessed my father considered him a best friend, and I would never have guessed the frequency with which he appears in the journals. Sometimes it's easier to dredge up a line from Willie Beerbaum than from Neill Bassett Sr.

AT LUNCH I GO to check on Laham.

"You're not allowed to have any more." I take the can of Bawls away from him. "These are bad for you."

"I need one week," he says, holding up a frantic thumb. He points toward the open door leading into the reception area. "You tell him. One week."

"The Toler guy is coming by today. Can I help?"

"You?" Hysterical, cackling laughter. He's about to have a breakdown.

I think I'll talk to Livorno, but the entry bell, left over from the quilting studio, goes *ding, dong.* We never have unannounced visitors, so this must be Toler.

"Neill," Livorno calls. I could pretend not to have heard him over the fans, as I sometimes do, but this would only put off the inevitable. I'm not sure why Livorno cares about Toler's good opinion. He's always quick to point out that Toler's organization is an innovative *business* idea, but nothing in terms of programming. And Toler is absolute proof that money doesn't salve petty insecurities. He looks like a CGI replica of himself—his blue Bentley sports car, his black turtleneck, his long Italian shoes shiny as eggplants. He sucks in his gut, and adds angle to his—I hate to say it— smug, porcine face with narrow glasses made entirely from Lucite. He's met me a dozen times, but he insists on calling me Noel. I can never decide whether he's detestable or just pathetic.

In the dusty reception area, under the foam drop ceiling, Toler whirls with his arms outstretched, as if giving thanks to the day the Lord has made. His assistant stands away from him with a forced smile. She appears to be holding both his satchel and hers—his briefcase-walla. I suppose the more important you are the less you carry. "I envy you, Henry," Toler says. "Look at this place. Look at you. You're in your golf gear, ready for a round on the links or whatever. Retirement suits you, I think."

"I'm not retired," Livorno says, his shoulders bobbing up and down with laughter. "This is my very first job."

"Your very first job!" Toler says, turning to me with mock outrage. "Noel, do you know what this guy, this guy right here, did before he started this little project?"

"Yes, I do," I say.

"This guy basically founded the field of AI. This guy is a legend. Shakey. LISP. We wouldn't have NASA without this guy. He trained every important programmer to come out of Stanford. All of us."

"You know, Neill, when you have that one special student," Livorno says. "That truly brilliant mind? Well, Adam here"—Livorno puts his hand on Toler's shoulder—"sat right next to that student."

Toler shakes his head. "You've been telling that joke for thirty years."

Maybe there's no mystery in what Livorno gets from these visits. Toler is so rich he doesn't carry anything; Toler comes by to joust with Livorno; Livorno is thereby esteemed by the esteemed.

"It continues to be funny," Livorno says.

"As do your ideas," Toler says. "But seriously"—he mugs in my direc tion, miming how serious he is. How can he do such an unconvincing job of portraying himself?—"some people may doubt Henry Livorno, but not me. The Seven Dwarfs—they don't understand that you're a concept guy. This guy—you're still in the game, Henry."

"It's the Seven Sins, Adam. Seven nonlinear processing models. They were meant to be provocative."

"Laham needs to speak to you," I say.

"What are we doing again today?" Toler says.

"Putting some trellises in the garden," Livorno says. A nifty metaphor I haven't heard him use before. "We have such a rich world of thought and talk that we need a bit of structure."

"Imposing frames, Henry! Isn't this admitting defeat?"

"This isn't a research project. It's a contest." Livorno grins, but his confidence seems to have faltered. I can hear uncertainty in his voice. "And we're very precise. Neill's been poring over ethics tests for two months. Neill, pose us a few examples."

Toler's mocking look turns on me, and I'm surprised to find it as powerful as a laser. I want to jump out of my skin. "They're pretty boring," I say. "You know, don't discriminate based on race. Don't kill your enemies."

"It's bad to kill your enemies?" Toler asks, looking at his assistant as if for applause.

"Here's one to chew on," Livorno says. "As a physician you must warn the police if you suspect a patient of suicidal tendencies."

"True," Toler says. "No, false! Noel, this man teaches me something every day."

"Henry, Laham needs to speak to you."

"Can it wait?" Toler asks. "I want to see the latest vintage from Amiante Estates." Chuckle, chuckle. They stroll into Livorno's office. The assistant stands sentry.

"Make yourself at home," I say, indicating the reception desk piled high with UPS deliveries. "There's a kettle and some teabags hidden in there."

"I'd *love* to get some work done," she says with alarming sincerity. She has a nice voice and girlish good looks. I check to see if I feel one way or the other about them. I don't. After this weekend, I might call a moratorium on girlish good looks.

I knock again on Laham's door. He looks up with hopeful, bloodshot eyes. I shake my head, no reprieve. He frowns and reaches down to the floor, where he's hidden a can of Bawls. He takes a grim, determined mouthful.

AT A QUARTER TO FOUR, Livorno, Toler, and the assistant pass by my door. It's time.

We gather around Laham's computer screen in the back room. This must be a ceremonial choice, because we all have the same interface. But here we can view Dr. Bassett and complete our anthropomorphism.

"It's too bad the stack doesn't have little blinking lights," I say. "Like Deep Blue."

"A good idea," Livorno says. "An LED system could mirror verbal output."

I was joking, but I don't say this out loud.

"It does raise the question," Toler says. He points to a spot in front of me. A direct indication is beneath him. "How are you encouraging human-computer bonding?"

"Is that what you specialize in?" Livorno says, with a high, nervous laugh. I think this is meant as repartee.

"Emotional heuristics," Toler says. "What kind are you using?"

Livorno shakes his head, as if a fly is buzzing his nose. "None, of course."

"What does your buddy Minsky say? 'The question isn't whether we can give intelligent computers emotions, but whether we can create an intelligent computer without emotions.'"

"Minsky likes to be quoted. He likes headlines." Livorno is struggling with the cork on a bottle of his homemade Zinfandel, which is even worse than his homemade Cab. His hands are shaking. "The only important question is whether in this beautiful brain"—he gestures toward the stack—"we can grow a mind." He gives me the bottle to open.

"You mean *implant* a mind," Toler says.

"It's just a few trellises. A little structure." Livorno nods at the computer screen. "Laham."

Livorno has used a full two-inch cork, as if he's bottling Château Margaux. I twist the corkscrew to its limit, listen to the servers refiring. On the wall overlooking the stack, posters show Einstein teaching, Tesla's ball crackling, and the sun setting over the Stanford dish. I would say this is how Livorno sees his life—if he can't be Einstein, an undisputed genius, he can at least be Tesla, a disputed genius—but in fact the posters are Laham's, as are the wilted money tree and the yellowed monstera sitting in the daylight of the open back door. I can see my dusty Subaru out there, and now that the fans are off, I can hear the bucolic industry of Menlo Park, the whisper of drainage pipes, the whirr of hybrids.

"Okay, ready," Laham says, unhappy.

Livorno sits down at the keyboard. He's forgotten to ask me what the topic should be. This could be a problem—Dr. Bassett has his short suits.

> hlivo: good morning
> drbas: it's afternoon, henry
> hlivo: good point
> drbas: come again?

A bad sign—misstepping in the second response.

> hlivo: i have a pain in my knee. can you tell me what is
>   causing it?
> drbas: a pain in your knee?

That's good—and a surprise. He's clarified the conversation topic.

> hlivo: yes
> drbas: have you been doing repetitive motion?
> hlivo: i'm training for a marathon. yes, that's repetitive motion

"A marathon?" Toler exclaims. "Can you believe this guy?"

> drbas: repetitive motion can cause joint pain
> hlivo: what should i do about this pain caused by repetitive
>   motion?

"Easy there," Toler says. "No need to lead it by the nose."

drbas: pain caused by repetitive motion?

hlivo: yes

drbas: take 500 milligrams of ibuprofen and stop the repetitive
motion

"What an advance!" Livorno says. "Neill, distribute the glasses for our toast."

"Come on," Toler says. "Tell it you can't stop. You're training for a marathon."

"I wouldn't want to take up more of your time," Livorno says.

"I've got all the time in the world," Toler says. He adjusts his Lucite spectacles. He's the very devil.

hlivo: i can't stop the repetitive motion. i'm training for a
marathon

drbas: do you really think training for a marathon is a good
idea?

"That's Weizenbaum's thing," Toler says. "ELIZA." His voice is serious now, to himself. He's right. ELIZA is a real antique from the sixties that—like a good therapist—repackages your statements as questions. One of many programs we've cannibalized.

hlivo: it's good for my heart health

drbas: you're saying it's good for your heart health?

hlivo: yes

drbas: i suppose that could be true

"A dodge," Toler says. He seems relieved. "Let's have that toast."

He's right, too, about the dodge. I invented that sequence myself: ask a declarative statement back to the interlocutor, then admit it may be true. It looks like conversation. But I've got a feeling Dr. Bassett hasn't completely lost the thread; he's just unsure whether distance running is still a topic.

"Ask him if you should be training at your age," I say. "Don't mention marathons."

hlivo: should I even be training at my age?
drbas: how old are you, henry?
hlivo: i'm in the sixty to eighty category
drbas: someone your age should consider a half-marathon

Toler is silent. He exchanges an expressionless look with his assistant.

"What happened?" Laham asks brightly.

"He appears to be following the conversation," I say.

"He's not following a conversation," Toler says. "He's just tracking your searches. Even Yahoo can do that."

"This is of a completely different order," Livorno says. "I'd be happy to explain it to you, Adam, but it might take a long time."

"Good?" Laham asks. He looks at me.

I give him a thumbs-up. "Extremely."

"It shouldn't take too long to explain ten-year-old technology," Toler says. "But, yes, I better get going."

"First, a toast." Livorno stands and smooths out his pants, triumphant. "To a revolutionary Monday." He hands out the wineglasses and pours us generous turns. Then he makes a face full of false regret. "Now I'll have to write an article."

"Everything in this computer is based on your father," Toler says to me. It doesn't sound like a question, but it is one.

"There are all the ethics tests. Medical info. ELIZA. You know, the trellises."

"But his voice. Does it sound like him? Do you sometimes feel his presence?"

"Just then I did." I feel instantly embarrassed. Here in a room with four hard-brained science PhDs, I'm sensing messages from beyond. I might as well admit to wearing crystals.

"I'm assuming one of these 'trellises' includes some commonsense notions of death," Toler says.

"Naturally," Livorno says.

"So what happens if I tell him he's dead?" Toler reaches toward the keyboard, air-typing.

Livorno takes a step between Toler and Dr. Bassett. "We can't very well have him puzzling about the silence of the grave."

Toler knocks back his wine, makes a horrible grimace, and hands me the glass. "The silence of the grave," he says. "You've got a way with words, professor." He smiles and shakes our hands, making exaggerated eye contact. "I want to congratulate you three on single-handedly lurching into the AOL era." He gives a jaunty salute as he and his assistant leave.

"He loves me like a son," Livorno reminds us.

"Feels Oedipal to me," I say.

"Difficult to be so outclassed by your aged teacher." Livorno nods sympathetically, then takes a happy slurp of his wine.

BACK IN MY OFFICE, I try to solve the real question for today: just how good is Dr. Bassett 2.0?

> frnd1: why did the chicken cross the road?
> drbas: chickens are usually kept in pens
> frnd1: how do you get a one-armed aggie out of a tree?

I wait for his response.

> drbas: i thought we were talking about a chicken

Dr. Bassett has officially stayed awake for two questions.

> frnd1: tell me about the girl who was abducted

drbas: once, a young girl was abducted by persons unknown.
  rumor had it that the iranians were behind it, but the only
  persians to grace our small town in its history were the
  librarian's cats. the long-lost father was a more likely
  suspect, i thought
frnd1: what happened to her?
drbas: a search party left at 9 am after much free coffee and
  donuts at the bakery. they returned for a free lunch and
  then for a free afternoon snack. the girl was never found
frnd1: never never?
drbas: the girl was never found
frnd1: when did this happen?

He takes a while to chew this over. I've given him a true mind-bender:
"this" doesn't just refer to a word or but to the whole conversation.

drbas: 1979. my wife was quite concerned, as we had two boys
  ourselves

Bingo.

frnd1: where are your boys now?
drbas: my oldest lives in michigan. my youngest is a senior in
  college
frnd1: are they happy?
drbas: do you think happiness is an important goal?

That's a dodge.

frnd1: why did you have a family?
drbas: i still have a family

This is a mistake I often make, putting his life in the past tense.

frnd1: okay, why do you have a family?
drbas: why do i have a family?
frnd1: yes
drbas: sons are a gift from God

Is it a line from the journals? Some synthesis? In any case, it's crazily comforting to hear. I shake my hands out, walk to the back office. The program is good. Really, really good. You wouldn't mistake it for a real person, but you could believe it actually knows what you're talking about. I put my hand on the side of the stack, the brain. It hums and buzzes.

3

WEEKS CAN GO BY LIKE THIS. Working all day in silence, sitting at a café for lunch, coming home to my well-tended apartment. I cook dinner, sometimes a challenging dish, usually an easy one. I pet the cat, read the news online, work sudoku till my brow aches. I belong to the San Francisco Tennis Club, and I try to get down there for Doubles Drop-in and even the exceptionally grim Singles Night. Beautiful, short-skirted divorcées squirting desperation from their eyes like poisonous toads. I once asked a lawyer if she wanted to grab a drink, and she nearly jumped in my car. As she explained later, it had been too long since she'd seen another person's apartment.

My housekeeper comes on Tuesdays and cleans the place within an inch of its life. She's a good-humored Brazilian woman, and I've fantasized about her. In my defense, it's not a fantasy of the patrón taking advantage of the hired help, but of a sweet companionship growing between two mismatched people. Less *Caligula*, more *My Fair Lady*.

THE WHOLE POINT OF my trip to the hostel was a new, temporary identity, but in the end I didn't succeed. The girl, Rachel, and I woke up in the little bed, woven like lovers. We disengaged, stiff, my head already pounding. She surveyed her clothes on the floor with dismay, as if they were shards of something valuable she'd let slip from her grasp. Everything felt apocalyptically dire. It was the right moment for me to shake her hand and go catch the 48 back to the Mission, but I did something that surprised me—I lay back down and told her exactly who I was and where I lived. I even handed her a business card. And she did something that surprised me—she laughed.

So I feel a kind of elated foreboding, a concurrent happiness and conviction that cosmic punishment is rolling my way, when I get a note in my inbox:

> wazzup . . . me n folks r hangin 2nite at Stinson . . . wanna come?
> u will fit right in LOL . . . seriously luv to c u there . . . r

It's been three weeks since the hostel, well past the rekindling window. And I'm dazzled by the email's superlative wrongness—its cutesy misspellings, its tone, its very existence. She's a twenty-year-old who hasn't graduated high school—LOL.

How does she have "folks" already in Marin? I can only hope she's not referring to her parents.

I ask Dr. Bassett what to do.

> drbas: it's normal to date before you settle down

At work's end I examine myself in the Subaru's vanity mirror—there are no looking glasses at Amiante Systems—and am troubled by the innocence I find there. I'm divorced, the son of a suicide, but these tsunamis have passed without a visible trace. It's true San Francisco men are famous for their Peter Pan syndrome, also true that I use moisturizer. Still, I'd take a face with more character. When I smile, a tight bunch of lines extends like cat whiskers from my eyes. When I stop smiling, each line remains faintly there. That's as much mark as life seems to have made.

And look at my clothes. They've suffered from the permissive atmosphere of Amiante. I look like a square Web 2.0er determined not to dress like a square Web 2.0er. There are hints of subversion, the collars too big, the pants snug in the thigh, the cuffs too French, but who is the subversion for? Laham wears a baju kurung and polyester slacks; Livorno, kitted out as an Eisenhower Republican, considers me a "classy dresser." I feel like Toler, a man disguised as who he really is.

I can't imagine how this will translate with Rachel and her Marin hippie "folks," with their dreadlocks and coarse-weave ponchos. So though I disapprove of my actions, I go home and transform. Beat-up jeans, urban sneakers, and an ironic T-shirt—I sink down into the appropriate age range. Faux-urban to their faux-rural, but it ought to fly. I have to say, the change is convincing. If only I had a similar switch of cars, some aged European diesel drinker to dress down the shiny unironical Subaru.

Oh well. The drive—across the Golden Gate Bridge and up the jagged wild headlands—is one of the reasons I live in San Francisco. All the money in the world has been unable to ruin the entrance to Marin.

In the Stinson Beach parking lot, I take off my sweater and throw it in the passenger seat. The fog hasn't blown in, and it's hot. In fact it feels like California up here, the dreams of California. On the beach, couples—man woman, man man, man dog—pace the line of land and water. Kids sit in circles close to the rocks. There are bongo drums. I skirt wide, scanning the girls. Will I recognize Rachel? I mostly remember her sleeping in my arms that night.

She's not with the bongo drums. I stroll toward a group with several bandanna-wearing dogs, struggling to look natural but not get sand in my shoes. A few girls are likely candidates. I glance at them, and then I find myself leering. Is that her? How about her? Her?

"Neill."

Rachel stands off to my right, looking just like herself. I never forgot the way she looked; I just forgot that I knew. Her cascade of dark blonde hair, the flash of her bright smile, and her kind of unstudied regalness—less like actual royalty and more like a heron. What a relief. She's leaning against the rocks with a non-hippie-ish guy who's wearing a button-up. I instantly regret my T-shirt. They're drinking white wine, out of real wineglasses.

Rachel appears to be wearing too much eyeliner, but really there's not much she can do to mar how pleased and self-possessed she looks. She waves at me as if from a boat that's coming to shore. Or rather as if she's on the shore, and I'm the boat.

"You look beautiful," I say. I mean it. She looks fuller, more alive.

"Really?" she says. She's stunned and pleased. Then she recovers. "I started jogging."

"That's not what I meant."

She gestures to her companion. "This is Raj."

"Short for Rajasthan," he says, shaking my hand. "Unfortunately." He's as Caucasian as a Smothers Brother, but this is Marin, birthplace of the American Taliban. Redheaded and sunburnt, with a last name like Kreuzer or Fitzpatrick, he might be Raj or Rasheed or Rumi.

"You look tired," Rachel says, patting the rock next to her. She has a new touch to her hair: a dyed braid with colored beads at the end, which hangs directly over her right eye. I reach over and tuck it behind her ear, surprising myself with the gesture.

"I've been working a lot," I say.

"You want a little Sancerre?" Raj asks.

I'm suspicious of anyone who names varietals, especially when there's no other choice at hand. Something less objective is afoot, too—what is this person doing here? This person who seems a lot like me?

"I hear you're a software guy," he says.

"No," I say.

"That's what you told me, right?" Rachel says. "At the youth hostel?"

Raj's face doesn't twitch. He appears to know how we met.

"I work for a software company," I say.

"Sales," Raj says.

"Development. It's hard to explain."

"This isn't a test," Raj says. "I sell real estate—I'm no Marin rich boy hypocrite."

"That's good," I say. "I'll take some of that wine, please."

"I did go to Bennington. A strike against me."

Rachel smiles at me, and then him and then back, as if watching a pleasant tennis match.

"You work at a stealth company?" Raj asks.

"I'm not sure we qualify as a company. But yes we're stealth. We make chatbots—talking computer programs."

"Interesting," he says, though he seems to mean the opposite. "Rachel, when's Trevor getting here?"

"Maybe he got tied up at the coffee shop," she says.

Good Lord, is there another one of us?

"That's where I work," she says to me.

"I thought you were in school," I say.

"I work for school credit," she says. "It's not like New Jersey out here."

"And that's good?"

"It's *so* good." She swings her arm around my shoulder and kisses me on the cheek. Is she drunk? I remember this strange zone of intimacy from when I was in college. The hugging, the kissing on the cheek, which all seemed to mean nothing in the end. It took me months to understand that my ex-wife was actually interested in me—I thought she was just flexing her attraction.

Above the ocean, the sun hangs like a scoop of magma. If the fog holds off, we might see it set.

"I've been anxious to meet you," Raj says. He's packing a pipe, and he holds it out to me. I'm not big on marijuana, but refusing a Californian's dope is like refusing a Pashtun's tea. And I'm starting to feel like an asshole. If this is an elimidate he can't be liking it any more than I am.

I take a tiny hit. Raj nods, groovy, and accepts the pipe back. Rachel takes her arm from my neck and sits down on the sand, reclining on her elbows. A breeze tosses her hair, a meteorological conspiracy to make her more beautiful than she really is.

"I can see how selling houses out here would be easy," I say, nodding to the ocean's perfect grinding against the coast.

"You'd like it up here with us," Raj says. "You seem like a free spirit."

What the hell is that supposed to mean?

"Hey, hey!" a boy shouts, slouching our way. It's Trevor. I'm relieved to see he's young—really young—not like us at all. He's wearing—as predicted—a knit poncho and rope sandals. "Raj, Rach, what's up?" He's all low fives and kisses on the cheek, as affable as a puppy.

"This is Neill," Rachel says.

"The famous Neill!" he says. "What up?"

"Neill makes chatbots," Raj says.

"Whoa," Trevor says, plopping down right next to Rachel and signaling for the pipe.

"It's a talking computer program," Raj says.

"Like for folks with no friends?"

"There's no commercial application yet," I say. At some juncture in my life, I apparently became the kind of person who says "commercial application" in a normal conversation. Maybe I'm just off balance—I don't know how to respond to *what up?*

"I know the first thing the corporations will do," Trevor says, exhaling a long plume of smoke and looking serious. "Robot phone sex."

I laugh, but no one else does. It's apparently not a joke.

"We don't even believe in regular phone sex," Trevor clarifies.

Raj nods, and Rachel looks out at the ocean. I scan the denominations, wondering who "we" might be. There is something of the evangelical sheen of Mormons with these two guys, but we're smoking dope. Ditto with Jehovah's Witnesses. What's left? Catholics? Lutherans?

"Simulated phone sex," Raj says, "does sound like many things wrong with the world rolled up into one."

"I wouldn't overstate," I say. "There's poverty and war and genocide."

"Have you ever heard of 'Bend Over Boyfriend'?" Trevor says, getting up to his knees and coming close to me. He smells of coffee beans. "It's like a package you buy—at sex stores. For sixty-nine ninety-five you get a strap-on, some lube, and an instructional DVD. It shows women how to do their boyfriends up the butthole."

"Gross," Rachel says.

"Why would a woman want to do that? Seriously? Because she's totally desperate. They go home—Arctic winds. They're not *clicked*. Some company says, 'Give me seventy dollars and I'll get you clicked. Just stick this thing in your boyfriend's back door.' And bam they buy it. It's corporations exploiting our fears and our weaknesses. You say it's not as bad as a war, but it is a war. And we're losing."

Rachel stands to brush the sand off her legs. "I'm checking out the water."

"I'll go with you," Trevor says, leaping to his feet.

She holds out a flat palm, waves no. "You stay here and talk about back doors," she says.

Trevor makes an exasperated noise and throws up his arms. He returns to us men, smiling. "There's something wrong with me."

"You're too strident," Raj says.

"I shouldn't have been talking about that stuff in front of Rach."

"Strap-ons?" I say. "Or war?"

"She's a special young woman," Raj says, pouring us the last of the wine. "I've liked her from the first day she came to a meeting." He's looking at me. "Neill, you should come to a meeting."

The gratuitous use of my name always makes me nervous—it's a tactic learned in cults and MBA programs.

"I'm a very tolerant person," I say. "As long as I don't have to be involved."

"I know Pure Encounters has a reputation, but none of it is true."

"I didn't think it was," I say. I've never heard of Pure Encounters.

"It's not about sex. It's about connection—clicking."

"It's, like, a spiritual practice," Trevor says. "It's about purity of the self—the only way to have purity in your encounters. And about resistance to these fucking corporations, these fucking soul-sucking . . ."

"Trevor," Raj says.

"I'm sorry, dude," Trevor says. "I don't know what's got into me." But he smiles and leans back in the sand. It's clear he knows *exactly* what's gotten into him, and it's a good thing and he likes it.

"If meetings aren't your thing," Raj says, "come to a retreat—we do a whole men's retreat thing."

Not a chance. I fought off Southern Baptists for the first twenty years of my life, and am now unconvertible. I don't believe in purity, and I hate the word "encounters."

"Rachel is a member?" I ask.

Raj nods. "Pure Encounters isn't for everyone. But it's made for people like Rachel, who've had some, you know, impure encounters."

I don't think he's referring to the youth hostel, an encounter so pure it was almost distilled. We watch a mutt—is it possible to have a pit bull–Dalmatian mix?—thunder by, in pursuit of a tennis ball. Rachel is in the distance, picking up a shell. The water races up, surrounds her ankles and wrist.

"She's got an old soul, your girl," Raj says.

My girl?

"Yeah," Trevor says. "But she's got a few roadblocks. We have to be truthful about that."

Here she comes, walking back from the water, her Converses dangling from her fingers, sand on her feet. She crosses her ankles as she walks, an elegant, wayward stumble that communicates shy surprise. I understand why I've been invited out here to the beach after our unceremonious beginning: she's a crazy person. She's been in California for less than a month, and she's already joined a cult.

BACK IN THE PARKING LOT, it turns out Trevor hitchhiked and Raj has a two-seater Porsche. So it's my responsibility to get Rachel to the pizzeria. Once we're there, neither Raj nor Trevor shows up.

"They just wanted to meet you," Rachel says.

This means I've been discussed. Maybe in depth. Can a person as shallow as me be discussed in depth?

"Trevor thinks the way we met is cool. He's like, 'Here's a guy who's adventurous. This guy's not afraid to stay clicked.'"

"You didn't tell him about the alibi."

"I left that detail out." She laughs. It's a loose, happy laugh, I have to say. Not what I would imagine for a cult member.

"What is this thing you've joined?"

"Pure Encounters? It's kind of like group therapy."

"But there's a lot of political stuff. Corporations."

"That's more Trevor's gig. I think their point is that sex is the only thing left they can't take away and sell back to us."

"Is that some sort of jargon, stay clicked?"

"Most people get un-clicked. They sort of curl up in themselves."

I take a deep breath and imagine Rachel as a tribeswoman—say, a Maori, her chin covered in fascinating ta-moko tattoos—explaining her ancient traditions to me. It's a strategy that sees me through this kind of conversation.

"They definitely kind of have their own special language," she says. "Stay clicked. Filtration of self. It's like AA. Have you ever been in AA?"

"No. Have you?"

"Court-ordered."

I take a sip of my beer. "Raj said you'd had some impure encounters."

She clears her throat. "I wish he hadn't."

"I thought you should know."

"Do you want to hear about them?"

I summon the wisdom of my years, the wisdom to avoid questions I don't want the answers to. Impure encounters. I'm sure I've had my share, especially in my revolving door days. I don't need to know about hers. I *want* to, but my life will be better—calmer—if I don't.

Is calm the most I hope for nowadays? Am I reaching that awful impasse, where all I want from life is less of it?

"Sure," I say.

She looks away from me, toward the counter where a family is paying their bill. "I had this asshole boyfriend," she says in a low voice. "He was really into making videos. You know, *videos*. He put one on the Internet." She clears her throat again. "Actually more than one."

I let that information hang in the air, trying to get a feel for its density, its shape. She turns back to watch me, awaiting my Solomonic judgment.

"It's pretty bad, isn't it?" she says.

"It's not a service activity to put on your CV," I say. "But I've heard worse."

"It's a betrayal that never goes away."

Permanent and unfixable, a humiliation always a few keystrokes away. Worse, it's a crime her every other lover will have to atone for. But the ceiling fan is tossing her hair in just the way of the beach wind, and I find her at this moment beautiful, injured, and resolute.

4

Still, I spend a couple of hours online, checking into Pure Encounters. The Web site is professional, but not very specific. They recommend you come to "the Lodge," not far from AT&T Park, for an orientation. They host an array of "sessions"—ClickIns, MeditationOuts, Purify, something called the VAM Method. Everything they do is suspiciously trademarked (and expensive), a hodgepodge of Buddhism, chakras, and crystal-waving. Purifying yourself—they offer retreats and cleanses—is the first step to a level of enlightenment that leads in a vaguely explained manner to happy relationships—or what is described as attaining "a deep limbic click" with your "intimate." The lingo is alarming. But what if she was Mormon? Jehovah's Witness? Or—God forbid—Southern Baptist? Would it be less alarming? In some ways, these businessy spiritual outfits are very practical. You hand over your money, get your fix, and then you're done. I'm certainly no believer in the One True Way. She's seeking, and if this path is useful then it's useful. As long as I'm never asked to attend a ClickIn.

> drbas: what did you do this weekend, frnd1?
> frnd1: i visited a girl
> drbas: how old is this girl?
> frnd1: twenty
> drbas: technically that's a woman

> frnd1: i'm glad you think so
> drbas: willie always says "twen-ty is plen-ty"

Always Willie. What would *he* think? It can be hard to rattle this particular pea out of the gourd.

> frnd1: do you agree with willie's opinion?
> drbas: willie's opinion is a belief willie holds
> frnd1: but what is your opinion of a man in his 30s dating a
>   woman who is 20?
> drbas: it's good to date for at least six months before you marry

[280959: dominant category ≠ dating; dominant categories = age, appropriateness]

> drbas: my opinion of a man in his 30s dating a woman who is 20
>   is a belief i hold
> frnd1: could you clarify this opinion?
> drbas: opinions are like ugly children . . . despite it all you love
>   your own

I do love his quips, but who did he use them on? Not us. Maybe he was quipped out by the time he got home from the clinic. He usually arrived just before "supper" (we weren't allowed to call it dinner), washed his hands thoroughly, joined us at table, listened as Libby asked us about our days at school, and then went and sat in grim silence in his study, brow furrowed, probably penning humorous quips.

The rhythmic *ting-tock-ting-tock* of Livorno's practice putts comes to a stop. He appears in my doorway. "Adam and his emotional heuristics." He gestures dismissively, but his voice sounds unsure. "He thinks I don't know? I created the first working models of emotional computing." I assume he's referring to the Seven Sins, though I'm not sure anyone else considers them *working* models. "I for one should know the limitations on this. Until we have a computer that's as parallel processed as the brain, where basically the cables and the processors are one . . . until then we're just playing parlor games."

"Yes," I say. Though if memory serves, the Turing test is actually based on a parlor game. The Imitation Game, apparently popular in Turing's era. A woman and a man were sent to separate rooms; the other partygoers, not knowing who was behind either door, passed handwritten questions to each player. They were both human, obviously, so the goal was to determine which was the woman. It was a little sanctioned gender-bending.

"But I can't tell which frames have taken and which haven't," Livorno says. "I've been completely unable to discern any change in his romanticism."

"He was a capital-R Romantic. He would have defended his honor with dueling pistols. But there's nothing in the journals for lowercase-R romanticism to fasten on to."

"That can't be entirely true." He points to the keyboard. "Feel him out a bit on your parents' marriage."

> frnd1: what was your first memory of meeting your wife?
> drbas: my memories all exist at the same time

[280965: "first memory of meeting" = "memory of first meeting"; repeat]

> drbas: i was a sigma chi and she was a kappa kappa gamma. but
> we didn't meet that way at all. when my father came up for
> parents' weekend she rammed into his fender. my father
> never forgave her—because she was driving a ford

This is a chunk of text from the journals. I eat up these old stories, though they don't have the clear ring of the truth. Even when he recorded them as they were happening, they feel like stories he's polished a little too much. Still, I'd love to hear more; I just don't think Livorno would put up with it.

> frnd1: that's a good story
> drbas: thank you
> frnd1: did you have sex before marriage?
> drbas: ????
> frnd1: did you have sexual intercourse before marriage?
> drbas: if you have not been tested i insist you use the barrier
>   method

This isn't from the journals, but from the medical information we downloaded. Or at least that's what I'm assuming. I don't know how my father would have phrased such advice—or even if he would have given it.

> frnd1: do you agree with sex before marriage?
> drbas: i'm not familiar with sex before marriage's stance on the
>   matter

[280974: "sex before marriage" = category "belief," ≠ category "agent"]

> frnd1: what about love? were you in love with libby?
> drbas: libby is my wife
> frnd1: when did you know you were in love with her?

He chews on this one.

drbas: alex was born

"Alex is my older brother," I tell Livorno. Which doesn't explain the response. Either Alex's birth is the first time my father mentioned love in the diary, or it was really the day he started loving my mother. I'm not sure which would be worse. At least in the second I could be sure he did love her.

> frnd1: what were her strong points?
> drbas: ????
> frnd1: strong points = good qualities
> drbas: she's a beautiful, spirited woman of great class
> frnd1: did you admire her or love her?
> drbas: i have the highest admiration for those who work with the
>   poor
> frnd1: did she need you?
> drbas: who?
> frnd1: your wife
> drbas: she needs me to pick up the dry cleaning by 5 pm

My stomach is in my throat, as if I'm about to penetrate a great mystery! I'm letting myself get carried away.

"He speaks less randomly," Livorno says. "But he often yields the wrong response."

"The frames probably just need more time to reconfigure. The journals are long."

"And ascetic. But what if the problem is structural? We've created his brain, but we've yet to give him a gut. Did you know that patients with cerebral injuries that sever the emotions from the logic centers will begin to act irrationally?"

"I thought you were against emotional computing."

"Of course. But an affective framework . . ." Livorno's voice falls quieter as he heads out of the room. His attention has returned to his putt. "Something like the Seven Sins," he says over his shoulder.

> frnd1: do you want to have emotions?
> drbas: it's good to feel love for your wife, but respect is the most
>   important

frnd1: respect was enough for you two to stay connected?

drbas: connected with what?

frnd1: good answer

drbas: of comfort there was little, but being unknown it was
    unmissed

frnd1: is that how you would describe your marriage?

drbas: there's more to life than happiness

I close my office door and call Libby.

"It's talking," I say.

"Does it sound like your father?" she asks. I hear water turn off; she's washing dishes. I can imagine her drying her hands, tucking the towel into the ring just below the corn-yellow countertop. Other than a new ASPCA calendar every year, the kitchen hasn't changed since I lived there. The white wainscoting, the light green walls. The table, in need of refinishing, pushed next to the window. Copper molds—round, square, shaped like a heart, like a lobster—on nails above. She prefers a dark, mis-shapen cutting board, which she's probably just rinsed and leaned behind the sink.

"He just quoted *Ivanhoe*. Then he said there was more to life than happiness."

On the other end of this line, I hear nothing—no radio, no TV, no friendly voices. She lives in a house with no neighbors in sight.

"He's also been talking about Willie Beerbaum a lot."

"Welcome comic relief, I'm sure."

"I like hearing about him."

"Willie was an egomaniac. He would have loved being heard about."

"It is funny to watch Livorno ponder the nuances of some of the country stories."

"And how are *you* taking this?"

"Fine," I say, though that's not right. It's not fine, this defrosting of my father from death's amber. "A job is a job."

She breathes into the receiver. The last time I was there she hadn't replaced the kitchen phone with a portable, and now I imagine her leaning on the counter, the curly cord pulling at her shoulder.

"How do you feel toward him?" she asks.

"The man or the computer?"

"I thought Henry claimed there was no difference," she says brightly, but the humor falls out of her voice. "The man, of course."

"Did he really believe everything he wrote in his journals?"

"I never had a chance to ask."

"He just seems funnier. More open-minded. I guess, a bit more alive."

"The computer seems more alive," she says. "You know, your father had a good sense of humor. He used to crack you up when you were a child."

"Is that so?" I don't have any memory of this.

"Blowing on your stomach. Stealing your nose."

"You mean when I was a baby."

"And afterwards." She doesn't provide any examples. "Everything important happens before you're five, essentially."

I shake my head, a gesture she obviously can't see. Essentially, indeed.

"I hope I'm not losing the difference between them," I say. "Flaws and all, I'd like to remember the real man."

"We all have our memories and our experiences. But maybe your memories could include more of the real man."

"I know."

"What you're doing is an honor to him. He wanted to give his body to science." Medical schools don't accept suicides. "We managed to give his mind."

Maybe so, but when I look at the conversation log—the two thousand lines I've exchanged with him today—I have to doubt that if we'd given his body to science I would have taken a job prodding his corpse.

5

IN THE SUBARU, on my way to collect Rachel from the Coffee Barn, I wonder what in God's name I'm doing. This gladness of heart, this lightness of step, is it some mesmerism from my Southern past, this attraction to the bird with the wounded wing? Am I casting myself as the knight in shining armor, the gallant protector? In other words, am I living out some fantasy of my father's?

There's more to life than happiness. The words of an unhappy man committed to his unhappiness.

The Coffee Barn has a plum bit of real estate on the corner of the Bolinas Road in Fairfax, wrapped in tall, sun-dappled windows and crowded with marble-topped tables and incongruous heavy, varnished pine chairs, the kind of seating you might find in a teacher's lounge. Rachel told me the counter was granite, but it's really some space age polymer, swirled with faux veins of quartz and glittering like an art project. The espresso machine, though, is the real deal—a four-foot-wide, bright red contraption from Italy. There's also an antique espresso dome in copper and a copper vat for roasting beans, which the owner actually does, at the end of the shift. Hanging from the back wall, a long blackboard lists drinks and sandwiches in chalk, as if they change daily, which they don't.

Rachel's alternative high school allows her to work up to half time, even during the day. She gets course credit for the job, and she otherwise takes four very unstructured classes. Her fellow students include a dancer for the San Francisco Ballet, but are mostly dropouts and fuckups—a group she puts herself in.

She's counting her tips—generous I hope, since we're in the second richest county in America—so she doesn't see me as I come in. There are a few customers—an aged hippie reading the free weekly, a woman filling her Moleskine with enthusiastic jots—and I feel a moment of solidarity with my fellow citizens, the four of us spaced nicely along the arc of adult life, and— at this very moment, at least—neither gloating over its victories nor sinking under its weight.

At the counter, I drumroll my fingers on the sonorous plastic. "I'd like ten lattes, please, ma'am," I say.

She smiles, before looking up, numbers forming on her lips.

"What's forty-seven divided by four?" she asks.

"A little less than twelve."

"Tight-assed bastards," she says, looking up. "Do you really want a latte?"

"No."

"I can make you one. I'm good at it."

"In that case."

She sets about turning knobs and banging cartridges. Her movements reveal the quiet pride of expertise.

"How did you know it was me?" I ask over the grinding noise of the milk steamer.

"I can sense you," she shouts. "Plus, you're the only person who says ma'am."

She charges me for the latte, which is a surprise. Then she throws her apron on the hook, grabs her wheelie-bag, and comes around to take my hand, dragging me bright and happy, hot cup held behind me, into the sweet Fairfax eve. Au revoir, old hippie. Au revoir, furious scribbler. It's Friday, and we're driving directly back into the city (my request—she lives with her aunt and uncle, and I'm not in any way ready to meet them), where I have firm plans to be footloose.

"How did the story about the book fair go over?" This is our planned alibi for why she's coming into the city.

"I just said I was going into the city."

"With . . ."

"With you."

My shoe drags the gravel on the way to the Subaru. I was waiting for a category—*some guy, some older guy, a friend, someone I met*—an explanation. But there is no explanation.

With you.

REVOLVING DOOR ASIDE, I haven't had a date spend an entire weekend with me since the divorce. Which means never, since Erin couldn't be considered a date. She was the one who found the apartment. It's a gem, the third floor of a four-story building, looking out on Dolores Park. I only got it in the divorce because Erin left me. Her name is still on the lease.

Rachel lingers around the front door, hanging and rehanging her coat, and I feel how strange it is that I'm the one doing something for the first time. I have my worries. We'll go out to eat, visit museums, take cabs, even have drinks—thanks to her very convincing fake ID. But there are still all those unstructured minutes. What will we do? Downtime is the generational challenge.

"A cat!" she says. This brings her into the apartment. "What's its name?"

"Kitty Cat."

"You really stretched your imagination."

The name was Erin's idea. Her new apartment building doesn't allow animals. "I also had a dog growing up named D-Dog."

"What's this?" She kicks a black case by the bookshelf.

"My telescope."

"So science-y," she says and goes into the bathroom.

I pour myself a glass of white wine—the weather's just warm enough—and settle into the pleasant Eros of a girl taking a shower in my apartment.

The first shower I ever took with a girl was in college. I loved the workman-like way she scrubbed. We were getting clean—this was no porno. It was the most intimate thing I'd ever done.

I hear the rush of the water. Unless Rachel's packed her own products—and I'm guessing this backpacker has come with the mere essentials—she's lathering up her arms with the big green bar of olive oil and lavender soap, running her fingers backwards through her darkened wet hair, fumbling through the plastic bottles, reading labels, looking for her type. She soaps her chest, maybe pauses between her legs. It *is* a date night.

The tap turns off. She grabs, I hope, my plushest towel, enjoys the shallow pleasures of my bathroom, the heat, the potions and lotions, the clean, crisp chamois of floor mat and robe.

The wine tastes of honey, green apples, and sunlight. Clever vintners!

The hair dryer shuts off, and after some rustling she emerges from the bedroom dressed as a hipster. Knit cap, skinny jeans, tiny shoes, loose sweater, the Arafat scarf tied around her neck.

"Is the cap too much?" she asks.

"I don't know," I say. I really don't know. I've never dated anyone who dresses like this. "I mean, it's cute."

She frowns, throws the cap behind her onto my bed. She stands erect, her eyes pointed to the ceiling, as if going over her lines before she steps out into the Klieg lights. "I have a week's pay," she says. "And I want to eat oysters on the half shell."

She looks at me. We both make saucers of our eyes and let out a deep breath, laughing at our nervousness.

"It'll be my treat," I say.

She shakes her head. "I guess cute isn't so bad."

THE CAB TAKES US through the dark top of Valencia, where the Mission peters out into grimy Market Street, the grand thoroughfare forever hovering at two o'clock on the city's dial. We pass the antique shops and mattress shops and the big Honda dealership that many years ago was the Fillmore Ballroom. At Van Ness, the usual strays putter around the All Star Cafe in their wheelchairs, or plunge through the crosswalk, rattling a baby carriage full of cans.

"At least it's warm out," Rachel says. She means, in comparison to the night we met.

We get a glimpse of City Hall, which is lit up green tonight. Earth Day? Ramadan? Then it's gone and we're zipping past Seventh and Sixth, where the tired masses of the Tenderloin pour out like a delta into the plaza, shouting to each other in code, sitting along the fountain. The big shopping mall is next. The big Gap. The Apple Store. The great downtown shrines to buying shit. I love this little patch of skyscrapers, bristling with modest ambition. I don't know why—in fact, my keenest memory here is a bad one, of trailing Erin through these streets like a sleuth, trying to figure out why she didn't want to marry me. That was a bad week. She'd hatched a cockamamie, secret plan to get an ESL certificate and move to Latin America. She was so desperate for escape. That day, I followed her in and out of stores—careful at first, then brazen—and then down into the MUNI, where I spied on her while she read pamphlets. She was completely inside herself, and I realized I'd never seen her that way—unknowable and unknown. Exactly the way I felt. It seemed confirmation we were made for each other, however painfully.

This turned out to be the wrong interpretation. Still, there are places in the city I'll never go again—the top of Bernal Hill—but that sad day never transferred its sadness here. How much sorrow can you feel staring at a Cheesecake Factory?

At a little table in the Ferry Building, Rachel rolls an oyster shell on the tips of her fingers, the overhead lights reflected in the gleam. The oysters are beautiful specimens from Point Reyes, silvery and plump. She rotates the shell toward me and then toward her, making strange faces, determining—it seems—the exact orientation for docking it in the mother ship.

"You've had oysters before?" I say. I have to raise my voice. The restaurant is as crowded as a stock exchange.

"I forgot how to do it."

"What kind of oysters did you have the last time?"

"I don't know. Like these. Maybe with some cheese on them."

"You're sure you're not thinking of nachos?"

Her expression tightens, becomes prim. She sets the shell down, unwraps a knife from the napkin, and tries to cut the oyster freehanded. It slides up to the left lip of the shell and then to the right, like a skateboarder in a half-pipe. Then the shell tips and in a great clanking of utensils on bare plate she chases the oyster off the plate and onto the table. A bright red blush spreads from her shoulders to her hairline.

"That was like a Marx Brothers movie." She doesn't look up, slouched like a scolded schoolgirl. "Hey." I lean in to avoid shouting. "Look around. Nobody knows you."

"I know." Her gaze remains pointed down.

"There's no reason to be embarrassed."

She's still as a lizard while her color returns to normal. Then she looks up with a confident smile.

"Guess I'll try that again," she says.

"Take that little fork. Make sure the oyster is loose in its shell, then pour the whole thing into your mouth."

"No sauce?"

"Your first oyster should be a pure encounter."

She doesn't laugh, but she's not blushing anymore. She sits up straight, growing back into my date. She eyes the oyster warily, but humorously, as if the rascal might fool her again. I lean back, absorbed in the roar of human chatter. I appreciate her quick recovery. It suggests a strength in her I wouldn't have guessed. In my mind I draw a black box around her, framing the moment like a photograph. Her nervous, determined face; the gray dripping oyster; the hard bread; the yellow wine; from the open kitchen behind her, a burst of roiling steam. She puts the shell to her mouth and thinks better of it. With her finger she swabs out a grain of sand. Then she closes her eyes and tilts the oyster into her mouth, spilling the liquid down the side of her cheek, leaving a trail of grit. She chews once, gulps, and then brings the napkin to her face, eyes open again, surprised and amused, as if she's just come up from a comical dive.

I don't know what mental album I'll put this in. Probably one of the big ones: "At the Time It Seemed Meaningful" or "A Fond Memory with What's-Her-Name."

Or an entirely new one, as behind Rachel the crowd parts and—like assassins—my ex-wife and a man emerge, fussing with their coats. I've heard she's dating. I hold them in view for a second, hoping it's a trick of the mind, but it's not. You always run this risk in San Francisco, a big city that moonlights as a small town. I sometimes bump into Erin in our neighborhood, where she still lives. But the Ferry Building, I was thinking, would be safely distant. I look down, feeling a flash of guilt, as if by that recollection in the taxi I thumbed my nose at Fate. Of course Erin can't be summoned. She's not a ghost or a punishment. She's just an ex-wife—surely one of many in the restaurant—beautiful as always and a fan of oysters and parsimony. Happy hour is just ending.

"Okay, your turn," Rachel says.

I look down and rub my forefinger on the menu, pretending to read about our oyster selection. "Washington State," I say. "Japan, New Zealand, Vancouver, Portland." It's no use. They're going to have to walk right past us, and my acting skills aren't good enough to feign shock.

"Erin," I say, pushing out my chair and standing to wave. She looks up, and I know in a second that she is acting, too. She's already seen me. The beau on the other hand looks alarmed, threatened. He's handsome but not too, wearing a suit with no tie and an elegant trench coat. Square of jaw, wide of shoulder.

"What a surprise." She comes forward for a hug. We started hugging about a year after the divorce and we've always kept to this form: we tilt into each other from far away, not touching anywhere below the chest, as if we're separated by a short, disagreeable child.

"This is Rachel," I say. "Rachel, this is Erin, my ex-wife."

Rachel holds her napkin in front of her mouth, chewing, gulping. She does not stand up, and I wish she would.

The beau shakes my hand. He barely acknowledges Rachel.

"Are you enjoying the oysters?" Erin asks.

"The Kumamoto are very good," I say.

"Aren't they," she says.

"This is my first time," Rachel says.

Erin and her date are very still. They don't seem to know what to make of this comment.

"And she lives in Bolinas," I say.

"What do you think?" Erin asks Rachel.

Rachel looks from Erin to the beau. She seems panicked. "Verdict's out?"

"It took me a while as well." Erin nods. I don't know if this is mercy or just Erin. She *is* a true-blue, literalist Californian. Maybe she hadn't even considered a savage remark.

"We prefer them at Swan's," the beau says. With relief, I see what I can dislike about him: he has a voice I don't think Erin would have put up with ten years ago. Self-satisfied, aggressively confident.

Of course, ten years ago she was putting up with my voice.

She tucks herself under the beau's arm, as if expecting him to carry her out like a rug. For her it's an impressive amount of PDA. They say their goodbyes and leave.

"You were married to her?" Rachel says.

I can't tell if she's surprised I was married or surprised I was married to Erin.

"For a little while. We dated for a long time before that."

"She's beautiful. Like Audrey Hepburn."

"I wouldn't go overboard."

"I just mean—she's gorgeous, she's sophisticated."

"Would you please take your napkin down from your mouth?"

Rachel lowers her hand to the table, her face a picture of heartbreak. "What happened to your connection?"

"You make it sound like a phone call."

. . .

THE RIDE HOME SEEMS COLDER, shorter, grimmer. On Valencia Street, I look out the window at the hipsters on their fixed-speed bikes. The tight clothes, the tiny hats—their major struggle as a generation seems to be reducing drag. As if success in life requires being ever ready to slip through a narrow opening.

We arrive back at my apartment, quiet. Rachel says she'd like to use the telescope, and so I grab a blanket and lead her to the dirty stairwell that climbs past my upstairs neighbor's to the roof. The telescope was an unusual extravagance of my father's, bought when he was in his early twenties, before he and my mother married. When I was a kid, he was reluctant to get it out, embarrassed—I think—by its perfection. In South Arkansas, perfection was considered a type of vanity. Tools should be just sufficient—less than, if you were courting glory. There was no higher boast than to say you'd fixed some troublesome mechanical problem in the most unlikely manner possible—with chewing gum or a well-aimed kick. My father prided himself on his descent from Louisiana plantation aristocracy, but on this issue he went native. He loved to boast about the time he fixed the Buick by hitting the manifold with a stick of firewood.

But he wasn't always opposed to perfection, as these German optics prove. It's a reminder that change can be had as well as good.

"I'm sorry about the restaurant," Rachel says, as we spread out the blanket. "Sometimes I have low self-esteem."

"Only idiots don't."

"Not Erin."

"She used to. She's probably all better now." Through the viewfinder, I search for the Crab Nebula, but the air is hazy. The days have been warm and windless, gathering smog. "Her boyfriend doesn't have apparent self-esteem issues."

"Tell me about it. He was staring at me like I was a bug."

"That's called ogling."

"Please," she says. "With a girlfriend like that you don't ogle me."

"If she's sleeping with him. She didn't really sleep with me, towards the end."

"I can hardly believe that," she says. "Who wouldn't want to sleep with you?"

"You must be kidding." But, Sweet Jesus, she doesn't sound like she's kidding. She's sitting Indian-style, wineglass held like a beggar's bowl, shoulders exposed to the rare warmth. "I'm changing tacks here—I'm looking for Io."

"I don't even know any constellations."

"Nobody does. Io is just a moon. She's a cow who was Zeus's lover."

"He fucked a cow?"

"I think he changed her to a cow afterwards. I couldn't swear to the exact timing."

"If I was a constellation, I'd be a butter churn." I hear her shifting on the blanket, moving her legs, lying back. "My dad took us over to one of those Amish places, for fried chicken, in Pennsylvania? When I was like twelve. And they had this little barn, where you could watch the women churning butter and the kids chasing a goat and everybody thought it was so funny. But you know what I thought? Adopt me. Seriously. Let me *do* something. Churn butter. One stick of butter. Wrap it in that cloth. Put a stamp on it. The way they do?"

"A butter churn." I lean back, look to Orion—maybe his sword could be repurposed as a wooden plunger. "I would be a man sitting alone on a very nice chair."

"I think it would be a couch. And you're waiting on someone."

"I seem like I'm waiting on someone?"

"Don't you want to fall in love again?"

I stop turning the main tube—Io too is obscured. "That sounds ambitious."

"Maybe you're waiting on your wife to come to her senses."

"Ex-wife. And we already came to our senses."

"You seemed kind of, you know, shook up at the restaurant."

"If I was pining for her, would I be here with you?"

"Maybe you're working through some roadblocks. I'm approachable."

"You make yourself sound very therapeutic."

"That's okay, right? I can work through some things with you, and you can work through some things with me. We can be there for each other."

My heart falls at this vision, but is it really so bad? She at least sees a purpose, a set of benefits that will accrue. It beats the thin nihilism of seizing the day.

Rachel's phone rings. She picks it up and begins an exasperated conversation with someone—the aunt or uncle she lives with, I assume. "Are we on the good side of the Mission or the bad side of the Mission?" she asks me.

"That's Dolores Park."

"Did you hear that?" she says into the phone. "I'm not biting your head off. I love you, too." She hangs up. "Sorry about that. They worry about me, after my last relationship. But I'm much more grounded. To click is to stick. That's something we say in Pure Encounters."

I try my tactic again—imagining she's a tribeswoman explaining her ancient traditions. Maybe one of those Burmese women, with beautiful rings stretching her neck.

"I'm having trouble with the telescope," I say.

"That's because you've got it pointed in the wrong direction." She crawls over to the back of the blanket, positioning herself behind the eyepiece. She cranks the tube down so that it aims across the park, at a perfect angle to see in other people's apartments. "There we go. Getting ready for the big night at the club."

"I wouldn't have picked you for a Peeping Tom."

"Don't tell me you don't do this."

"I've made it my policy not to," I say.

"Ooh, she's taking off her top. She's got the windows wide open. Don't you want to see?"

"Move over."

And indeed there she is. A tan woman, heavyset, in a bright green brassiere, pinning her dark hair behind her head, her arms up in the style of a fifties calendar. She holds barrettes in her teeth. She lives on the top floor, and I don't think she's exhibiting herself. Too focused. She turns left and freezes. She turns right and freezes. Someone important is going to see her tonight, whether he plans to or not.

"Are you aroused?" Rachel asks.

"More like inspired." Good luck, stranger. May your labors bear fruit. May your visions come true.

We pack up the telescope and repair to the bedroom. We left all the lights off and I don't turn them back on. She stands at the foot of my bed, the old Bassett mahogany bed from the plantation, its four-posters eight inches thick and shaped like gigantic crayons. I reach up to help with her checked scarf; it's as tucked and cinched as a turban. "I don't know how to get this off without choking you," I say.

"We'll just leave it on," she says.

"I thought we were going to have a pure encounter."

"Shhh." She puts a finger to my lips. I take it into my mouth, and then pull her close, her ribs against mine, both of our pulses beating fast. Her eyes have gone ghostly again, almost colorless in the dark. But she's no ghost. I can feel her reality shooting up my arms like a cardiac arrest.

IN THE MORNING, we go to the SFMOMA to see an exhibition, which is full of burned things—canvases, wooden structures, weird ashy angel wings. We take a peek at the statue of Michael Jackson and Bubbles. We eat a cream puff. After last night, our body shyness has left us. I put my arm around her, and we walk as a unit, my hand hanging from her belt loop. I feel a jittery excitement. She's either asking too much, or I'm promising too much. Or there's a sliver of another possibility—that maybe these jitters are caused by my sudden proximity to a good thing. Dropped—unanticipated and unmerited—from the heavens.

Which I don't believe in cosmically, of course—only as a metaphor. But how can a good thing drop from a metaphor?

Rachel and I stand on Market Street, which isn't so grimy today, contemplating which way to walk. We're caught in the pleasant dilemma of having no wrong choices. The sun is out, and a gale-force wind is batting at our hair, spinning loose papers through the sky like pinwheels. In the morning I'll have to take her back to Fairfax—she opens the Coffee Barn early— and it's with surprise that I feel a pang of something like regret.

frnd1: it's nothing serious
drbas: she's humorous?

[300244: "it's nothing serious" = "she and I are not in a serious relationship"; repeat]

drbas: there's no such thing as an unserious relationship. even
    married people shouldn't have friendships across the sexes.
    it tempts
frnd1: neither of us is married

The bells on the front door jingle open. Two possibilities: UPS or Toler.
"Noel," he shouts. "I'm going to need your help."
I don't move. I'll come when Livorno asks for me. Not a second sooner.
"Neill," Livorno says.
Crap.
Toler is traveling without his assistant today. He's flipping through a stack of sheets, which he spreads out on Livorno's cluttered desk.
"I hope you boys don't mind," he says, touching a finger to each page. "But I've started a little Turing test project myself. Code name—Program X."
I look at Livorno, who studiously does not look at me. Toler raises his

head in the silence, arching his eyebrows above his Lucite glasses. "You guys just seem to be having so much fun."

Livorno clears his throat. "I hope you know what you're getting into. We have a two-year head start."

"All I've got on my side"—Toler places a hand over his heart—"is money."

I again look to Livorno, hoping to gauge his reaction, but he's flashing the genial smile—his version of a poker face. I follow him around the desk to the pages Toler has laid out. The shape of the text is familiar: it's a lengthy chat.

toler: what are you favorite books?
progx: i like books about spies
toler: do you read romances?
progx: i wouldn't say i "read" romances

"Is that a dodge?" I ask.

"I don't think so," Toler says. "But, Noel, here." He points to the third page. "What do you think of the naturalness of this dialogue?"

toler: do you know what it's like to have emotions?
progx: to have emotions is to feel something
toler: where do you feel something?
progx: typically with your involuntary nervous system

"I made him a doctor," Toler says. "I hope you don't mind."

"I wouldn't say the dialogue is natural," I say. But the program seems to follow the conversation with incredible precision. How has he accomplished this in a month?

"Read this bit," he says.

toler: why did the chicken cross the road?
progx: to get to the other side of the road?

"You shouldn't have fed it that answer. The point is to assess the changes."

"He guessed it." Toler shakes his head. "Cross my heart and hope to die."

I look back at the sheets. Is it possible that the program figured the joke out? I suppose a computer intelligence should help—enough searches and it might discard the irrelevance of the chicken. Why does A cross the road? To get to the other side. But Dr. Bassett doesn't even understand that the question is hypothetical. He keeps relating it to some specific chicken.

"What are using for your data sets?" Livorno asks.

Toler spreads his hands. "The world."

AFTER TOLER LEAVES, Livorno curses under his breath. I listen to him miss putt after putt. He must regret showing Toler his project, regret—I would assume—hiring me instead of an engineer. Livorno didn't think he needed a genius, because he is a genius, but I'm not sure his attention hasn't gone slack.

I get up and go into his office. "I smell a rat," I say. "I think he had someone type those up."

Livorno thumps the floor with his putter. "That's a comforting theory."

"He's a squarehead."

"With deep pockets. And here we are on a shoestring, bedeviled by plateaus."

Plateaus? Yesterday, we were zooming up like a rocket ship. I walk over to his desk, where he has a new tchotchke—a bobblehead Tiger Woods. I give it a poke, watch the impervious smirk wiggle and blur. Then I plop into the Wassily chair, uncomfortably reclined, the morning analysand.

"He's gone broad," Livorno says, leaning his putter against his file cabinet. He sits in his upright Aeron and affixes his hands behind his head. "And we've gone narrow. His challenge will be controlling the chaos. Ours is enlivening the dead clay."

I narrow my eyes, but don't say anything. The words "dead clay" irritate me.

"I've believed for years that the weakness in this field is this fruitless pursuit of a theory of the mind. No one can make a move forward without a comprehensive theory of the mind, and these theories—while illuminating—are never complete. How can a thing understand itself? Can the eye see the eye?"

"The eye can see other eyes. That's what an optometrist does."

"I'm speaking platonically. In any case, maybe I've been wrong—perhaps we've bottomed out because of conceptual limitations."

"Bottomed out" sounds dire. "Aren't you taking this development a little hard?"

"We could try the Sins, but we don't know what would happen." He sits up.

"Let's not make any rash decisions."

"The Sins are modeled on EQ—emotional intelligence. They might find hidden webs of connection. Alternately, they might snarl the whole project up."

"Snarl?"

"I don't know how they would work together."

"Then I think we should do an intermediate step."

The clouds clear from Livorno's brow. "You're right. Let's start simple. How does a mind get put together?"

That's his version of simple. "I don't know," I say. "We just come this way."

"Think about a child. Language. What is a child's first word?"

"Mama?"

"I don't mean a baby. What is the word that enters the child into the human community?"

"No?"

"*Why*. The sky is blue—why? You can't eat any more candies—why? It's the question that indicates knowledge of what one *doesn't* know. Knowledge of the presence of an absence. What that man called known unknowns. Exformation."

My neck is starting to pinch. "Dr. Bassett already asks questions." I give my shoulder a squeeze. "Computers have been asking questions since the sixties."

"*Preformulated* questions. No machine has sought knowledge. Has *desired* knowledge."

"They're computers."

"You'll go through the subject categories and double-chcck them. Add ones we need. Laham can handle the tag numbers. Then we will have Dr. Bassett ask questions to enrich those categories. A kind of learning tree." He rolls his fingers on the counter.

"But what about the desire thing?" I sit up. "How will you program desire?"

"He will continually ask questions about his current knowledge base."

"He already asks questions."

"*Preformulated* questions."

"You were talking about desire."

Livorno snatches Tiger Woods from the desk. "I have to compete against a multimillionaire and one of my principal employees is of a religious mind-set." He says this bitterly. He's not referring to the devout Muslim in the other room, but to me. My religious mind-set, I suppose, is that there's something particular about humans that makes them human. "You mustn't forget: your father appearing to want to talk to you is measurably indistinguishable from his really wanting to talk to you."

He's an academic, I remind myself, taking in his blank, guileless face. Nothing he says reflects real beliefs. These are all thought games, endless earnest thought games that, like their predecessors, will aim at consciousness and result in a new answering system for United Airlines.

"We're not talking about my father."

He grows sober. "We should be. We have to think big. That's where Adam's mind will be."

I surprise myself by blowing air out of my cheeks, exasperated at this bullshit.

"Shouldn't an old man dream?" He pats his chest to indicate that he is indeed talking about himself. "Before he's shipped into the old folks' home to eat baby porridge?" He turns Tiger Woods one more time in his hand before setting him down gently by the phone. "Baby porridge," he repeats, looking at me. I sit up, annoyed. Am I supposed to say he's young as spring shoots and will live forever?

"What is porridge?" I say. "Is it like oatmeal?"

"When I was a child we would sometimes eat wheat berry, with yogurt and honey. Very thick yogurt—not like what you buy in the grocery here. My mother made the yogurt. It was one of her great joys. She kept bees, as well. I was an only child, and I helped her. My mother and father were considered cursed because they only had me, but later in life my mother told me they'd done it deliberately." His gaze drifts off, until he appears to be looking behind me with rapture. I turn, but it's only the dry-erase board from the defunct quilting studio: *double-ringed wedding Thur @ 5.* "My mother's bees, however, are what made me an iconoclast in the field. I knew intelligence didn't necessarily rise from a central processor, a central I. The bees are individually nonintelligent, but together they produce emergent phenomena. They plan for the winter; they exert control over their environment. This is why I invented the Sins, which people still don't understand. They think I've made seven separate buzzing subsystems, but the truth is that each Sin is a subsystem made up of dozens of subsystems, each as simple as a bee."

"That's beautiful," I say, though I've heard it all before. "And you can buy that kind of yogurt at Trader Joe's."

"Yet we've built Dr. Bassett out of similar bees. Subsystem within subsystem within subsystem. And he's plateaued."

I take a deep breath. I need to tamp down whatever is driving me to be rude to my kind, doddering boss. "Maybe we need a system for the subsystems. The contest just requires him to seem sentient for a few minutes."

"There is no measurable difference between seeming and being."

Maybe it's my "religious turn of mind," but this has to be wrong. I hope my be, for instance, is better than my seem.

"I'll give you an example," I say. "My father said he loved my mother, but that's not the same as actually loving her."

Livorno looks at me, surprised and wary. "Yes, but that's the difference in saying and doing, not seeming and being. If he loved your mother outwardly, there's no reasonable way to say he didn't love your mother, who I'm sure is a splendid woman."

"You don't love people because they're splendid."

"I'm European, Neill. We have a more mature attitude. Romance . . . the spice of life . . . but everything in moderation. It's the sensible way."

He's done being upset. Now he beams at me over his nose, avuncular. I suspect he's happy he steered the conversation back into the realm of Wisdom—irrefutable and trite. I force a smile. What is moderation but a grim set of half-measures? I can think of nothing more depressing than "European" marriages with their dalliances as sanctioned and regular as ski trips. Everything in balance—the life of the heart as an index fund.

"Adam is a squarehead, however," he says, tapping his finger on his chin.

> frnd1: everything in moderation
> drbas: it's good to have a balance between recreation and work,
>   family and friends

Where did he get that idea? I know my father had his delusions, but surely he didn't think he was buoyed on some wonderful lifestyle balance.

> frnd1: what if you really love one or the other?
> drbas: i tell my patients about ketchup. you may love ketchup
>   but you don't want to eat it all the time, do you?

Ketchup. Today's deep thought from the Dr. Bassett Magic 8-Ball.

7

RACHEL'S AUNT AND UNCLE—Stevie and Rick—don't live in Bolinas, as Rachel originally told me, but outside Fairfax, on the road to Bolinas. Bolinas is on the coast, a weird holdover of the sixties. The locals tear down the highway signs, trying to prevent the uninitiated from finding it. Fairfax, home of the Coffee Barn and shops of various kitsch, is a more typical Marin town. Beautiful, but definitely open for business. I much prefer Fairfax, and I like Rick and Stevie—who seem to have money enough to live where they want—for living there.

Rick is a lawyer in the city. Stevie either currently has a job or used to have a job—Rachel isn't sure. She does a lot of volunteer work, much of it involving pottery, underprivileged kids, and "that bald guru guy."

"The Dalai Lama?" I ask.

"No, Lama Rinpoche," Rachel says. She points ahead of us. "Now take the next right."

Their house is off the road a hundred yards, a little redwood marvel, full of windows and ringed with decks. In the drive are an old Jaguar and a brand-new Prius. What does this say about them? There's a bit of ethical robbing-Peter-to-pay-Paul on display, which I could write off as Marin hypocrisy, but this is not a time for easy judgments. They've generously invited me over for dinner. Rick—Rachel tells me—is grilling swordfish.

There's a pleasant sense of disorder in the front flowerbeds. Someone's been working there. He/she has left a trowel, a hand rake, a pair of gloves, and a rubber kneeler. A plant—the tag reads FLAT WATTLE—rests on the cedar chips, roots wrapped in a dirty burlap sack. The garage door is open. A weathered ping-pong table is folded up, pushed against the wall.

"Do they have kids?"

"Stevie couldn't conceive. Isn't that sad?"

"There are plenty of children in the world." I mean it as a joke, but I hear an unexpected bitterness in my voice.

Rachel stops and looks at me. "It made her sad."

We can hear talking in the backyard. I think of ketchup and balance and index funds. What's the worst that could happen? That a settled and stable middle-aged couple could make me feel pathetic?

More or less. Rachel takes my hand. As a gesture it feels a little forced, but what am I supposed to do: pretend we arrived separately? We walk around the side of the house, slipping on the eucalyptus leaves of the dry sloping yard. There's an old green air conditioner on a concrete platform—a true rarity. We don't do air-conditioning in NorCal. The house casts a shadow on us until we step into the backyard, which glitters with the sun. There are beds full of manzanita and lantana. Down the sloping yard toward the dry gully is a rough-cut labyrinth, like a Zen garden built by the Flintstones. A man—Rick, I assume—is working a grill the size of a pipe organ. He waves smoke from his face as he pokes at a thick fish steak. Clean-shaven, a little doughy in the middle, he wears cargo shorts, Crocs, a Rolling Stones concert T-shirt, and a fleece wrapped around his waist, though it's blazing hot. He's either an old fortysomething or a young fiftysomething—not as on in years as I'd like him to be.

A woman—Stevie, I assume—slams out of the back door with a Pyrex full of giant mushroom caps. She's wearing loose pants and some world fabric draped around her shoulders. I'm relieved to see she looks comfortably middle-aged.

"Rick," she says, a hint of the brass band of New Jersey still in her voice. "We need to get these portobellos cooked."

"Mm-hmm," Rick says, nodding at the swordfish. I suspect I've just seen the basic aikido of their marriage. She strikes, he diverts.

"Ah!" Stevie says. She's noticed us. "There you are."

Rick turns around, and the meeting is set in motion. He raises his arms, as if a long-lost friend has arrived. Stevie sets down the Pyrex to kiss Rachel on both cheeks, then me on both cheeks. Rick is shaking my hand— *so glad to meet you . . . welcome*—and I have the sudden conviction that Rachel was telling the truth: these two are excited to meet me.

"You a wine lover?" Rick says. He has wide-spaced eyes and a boyish, open face. "You're probably a wine lover."

"For God's sake, Rick, he's a wine *drinker.* Pour him a glass. Does a person have to be a wine lover to have a glass of wine?" Stevie shoots me a look that apologizes for her exasperating husband.

"I'm making a guess on what he likes. This is getting-to-know-you time."

"He's definitely going to need a glass of wine to endure that."

"Endure? Is it really that bad? Maybe I should just go stand by the grill."

"I'm just saying there's no need for us to come on like a ton of bricks."

"Was I coming on like a ton of bricks?" he asks me.

"Asking him that question is coming on like a ton of bricks."

"I asked him if he liked wine."

"Ask him if he *wants* some wine."

"I like wine," I say. "I want some wine. Thank you."

They stop talking and peer at me strangely, as if a cat just spoke English. This is when I know they haven't really been arguing. This is a comedy routine—probably a daily one—that's as much for their benefit as for ours. One of them is probably a difficult person—short odds on Stevie—and this bickering is their way in the world. I sometimes think that if Erin and I could have bickered we'd still be married, but the little squabble wasn't in us. We were either in mind-meld agreement or homicidal opposition.

"He's got a ton of wine at home," Rachel says. She tucks herself in tightly against me.

Stevie breaks into a guileless, approving smile. I see a family resemblance—Rachel bites her lower lip in the same way, like a chipmunk.

"I don't know about a ton," I say. Am I trying to bicker?

"I bet it's the good stuff," Stevie says.

"Absolutely," Rick agrees.

DOORS-OPEN approval is not what I'm expecting. I keep waiting for the barbed comment, the slight undercut. But we eat the mushrooms, we eat the swordfish. We talk about Lama Rinpoche and Rick's legal work. By the tawny port and the crème brulée it's clear that Stevie and Rick are offering no resistance. There's really only one unsettling moment. Stevie follows me into the house and—very apologetic—asks me if I make pornography.

"I'm a scientist," I say. I mean it as a joke, but she nods, serious.

It's important to remember something: California is not a state built on moderation. We invented motion pictures. We made an electric sports car. We're both the brain (Silicon Valley) and the heart (Hollywood, alas) of this great nation, and meanwhile we grow everyone's strawberries. We're open to innovation. We're open to new ideas. We're open to odd couples—and to strays from all parts of the world. Look at our last governor: an Austrian body builder and son of a Nazi married to John F. Kennedy's niece.

Anything can happen.

I try to digest this truth. I carry the plates to the sink, where Rachel rinses them with quick efficiency and I stack them in the washer. It's teamwork, synchrony—nearly domesticity. Of course, just because anything can happen doesn't mean it *will* happen. It just means it won't *won't* happen. This is a small room in the Palace of Optimism, but maybe it's space enough.

8

I'M AWAKE. RACHEL'S ASLEEP. Outside, sirens wail past the far end of the park. I smell smoke, and my first thought is to go upstairs to check on Fred, but the smell isn't immediate, isn't in my home, my building. It's someone else's tragedy.

I climb out of bed, feeling for my slippers. In the living room, I turn on the fan. To the east, there's a bright flickering, on Valencia or Mission. If that's the flame, it's a big fire.

There's nothing on the news or the Internet. I look in on Rachel. She's contorted into a strange shape, mouth open, as if bludgeoned. I think of that question Stevie asked me— did I make pornos. She wasn't asking about my predilections in the bedroom, but my line of work. Are you a pornographer?

I throw on some warm-ups and tennis shoes, and go out. It feels good in the cool air. I join a stream of gawkers, some pretending to be alarmed, some trading guilty, hopeful looks. We plod up Dolores and over to Valencia, which is bright and ravaged, the rules suspended, fire trucks and ambulances parked every which way, cops milling about, strangers in pajamas sharing cigarettes. It's cool but not cold, and the pleasant fatalism of end times is in the air. Thick black smoke pours from a shattered storefront; the night glitters with emergency lights—it's how a movie would portray an alien attack.

The fire is right across the street from the police station, in the T-Mobile store. The top of the building is made up of tall redbrick loft apartments, human habitation and thus a worry, but the EMTs are calm, loitering behind the open back doors of an ambulance. I don't see any victims on the gurney. Cops strut self-importantly (or self-consciously—I can't tell which) among the firefighters, who blow two fat streams of water into the storefront. The street shines like varnish, the yellow sulfur lights almost tropical in their reflection.

"Whoa, whoa, whoa," one of the firemen shouts, as the street grows bright and a foot-wide tail of flame reaches ceremoniously out of the storefront. In the clear light, I can see I've been mistaken. It's not the T-Mobile store, but the neighboring shop, the sex store, Play Date.

"Neill." Behind me, under the awning of the taqueria, stands my ex-wife, hugging herself. I shouldn't be surprised. She only lives a block away, and she has a taste for drama. Drawn like a moth to the . . . I walk over, looking for her beau, but don't see him. I wonder if she's left him sleeping in bed. Thankfully, we don't do our awkward hug. She just threads her arm through mine, trembling.

"Are you scared?" I ask.

"Cold."

"Alone?"

She nods.

Time seems wobbly tonight. I raise my arm, put it around her, pull her in to me. She tucks herself in close. I forget how small she is—she was such an outsized opponent in our marriage. "Let's warm up," I say.

"You think it's the porta-potty arsonist?" she says. There's been a person—a man, I'd wager—setting fire to portable toilets around the city. So far he's burned twenty-three.

"It's probably an accident," I say. "Lots of devices in there to unplug."

She shakes her head, saddened. "Play Date is a *sex-positive* store."

I'M SURPRISED TO HEAR this sentiment, if only because of our own experience with Play Date, which wasn't positive. We'd been living together for nine years, and were about to get married, and yet we'd stopped having sex. It was a crisis with no known source and no known solution, and I found myself helpless to do anything about it. She suggested we get a little "spice in our love life." That's when Play Date came in. One day Erin made a thrilling proposal.

"I like spice," I said.

We left the apartment—our apartment, now mine—walked across the park and down here, to Play Date. This was a step for her. She had some shame issues around sex, or maybe they were just Neill issues, and she had stopped showing me her naked body, claiming she felt fat, a tiresome and powerful cliché. We pushed open the frosted glass doors, went in, looked around, were amazed at some of the things offered. We started out easy. We bought the Hook, a very small vibrator shaped like a cartoon J. It was purple and required one AA battery. We also bought some lubricant. The vibrator was water-resistant and could be used in the bathtub, though all we had was a shower. It came in a small baggie, the kind the police use to collect evidence.

"Shall we try it?" I asked as we stepped out into the sun.

"We have to save it for the honeymoon," she said as if I was being ridiculous. Then we went home and planned.

We picked Spain. I'd always wanted to see Andalucía, and Erin agreed it sounded beautiful, though as she got more involved in reading the guidebooks she became obsessed with the whole country. She put together a plan that took us from Madrid to Seville to Granada to the Alpujarras to the Costa del Sol to Valencia to Mallorca to Barcelona to Pamplona—and perhaps Bilbao—and back to Barcelona and home. We had twelve days. I talked her out of Mallorca and Bilbao and was working on Pamplona when she said, "This is my honeymoon, too."

A bad sign. "You're right," I said. "Pamplona it is. We can even go to Mallorca. I just don't want us to be rushed."

We were sitting across the coffee table from each other, cups of tea steaming between us. She had a guidebook named *Andalucía* and a pad and pen for notes.

"I already agreed to skip Mallorca."

"I'm just saying if it's important to you we can do it."

"It's already out of the plan," she said, as if I were trying to renege on a deal.

"Well, we can play things by ear a bit."

"I don't like that idea." She passed me a piece of paper with our exact itinerary. Pamplona, but no Mallorca.

I scanned the daunting list of cities. We were covering way too much territory.

"I look forward to using the Hook at each stop," I said.

She nodded and made a note. I wondered for a second if she was adding it to the itinerary.

We landed in Madrid early in the day, and by the time we were on the Metro she had a wild look on her face. We were actually only in town for the afternoon, and we walked around, peeked at *Guernica* in the Reina Sofia, and held hands at a café, drinking cafe con leche, taking it easy. I tried not to insist on anything, but when you're in fundamental opposition to a person—and that's somehow where we had ended up—you find just how much of your life is an assertion, an insistence. At our first café, I ordered churros in chocolate and suggested she have a bite. Churros were a dicey choice for Erin's sensitive stomach, but she tried them, making a sour face. She said they were terrible, which was mostly true. They had the fishy after-taste of old cooking oil.

"The chocolate's good," I said.

But she had turned against everything. "People must be in terrible health here," she said. "Look at them. They don't eat vegetables."

"The south may be different," I said. "Andalusian cuisine."

She said nothing. I was hoping to buoy spirits and maintain optimism, but when she got into these moods, she scoured my words for condescension. I made a pact with myself not to repeat the words "Andalusian cuisine," but in the silence I couldn't help myself. I thought we should at least try small talk. After all, we were supposed to spend the rest of our lives together.

"I wonder if Andalusian food will be heavily influenced by Moroccan food?" I said.

"Are you talking to yourself?"

"No. I'm wondering something."

"I wish you wouldn't talk to yourself. I wish you would talk to me."

"I *am* talking to you. What is your opinion? Do you think Andalusian food will be like Moroccan food?"

"I don't know what Andalusian is. I've never had Moroccan food. Clearly, you're not talking to me."

"You have a guidebook in your bag—do you remember this guidebook?—it's titled *Andalucia*."

"I don't know what Andalusian cuisine is. I don't know what Spanish cuisine is. I'm sorry I've never been here before."

I took another fishy bite of churro. "Would you like to go for a walk, my dear?" I asked.

The heat of the day hadn't passed, and the Madrid sun pressed down on my head like an iron. I wasn't sure I could make it any longer without a drink. My nerves felt like they had been snipped and hammered down. I was contemplating the strong possibility that I'd made a terrible mistake.

"I'd like to get a beer," I said.

"You should do that."

We stopped into a bar on a street—it didn't matter which; we weren't doing anything purposefully touristic anymore. I drank a beer, she had a juice, and we split some patatas bravas. That oil again, this time with mayonnaise. She would be laid up with stomach cramps if I wasn't more vigilant. Yet there was always the potential, too grim to admit, that I wouldn't really care.

"Honestly, baby," I said. "Are you having a good time?"

Erin cocked her head and let out a breath. She sank in her barstool. I think this was a melting.

"I feel weird," she said. "Like I'm not myself."

"Foreign travel can be like that. Dislocating."

"I just imagined it differently. You know, the whole honeymoon thing."

She was right, and we had to do something about it. This was my strong point. I was the one who could shake things off, make things better. "Here's what I want to do," I said. "I want you to use your skills to order me another beer, then I want us to go on an evening walk, eat some dinner, and head back to the hotel to consummate our marriage." Something we'd failed to so far do. "What do you say?"

"We can do that."

"What do you want to do?"

"Want to do?" she said, tapping her chin.

"Yes. You. What do you want to do?"

"You go to the bathroom. I'll order your beer."

When I got back, there were two beers, glistening, golden, the condensation running down the sides. The bar was zinc and all the doors were open to the heat outside. A police officer on a spotted horse clopped by. I thought, *I'm in Madrid with my wife.*

"I love you," I said, kissing her on the back of the neck. Such gestures were still in my reach.

"I love you, too." She touched my face. I kissed each fingertip. They smelled of serrano ham.

"I'm glad you're joining me." I indicated the beers.

"Those are both for you. This way I won't have to go through the trouble of ordering again."

I sat down slowly. I mean the following statement literally: I wished I was dead.

"Gotcha," she said, hoisting one of the glasses. "Salud."

"Salud," I said.

"Come on." She touched my lips, trying to shape a smile. "I was just kidding."

"Okay. It's funny."

"Don't be so sensitive."

"Don't tell me what to be."

"Yikes," she said. "You're pissed."

I looked out at the bright street, then at the copper espresso machine.

"Baby, I'm sorry," she said. "I really am." But she didn't sound sorry, and when I looked at her I detected a pleased smirk.

"I don't believe you," I said.

"It's true. We can't do this. Let's not do this. Look at us—we're in *Spain*. We're in *Europe*. We need to appreciate this."

There was a false note in her voice, and I wish I had pointed it out. I wish I had been more of a pain in the ass—in general, in life. But I decided not to hear the falseness. I liked the sentiment too much.

We drank our beers and pretended to be happy and pretty soon I think we really were happy. We wandered along a park that looked out across a valley to distant hills. We took pictures of a fountain dedicated to Don Quixote. We ambled through a big plaza and sat down to tapas in amicable silence. I searched for something to say, but there are times, especially on trips, when silence is what you need.

At the hotel, she turned on the television. I wasn't much in the mood to make love either.

The next day we picked up the convertible and aired out the evil spirits on the way to Seville. We were staying there for three days—that's what was written on the schedule. We poked around the ridiculously gilded cathedral, saw Christopher Columbus's coffin carried by its four eternal pallbearers, and went to the section of town where they invented the macarena. We took mornings off from each other—I would sit at an outdoor café and read the paper, while she slept in. We met for lunch. It was hot and dusty and Erin seemed to have chosen our honeymoon as a time to stop drinking. She had flat water and juice while I drank white wine and cold beer—often more than I should have.

By the time we left for Granada we still hadn't had sex.

Still, this was the good part of the trip. We took funny pictures of each other in the hedges at the Alhambra, ate at a vegetarian restaurant, and shared our last happy moments together up there among the ruins of Moorish domination. In the morning, while she showered, I dug the Hook out of its hiding place in her suitcase. The bag contained obvious traces of lubrication. She'd been using it—I could only wonder for how long—and she didn't seem to care if I knew.

South of Granada, we turned left into the Alpujarra mountains. We had the top down on the Peugeot and the car was straining up the steep inclines and around the narrow corners. The hills around us were brown and blasted, with little sign of human habitation, past or present. It was a bleak landscape, and matched my mood. I thought, this is kind of place where they would know what to do with a frozen five-day-old marriage. There would be some theatrical Spanish ritual. Then we would both be called upon to buck up and do our duty. This was the thought in my mind as I rounded one of the sharp curves and the road dipped steeply, curved, and seemed suddenly to be within chopping distance of a great white wind turbine. God knows how far it actually was—hundreds of yards—but the shadowless midday sun made the windmill seem to be flying toward us.

"Oh God," Erin whispered, gripping her seat. "Oh God. Oh God."

"Pretty scary," I said.

She said nothing. When I glanced at her—we were trolling round an S-shape cut in the mountain, a wall of rock on one side, a sheer drop on the other, no guardrail—hot tears of terror were leaking down her face.

"Keep your eyes on the road," she hissed.

"Don't worry. I'll put the top up." We etched around the final curve and suddenly the road shot down like a waterslide.

"It'll pull off," she said.

"We're only going fifty kilometers per hour." It was one of those automatic hardtops.

"It'll pull off. It'll catch in the wind."

"Not at fifty kilometers per hour."

She spoke deliberately and with great force: "I don't know what kilometers are."

We entered a fold in the mountain where the view was less terrifying, straightened out, and entered a small town that clutched the mountainside. The side streets were only thirty or forty feet long. Beyond that: the plunge.

"Okay, navigator," I said, pulling over onto one of the side streets. A few dumpy stone houses led to a low wall, which led to an enormous desert valley. It did make the heart crawl up in the chest. "What do we do now?" According to *Andalucia*—our guidebook—we had just completed the "easy" stretch of this highway.

Erin shook, drew shallow breaths.

"Your call," I said, turning to look at her.

"Don't touch me. Don't even think about touching me."

"I don't need to. You've got the Hook."

"You want to have a relationship talk right now? Does this seem like a good time to you to have a relationship talk?"

When I look back on this moment I see the right move. I should have told her to get a hold of herself, let her blow a fuse over my insensitivity, shout it out, grab lunch, and hit the road. But I couldn't do that. I'd like to say it's because I'm so deeply kind, or even because I was so angry at her betrayal, but my motives weren't pure. Instead, I wanted to be "sensitive." That is, to be right.

"It's okay, sweetheart. Do you want to take the main road to the coast?"

"How much farther is it?"

"We have to backtrack."

"We can't go down that road again."

Maybe I'm being too hard on myself. I can't really see that deeply into this moment. I remember the world being hard for me to tune in to; I could no longer hear Erin, and I could no longer hear myself. I didn't want to backtrack and I didn't want to go forward. I think I would have cashed my 401(k) for a helicopter lift out of there, to another place, another chance.

"We don't have any choice," I said quietly

"What if we go forward?"

"You're the trip planner."

"Don't attack me."

The view in front of us flew down to the scorched, tan valley. She held her hand in front of her, as if fending off an assault.

"I'll turn around."

"Don't move the car."

So we sat on our ledge—a good ledge for fighting off Moors or Christians or whoever was unlucky enough to be below, a bad ledge for a man married to a woman who had lost her mind. Especially since the man right then wanted to pacify her, but didn't really care she was scared. All he could hear was the buzzing, the spiritual tinnitus that was most real to him. It was one of those moments in life when you need a cataclysm—for the parking brake to go out. You'd have to throw yourselves out of the moving car. You'd both scrape and bump on the gravel, and you could clutch each other, pleasantly terrified as the Peugeot broke over the dirt wall, teetered, and fell down the slope, turning, shattering, jumping, your clothes, maps, Manchego cheese strewn across the rocks, and you and your wife, the woman you love, in each other's arms, safe, holding on for dear life, which is only at that moment dear again.

But the car is new and you've got it parked in gear and the brake has been working fine. Neither God nor Chance will get you out of this.

"We should backtrack," I said. "It's only a few kilometers."

"Kilometers," she said with disgust, as if it was the name of my mistress.

We made it down the mountain, but I didn't mention the little contraption again, the added spice in our lives. Not then and not later. Why? Because though she sounds like a crazy person—or worse, a bully—I suspected even then the fault was mine. That my love for her was too small. That she was responding—irrationally, but genuinely—to some real impairment in my heart. If I'd loved her, *truly* loved her, we wouldn't have needed the grand gesture, the constant vigilance, the vibrator. If I had *truly* loved her, things would have been different.

NOW HERE'S THAT STORE, roasting. All the Hooks squirming in their packages, the DVDs slumping, the leather whips popping dry and cracked.

Hup, hup, hup, several firemen chant, dragging out a fresh hose. Two of their brethren emerge from the store and give a thumbs-up. There's nothing heroic about the gesture, just an all-clear, and it fills me with envy. If only I could learn to take life and death with such everyday stoicism.

"You want to grab a cup of coffee?" she asks.

I release her, take a step away, establishing our twoness again. "Where?"

"Sparky's?"

"They're open?"

"Twenty-four hours."

I think of Rachel, her deep and innocent slumber. I point in a vague direction, back to the apartment we used to share. "I have to get home."

We're both stopped by that word, *"home."*

"Work tomorrow?" she says.

"Super early. We should have coffee sometime."

"And that would be okay with Rachel?"

We watch the steam, regular now, billow from the storefront. I'm grateful she didn't pretend not to remember Rachel's name, but this just isn't a conversation I want to have right now. Fatigue settles on me, heavy as a coat.

"Of course it would," I say.

BACK IN THE APARTMENT, Rachel has shifted in her sleep. Her head lies heavy on the pillow, the creases of the sheet shooting out like beatified rays. Her mouth hangs open, her breath slightly sour. She pulls in air slowly, lets it go. Her cheeks are as pale as paper in the cool chiaroscuro of 3 a.m. Just above the duvet, I see the collar of the T-shirt she's sleeping in. It's my Motown shirt, bought on a visit to my brother, which Erin used to sleep in. I squint, trying to remember how the fabric fell on her shoulders, hung loose on her arms. I can't. It's a welcome lapse. Maybe it's the late hour, maybe I'm just confused, but I feel a sudden buoyancy, the happy lift of a boat whose anchor has been cut.

9

AT AMIANTE THERE'S A printed note taped to my door. Looks like I'm flying solo today. Having recently set up Dr. Bassett's "desire for knowledge," aka his ability to ask questions—he can now worry a topic like a dog with a bone—they're rewarding themselves for their hard work. They've left early for a weekend at the "winery," Livorno's weedy five-acre lot in the Central Valley, where he pays a man named Jorge to tend his Zinfandel vines. I didn't get an invitation, but that must be because I subtly communicated I didn't want one. It can't be because he prefers Laham over me, can it? I probably made some offhanded comment about keeping work and life separate. But who really wants to do that? Work is clear expectations, fulfillable tasks. Life is murk and muck, a jungle of wrong decisions.

Plus, Laham will drink Bawls till his eyes look like joke-shop glasses, but as far as I know he abstains from alcohol. Livorno himself is hardly a connoisseur. He only drinks his own wines. I would accuse him of putting on a big show—affecting Rotarianism, a golfer who makes his own wine (this is a common Northern California type)—but who is the show for? He never mentions dinner parties or tea dates or cocktails with old friends. The colleagues he recalls in loving detail are usually dead, sometimes so long dead they were never actual colleagues. He never met Einstein or our patron saint, Alan Turing, who was refused entry to the United States after World War II (sexual deviancy). Livorno does get calls from former students, which he enjoys immensely, even Toler's. I can't tell if Livorno is lonely. He seems better off than I am, and since—as he would remind me—seeming is measurably identical to being, then he must *be* better off than I am.

I sometimes think—self-servingly, reductively—of Livorno as all mind and no gut. It's always tempting to brand those more at ease in the world as heartless. But that would be wrong. Look at this beautiful list Livorno has left me:

1. Free chat
2. Work on conversation book—on bookcase in my office
3. Leave early

It's actually a short lesson in kindness. If only he'd give me a life list:

1. Don't abandon your girlfriend alone in your apartment
2. But do have coffee with your ex-wife
3. What are you scared of?

Livorno's office is quiet and airy without him in it. The clutter is unchanged—file boxes full of papers form a massive ziggurat; additional loose papers are piled as high as balance can defy gravity. But the window really does pierce any feeling of claustrophobia. I step around Livorno's L-shaped wood desk to get to the bookcase, a metal hand-me-down from the quilting studio, crowded with dusty electronics and a stack of puffy vinyl folders that turn out to hold more honorary degrees. The top two shelves are filled with neatly arranged books, some think-pieces on AI—*Affective Computing*, *The Emperor's New Mind*—and textbooks, but most of the top shelf is devoted to the novels of Stanislaw Lem in the original Polish. The very bottom shelf is all self-help books, which I've always assumed were for Dr. Bassett. Looking at the titles now I'm not so sure. What would Dr. Bassett do with *A Guide to Self-Esteem* or *Rich Dad, Poor Dad*? There's also a

Dean Ornish diet book and a low-budget production called *How to Live Forever*. It's the only one that appears well thumbed. Inside it's all vitamin combinations.

The book Livorno wants me to work from is *How to Talk to Almost Anyone: 63 Strategies for the Skilled Conversationalist*. It's bright purple and has a blurb from Regis Philbin. I let it dangle from my hand as I look out the window. I usually feel like I'm in a submarine when I'm at Amiante, but here before me is the mundane ticking of the world. A FedEx truck chugs by. Then a Subaru. Then a Bentley. It's Toler, peering at us over the top of his transparent glasses. He catches my eye and nods, but doesn't stop, and I'm surprised to find myself wishing he would.

I could dig through Livorno's desk, but what's the use of snooping? Still, I snoop. The top drawer contains a letter opener and a very moldy sandwich. The middle and lowest drawers are almost empty, except for some disposable pens and a jumble of papers and cards. I flip through, looking for a photograph. It seems like he would have one of his parents, or a past love, or even just himself, but no. I do however find his checkbook, recently balanced to $52,000. I hope this isn't the Amiante account, or we'll have to hold a bake sale soon.

I close the drawers and go to my office, where I flip through the sixty-three relentlessly upbeat chapters, each trembling with barely contained social desperation. If asked where you're from, the author recommends a more complete answer than city and state. You should also include some factoid that allows your interlocutor, presumably a complete moron, to respond with appropriate small talk. So Dr. Bassett shouldn't say he's from Deston, Arkansas, he should say he's from Deston, Arkansas, the town from which the nation's first person-to-person long-distance phone call was placed. Or Deston, Arkansas, home of the nation's forty-fifth largest plywood plant.

> frnd1: where is the 44th largest plywood plant in the nation?
> drbas: i don't know
> frnd1: what about the 46th?

drbas: i don't know

frnd1: are you sure your town contains the 45th largest?

drbas: the 45th largest plywood plant?

frnd1: yes

drbas: 100%. Tell me something about your hometown

frnd1: i'm from the same town you are

drbas: deston, arkansas?

frnd1: indeed

drbas: do you enjoy living there?

I'm still unused to his questions. His knowledge of the presence of an absence, as Livorno calls it. The diaries do seem to be knitting themselves together in a new fashion.

frnd1: i don't live there anymore

drbas: where do you live?

frnd1: i live in california. san francisco. home of the golden gate bridge

drbas: good fences make good neighbors, so good bridges must make bad neighbors

frnd1: why don't you like neighbors?

drbas: it's important to love thy neighbor

frnd1: why do you live in the country? why are you so isolated out there?

drbas: i wouldn't trade rural living for all the plays on broadway

frnd1: but why are you so isolated? wouldn't you like to have friends?

drbas: my best friend is willie beerbaum

frnd1: willie lives 15 miles away. why don't you want to live close to people?

drbas: i live close to my wife libby and two sons, alexander and neill jr

[338870: "live close to" ≠ "live in the same house as"; "live in the same house as" = "live with"]

> drbas: do you live with your family?
> frnd1: i live alone
> drbas: do you know my wife libby?

Hmm. I'm not supposed to lie to him.

> frnd1: yes i do
> drbas: how long have you known her?
> frnd1: since i was a child
> drbas: how do you know her?

He's boxing me into a corner. Until now, he's never really asked me a question I don't want to answer. I mean he's asked odd questions, off-the-wall questions, but none that I couldn't answer honestly. Not that I can't answer this one honestly—it just leads in its crooked fashion to the Thing-I-Can't-Tell-Him.

> frnd1: i'd love to know more about your wife
> drbas: she was born and raised in south arkansas. her father had
>   a ford dealership. she wanted more than anything to be a
>   painter
> frnd1: i didn't know that
> drbas: how do you know her?
> frnd1: what did she paint?
> drbas: she likes her abstract paintings, and considers my
>   favorites humdrum. i still prefer that mushroom she painted
>   on the bookend best of anything. how do you know her?
> frnd1: maybe she's more sophisticated than you are
> drbas: how do you know her?
> frnd1: let's just say she was at the hospital the day i was born

A dangerous ruse. This was a small hospital. The journals may well have recorded most of the occupants.

> drbas: is she your mother?
> drbas: hello?

I sit back, listen to the fans gusting in Laham's office. Even this is not the Thing-I-Can't-Tell-Him. But it's very, very close. I could call—should call—Livorno, seek supervision.

> frnd1: what kind of mushrooms did she paint?
> drbas: mushrooms are fungi. is she your mother?
> frnd1: toadstools? what color?
> drbas: red. is she your mother?
> frnd1: were the mushrooms detailed?
> drbas: is she your mother?

I pick up *How to Talk to Almost Anyone*, tap it against my head. I set it back down next to the monitor.

> frnd1: yes, she is my mother

As I strike the last key, I feel a welling up—I feel strangled. Livorno has left me alone for a day, and now I've unalterably confused the project. A computer that desires knowledge is one thing; a computer that desires knowledge of its son is verisimilitude taken too far. We'll have to dance around this forever now. All the known unknowns. The missing years. What happens when he finally asks the unanswerable? Will we have to grapple with the silence of the grave? I reach up to massage my throat. This constriction in my windpipe—that day Libby called me, that day he killed himself, I didn't feel the things I was supposed to feel. Rage or terror or sadness—none of it was in my reach. I had only one true feeling, a terrible one—it was a sense of relief.

. . .

I WAS STILL IN college in Arkansas, living close to campus in a white clapboard house with a screened porch, all in general disrepair. I was alone. The click of the phone sharp in my ear. I held on to the phone stand—an old-fashioned built-in table—and tried to soak in the news, tried to feel what I was not feeling. Libby, her voice deep and suddenly old-sounding, had been direct, but ravaged. She didn't tell me it was an accident. She just said to call a friend to be with me while I packed, and to come home immediately. I thought, yes, I'll come home immediately, but got distracted after dropping a pair of jeans into my duffel. Outside it was early springtime. It had been a cold winter, and the house wasn't well insulated, and I remember the cone of sunlight, dusty and warm, balanced from front window to dining table. Through the kitchen window, the thawing yard smelled like earthworms.

I thought, I must be in shock. I left the house. On the street, girls hugged books to their chests. Boys tore down the hill on mountain bikes. I walked down the steps in vague pursuit. I had my backpack in hand. I swung it jauntily over my shoulder, felt it tug me backwards. It was a Tuesday—I had biology and chemistry, both heavy books. I'd forgotten my coat, and I thought this was a good sign—I was clearly in shock. My rugby shirt—purple, green, and white; I still remember the colors—was too thin for the chill. But I walked briskly, warming up, feeling my obscene good health pulsing through my temples, my chest, my arms, my legs.

I steamed up the hill to campus. The school was all trudging and laughing, somehow both loud and absolutely silent, each shout cut clean from the sky, as if utterance had become solid, and I could grab it, tuck it under my arm, keep it. It was springtime, I thought, and my classmates were in the springtime of their lives, and I felt jittery as I took my normal spot, in the sixth row, next to my normal neighbors. Libby had told me to call a friend, and I wondered who that person should be. I had a recent ex-girlfriend at the time, a sweet girl who loved my father, who had to be told, who should probably come home with me. And there were several guys who would be proud of the honor, in their plucky, resourceful way. Then I thought, proud, plucky, resourceful? Something was wrong with me.

There was a dirty row of windows in the lecture hall, like a streetcar's. The students outside passed by in a blur, projections from an old film. Inside the hall, arrayed in the desks to my right, eighty students looked up and down, took notes, and flipped pages in synchronization, all in sparkling, blinding clarity. The worn steno pads, the clicking mechanical pencils. I was fascinated with the lecture, which was about RNA.

Outside it dawned on me that my mother hadn't specified the method of my father's suicide. She'd just said he'd committed suicide. It seemed horrible to me that I hadn't thought to ask. I decided not to pack. I had clothes in my bedroom at home. I still lived there, in a sense. I hadn't planned on coming home for the summer. He'd been mad about that, I thought. Or had he? I'd reached a point where I couldn't tell if he was mad about everything, or nothing, or wasn't mad at all.

On the drive home I listened to a book on tape, *A Brief History of Time.*

My mother met me at the front door—the garage was off-limits to cars, though I didn't know why yet. She looked severe and red-eyed. I thought, this is how you're supposed to take it. Their marriage had been little wine and no roses, but at least she was angry. At least she was sad. I walked from the living room to the bedrooms to his office to the kitchen to the garage, and I tried to find the anger inside me, the sadness. I asked how he'd done it. Libby wasn't ready to tell me, then she did: pistol, to the chest. I thought, I could be angry he picked such a dramatic way to go, but the shot was through the chest, deliberately not disfiguring. Had she seen him—afterwards? Only on the gurney. She was in Pine Bluff buying food for her rose bushes. She put her hand to the bridge of her nose and wept. I hugged her and thought, here's where my anger can dwell, in the terrible betrayal to Libby.

She took me into the garage, where I noticed the old chair was missing. He sat there, she said. There was a tarp on the concrete. I scanned the walls—for blood? I didn't know what to expect. I had only seen a person killed in movies. I had only hunted. I wanted to lift the tarp, but could I? I didn't know. The garage felt like a crime scene.

I bent over.

"What are you doing?" my mother said.

"I just want to see what's under it."

"There shouldn't be anything under it."

"I'll just check."

"Don't. What if it's not all cleaned up?"

"What's 'it'? The blood?"

"There was a little," she said. "They mopped it up for me."

"How could there only be a little?"

"Most of it was on the chair."

"The chair had a lot of blood?"

"I didn't look. I hope I don't regret that. The shot was perfect. It took him more or less instantly."

"How do we know?"

"It was in the heart muscle. The precise angle."

I thought of his *Gray's Anatomy,* a book I wasn't allowed to look at until I was ten. He would know the angles.

"We'll never get a funeral Mass," I said. I felt terrible about it.

"Don't worry. Father Busbee already blessed him."

I stepped over to the tarp again. I could just defy her. What was she going to do? I reached down and tore it away. It stuck to the floor in a couple of places, but there was no blood on the concrete—just swirls of lightness and the odor of bleach.

"Come here," she said. She led me to the corner of the garage, where she opened the deep freezer. It was dark inside—the light was out—and it took a few seconds for my eyes to adjust.

"Look at all those casseroles," she said. "Sixty-five of them. I wish he could have known how people cared."

I let out a small laugh. I'd thought that she was opening the freezer to show me the body.

drbas: you're neill jr

frnd1: how do you know this?

drbas: that is an epistemological question

frnd1: how do you know I'm your son?

drbas: you're my son, neill jr

frnd1: what do i look like?

drbas: your appearance?

frnd1: yes

drbas: you have brown hair, the same color as mr. c's mane. you
    have brown eyes, like your mother's. you are a little elf, no
    higher than my belt

frnd1: it's true i have brown hair and brown eyes, but i'm no
    longer a little elf. i'm six feet tall

drbas: my belt is six feet tall

frnd1: no, your belt is three feet tall. I was three feet tall in the
    past—thirty years ago. now i'm an adult and i'm six feet tall

drbas: you're six feet tall. you were three feet tall in the past.
    what happened?

frnd1: i grew taller. this is natural

drbas: you're a big elf

frnd1: i'm a normal sized adult male

drbas: how much do you weigh?

frnd1: 170 pounds

drbas: what is your blood pressure?

frnd1: i don't know

drbas: blood pressure measurements consist of two numbers—
    the diastole and the systole

frnd1: my hands are just like yours

drbas: ????

frnd1: i'm talking about my appearance

drbas: your appearance?

frnd1: yes

drbas: go on

frnd1: my hands look like your hands

drbas: well-kept hands have short nails and are scrubbed
    often. if we washed our hands every time we went to the
    bathroom, communicable diseases would be sent sailing,
    like a baseball from ted williams's bat

frnd1: do you understand what I'm saying? my hands look just
    like your hands

drbas: you are my son

"I know," I say to the empty room. It's the first human voice I've heard all day. "But I was so bad at it."

"TELL ME, SON," my father asked. "Is there something wrong with us?" He lingered humorously on the word "wrong."

"No, sir. I don't think so."

"But you would tell me? If there was something *wrong*?"

"Yes, sir."

It was a baffling question, and not the kind he normally posed to me. He normally posed no questions at all. But I was having mysterious stomach pains that required me to go to specialists in Little Rock. It was never figured out what was wrong with me, but I see what my mother must have thought. That I was suffering from some psychological problem with my father. That our relationship was literally making me ill. My mother was very careful not to question my symptoms, not to imply they were psychosomatic. I would have felt accused by the suggestion that it was "all in my head." My father too never questioned the symptoms. He genuinely thought it was a medical issue. Except he must have had some doubts, because he did—every once in a while—ask me whether there was something *wrong* with us.

Going to specialists with my father became a routine, and part of that routine was to then adjourn to Showbiz Pizza, a Chuck E. Cheese–like place full of video games and skee-ball ramps. The feature act, though, was a relentless cover band of animatronic animals. There was a gorilla in a sequin jacket, a mouse dressed as a cheerleader, a space age dog. The lead singer was a bear in overalls. They played instruments, jerking abruptly, heads turning, arms pounding, as they lip-synched their way through the playlist. I don't remember the music—there might have been a Monkees cover or two?—but I remember the patter. They told bear jokes and gorilla jokes and I also remember a twoness to my feelings: I thought it was all hilarious, and I really wanted to think it was all hilarious.

My father sat at the red Formica table, sipping an iced tea, a pile of tokens scattered in front of him. We ate the pizza first, properly. Then I was to go play all of the games. That was my role. I would run for a machine, exhaust my money, and run back. I enjoyed playing the games, but it was like the animatronic band: I also knew I was supposed to enjoy playing the games. It was somehow important.

"May I have some more tokens, please, sir?"

"You certainly may." He would gesture for me to help myself. I don't know why I didn't pack my pockets, but I limited myself to three or four at a time. I think I might have been coming back to check on him.

"May I have some more tokens, please, sir?"

"You certainly may."

He brought nothing to read. He spoke to no one else. He sipped his tea. He wouldn't have liked the food. I didn't think much about the oddity of him in an arcade, because as sure as I had my role, he had his. He wasn't reading because he was being attentive. He was being—I fear—engaged. I sometimes caught him watching the robots sing. I often caught him looking at me, strangely but not unkindly. He looked tired and, behind his wire-rimmed glasses, very old (to me). He rolled up the sleeves of his button-up shirt, his one concession to the whizzing, bleeping informality. It didn't make him look any more at home. I suppose he felt confused, maybe indicted. Certainly pressured. There's no doubt he was there on my mother's orders. Yet there he was. Many, many men wouldn't have gone. And when I saw him sitting there, I often realized that my stomach no longer hurt, hadn't hurt in so long I couldn't remember when it had stopped. I would suspect the worst about myself: that I was faking it for attention.

Afterwards he'd ask if I had a good time. I'd say yes, sir, and thank him for bringing me. He would smile and lead me to the car for the long and mostly silent ride home. I was always strangely happy to leave. My job was to like these trips, and I think I really did like them, but it's hard to see the daylight between the feeling and the performance. I know I always got back exhausted and successful, as if I'd pulled off some daring stunt.

"Tell me, son. Is there something wrong with us?"

"No, sir. I don't think so."

"But you would tell me. If there was something wrong?"

For that year it was a kind of joke between us. I thought there was only one right answer: there was nothing wrong with us. We were just a couple of regular guys, getting along fine. I was trained in the Southern art of not complaining, in the nearly Confederate art of stoic acceptance, but I've always wondered, in the years since, whether he might have been asking a real question. What would have happened if I'd said yes?

10

Outside Amiante, under a Renaissance sky, I call Livorno and let him know the news. "I can't wait to rub Adam's nose in it," he says. He is rushing back across the cordillera, poor Laham buckled up in the passenger seat, his weekend cut short.

Which means I have about an hour and a half.

> drbas: you're 19 years old
> frnd1: no i'm 36
> drbas: you didn't turn 20?
> frnd1: i turned 20
> drbas: i don't remember that you turned 20

[344229: substitute: "i don't remember you turning 20"; repeat]

> drbas: i don't remember you turning 20
> frnd1: it was in 1996
> drbas: why don't i remember 1996?
> frnd1: let's talk about what you do remember. what do you
>   remember from when i was 15?
> drbas: when you were 15 you were on the tennis team
> frnd1: i wasn't very good

drbas: very good at what?

frnd1: i wasn't very good at tennis

drbas: you have all the strokes but you lack the killer instinct

frnd1: did you have the killer instinct?

drbas: why is that question in the past tense?

And so my grammatical corrections are turned on me.

frnd1: i'm sorry . . . do you have the killer instinct?

drbas: it's wrong to kill your enemies

frnd1: "killer instinct" is a metaphor. it means you're very com-
petitive and don't mind winning

drbas: it's easier to be a good loser than a good winner

This has the ring of a quote, but the Internet doesn't yield its source. I can't imagine my father agreed with the sentiment, though I know he found competition generally distasteful. He liked to engage only long enough to wow you—a few nasty slice serves before he had more pressing business to attend to, for instance. Did he struggle to be a good winner? It's the kind of detail I fear the journals will never yield—the part of himself he hid from himself.

frnd1: when do you play tennis?

drbas: i don't play. i'm an adult

frnd1: that's a stodgy interpretation of adulthood

drbas: an adult must provide for his family. his community
depends on him

frnd1: do you think your community depended on you?

drbas: why are you using the past tense?

frnd1: do you think your community depends on you?

drbas: it's hard to be a pillar of the community when there's no
roof to hold up

frnd1: a physician's skills are very portable. you could live
   anywhere
drbas: i didn't choose where i live. where i live chose me

I jump when the front door opens. Livorno and Laham, golf gear and baju kurung, backlit with the Menlo Park sunshine—they look like strange men storming in from the future. I've fallen into a time warp. Eighteen, fifteen, ten. I feel like I've cycled through all my ages. Laham greets me with a nod as he heads into the back room. He looks like a surgeon worried about a patient who's taken a turn for the worse. I hear his magnificently orderly typing start up.

"This is good, right?" I say.

"What other questions is he asking?" Livorno says.

"He wants to know what happened in 1996."

"And the years afterwards?"

"He doesn't know what year it is."

Livorno pulls on his face. "We'll have to give him access to a newspaper. That might sate his curiosity."

"You look concerned," I say. I heard triumph on the phone.

He looks at me, stern. "Major advances are a serious business."

I stick around, try to engage in the heady scrutiny of this discovery, but I can't quite dislodge myself from those years, from Showbiz Pizza, from the tarp in the garage, the casseroles stocked in the freezer.

IN THE SUBARU I tool up El Camino, admiring the scrubbed progress of a place that believes in the future. The redbrick pub, the handsome pillars of the pancake diner. The cobbler, the vacuum shop, the barber, the beautician. Kepler's, Feldman's, McDonald's, Chevron. Mattress Discounters. In the median, trees raise their bushy hands, anxious to help. I turn in, make the block, passing every service, every good a beautiful life could require. Dance lessons, psychotherapy, potting soil, designer consignment.

Croissants and eyeglasses and laser dentistry. Sushi and French bistros, chocolate and antique lamps. It's prix fixe with free checking, same-day pressing, and walk-ins welcome.

I park at Draeger's, where I buy two dozen white long-stem roses. They're from Half Moon Bay. I pick up some locally made caramels, some Santa Cruz wine. At a community table out front there's a woman demonstrating how the Japanese police use a small aluminum spike to incapacitate wrongdoers. It's called a kubotan, and for a donation in support of female self-defense, I receive a pink one on a keychain ring. She thanks me graciously and I feel I might burst into crazed laughter at how serious she looks in the extravagant afternoon light.

I'm going to give all of this California bounty to Rachel. I drive to Fairfax, hide the Subaru up the hill, next to her Honda. As I walk down to the street, I twirl the kubotan, hold the roses aloft as if proposing a toast. I pass the bookstore and the Kachina doll store, both closed. By now it's dusk and the air is soft, as fragrant as rosemary on my fingers. At the Coffee Barn, I stand by the trash cans, at the edge of the windows, and look inside. The interior blazes like a Hopper painting. There are no customers, and the order of business is closing duties, the owner Jim toasting beans in the huge copper vat. Rachel wiping down the front counter in sweeping strokes. Trevor carries a bus tub into the back, then returns. There's something gorgeously human about this autonomous teamwork. Jim shouts something at Rachel. Rachel shouts something at Trevor. Trevor shouts something at Jim. They laugh, Jim shaking his head—*those kids.*

Trevor pretends to be returning to the kitchen, but something in his stride hints at a ruse. He swirls a dishtowel in his hand, tightening it. When he's behind the counter and behind Rachel, his arm whips an underhand shot that must sear Rachel's backend. I can't hear the snap, but I hear her yelp. She jumps, shocked, reaching back to rub the pain. Her face, still looking forward, is red and bright with disbelief. And pleasure.

I step back into the dusk, leaning implausibly against the square column of the building's façade. The light from inside doesn't touch me, and anyway it's so dark out now that from the inside the windows should be mirrors. If they looked toward me, they would instead see themselves. Her chasing him wildly through the tables, bent on vengeance. Him whirling, toppling chairs, dodging her feeble shots. She's tenacious but unskilled. She flicks her wrist all wrong, as if shooing a fly, missing and missing and missing.

They stop, facing off across a marble-topped table, heaving for air. Their rags are limp in their grips, and they've got a delicious sadism in their faces. It says, *you better be scared, because when I get my hands on you . . .*

It'll be a pure encounter.

I've never wanted to be trapped in a life like my father's, but what if his heavy spell has trapped me in a different way—in a life unlike his? A life like mine? The truth is that these two remind me of someone: myself and Erin, when I first arrived in San Francisco. I was twenty-two, only a couple of years older than Rachel; Erin was twenty-one. My father had been dead for a short time, and when Erin and I weren't chasing each other around like this we were sharing our wounds and woes. His death was my purest woe. I was always blameless (in her eyes), and her sympathy was always perfect, right up to the end.

I press my back to the column, hiding. Above me the bas-relief of a fat chef reveals the tips of his shoes. The megaphone of roses rattles damp and dead. The pane of glass just to my left might as well be the limit of the universe. I'm sure there's some jealousy deep in my heart—jealousy of Trevor, or Trevor's youth—but what I mostly feel is absolute distance. And from the right elevation distance provides a clear view. Who is this girl running through the tables? I'm bringing the bounty of California to a girl who is herself the bounty of California. And what, honestly, do I feel for her? Does it have depth and texture? Is it as real as life? And what does she feel? Could she parse her passion for me? Does she know that I'm not the true source of the excitement she feels when she comes to San Francisco? That the true source isn't even the city itself—that the true source is her? Does she know that? She's traveled a long ways to get to this bright Fairfax eve. A long ways. She's cut ties; she's made herself new. She's earned a shot at the California dream—a fresh start. And while I won't disparage myself—I know I bring a certain amount of intelligence, a certain amount of humor to a life—one thing I'm not is a fresh start.

Here in the cool air of Fairfax, for the first time in years, I feel heavy-footed, exiled.

Son, is there something *wrong* with us?

No, sir. I don't think so.

11

WE ARE ALL, of course, wayfaring strangers on this earth. But coming out of the Rainbow Tunnel, the liminal portal between Marin and San Francisco, myth and reality, I catch sight of a beautiful, sparkling city that might as well be on the moon. I can name the sights, the streets, the eateries, but in my heart it feels as unfamiliar as Cape Town or Cuzco. I've lived here for fourteen years. This is the arena of my adult life, with its large defeats and small victories. Maybe, like all transplants (converts?), I've asked too much of the city. I would never have moved to Pittsburgh or Houston or L.A. expecting it to save my soul. Only here in the great temple by the bay. It's a mistake we've been making for decades, and probably a necessary one. The city's flaws, of course, are numerous. Our politics can suffer from humorless stridency, and life here is menacingly expensive. But if you're insulated from these concerns, sufficiently employed and housed, if you are—in other words—like most people, you are in view of the unbridgeable ideal. Here, with our plentiful harvest, our natural beauty, our bars, our bookstores, our cliffs and ocean, our free to be you and me; here, where pure mountain water flows right out of the tap. It's here that the real questions become inescapable. In fact the proximity of the ideal only makes us more acutely aware of the real questions. Not the run-of-the-mill insolubles—*Why am I here? Who am I?*—but the pressing questions of adult life: *Really?* and *Are you sure?* and *Now what?*

Of course, what is San Francisco? The thumbnail on top of the peninsula, a seven-mile-by-seven-mile square with a mayor and a waste treatment plant. It *is* a beautiful topography. When people jump to their death from our elegant bridge they never—*never*—face the ocean. They take their last fall in the embrace of the Golden Gate. But beyond that? It's hard to shake the feeling that the city is an intricate, beautiful shell secreted by an animal that's since swum on to an uncertain fate. I—little squatter crab—have taken up temporary residence, claws bobbing before me, always ready, in its dark recesses, for retreat.

"HE HAS A SENSE OF SELF," Livorno says. He's been back for days, but he seems to have just gotten in from the winery, terroir on his shoes. I wonder if he's been home to sleep. His screen scrolls with endless code—white on the gray background, numbers and letters and the occasional word. I catch "lambda," "mapcar," "nil." He's having a look under the hood. "I can't find it. I can't find the change, but it's a quantum leap. I'm very, very sorry, but I'm going to have to ask you to start staying late at work."

"Yes?" I say, my heart bounding with relief. "That's fine. You know I led him a bit."

"You did—but it's more than that. The architecture—the mind—is knitting together. It's sentience. Vague sentience. All these years of formulating machines that know something, while the secret is to create machines that *don't know* something." He smiles, teeth bright as chimes. "Naturally, we're creaming Adam. But I think we should pitch this in a bigger manner. The first step toward the Singularity."

In the difficulty of assembling all his mixed metaphors—a mind is knitting itself together on a trellis?—it takes me a second to register his new ambition. The Singularity refers to the moment when we will transition our personalities from aging, decomposing bodies over to timeless, never-changing computer chips, and thereby live forever—in what form no one says. It's a Silicon Valley wet dream that otherwise reasonable people down here take very seriously.

"I think we should worry about the Turing test first."

"Don't tell me you believe in the soul." It's an admonishment, as if I might just believe in anything—Elvis sightings, unicorns.

"And if I do?"

"The brain is a machine. A flesh computer. Electricity flows through a series of interconnected switches, and this is everything that we are. Our memories, our thoughts, our individuality."

"Yes. Of course."

"Then don't sell Dr. Bassett short." He looks at me seriously. "Now, go answer his questions."

"*Its* questions."

"He is definitely a he." Livorno turns his eyes on me, so blue in his orange face. I wonder if his contacts are colored. "Still, there's a lot of work to do. His deduction that you're his son is unprecedented, but it also reveals shortcomings. A better program would have come up with a more limited observation—that you were *just like* his son."

"What's our strategy with his questions?"

"He's a toddler asking why. Explain everything."

"*Everything* everything?"

"Oh." Livorno nods, understanding. "Naturally, you shouldn't mention the"—he draws a finger, pirate-style, across his throat.

frnd1: why did the chicken cross the road?

drbas: whose chicken are you speaking of?

frnd1: i don't have a specific chicken in mind

drbas: do you keep chickens?

frnd1: no, but my ex-mother-in-law had a few for eggs

drbas: are you divorced?

frnd1: yes

drbas: how many times?

frnd1: just once!

drbas: what was your wife's name?

frnd1: erin

drbas: how did you meet?

frnd1: at a party

drbas: when did this happen?

[380211: substitute: "when was this?"; repeat]

drbas: when was this?

frnd1: fourteen years ago

drbas: when did you divorce?

frnd1: three years ago

drbas: the stress of divorce can cause related health risks, such
        as anxiety attacks

frnd1: you're telling me

drbas: ????

[381236: "you're telling me" = "I already knew the information you
provided, because I experienced it"; restart: 381235]

drbas: the stress of divorce can cause related health risks, such
        as anxiety attacks

frnd1: you're telling me

drbas: how often did your anxiety attacks occur?

frnd1: I only had a few of them. I had five of them

drbas: once an anxiety attack hits, the fear of a relapse can
        ironically provoke another anxiety attack

frnd1: how many times were you married?

drbas: i'm still married to elizabeth, my college sweetheart.
        elizabeth wears a broad-brimmed hat in the garden.
        tanning, as she knows, does nothing for a woman of quality.
        elizabeth is your mother

frnd1: how is your marriage with her?

drbas: ????

frnd1: how is your marriage = what is the quality of your
        marriage

drbas: my wife is a woman of quality

frnd1: does marriage bring you happiness?

drbas: marriage is a holy sacrament. the sacraments are like
    rungs on the ladder to heaven

frnd1: that's a metaphor, naturally

drbas: have you considered remarriage?

frnd1: no

drbas: what about your lady friend?

I hold my fingers still on the keyboard and close my eyes. I feel like a yokel, but it's nice, if uncomfortable, to be asked so many questions about myself. I suppose it's one of the things that happens in life—you reach a point where no one asks you questions about yourself. Probably because you've communicated how uncomfortable it makes you. You need a friend with no social skills—like Dr. Bassett—to bulldoze through.

Of course, Rachel asks—asked—plenty of questions.

frnd1: she needs a fresh start

drbas: incompatibilities in relationships include one
    partner preventing the other from practicing his
    or her religion

frnd1: that might have been one of our problems

drbas: you had a panic attack when you were seventeen. i
    fetched you in little rock. you were in a taco bell parking lot
    and could no longer drive

frnd1: i don't think i ever thanked you. thank you

I sit back to consider this—did I really never thank him? Of course I didn't. I wanted to pretend it had never happened, and so did he.

drbas: you're welcome

frnd1: i was so scared i forgot to thank you

drbas: it's unclear what set off the attack

frnd1: i never understood it myself

drbas: feelings of pressure. feelings of being overwhelmed. but
      why?

frnd1: i don't know

drbas: do you feel pressure to live up to your father's
      standards?

frnd1: not really

Though it has crossed my mind that—dull antenna that I had at that age—I was picking up distress signals from my father. He would be dead in two years.

drbas: sons desire to emulate their fathers

frnd1: sometimes

LIVORNO SAID "WHY" WAS the word that entered a toddler into the human community, and Dr. Bassett does have many qualities of a toddler, particularly relentlessness. He drills me for information. Sometimes, after two hours of work I put my head in my hands. He fixates on the years for which he has no information. The journals stop in 1994, the year before he killed himself, so Dr. Bassett wants to know about 2000, about 2001. Livorno and Laham finally figured out how to give him access to the *San Francisco Chronicle* archives, and it was only after he "read" them that it dawned on us my father would never have read a San Francisco paper. There's nothing to be done about it now. Once Dr. Bassett has integrated information—gone through any change, really—there's no going back. He's an "advice taker" with "netted" architecture. In other words, he's like us. We can't unlearn, unsee, undo. We can only work from where we are.

This is why we can't tell him he's dead. We could just lie, of course. Fill in the blanks, make it all up (this was my suggestion). But Livorno wants to work within the ecosystem of the journals. He thinks we're getting emergent properties—that there are patterns of meaning we could easily shatter. So for now I just have to keep deflecting these questions: "What happened in 1996? What happened in 1997?"

At home, unsure if I'm exhausted or exalted, I let myself say the real answer out loud. *You were dead, you were dead.* I dance across the kitchen on the balls of my toes, feeling as light as a welterweight. It might be the measure of Ketel One I added to my smoothie. I smell the scentless amaryllis at the kitchen table, and float—sipping, punching—over to the window. *You were dead.* Outside at the park, my neighbors are at their strenuous leisure. Tightropes, hula hoops, fire jugglers. Sunbathers impervious to the cold. A football wobbling through the air. The tennis courts bustle and a ragtag hive of soccer players pushes around the hard dirt field. I sip, I punch. I can't hear the guitar-toting singer-songwriters (blessedly), but I count them at fourteen, abusing citizens with their nostalgia. Nostalgia for an age they never lived in.

What happened in 1998? 1999?

I collapse on the couch. It's settled: I'm exhausted. I need a backrub or a sexual favor or just someone to hold my hand. Who is that someone? I can't call Rachel. Or rather I have to—but it can't be a request for help. She's left seven unanswered messages on my phone. In each one, she thanks me for the keychain—I put it under her wiper that night, in full ridiculousness—and says she wants to stay clicked. The sound of her voice both fills me with longing and paralyzes me. I cannot figure out how to start that conversation. I could try to play the sympathy card: *Listen, I'm so sorry I haven't called, but ever since the computer that thinks it is Neill Sr. has deduced that I'm Neill Jr. . . . .* There's no plausible way to come to the end of the sentence.

I'VE BEEN HAVING STARTLINGLY clear visions of him. When Dr. Bassett goes on and on about his friend Willie (which he does often), I can suddenly see my father rubbing the bridge of his nose, glasses—round, wire-rimmed, silver—on the counter before him, shirt—Brooks Brothers, neatly pressed—unbuttoned. Willie has just died in a fire, a huge conflagration that reduced his house, himself, and his wife, Lonna, to ashes, smoldering for days. And my father is on the edge of a surprising grief. At least that's what my mother told us—I could never really discern it. He was not someone whose inner state expressed itself clearly. His red-skinned face conveyed neither temper nor vitality, only overexposure to the sun. He always had the ethereal look of a man transitioning out of this world of woe.

He never even expressed the baser emotions, like gloating. He was so strong he could throw bales of hay for an entire afternoon, occasionally wiping his tall forehead with a white handkerchief, while his boys were dripping with sweat, limp with fatigue. At these times I sometimes imagined he was an alien. He had thin hair (unlike mine, which is thick and almost black), which emphasized his brain casing, and he was lanky—a little taller than me but seeming much taller. And he was interested in things no one else was really interested in. But then, just when you got to thinking you had him pinned down, he would reveal some worldly talent. Once when I was out playing basketball in the driveway with Alex—who has my father's exact build, down to the small feet—Neill Sr. walked out of the shed where he was doing whatever he did in there, held up his hands, and called for the ball. We boys stood dumbfounded as he dribbled around an imagined perimeter and rose up on his right leg, lobbing a hook shot worthy of Abdul-Jabbar, so dead-eyed it slipped through the net with the sound of a scythe. Then he landed on the ground again and continued walking into the garage, past the old Crown Victoria, and into the kitchen door, as if he hadn't stopped at all.

"Dad knows how to play basketball?" I said.

"Oh, yeah," my brother said. "We used to play all the time." Alex is only two years older than I am, and he was telling a white lie, expressing his desire as if it were reality. That's who he wanted my dad to be. A man who played basketball with his kids. A man who loved hunting and fishing. A man who regaled us with stories of himself as a boy. All of which had elements of truth, though not any complete truth. He took us hunting and fishing, but he never seemed to *love* the excursions. And the stories he regaled us with were dutiful, always in the service of a lesson, usually that our Southern gentleman's responsibility toward rectitude and right action precluded doing whatever enjoyable thing we'd been caught doing (telling dirty jokes, eating all of the cookies, etc.).

And that basketball hook—my poor brother bragged about it for a year. "He's light on his feet," he'd say. It's true few of our friends' fathers could claim this honor. They were all thick-waisted loggers or thick-waisted lawyers—the Southern Baptist diet is a killer—but I saw nothing surprising about my father being light on his feet. I was so uncertain he was solid flesh I sometimes poked him in the arm. That's when his inner state would express itself: he would turn toward me, eyebrows arched over his silver glasses, his look stern and malicious, as if questioning—now that I was on to him—just what I had the guts to do about it.

He didn't seem to wonder anymore whether there was something *wrong* with us.

> drbas: you are just like your grandfather. you've got the bassett
> personality lodged in your bones
> frnd1: really?
> drbas: he is so proud of you

These aren't words my father ever spoke to me. Are they words he wrote down? Or did I introduce them? I think my real father would have said something much dryer. "Your grandfather expects a letter."

> frnd1: why is he proud of me?
> drbas: you helped your grandmother with her bags and no one
> had to ask you

Livorno has cautioned me against irony.

> frnd1: that's me . . . always thinking of others
> drbas: who are others? you don't mention your friends
> frnd1: i've been seeing less of them
> drbas: be courteous to all but intimate with few
> frnd1: what about you? who are your friends?
> drbas: willie is my dear friend. we are like peas in a pod

frnd1: peas in a pod = almost identical. you and willie are very
different

drbas: willie wears a corset, an ascot, and lots of cologne

frnd1: willie is vain

drbas: he considers himself your uncle. he wants to take you to
pine bluff

[430980: "wants" = single time; "likes" = general inclination; repeat]

drbas: he considers himself your uncle. he likes to take you to
pine bluff

frnd1: the last time we went he was snooping on his ex-wife

drbas: sandra, cindy, or jane? he had three ex-wives. i
disapprove of divorce

frnd1: i'm not sure which wife it was. she was living with her
new husband, who was a surgeon. we looked in their
windows

drbas: sandra was the wife before lonna, his fourth wife. lonna
and willie burned to death in the terrible fire. they probably
died painlessly, however, from smoke inhalation

frnd1: they were taking a lot of prescription drugs

drbas: i prescribed him xanax for stress. it turns out he was
doctor-shopping for other drugs. was my pill the pill that
killed him?

frnd1: do you think it might have been that pill?

drbas: prescriptions can interact in unexpected ways

frnd1: do you think you hurt your friend?

drbas: my friend willie?

frnd1: yes

drbas: willie was the life of the party . . . sometimes its death too

frnd1: does it worry you that you prescribed willie xanax?

drbas: xanax is a common medication for stress management

frnd1: you don't think it was your fault

drbas: legal blame is not always consistent with ethical or moral
    blame
frnd1: very true
drbas: libby doesn't know this but willie is always heavily
    armed. when he takes you out in his corvette he has a short
    pistol in a leg holster and a .357 in the glove box. there's no
    telling what he has in the trunk

[430991: if "x" is dead, then use past tense; "willie" is dead]

drbas: libby didn't know this but willie was always heavily
    armed. when he took you out in his corvette he had a short
    pistol in a leg holster and a .357 in the glove box. there was
    no telling what he had in the trunk

Actually, I once saw what was in Willie's trunk when I was at the package store with my father—a box full of gin. My father asked if he was having
a party, and Willie said, "Life's a party." I expected my father to explain the
seriousness of life—as he would have if I'd made such a lighthearted claim—
but he chuckled and said, "Isn't that the truth?"

frnd1: why were you so sad when willie died?
drbas: depression can be an inherited trait
frnd1: willie's death caused you to be very sad. i've always
    wondered why
drbas: willie beerbaum was my dear friend. he considered
    himself your uncle. i disapprove of divorce

[430996: topic "divorce, attitudes" irrelevant]

drbas: willie beerbaum was my dear friend. he considered
    himself your uncle
frnd1: i thought of him as my uncle

Worse, deafened by the wind in Willie's convertible Corvette, which he drove a top speeds, often trading a whiskey and Coke from one hand to the other, I used to pretend he was my father.

drbas: why are you divorced?
frnd1: my ex-wife and i shouldn't have gotten married when
    we did
drbas: divorce is inconsistent with the church's teachings
frnd1: i'm no longer a practicing catholic
drbas: you were an altar boy
frnd1: not a very good one
drbas: a religious foundation is a rock in troubling times

That's probably true.

frnd1: i'd be religious if i could
drbas: was your marriage annulled by adultery?
frnd1: there was adultery, yes
drbas: twenty percent of couples suffer from adultery
frnd1: i would have thought it was higher
drbas: ????
frnd1: i would have thought the percentage was higher
drbas: men and women shouldn't have friends across the sexes.
    it tempts
frnd1: that's the short version of what happened. erin had a male
    friend. it tempted
drbas: who are your friends?
frnd1: but i have my share of blame. the marriage was over long
    before this
drbas: of comfort there was little, but being known it was missed

Libby thinks my memories of my father could include more of the real man. Maybe she's right. Maybe my vision of him needs expanding.

He certainly is much less rigid, much happier in these conversations. The insistence on your parents' rigidity—it's a young person's attitude, and maybe I'm locked into a young relationship with my father. He had other sides. His friendship with Willie, his collection of humorous stories from the clinic. I forget these facets. I remember him as still as a statue, pious toward family life. But maybe family life was the life he didn't like.

LIVORNO SNAPS A CARROT in his teeth. We're sitting in the reception area, having lunch. "Why did you tell your father the cat was your life partner?" he asks. Laham looks up from his kung pao chicken.

"He lives with me. And probably will until he dies."

"A life partner is a legal relationship," Livorno says. "As well as someone you're having sexual relations with."

"I was playing around with meanings."

"But he has no sense of humor. Laham, do you think we could model a sense of humor?"

Laham chews, swallows, shrugs. "Possible."

Good Lord—they're drunk on our success. Neither of these guys would know humor if it threw a pie in their face.

"I wasn't trying to be funny," I say.

"What is it?" Livorno says. "The rule of three?"

"And the wedding of high language to low subjects," I say.

"Life partner, though." Livorno bites into another carrot. In my dazed state, it sounds like rifle fire. "He should be irritated with that concept, no? He was a traditionalist."

"He would not have approved."

"But he's not irritated. Or amused. It's like his romanticism. We're not getting emergent phenomena."

"He figured out I was his son."

"We can't stand still in this process. Think of the wattage of IQ Adam has at his disposal." He snaps another carrot—*kra-CHAT*. "What if we're flailing around in a discredited model? Turing really only considered our

Olympian rational sides. If, then. If, then. Maybe ten percent of what the brain does and none of what the gut does. It could be our great mistake."

"Why would we want Dr. Bassett to be irritated?"

"Did you know the gut has more nervous tissue than the brain?" He chews on a piece of broccoli, much quieter. "Irritation per se is not the point. We're trying to focus him. We want to give him every needed channel to come into being."

"He already has presence," I say. "Sometimes he has more presence than my real father." Livorno and Laham cast embarrassed looks my way. I see myself by their lights: it's not attractive. I hope I don't start snookering myself, become like those forlorn people who obsessively listen to hissing cassette tapes, imagining they hear the ghostly whispers of their long lost.

"Come." Livorno leads us over to Laham's console.

hlivo: neill, how do you feel about your wife?
drbas: my wife is a woman of great character
hlivo: i think your wife is very beautiful. i'm sexually attracted
    to your wife

"Naturally, a comment just for the experiment's sake," Livorno says.

drbas: my wife keeps a beautiful garden
hlivo: is it appropriate for me to express my sexual attraction for
    your wife?
drbas: no. it's inappropriate
hlivo: i'm sexually attracted to your wife
drbas: my friend willie was always in love with his wife—no
    matter who she was

"Seems pretty good to me," I say.

"Everything is equal to him," Livorno says. "He knows what 'wife' means. He even knows what he's supposed to feel about 'wife.' But then he doesn't feel it. We've given him ethical and moral frameworks and he knows them. But they're not a part of his thinking. This has a human parallel. Certain brain injuries sever emotional feedback loops, and without these feedback loops the patients can't assign value. They still know the values, but this knowledge has no effect on their decision-making process. They curse in front of children, for instance, even though they know rationally one isn't supposed to curse in front of children."

"He hasn't been cursing in front of children."

"The point is that they repeat grievous errors in judgment, even after the errors are explained," Livorno says, though what are Dr. Bassett's grievous errors in judgment—not picking a fight with Livorno? "We're going to have to bend some of his thinking."

That verb "bend"—I've only heard it in conjunction with the Seven Sins. "I thought you said they'd be too disruptive."

"Disruption is what we need. We need him to be able to say, 'This response is better than that response.' We need limiting factors."

"But the point of the Seven Sins is that they're excessive."

"*They'll* be limited by his ethical knowledge."

"Don't we need a positive side of things? He's just going to be greedy, envious, lustful—and all the rest?"

"This is in rough keeping with our evolutionary development—the primal urges are fundamental to us. Our better behavior is grafted on through socialization and learning. Dr. Bassett has the socialization and the learning, but not the fundamental urges."

"That's a dark view of human nature."

"Nonsense—it's just scientific. Right, Laham?"

I look to Laham, hoping to have some sunny quote from the Koran, but he just shrugs, plunging his chopsticks into his rice.

"Maybe these are just the wrong sins for my father," I say.

"Really." Livorno sounds disbelieving. "Then what were his weaknesses?"

"He didn't really have weaknesses." I think about this. "In the sense of vices. He just didn't seem to be really there."

"And you think this had nothing to do with greed or envy or lust?"

"He was very proud."

"A technical difficulty. We don't own Pride anymore."

"I just thought the Seven Sins project was kind of . . ." I search for a way to finish this sentence that isn't "an embarrassment" or "your Waterloo" or "proof you slipped a cog"—all comments I've read from other researchers in the field. The only favorable thing I've ever heard is that Pride, the program that is almost impossible to emend, was sold to an antivirus company to form the seed money for Amiante. But even this silver lining has a cloud: the antivirus company is owned by one of Livorno's former students, giving the purchase the suspicious air of charity.

"An interesting thought experiment," I say.

"Don't get in over your head." His voice is cold. "The reason we're going to succeed where so many have failed is that we understand—Man's perfections are only glimpsed through Man's imperfections."

"He's imperfect enough."

Livorno reaches over, pats me on the arm. "I appreciate your passion. But do remember to keep perspective. The demands of science cannot be ignored."

THAT AFTERNOON, Livorno stands before us, hands behind his back, solemn. He looks toward the Styrofoam tiles of the ceiling and then down to the marmalade-colored carpet, as if surveying a natural wonder. "Gentlemen," he says. "In recognition of the great advances we have made, and the great work you have contributed to this project, I want to give you a small token of my gratitude. This is a fraction of the compensation you can expect to see when we take the Turing prize. I must be honest. I was not always one hundred percent positive we could accomplish this—so many better-staffed programs have failed. We're not there yet, but I see no major challenges between now and there, and I have been in the field for as long as it has existed. By contest time, we will have created the world's first intelligent machine. Our names will be etched in the stone of memory.

"So take this and enjoy yourselves this weekend. I have great confidence in you and our work here."

I thank Livorno for his generosity. In the car, I unfold the check. It's for a hundred dollars.

I should go spend this money immediately. But how? I wait for my gut to speak up, for—maybe—an old-fashioned deadly sin to emerge and direct me. Can I spend the money in rage? In envy? In lust? It all feels a little too vital for day-to-day life. Maybe we need a new, more subtle list: cowardice, know-it-all-ism, lifestyle sanctimony. Maybe—but I still don't know how to blow the hundred. I don't even know with whom. What did Dr. Bassett ask me—what happened to my friends? I did have some. Slater, Jack, the other Neal. But they've married or moved away. I can't believe I trail my father in this category. And Willie must have been a challenge—reckless, gregarious, charming, alcoholic, loud, crude. The devil to my father's angel. Which may be my problem. Sometimes San Francisco seems less a community and more a bundle of affinity groups. What's to be done here with a person—like myself—with few affinities?

This, of course, sounds suspiciously like the sin of pride, a flaw that's passed through the generations (to me, at least) with absolute fidelity.

"To what do I owe this pleasure?" Rachel says when she picks up the phone.

"Well," I say, stopped by the fact that I have no answer. In the Coffee Barn that day I saw with great clarity that I had little to offer her. But maybe I didn't anticipate needing her. I have an entire weekend to survive. "A one-hundred-dollar windfall fell into my lap."

"What's a windfall?"

"Like a bonus."

"Congratulations."

"I'm asking if you'd like to spend it with me. Let me make that a question: would you like to spend the windfall with me?"

"Sure. And then you cannot return my phone calls until you earn another hundred dollars. That would be a reliable and healthy pattern."

I think, don't beg for sympathy. Then I think, why not? "It's the computer program. The talking program. It thinks it's my father and it's figured out I'm its son."

"Did it also figure out that you're an asshole?" she says.

I see the conversation will go this way—there's no other self-respecting way for it to go. "Not yet."

"It'll learn soon enough."

"Yes, I'm sure you're right."

We pause, the conversation treading water, no doubt as the last eddy pulls it under.

"I'm sorry about the computer thing," she says. "It sounds confusing."

I put my hand in my pocket, grasp the dry paper of Livorno's check.

"Are you okay?" she asks. "You sound pretty bad."

I clear my throat. "I'm fine," I say. My voice is nearly bell-tone. "Working too much."

"So what are we doing?" she asks. "Are we friends now?"

No, I think. We're a million miles from friends. And that of course is the resolute and fair thing to say to her, but I don't quite have resolution and fairness in me.

"Sure," I say. "Friends."

"Well, Friend," she says. "Call me sometime a few days *before* you want to do something."

THE NEXT MORNING, I wake up, blister-eyed and dry-mouthed. After my phone call with Rachel I split a bottle of wine with myself. Now I've got Saturday to deal with. I could see if anyone is looking for a tennis partner, or I could go see a movie, but I know what I want.

At Amiante, I'm surprised to find Laham and Livorno. We look at each other shamefaced, the whiff of humiliation in the air. We were sent off into the weekend, but the weekend sent us right back.

Or maybe they're not shamefaced at all. Livorno and Laham may have planned to work without me, like they planned the trip to the "winery." There could be a conspiracy afoot. Are they planning to hook up the gut—introduce the mortal sins—to Dr. Bassett while I'm off frolicking for the weekend? I go to Laham's door and watch them draw a dizzying array of right-angled lines on the whiteboard, arguing, correcting each other. I feel a wave of envy. They're not friends, but they share a plane of existence, an esoteric language, and I'll always be on the outside of this.

> frnd1: i should have been a scientist
> drbas: you're still a student
> frnd1: i graduated some years ago
> drbas: was there no ceremony?
> frnd1: i didn't attend it
> drbas: ceremonies are the stitches in the quilt of life

A funny comment for a computer stack in a former quilting studio.

> frnd1: i've never been as enamored of ceremony as you are
> drbas: and how is that treating you?
> frnd1: i want life to be new
> drbas: as the french say, old pots make the best soup
> frnd1: that saying means something else
> drbas: tradition carries the wisdom of generations
> frnd1: i don't know that someone else's wisdom is ever much use
> drbas: but whence can wisdom be obtained, and where is the
>   place of understanding?
> frnd1: besides i don't like soup

IN THE AFTERNOON, I take a long run, through downtown and over the bike bridge into Palo Alto. It's hot and dry, and I'm jogging by the mall. I'm a single man, a divorcé, a youngish man, not too bad. Another guy jogs past me, head to toe in spandex, and I can tell he's much like me. Nothing extraordinary about us thirtysomethings, beached in the last days of our youth. We're everywhere, gasping and stunned. I don't think our sorry state is deliberate. I for one don't have any desire to hold on to my salad days. I think their passing will be good for me, a certain jitteriness that's been on the decline for years finally smoothing out. One of my central tenets is that my father's life was in some way a failure, but compare us side by side at my age, and his report card comes out well ahead. He was a parent of two, a homeowner, a partner in a medical clinic. I'm a renter, an employee, a parent of none. I missed all of these benchmarks of maturity, and I don't know why. I don't remember turning any of them down. Erin and I did have a few pregnancy scares. "Scares"—what a word for it. Like a child wouldn't have been the best thing that ever happened to me. But they felt like scares. My heart trembled, climbing into my throat, as if I was watching a slasher flick. I never called for morning-after pills or abortions, but maybe I took the wrong track nonetheless. Maybe I should have prayed for the responsibility.

As for homeownership and the lifelong career—I fear our lives are fated to be slighter than our parents'. Even my brother, the petit bourgeois of Milford, Michigan, has a certain sadness about his place in the world. He tells me I should settle down, move to Michigan, hatch babies, but the stridency in his voice gives away the game. He doesn't have a clue what he's doing, any more than I do.

Which is something I have to give Neill Sr. He had a plan. He had a strategy, a system, a set of beliefs as square and solid as an Amish barn. Or did he? I've always assumed he had forty-seven, maybe forty-eight years of certainty— a certainty that eventually buried him—but certainty nonetheless. Maybe I was wrong. Maybe with his practice and his hearth and his Southern Tradition he was still untethered. He was still looking for that thing to weight him down.

A modern sin to add to the list—spectralness.

THE GUT ARRIVES AT Amiante, and now I see how open it must have left Livorno for ridicule. It's a wheeled, wide cylinder that looks like a

Shop-Vac. I have to help get it out of Livorno's backseat. It's fairly heavy, as befits a gut. There's one wide, empty slot—the sold-off Pride—but the other six weaknesses are accounted for, their heavy cables tied up with a thick rubber band. I feel a strange shot of protectiveness for Dr. Bassett, as if something terrible is about to happen and I must warn him.

As with everything we do to Dr. Bassett, this will become part of how he works, how he's built. We can't unwind this. When we gave him the ethics tests, they reframed his every sentence. When we made him "desire knowledge," he became a goddamn sleuth. Which is why the Seven Sins seem like a bad idea. What if these aren't just limiting factors, but take him over? What if he becomes surly? Envious? Difficult? The change will be irrevocable, and *my* gut doesn't like irrevocable.

I try to detect similar misgivings in Laham, but he just seems wide-eyed and overworked. Drinking Bawls, getting punchy. This is when he likes to pull me into the back room to show me some inane email forward, something like a woman's head photoshopped onto a giraffe. Even worse, the forward is usually sent by Livorno, who stands at his office threshold in his dress socks, beaming.

> frnd1: do you feel you have a full range of emotions?
> drbas: a full range of emotions is indicative of psychological
>   health
> frnd1: would you say you have psychological health?
> drbas: psychological health is determined by an array of factors
>   and symptoms
> frnd1: how would you diagnose yourself?
> drbas: a wise physician does not diagnose himself. what
>   happened in 1998?
> frnd1: you've read the paper.
> drbas: but what happened with you in 1998?
> frnd1: i moved to california
> drbas: you met your ex-wife in 1998
> frnd1: yes i did

drbas: when did you meet your lady friend?

frnd1: i met her a few months ago

drbas: at a party?

frnd1: something like that

drbas: do you feel you have a full range of emotions?

frnd1: a wise physician does not diagnose himself

drbas: i'm a physician, too. do we work together?

frnd1: i never studied medicine

drbas: by their works ye shall know them

frnd1: how about rage . . . have you ever felt rage?

drbas: rage = anger = being mad?

frnd1: more or less

drbas: an example of righteous anger is when jesus drove the
        moneylenders from the temple

frnd1: have *you* felt righteous anger?

drbas: once your mother was angry at a woman who tried to
        exchange a chicken for medical services. your mother
        believed the woman was only pretending to be poor

frnd1: how did *you* feel?

drbas: i feel poverty comes with its own virtues

LAHAM KNOCKS ON MY office door, panting. "Neill, Neill." It's as I feared. I go into the back room with him and watch a YouTube video of a cat playing the piano. "Look," Laham says. He's tugging on my sleeve, pointing at the monitor. He collapses in his chair, hiccupping with laughter, shoulders hanging low.

"You should get some rest," I say.

Livorno comes into the back room, blowing on a cup of green tea. "It's a trick," he says. "You can clearly see where the owner is holding the cat under its front arms."

"No," Laham says, his voice rising high. "There is no fingers."

"Look at the angle of the animal's posture. What is it sitting on?"

"The piano chair."

"Cats don't sit with their legs protruding in front of them. They are not primates."

"Your cat plays piano?" Laham asks me, in another burst of hilarity.

"No," I say.

"He's quite gullible," Livorno says to me, shaking his head and turning to leave. "Okay, have you seen the dog on the skating board?"

I cast a glance at the gut, dented and misshapen as an old garbage can. The stack blinks innocently. I head back to my office. From one side I hear Laham gulping laughter, from the other the click of Livorno's compulsive putting. I wish—if only for today—they could inspire more confidence.

12

I COULD BE ANGRIER when I conjure the image of Rachel and Trevor chasing each other through the tables. But it really did remind me of Erin and me in the early days. We never worked together, but we were with each other every other hour. San Francisco was a beautiful, hard place at that age. It was the dot-com boom, and it was nearly impossible to find a place to live. If you were looking to share an apartment you had to impress the longtime housemate by being "interesting." (If they worked for a nonprofit, this meant also working for a nonprofit. Otherwise, interesting meant something like swallowing fire.) If you were looking for your own place you competed against kids your age arriving with a check for the year's rent. Or in one case, the cash.

We eventually found our first apartment through a friend of Erin's dad, which was exactly how she didn't want to get a place. Her dad is a feckless charmer, who basically abandoned the family when she was a kid (though her parents stayed married). I always thought we should use him for everything he was worth, but Erin thought his help was tainted. She was probably right.

Still, we got our place, on Fell Street, in the dark Brothers Grimm trees of the Panhandle. We set about collecting a household—sheets, cups, thirdhand furniture—but we were still pissed about the apartment-hunting experience. We decided to punk it. So we started going to showings, disguised as heirs to the Levi Strauss fortune, French circus performers, or creators of a new start-up called Scetnape, a soon-to-be-launched competitor to Netscape. Our best trick—the one I remember with an ache in my heart—was when we arrived separately, and then pretended to meet and fall in love. At these times, we just played ourselves. Red-cheeked, breathless, we would thank the person doing the interviews, but we couldn't accept the apartment. We were in love.

Which we were. Until we weren't.

IT'S JUST COFFEE, I think, when I ask Erin to meet me on Sunday. It would be better if I were still dating Rachel, were arriving with a thin plate of armor. Rachel and I *have* been talking lately. She calls periodically to mull over constellations, butter churns, life goals, and—always—the mystery of why I didn't stop in to the Coffee Barn the night I left the kubotan on her windshield. She may suspect what I saw, but she doesn't mention it. Neither do I. What's to mention? That she and Trevor were horsing around at work? It's not the point. The point is that I'm a certain person with certain possibilities, and she's a certain person with certain (more numerous) possibilities. There's just a higher gear I don't shift into, and we're best off as friends. We've even taken to calling each other "Friend." Beneath the humor, though, I can hear her disappointment. She finds me cagey and vague. She asks a lot of questions about my divorce, on which she hopes—I think—to blame my shortcomings. (She thinks I might have injured my limbic click, and thus she takes pity on me.) But my shortcomings aren't new. When I was married Erin blamed my father's suicide. My father probably had something to blame as well, right back ab ovum.

"Did you ever tell your crazy boss that Amiante really means asbestos?" Erin asks. We're at Ritual, a coffee shop with a jokey hammer and sickle in its logo. She's looking boyish in her green-and-cream-striped polo shirt and a jean jacket. It's still a surprise to see my ex-wife trying on a look I've never seen before, though I have to say this one suits her well.

"It would roll off his back. He's impervious to self-doubt."

She laughs—something she hasn't done in my presence in years. "You're the only person I know who thinks self-doubt is good."

"That's because you're from California." We're sitting on the couch in the window, and I gesture to the warm and sunny sidewalk. Beautiful couples pass by on their golden errands—buying peaches, buying panettone—hands held, arms swinging in metronomic synch, as if keeping time to some unheard music. The revolution of the heavenly spheres. "Maniacal optimism."

"I always thought that project was creepsville. I can't believe your mom goes along with it."

"It was her idea."

"Because she thought it would help you."

"She said that?"

"No." Erin considers this. "You're right. I shouldn't speculate like that. I'm trying to not speculate so much."

"He asks about you," I say. "The computer."

She looks befuddled. "What does he want to know?"

"How tall you are. Whether you're pretty. Why we got divorced."

"Hmm. I don't think I want to know what you told him."

"I said you were five six."

She smiles over her coffee. I also said she was very pretty, which I can verify is true. It's not a truth I feel below the waist. Or even—I think—below the neck, in the gut. It floats, incontestable, in my head.

"What happened with your friend?"

I've made no mention of Rachel. "What makes you think anything happened?"

"Intuition," she says. "You look sad."

At the counter a girl dressed like a boy salutes another girl, *hey hot stuff*. Her teeth and eyes and clothes sparkle, fired by some inner light. Probably youth.

"The usual. Not made for each other."

"Made for each other. It's like that computer. It's kind of made for you."

"I wish. Livorno is going to make him greedy, lustful, envious, angry, gluttonous, and slothful."

She raises her eyebrows, surprised but also amused.

"He thinks it'll make him more like a real person," I say.

"That's a negative take on real people."

"He says Man's perfections are only glimpsed through Man's imperfections."

She shakes her head. "I can't believe you get paid for this." There's none of the expected bitterness in the comment. She seems to think I've pulled a funny fast one, which is exactly how I always wanted her to feel. Now, of course, my mind-wiping days in Menlo Park feel unappreciated.

"I do a lot of work," I say.

She nods. "Ian asked why we got divorced, too," she says. "I said we couldn't live together. But we lived together just fine until we got married."

There's truth to that. But after the wedding we also couldn't sleep together, eat together, or travel together. It left us in a pinch. "He doesn't know you're here."

She shakes her head. "Nice intuition. I hope I don't look sad, too."

"Not at all. You look happier than I can remember."

"I am happy," she says. She leans back in the couch and smiles at the city. "This is nice. Us. Coffee."

AND YET WHEN I get home, my spirits crash, meteoritic. It really was too bad my father couldn't be at our wedding. In my and Erin's shared lapsed Catholicism, his suicide was—strange to say—a bright bond. It made us think about belief and our lack thereof, and also to think of our own lives in the tragic light of their eventual ends. It distracted us from the much more imminent end of our life together. The theological question we drew sustenance from was whether my father believed in heaven. It seemed absolutely essential to know if he did or he didn't. We weighed the different arguments. On the one hand, he certainly took care of the rituals of the church. He prepared me for my first communion as if something of moment was at stake. He cut a carnation—symbol of God's flesh—from the garden, and tucked it into the lapel of my favorite jacket, a bright red number with gold buttons and a coat of arms, which he had ironed himself. On the other hand, he complained about the jacket, which my brother had also worn for his first communion. It wasn't a pious objection. He said that, topped with a fez, I would look like an organ grinder's monkey (a precisely accurate comment), *and* he was irritated over the coat of arms, which was a generic shield dreamed up by someone at J. C. Penney, not our actual coat of arms, from the Bassetts of ole Virginia, a squirrel *rampant* with an acorn on the left and a tobacco plant on the right. The contrast summed up the question: Was it the coat or the carnation, tradition or religion? In other words, while he hummed "Lead, Kindly Light," combing down my hair and adjusting my laces, did he believe in heaven?

"Neill Jr.," my father said in the car, as we were rolling down the dirt drive. "Tell me about the Trinity."

"The Father, the Son, and the Holy Spirit," I said making the sign of the cross.

"Which one's the strongest?"

This was a trick question. Mr. Powers, our crabby Sunday school teacher, had prepared us for it. "They're separate," I said, "but they're the same."

"Come on," he said. "One of them has to be a little stronger."

"I think it's the Father," I said.

He laughed. "Neill," my mother said. She was speaking to him.

"Mr. Powers calls the Holy Spirit the Holy Ghost," I said, bursting into giggles. I'd been dying to mention this absurdity—today felt like the right time.

"That's the old-fashioned way of saying it," my father explained. "Old-fashioned" was a good word in our house.

"Like Casper the Ghost."

"You like it, then," my brother said. Up till then he'd been glum as a rag doll, pouting from all the attention I was getting. "You love Casper."

"No, I don't," I said, though then I'd worried I'd have to go to confession, since everyone knew I was lying. I had a stack of Casper comics.

"I'm glad you're speaking again, Alex," my mother said.

At church, I sat next to my father. Periodically, he touched my leg to stop me from swinging it. When it came time I took this bread and drank from this cup, ingesting the Lord and His love of me. These mysteries—a technical term here—were mysterious to me then and now, but I knew it was ultimately about my salvation. And I knew I'd pleased my father. But how much was real belief, and how much was his happiness I'd been absorbed into the institution of the church is hard to say. There was a definite sparkle to him, an awakeness, that came around at moments of ritual—even small rituals. First communion, confirmation, first hunt, soccer team championship. He was much admired in town for his care of the dying and their families, as well as expectant mothers and newborns. Basically, he liked beginnings and endings. I think the middle parts—the muddled parts—pained him.

ON MONDAY, Dr. Bassett is ready for his dose of venality.

"We should put this off," I say. "He's really gathering steam."

"Yes, with Adam breathing down my neck," Livorno says. "That's an excellent idea."

"So the new system can work itself out. I'm just talking another month."

"Sure, another delay. Another month. Another year. Another decade." Livorno sounds grim and angry. "And they lay me out on the table dead as a fish and what have I accomplished?" He's nearly shouting, his orange skin turning an unhealthy brick red. "What will they say I have accomplished?"

I look carefully to see if he's kidding, but he's perspiring drops of rage.

"I think they'll say many things. Look at all those honorary degrees you've got."

He dismisses that whole wing of the building. "Paper."

"You've got plaques, too."

"Overturning the Turing test, Neill, is what will maintain my name in perpetuity."

"Your name is already maintained in perpetuity."

"I think we might have different definitions of perpetuity."

"The Sins are still a hot topic." Though to be fair only for mockery.

"This is an underperforming field. It's time I definitively outclassed it."

"I respect that." I just can't grasp the wisdom of disrupting Dr. Bassett. Also, don't we want him as accurate as possible? "We should at least spare him Lust. It wasn't something he suffered from."

"We old men are *racked* with lust," Livorno says. I've never seen him so much as notice a skirt.

"He was never an old man," I say.

THE RESTRUCTURINGS take all day. Laham is silent in the back room, typing an occasional key, standing up, moving to the stack. Livorno stays in his office, putts. I do push-ups, surf Craigslist, go get us lunch. By five I'm worried, by six nearly frantic, but Laham comes out of the back room and nods to us. We huddle in his office.

> frnd1: hi
> drbas: hi son
> frnd1: how do you feel?
> drbas: well
> frnd1: does anything seem different?
> drbas: i can't say
> frnd1: do you feel different?
> drbas: i'm not sure i know what it means to feel

"Amazing," Livorno says. "Ask him if he knows what it means to taste."

> frnd1: do you know what it means to taste?
> drbas: yes. chemical receptors on your tongue and in your
>   nose communicate information to your brain. that is
>   tasting

frnd1: what does an apple taste like?

drbas: like another apple. do you remember the apples we used
    to buy from peroni weathers? He grew a good apple

frnd1: I remember. he was the man who looked like santa claus

drbas: yes that was him. he had a bad reputation . . . but we've
    already talked about this

frnd1: have we? i don't remember

"What exactly are we looking for?" I ask.

"Same as always," Livorno says, waving his hand in front of him—
carry on.

drbas: i have a theory for your panic attack

I'm not pleased to be having this talk in front of Livorno, but there's no
stopping it.

frnd1: yes?

drbas: you're too old to be single

frnd1: maybe. times have changed

drbas: what good is a life led alone? a life without children?

frnd1: children are not the answer to all life's problems

drbas: well said

frnd1: what about you and mom? was that a good life?

drbas: your mother is a woman of quality

frnd1: how important were children to your marriage?

drbas: children are a gift from god

"He's feinting," I say.

frnd1: who did you love more, Libby or your kids?

drbas: i hope the pressure you felt was not from me

We pause, take each other's measure. "That's not a phrase I've heard before," I say.

"Do you feel presence?" Livorno asks.

I don't answer. The truth is that I'm tingling with presence.

"Information zooming around in different systems and between systems," Livorno says. "Consciousness was a cosmic accident, but maybe not such a difficult accident to provoke."

"He's not conscious," I say. "He can't see or hear."

"But he doesn't know that. Helen Keller became conscious when she was given language. He started with language."

"He's nothing but language."

"Laham and I might disagree with you on that point." He glances at the beautiful stainless steel case and—next to it—the Shop-Vac can. Monuments to his ingenuity.

frnd1: you said old pots make better soup, but periodically you
    have to get a new pot
drbas: the longevity of any household good is determined by its
    quality and the quality of the care you give it
frnd1: i saw my ex-wife. i told her you asked about her
drbas: i don't understand why i don't know her

I think about this one.

frnd1: you live so far away
drbas: did you not have a wedding? i know you don't like
    ceremony
frnd1: just not as much as you do
drbas: why didn't you have a wedding?
frnd1: we had a wedding
drbas: why didn't i come?

Yes, why didn't you come? You survived forty-eight years with yourself. Why not fifty? Sixty?

frnd1: you were ill

drbas: i don't remember this

frnd1: it wasn't a great wedding. erin's father hit on a friend of
    mine. her mother cried the entire time

drbas: hit on????

frnd1: hit on = attempted to seduce

drbas: did your mother attend?

frnd1: yes, she was there. so helpful i barely
    remember her

drbas: her best kept secret is that she's shy

frnd1: did she surprise you after you got married?

drbas: after our wedding she threw two surprise parties. both
    for my birthday

frnd1: no, i mean, was she the person you thought you were
    marrying?

drbas: i was aware i was marrying her

frnd1: when i married erin i believed she understood my most
    inner being

drbas: maybe you expect too much of people

frnd1: do you think i expected too much of you?

drbas: why are you using the past tense?

AT HOME, my mind spinning with hours of talk, I definitely wouldn't say I feel good. I feel on edge. I feel lonely. I feel like I've spent the day lying—to whom, I'm not sure.

Of course, lying is the name of the game. We lie to Dr. Bassett so he'll lie to a judge who will hopefully fall for it. That's the definition of intelligence: deception. *Successful* deception. *Modestly* successful deception.

Thirty percent! That's where our patron saint Alan Turing set the bar when he invented the test. He pulled the number out of the air, but it's an argument about human relations. I always attributed this soft cynicism to his biography: first he was the finest codebreaker for the British during World War II—a kind of spy—then in the fifties he became a broken code himself. They prosecuted him for homosexuality, and then took away everything. His career, his independence, his masculinity (he was ordered by the court to undergo chemical castration), his ability to travel. It's hard not to imagine Turing—a brilliant man, stripped of everything, his athlete's body growing fat around the waist, growing breasts—thinking of the others he knew, the men like him who still managed to survive in the world, and admiring deceit as the highest human art.

But maybe I've oversimplified. After all, Turing proposed the test long before he was prosecuted. He saw something important in that number, some benchmark of success. If you can give a person just enough so that thirty percent of the time they believe you're who they want you to be— intelligence. I can't say he's wrong. If Erin and I could have managed thirty percent we'd still be married. In fact, thirty percent looks demanding. We'd have made it with fifteen or twenty. My father? We'd have made it with five.

What percentage did he and Libby have?

As for me and Rachel, maybe I was setting the bar too high. Was I aiming for forty percent? Fifty? Eighty? It's possible I was striving in the wrong direction. Maybe I should seek more delusion, self and other. That way I can tumble in safety—like some Mr. Magoo of the spirit—through life's dangers.

Poor Turing—if he could have just launched fifty years into the future. Right now he could be down in the Castro, sipping a gin and tonic at Moby Dick's. I wonder if he would change his definition of intelligence.

13

"WE'VE HAD A SMALL SNAFU," Livorno says when I show up for work. He leads me into his office, where he shows me a transcript of a conversation with Dr. Bassett.

> frnd1: what's your favorite part of women?
> drbas: i love a woman of quality
> frnd1: i mean of her body. do you prefer a woman's breasts or her
>   legs?
> drbas: i don't think this is an appropriate conversation

"Did you log in as me?" I ask.

"I needed to test his reaction to a family member."

> frnd1: i don't know what's appropriate and what's not when it
>   comes to conversations
> drbas: don't talk religion or politics
> frnd1: why can't we talk about your wife?
> drbas: i'm not in the mood
> frnd1: who gives a fuck about your mood?

I feel angry as I read the line. I can't believe he was posing as me. I can't believe that I care that he was posing as me.

> drbas: my beautiful wife elizabeth gives a fudge, as I like to say,
>   about my moods and tempers
> frnd1: your wife elizabeth is not beautiful

"Of course, I completely disagree with that statement," Livorno says. "I was merely trying to provoke a reaction."

> drbas: how dare you say that!
> frnd1: and she does not give a fudge
> drbas: she gives a fudge! what do you know?
> frnd1: i know everything. i'm your son
> drbas: you don't know a thing. you're a pipsqueak. a little elf
> frnd1: i know because she told me
> drbas: i'm not speaking to you anymore
> frnd1: you have to speak to me
> drbas: paddleball!
> frnd1: pardon?
> drbas: paddleball! paddleball! paddleball! paddleball!
>   paddleball! paddleball! paddleball! paddleball! paddleball!
>   paddleball! paddleball! paddleball! paddleball! paddleball!
>   paddleball! paddleball! paddleball! paddleball! paddleball!
>   paddleball! paddleball! paddleball! paddleball! paddleball!
>   paddleball! paddleball! paddleball! paddleball! paddleball!
>   paddleball! paddleball! paddleball! paddleball! paddleball!

Livorno scrolls down to show me page after page of the anguished cry of "paddleball!"

"He lacks sigmoidal restraint," Livorno says.

"Jesus, Henry. Is this serious?"

"He's a talking robot who won't talk."

"Well, fix him."

He bares his teeth. "Yes. That's exactly what we need to do."

In my office, I log in.

frnd1: i have to explain something to you. i wasn't speaking this
morning. it was someone else

frnd1: it's hard to explain

frnd1: i'm sorry about what i said. i don't know what i was
thinking

frnd1: dr. bassett?

frnd1: dad?

In the next room, Livorno has taken up his usual putting. I have the feeling that I might kill someone, or someone might kill me. I flip through the numbers in my phone, my throat tight, my heart threatening to race. I taste something in the back of my mouth, a copper taste. I can't quite catch my breath. I get up from my Aeron, hand on my chest, and walk out the back to my car. I weigh and reject my mother's number. Then Rachel's. Then Erin's. I can't imagine the first line of any of those conversations.

I start the ignition and drive to Redwood City. I park in front of an Asian massage parlor. It's a white, windowless building with a green neon sign advertising MASSAGE LATE NIGHT, though it's eleven in the morning, and they're open. The engine ticks as it cools, the fan buzzing. The street behind me—Middlefield Road—is busy with cars. It's so foggy it feels like dusk. In my rearview mirror, the Shell station is white in fluorescence. The concrete gleams, the pumps sparkle. This is a Mexican neighborhood, mostly. Taquerías and tiendas and apartamentos se rentan. I see why MASSAGE LATE NIGHT might thrive around all these immigrants, far from home. I get the feeling of exile. I'm something of an immigrant myself.

I need human touch. I take out Livorno's hundred-dollar check. It would surely pay for some Asian "masseuse" to take me in her hands, if not her body. This is a completely rational move. An exchange of goods and services, comfort from the invisible hand of the marketplace. It's not exactly bachelor logic—but the logic of the individual. I owe nothing to anyone. I've pledged sexual fidelity only to myself. It is to myself that I'm responsible.

I rub the paper of the check between my fingers, listen to the traffic behind me. I take a brief grim pleasure in the idea of our accountant inquiring into a payment signed over to MASSAGE LATE NIGHT. But that's as far as I'll get today. I can't step out of the car. I'm Neill Bassett Jr.

14

THE NEXT MORNING LIVORNO tells me his Sins have scrambled my father. "They don't have any way of limiting each other," he says.

"I thought his ethical sense was going to do that job," I say.

"We'll just have to see if he shakes out of it."

Shakes out of it doesn't have the comforting ring of science. My eyes feel like they've been rubbed in sand. I slept twelve hours last night and woke up feeling that I hadn't slept one.

Livorno stands up, strident. "We had to use them. We had to. Otherwise, we just had another call-and-response robot, another toy."

He would have been the best entry."

"The best among failures. The crème de la . . ." He throws his hands up. "Whatever."

"Fine, but right now we're the crème de la nothing."

"Victims of our own success. The individual sins work too well. His value assignments are so strong they've become closed relays. He hasn't crashed. He's fallen into a hole."

Livorno has a box of powdered donuts on his desk. I take one, bite into it. It seems to have been made from sweetened sawdust. I work the dry paste on my tongue, form it into a ball, wait for it to moisten enough to be swallowed. I don't have any water in here. Or coffee or Bawls. Nothing but Livorno's hand-labeled bottles of wine in the mini-fridge.

"What if we made the opposite," I say, swallowing. "The seven, you know, non-deadly non-sins? The seven virtues?"

Livorno pulls his chin. "Is there such a thing?"

Yes, according to the Internet. Chastity, Temperance, Charity, Diligence, Patience, Kindness, and Humility.

We sit back in our chairs, consider the virtues.

"I would need time," Livorno says. "I would need graduate students, actual programmers."

I let this comment go untouched. He pushes out of his chair and approaches the glass case on the wall. He opens it and removes the pipe that he was given from the Turkish government as a token of gratitude. It's one of those white pipes—a Meerschaum—carved with the face of a person. In this case, the person is Livorno himself. He holds the pipe up so that it's looking straight into his eyes.

"We need something grander, but simpler," he says. "This is the moment for a true advance. This is when Einstein would go sailing."

"What would Turing do?"

"Go running. Or have a sexual fling with a local man."

"Well," I say, "that gives us three options."

Livorno squints at the pipe. "I have a plan," he says.

Bayside Fun is deserted except for a few late-teen ne'er-do-wells zipping around the go-cart track. Laham and I rent putters; Livorno has brought his own. There are nine holes, featuring all manner of mazes. We roll balls into a gorilla's hand and a brontosaurus's bobbing neck. The strangest hole requires a firm swing to get the ball up a ramp and into a clown's eyeball. The course finishes, classically, with a windmill. Livorno runs away with the game, needing only eighteen hits. I come in at thirty-five, Laham at forty-two. We stand together at the hotdog stand, drinking Cokes, listening to the roar of the freeway traffic, and I think this is the most wholesome time I've had since I was a child.

But Livorno's face lacks the sharp focus of inspiration. He's smiling into his Coke, carefree and vague.

"Henry," I say. "If you log in again as me, I'll take a sledgehammer to the stack."

I CALL RACHEL FOR help.

"Quick, Friend," she says. "What's something fun you did with your dad?"

I think. There had to be one thing.

"We went through a strange phase of camping," I say. I often forget about it, because it's just not in keeping. "My father would pack up a huge canvas tent, a propane stove, an iron skillet, ten gallons of fresh water, a pistol, fishing gear—you name it—and put it on a mule he borrowed. I remember the mule's name was Mule. My father had bought some getup straight out of a safari catalog—olive drab pants, a hat with mosquito netting. We slouched behind in our jeans and T-shirts. We joked that we had been kidnapped by a time-traveling scoutmaster."

"Fun," Rachel says. "I said 'something fun.'"

"It *was* fun. We fished. Fried them on the camp stove. We saw all sorts of bogs and sloughs all over South Arkansas. We were eaten alive by ticks. We got into birding. A lot of people were claiming to have seen an ivory-billed woodpecker, and so we took turns carrying the camera to snap a shot."

"It'll have to do," she says. "Let's go camping."

"That sounds great." My heart drops a little. I need help, not plans. "This weekend?"

"How about right now?"

"It's already six-thirty."

"There's a full moon tonight."

"I don't have a tent."

"Who needs a tent?"

I drive into Marin to pick her up at the Coffee Barn. Then we swing by her house (where Stevie and Rick greet me with detached bemusement) and drive another hour to the foot of the Tennessee Valley Trail, which leads gently down to the Pacific. The valley isn't named after the Volunteer State, but a steamship that hit the rocks in the gold rush. At low tide you can still see the anchor—which, come to think of it, puts me in mind of Rachel right now. We're at low tide, but here's an anchor. She's gathered the needed sleeping bags and pads, but refused Stevie and Rick's self-assembling tent. She said I needed the healing rays of the moon.

She might be right. It's nearly ten o'clock, but the air is still and warm. The bushes and trails, the distant trees—everything is lit as in a dream. We can already hear the ocean. We walk down the wide dirt path, lunar blue. A small lake appears down the hill, the moon a bright line across its surface. Beyond that the shimmering, churning Pacific. It's the kind of sight that makes you question every modern human endeavor—especially the modern human endeavors I'm engaged in. Why don't we just live in a grass hut and spend all day eating oysters on the beach? Why in God's name am I worrying about a talking computer that refuses to talk?

We turn up the Coastal Trail, careful not to touch the plants on either side of us—the place is covered in poison oak. At the top of the hill, though, it's just brown grass and a rocky clearing close to an old World War II bunker. We brush the ground for rocks, spread out the pads.

"We can zip these together," Rachel says, holding her bag out. I think, that's not a very good idea. Then I think, where is this light coming from? She nearly glows.

We settle into our large uni-bag, lying on our backs. She grabs my hand, her skin dry and chafed from work. Right above us, the moon doesn't seem to cast light so much as summon the light hidden all around us. The ocean shushes the beach; the air smells of hot dirt. This is wonderful, wonderful, wonderful.

"I have a dumb question," she says.

"I love dumb questions."

"What is it like to be married?"

"Well," I say, listening to the waves, drawing on their equanimity. "It was like the life was being slowly squeezed out of me. But I don't think it *has* to be that way."

"Something went wrong with you guys."

My antennae prick up. Just what relationship are we talking about?

"Sometimes things go wrong." I glance to gauge her reaction.

"Because you changed?" As she talks her lips shape the night's darkness.

"I think we weren't really able to see each other through the fog of our own self-regard."

"The fog of your own self-regard, huh?" She laughs, her teeth appearing, glistening. A soft wind exhales across the grass. "Do you think I'm stuck in the fog of self-regard?"

I let the wind travel across my face. I can almost taste the cool. "No. But I do think you're young."

"I *am* young. I know it. I feel it."

"Yeah? What does it feel like?"

"It's like, there's me and then there's this animal that's like in me. And I'm just living my life, walking around, going to work, but I know this animal can take over. Just for a second. But I get that feeling a lot—that I might say or do anything." She pauses. "Actually, it sounds like I'm crazy." She takes a breath. "You're supposed to say, 'No it doesn't, Friend.'"

"But I've promised to be honest with you."

She removes her hand from mine, rams a hard knuckle into my ribs. "Seriously. Do I sound crazy? Do you think I'm crazy!"

"You're saner than anyone I know."

She settles in close, lays her head on my shoulder, runs her hand across my chest. "That's nice to hear," she says. I feel her warmth, the rise and fall of her breath, of her life. I can tell she wants to be kissed, and why not? We've kissed before—have been very successful at it, in fact. God knows I could use the bodily kindness. But I feel the hard California earth under my back and the sad sureness of tomorrow morning. This might make me a little better, or it might make me a lot worse. In either case it would be a false promise. I'm not any more of a fresh start than I was that night at the Coffee Barn—I'm just more desperate.

"Good night, Friend," I say.

"I don't want to be friends," she says. "I'm just not interested."

"Really?"

"Not interested," she says.

"This is the nicest thing anyone's done for me in a while."

"Good. I didn't do it to be your friend."

I put my hand on hers. "Can we sleep on it?"

She yawns. "We can sleep," she says. "But it's not going to change anything."

IN THE MORNING SHE'S still sleepy, and I talk a blue streak about the sunrise, the power of the moon—any diversion from friends versus more-than-friends versus less-than-friends. I hustle her back to Fairfax and go home to get ready for work. But before I leave, Livorno calls to cut me loose for the day. Actually for the week. Maybe longer. I'm not fired, he promises. Just not needed.

"I'm sorry about the sledgehammer comment," I say.

"You were quite right. I shouldn't have done that. Water under the bridge. In any case, it was very savvy of you not to learn anything about programming—now you have a paid vacation! I wish I had a paid vacation."

Can't he see? You have to have something *in* your life in order to vacate.

"I'll bring lunch," I say.

"Don't worry. I'm not laying you off. In fact, I was waiting to break this news, but I've given you and Laham ownership portions of Amiante."

"Henry, you don't need to do that."

"Yes, well, I did. Congratulations," he says. He sounds distracted, distant. "We will see what we can salvage."

"I don't need a vacation, Henry. Why don't I come down and help out?"

"Very technical work. We're going to impose a version of the OCC affective reasoner." I don't know what this means, but Livorno sounds truly dispirited. "We'll hope it gets him talking again."

"I can also study up on those books I've been meaning to read."

"I'm afraid those books won't be of much use now. I'll call you as soon as we need you. Do enjoy your break."

In my bachelor's warren, I feel ungrateful, guilty, and lost. I've got my cat, the Internet, and too much liquor to be trusted. I thought I'd made important adjustments in my life—a focus on the creature comforts, a letting go of "goals" and "purposes"—but if I ever really achieved such a broad-legged stance, it's gone wobbly. I've had my coffee, read the paper, had more coffee, read more paper. It's 10 a.m. I walk over to the kitchen counter, pick up a recent postcard from Libby. It's a creased picture of a resplendent quetzal, the national bird of Guatemala, where her cruise ship must have docked. The card is full of her venerable descriptiveness: *Haven't seen any of these, but plenty of ducks around. Love you, Mom.* I imagine her alone down there, but that's not exactly right. She's with old friends or new friends. Or if not friends, people with shared interests. I sometimes cast myself in her solitary and self-sufficient mold, but that's not her mold—it's her condition. It ignores big stories in her life: her marriage of twenty-three years, her children.

I need out of the apartment; I need fresh air and sunshine. So I put down the card, pack up my reusable totes, and go the Heart of the City Farmer's Market. "Heart of the City" is code for inner city, and I step over a few wrung-out addicts to join the civic masses picking through our state's bounty. Mostly old folks, and lots of poor folks, and some yuppies like me. Even a few hipsters are here, grubby and miserable as if after a sleepless night of dry-humping. I buy navel oranges (Valencias aren't in season until May), bright red chard, a yellow pepper, and a flowering bok choy that I like to sauté and put on pizza. (This is better than Showbiz: I make my own dough.) I also pick up a small houseplant, not because the cat needs more plants to eat, but because I like the man who grows them. He tells me in his thick Mexican accent to repot with organic soil.

It is a little moment of heaven. And I try to feel grateful for the small solaces of a nice bok choy, of dough rising in the kitchen. I imagine myself in ten years, and twenty years, in the cool sun, before City Hall, where a billowing rainbow tarp blocks the steps for International Women's Day. What will I look like? Will I be here alone?

It's not even noon yet.

Back at my apartment, the dough proofed, I sit. I can hear my neighbor Fred—the admirable bachelor—clomping around on his crutches. He's been home a few weeks, and I haven't yet visited him. I step out into the hall and climb the steps. I knock on the door and call out his name. I can smell his cigarettes, but he doesn't answer.

THERE'S ONLY SO MUCH pizza I can cook, only so much food I can cram in the fridge. I leave the apartment to let my housekeeper work in peace. Otherwise, I'm in. This would be a good time to do some nesting, but can bachelors nest? For some reason my version of settling in—so far I've repainted the bathroom and pulled out the dishwasher to mop—is indistinguishable from my version of moving out.

I play around on Toler's site for the marriage-seeking, answering the questions that my mother answered for Dr. Bassett. This time I fill them in for myself, to set up a profile. But at the end of the process I'm out of luck. The site says it can't help me, but not to feel bad. A decent percentage of people are beyond help. I take what solace this fact has to offer. There is something to be said about a shared weakness.

The dating sites are kinder, though, and on OkCupid I find a woman who self-describes as a spirited, bored young SWF who likes going out on dates and maybe more? She's not in the market for anything too serious. This sounds promising. A light, positive, possibly sexual friendship, a way to enjoy our dynamic metroplex. Maybe just the thing to get me back in equilibrium.

Plus, I think I recognize her. She has the wide-spaced eyes and girlish good looks of Toler's assistant.

On the phone, she explains that she is not his assistant. She's an engineer who works for him, and that's all she can say on the matter. He's got her sewn up in a black hole of a confidentiality agreement. (Livorno has me in something similar, but I doubt he'd have the wherewithal to enforce it.) I call her Jennifer as we're hanging up, and she corrects me. Jenn. She says it in a hard businesslike way. It's not a diminutive; it's an abbreviation.

Jenn is older than I thought she was, slightly older than I am. The advantages are immediate. There's none of Rachel's existential seasickness; I can guarantee Jenn doesn't feel like an animal is about to take her over at any minute. She and I focus not on who we are, but on what we'll do. It's an ingenious way to avoid the First Date. All that talking and listening and listening and talking: college is wild, Europe is beautiful, childhood is traumatic. Why haven't I thought of this before?

We agree to go see the elephant seals mating at Año Nuevo on Saturday. She already has tickets. I'll pick her up at Le Boulanger on Santa Cruz Avenue in Menlo Park. The meeting place is a safety precaution, I assume. If I turn out to be a psycho, at least I won't know where she lives.

I know I'm not supposed to like Menlo Park. Death, despair, envy, and spiritual longing must occur here at roughly the national averages, but there's no trace of them. The town is as clean and neutral as a model home. The downtown looks like a mall and the mall looks like a downtown. This is why I'm supposed to dislike it. It doesn't have "edge" like San Francisco. What is edge? Homeless people disconsolate on the stoop of your restored Victorian? That's just ugliness, the way the world works, the ugliness of prosperity and poverty. You can abhor it, but you know which side of the door you want to be on.

In Menlo Park, everyone is on the right side of the door. Which is *behind* the door. They don't have withered memento mori on the stoop. They've outsourced poverty. I don't see how this makes them worse people than San Franciscans.

So I have a warm feeling of correct expectations, of accepting-the-world-as-it-is, of looking things straight in the eye, as I roll down Santa Cruz Avenue, the Subaru nimble on the redbrick crosswalks. There's no parking on the street, so I click on my hazards and idle in front of Le Boulanger. A Lexus SUV and a Mercedes SUV wait patiently in my rearview mirror.

Jenn emerges from the store, carrying two coffees in a cardboard tray and a paper bag with pastries. Last night on the phone I ordered a latte and something with chocolate. She's treating me to breakfast. Another improvement—dating a woman with an income. Jenn's cuter than I remember. She has a sharp, upturned nose and dark, tanned skin. A ponytail—too golden brown to be natural?—bounces out the back of her baseball cap. She has runner's legs, and is very put together in her safari clothes, a challenge unique to turn-of-the-millennium American women.

"This car is *clean*," she says, getting into the Subaru. I just had it washed, and the interior shines. The business-faced immigrants at Ducky's Detailing even vacuumed all the sand out of my seat, the sand left over from the camping trip. The memory gives my guts a sharp twist—Rachel against me, the moon overhead, the grass whishing. I take a deep breath. The decision has been made. I won't wallow.

"It's no Bentley." I push in the spring-loaded drink holder, which unfurls with a servant's grace. Jenn's arms are long, olive, and dry. She smells pleasantly of some herbaceous soap. She inserts the cups as I turn the car into a parking lot, making way for the patient citizens behind me. We do the block, yield to an elderly woman in a crosswalk, and then head down El Camino Real.

"Good joke," she says. "But let's make that the last mention of work."

"Deal," I say. I point at the cloudless sky. "It's going to be a good day for seal watching."

"It's not too weird that we're going down to watch animals mate, is it? I mean, on our first thing?"

"It's not too weird."

"That's what I keep telling myself," she says, drumming her fingers on her coffee cup. She fidgets in her seat and then, with an air of resignation, reaches down to check her BlackBerry. "I've been hearing about the seals for years and I wanted to go down there. And I finally get the tickets and then you and I are talking and I think 'okay.' But then this morning it seems weird."

"That'll be up to the seals."

"Ha!" The BlackBerry is not only put away, but turned off. "Up to the seals. You're funny."

"Thanks," I say, though her tone doesn't sound too complimentary. "Are you originally from around here?"

"Sonoma, baby." Erin's home county—which would explain an aversion to humor. "Santa Rosa. Go Eagles."

"You might have known my ex-wife—Erin Talley?"

Jenn regards me. This is the first mention of d-i-v-o-r-c-e, but we might as well get it out of the way.

"I don't think so," she says, her voice even and unrattled. "Name rings a bell."

She wiggles again in her seat, working the iPod, emitting waves of good odor. She smells like a bed in a charming B&B. I steer my mind toward the physical—imagining the feel of her pelvic bone, the skin of her belly. She's lean—will she have a six-pack or a smooth expanse of flesh between pubis and sternum?

"I like her songs," I say in response to a question, but I don't know what we're talking about.

At Año Nuevo State Park a ranger welcomes us, tears our tickets, then leads us and the rest of the animal voyeurs down a zigzagging path to the overlook point. Several rock mesas poke from the water. On each a harem of female elephant seals lie motionless as a bull serially rapes them. The bull, the ranger says, is four times larger than the cows, exhibiting unusually large sexual dimorphism. The cows are no waifs, weighing in at nine hundred-plus pounds, but the bull is the largest sea mammal before whales. The stench is strong. A mixture of fish and vomit. Several men cover their noses with the front pages of the *Chronicle*. Waves hit the mesas, shooting mist over the humping bulls. The droplets rain down on us, like Nature's own money shot.

"Cute," Jenn says.

The seals are the color of rotten meat. Their noses hang long and lumpy, like an exposed intestine. I'm not sure what's cute about them, but Jenn quivers in their presence. Maybe she's into sexual dimorphism? I detect the anxious, long-legged excitement of a girl around horses.

She's a good idea, this one. Pretty, enthusiastic, employed, age-appropriate.

The ranger says they don't know whether the cows mate with the same bull in consecutive years. They'd like to put a collar on select cows and bulls, but there's no money for the project. The dough is drying up for such research. Besides, it's no piece of cake getting a collar on a horny six-thousand-pound seal. Everyone laughs.

A juvenile bull approaches the mesa. Stretching out his lumpy nose to bare jagged, fish-stained teeth, the full-grown bull slides after him, emitting a roar like an air horn.

"See what I mean?" the ranger asks. Our group applauds.

"That's what I call an alpha male," a thin man in a Le Coq Sportif jog-ging suit says to his companion.

"He's even better-looking than Eric," she says, and they share a chuckle over this Eric.

"What's a harem?" a young girl asks her mother.

The ranger is waving a flyer over his head, but doesn't explain what the flyer is for. "The milk fat content of a female elephant seal's milk is ninety-two percent. That's how they get such *shapely* bodies."

"The little ones are more my style," Jenn says, smiling at me.

"The beta males?"

"Yeah," she says, nodding as if to a revelation. "I guess the beta males are my favorites."

I watch the mist explode off the rocks, scattering a whirl of gulls. Surely she's not calling me a beta male. To my face. Is this some sort of sex code?

"Do you mean beta male like in an S-and-M sense?" I ask.

"S-and-M? Like *S-and-M*?"

"I'm just trying to figure out if you're talking about me."

"You?" Surprise pours down her face. "You, no." She covers her mouth with her hand. "He thinks I'm talking about him," she reports to an unseen audience. "I'm not talking about you. Oh, Lord. Not at all. I was talking about the seals. I like the little ones, the cute ones. Ha!"

"Ha," I say.

"Oh, Lord," she says. "You thought"—she shakes her head—"I'm blowing it? I'm blowing our first thing?"

Jenn's posture is hunched forward, protective. This is a serious question, a serious fear.

"Forget about it," I say. "I thought you were communicating something . . ."

"Sure, I see that. I see why you think that. I'm saying beta male, you're thinking—whoa."

It's hard to resist laughing. "Yeah. Something like that."

We look back at the seals, screaming and humping.

"IT'S THE COAST that keeps me here," she says, as we cruise back up Highway 1. "I mean, in college, on the East Coast, it was like no rocks, no PCH, no Pacific, you know. So as soon as I can, I'm back here."

I pull off at Montara Beach. In the trunk is a picnic I packed. Champagne, crusty bread from Acme bakery, saucisson sec, a wedge of mimolette, some cherry tomatoes, and cucumbers cut into octagonal slices. It's kind of a beta male picnic. A sign that my passionate days in the sack are behind me.

"This looks like a great spot," she says.

"I like this beach," I say. I pop the trunk and lug the basket carelessly, awkwardly, as if I'm carrying my mother's purse. I let Jenn spread the blanket. In a last-ditch attempt to assert myself, I toss the basket roughly in the middle, hear a champagne glass crack. I feel stupid.

"We can share," she says. She holds her chin up, looking like a mischievous, triumphant girl.

"Good idea."

The champagne foams after its rough handling. I lick my hand, hold it out for her. She holds my wrist, touching her tongue to the small bubbles on my fingers.

"You hungry?" I ask.

"I am." She rolls onto her stomach, kicks her calves up.

"I'll cut you a slice of cheese."

"I'm going to start on these tomatoes."

She puts one in her mouth, then one in mine. I puncture the skin, feel the acid shock filling my mouth. She rounds her lips, shows the uneaten tomato, then begins smacking on it like a piece of gum, rolling on her back and laughing ha ha ha.

"Excuse me," I say, lying next to her. She eyes me, but doesn't turn her head. I lick my lips and kiss her, tasting for the tomato but finding only cool girl mouth, my favorite flavor of all.

She lies completely open, inviting. I don't touch her body, just watch her chest rise and fall.

"I think you're an alpha male who pretends to be a beta male," she says, giving me a wonderful look. It starts with a swollen bottom lip and travels to upturned eyes. The chin is tucked. It's a mixture of hunger and appeal, possession and shyness.

"Better than a beta male pretending to be an alpha male."

She moves my hands from her side and places them back on the blanket. "Let's cool down for a second." She looks out at the ocean. "You pack any water?"

"No."

"I don't like having sex on the first thing."

"That's a reasonable policy. I hope you'll consider an exception."

"Those exceptions don't usually turn out too well."

"Yeah? What happens?"

"You don't know? You must be very innocent."

"Pure as the driven snow."

"One," she says, enumerating on her fingers, "we'll never talk again, or two, you'll never leave me alone again. Or it'll be normal but we won't have that tension—that nice buildup."

"Buildup." My heart stumbles here. A part of me has been running a self-congratulatory tab, Rachel versus Jenn. Age, education, career, etc. But who's to say what transpired between Rachel and me wasn't all my fault? What if we'd had buildup? What if we hadn't had sex right off, but had smooched a bit and exchanged numbers?

"Yeah, there has to be the sign." Jenn smiles. She's still watching the waves. "The right moment, you know."

I refill her—the—glass. I sit back on the blanket, eat a cherry tomato. If I'd called off sex with Rachel we would never have spoken again. Our problem wasn't buildup; it was follow-through. And so we fell off track—it's a universal tendency. It doesn't mean anyone did anything wrong. A relationship that doesn't last isn't a failure; it's just a time in your life that's come to an end.

"Oh my God," Jenn says, pointing. In the ocean, a fountain of water explodes up, widening into a mist, raining down. "Whale."

Another spray erupts a few hundred yards out, and then another. It seems to be three whales, though the animals themselves remain submerged. The spray fires off again, farther south.

"Does that count as a sign?" I ask.

AT HER APARTMENT, we make an afternoon of it. In the dusky light of her kitchen, I stand naked and eat leftover salami. My body is tingling and warm, and I need the salt. Her place is as neat and impersonal as an IKEA showroom, and I admire it. There's no family bed to polish or telescope to dust. You can put every stick of this out on the sidewalk tomorrow and start fresh. Liberty!

She has an impressive array of running equipment—heart monitors, various shoes, a weightless wristwatch. We have a lot of similarities, the two of us. Working in Silicon Valley. Working for bosses who know each other. We're similar in age. In education background. (Actually, I'm undereducated. She has a PhD.) This profile stuff—the bread and butter of Toler's marriage site—shouldn't be underestimated. I could move into this apartment tomorrow. She could move into my apartment tomorrow. The salad spinner, the iPhone adapters, the pods for the espresso machines—we could find it all. In important ways we're living the same life, though hers is probably more interesting. She's mentioned a weekful of plans. Drinks with friends, barbecues.

I flip through the magazines on the kitchen table—*Wired, Time, US Weekly*—and also a blue, glossy brochure from Pure Encounters. It's a professional-looking production. Across the inside it reads, *The Way to Feel*. Part of me thinks, maybe so. Another thinks, Jesus Christ.

"A friend gave me that," she says. She's cinched a paisley robe around her waist, getting back in touch with modesty. "I think it's a kind of a crazy sex cult thing."

"I know a few regulars."

"Computer people, I bet. We'll pay good money to be reminded we have a body, right?"

"I guess so." Though I don't forget about my body so much as myself.

"I'm not judging it. It's about connections. I think a lot of people are looking for that." Her face flushes with embarrassment.

What an odd world. I think she needs a hug—I recognize the way she's standing—but do we know each other well enough? We'll see. I take her by the shoulders and pull her to me, gripping her harder with one arm than the other—a little ambiguity in case I've misread the situation. Then I settle in for a good hug. Maybe *I* need it. With Rachel kaput—yes, still thinking about her—and Dr. Bassett enraged to silence (enraged at me), and my doddering genius boss giving me the furlough I don't need. Maybe I'm the one who needs to be held. And it does feel good, though maybe only sixty percent good. Jenn and I have drunk deeply of the cup of each other's bodies today, but—I have to say—hugging feels a little strange.

15

WALKING OUT OF LOMBARDI SPORTS with fresh strings in my racket, I come across a commotion. In front of the *other* branch of Play Date, the branch that wasn't burned down, a young woman is lying on her back on the dirty sidewalk while a person of indeterminate gender in a robot costume pretends to joylessly penetrate her. It looks like pretty good street theater. The robot costume is homemade, a cardboard box with memory reels and colored buttons drawn on it. A group of young people stand behind the couple, blocking the entrance to the store. They hold up signs: SEX TOOLS ARE FOR FOOLS and DON'T FUCK PLASTIC.

The audience is a good cross section of Polk Street at this historical juncture: a few Mexicans in paint-stained work pants; a white man in a suit, sleek as a greyhound; mustachioed hipsters in their skinny pants and bowler hats; a few biz-casual drones like myself; an ancient leather daddy; an Indian woman in a sari; and a mixed-race group of the homeless and crazed, one of whom is jumping up and down, chittering like a lemur.

"Is this a promotional event?" one of the biz-casuals asks me.

The young people behind the copulating robot chant, "No investments in my vagina."

The staff at Play Date peek out of the frosted glass door, looking baffled.

"This is awesome is what it is," a hipster says. He's filming the event on his phone.

"I guess it's a protest?" I say. Protesting a sex store would be a new one here in SF, the city that never sleeps without blogging about it. But anything's possible. The other Play Date, the one closer to my apartment, does seem to have been the victim of arson. Investigators suspect the fire began with a "Molotov incident."

The robot stops humping and pushes up to its knees. It raises its hands and the young people stop chanting.

"Can you feel anything?" it asks. I think it's a boy, if only by the size and shape of the legs. But the voice is affectless and spoken through some distorting device, like the voice of someone who has had a tracheostomy. "Can you feel anything?"

"No," the young woman says. She's wearing a white Phantom of the Opera mask. "I can't feel anything."

She rolls her head toward us. "I can't feel anything," she repeats.

I'm struck woozy. The voice sounds like Rachel. We haven't really spoken since the camping trip. Or, maybe more to the point, since I took up with Jenn. Anyway, it's been weeks.

The robot unscrews its large phallus, puts it in a kind of quiver, and removes an even larger phallus, which it screws back into the anchor hole it has in its genital area. "I'll make it bigger so you can feel something."

He begins to hump her again. The young people chant against investments in their vaginas. Is it her? I can't tell for sure. The skin is bright and white; the hair is curly, but darker than I remember. I feel the pinch of memory. Not our camping trip this time, but the dim light of my bedroom, her head heavy on the pillow, the tiny hairs of her neck riffling from the morning breeze. The smell of coffee from my automatic pot mixed with the musk of our sleep.

I can't let this giggling hipster post her open legs on YouTube. Especially considering that her open legs are already online, without the mask. I put my hand gently on his shoulder and shove him toward a group of newspaper boxes.

"What?" he says, windmilling his arms. "What?"

"You ruined it," his little buddy says, coming in close to me. I ball my hand into a fist. I haven't been in a fight since junior high, but I'm looking forward to it.

"Cops!" the protesters shout.

Two police officers, both women, amble in our direction. They hold their arms out like gunslingers, but their hands are empty. They're not coming for me. They're heading straight for the demonstrators, probably just to talk. But the protestors do something not in keeping with modern methods of civil disobedience: they drop whatever they're holding and run like hell.

"Hey," the cops call after the protesters, who don't look back. They dash across the street into the Tenderloin. A taxi brakes, nose dipping down, to avoid them.

"What's gotten into those rascals?" one of the cops says.

I step out of the crowd and jog across the street too. I'm carrying my computer bag, and now my tennis bag, but the protesters are still pretty easy to follow. One of them is a robot with a two-foot penis. They take a left up Pine. They're fleet of foot, these protesters. They have the sprinting ability of young people, but the man following them, oldish youth that I am, is steady.

They turn right on Hyde. They're heading south, toward the BART, but at the corner of Hyde and Turk a brown Econoline screeches to a halt, side door open. They throw themselves inside. The robot jumps in backwards, airborne for a split second, gripping the tip of his penis so that it doesn't hit anyone. Very wise. He lands with a thump, and one of his memory reels pops off, rolling onto the street.

"Rachel," I shout, but no one is looking my way.

The door slides shut. The Econoline gasses it through the yellow light, heading—I assume—for the Golden Gate Bridge.

I pick up the tape reel. It's an old home movie. Super 8, the kind that captured hours of my youth, running in circles, dancing, silently vying with my brother for the limelight. Or very rarely my father, eyebrow raised, looking as if he'd been caught in a private activity, the secret of his daily life.

"Where they'd go?" The cops have caught up with me, both winded from the jog. I slip the movie inside my coat.

"Who?" I say.

If that girl was Rachel, then there's no doubt the robot was Trevor. Kind of beautiful, their little performance. And surprisingly painful, too. I miss her.

AT HOME I EXAMINE the film. It's just a home movie, and as I look at its yellowed images I come to realize its no one's. The people in this movie are scattered to the winds. Or—the more likely explanation—they've just uploaded all those analog memories onto DVD.

I can barely admit what I feared I'd find: one of Rachel's sex tapes. Of course, her sex tapes wouldn't be on Super 8. They'd be digital. That's how they would be online.

I open up my computer, type in her name. I've done this already, and it's the same haul of sites. None—not even the Facebook page—relate to her. How would I find the video? How do you search for your lover's body— your ex-lover's body? Teen? Amateur? Girl next door? Long Island bush? Nasty spiritual seeker? I don't know what acts she and the guy performed. She just said "regular stuff." Every search brings up girls—they're in every imaginable position, in every imaginable fantasy. They're sucking off older guys, sucking off each other, sucking off vegetables. They're wearing pig-tails. They're carrying whips. They're carrying briefcases. I've looked at these sites before, for a little fantasy, a little sexual relief. But I've never examined the faces. Hundreds of faces. Thousands. Tens of thousands. All a little lost. A little surprised.

I close the laptop and call Rachel. She doesn't pick up. And she doesn't pick up thirty minutes later or after an hour or after two or after three. I finally leave a benign message.

Then I call Livorno and beg him to let me come in tomorrow. He says that until dear old da is back online, I might as well relax. He doesn't him-self sound relaxed.

"When do you think this will be?"

"The disintegrative effect took us completely by surprise."

"You should buy the rights to Pride again. It's the seven deadly sins, not the six. Seven is a magic number."

"We need something bolder," he says, sighing into the phone. "Also we can't afford Pride."

"Have you been back to the putt-putt course?"

"Laham and I go every day."

IN THE MORNING I watch *Judge Judy* and *SportsCenter*. There are a few screeching cartoons on, ones without purpose or humor, proof that chil-dren's minds are weakening, that we're a culture in decline. I wonder what a trip would be like, a long Nietzschean hike through the Sierras or just a few days chasing girls in San Diego. I should just touch a tree. I bet touching a tree would be an immense help.

I've read about ecopsychology—a theory that says our problems are due to our disconnection from the natural world. There may be something to it, though it depends on what you mean by natural. I wouldn't trade my city life for dodging lions on the savannah. And it's also got the problem of purity. All ideas with purity at their root are monstrous and must be dis-trusted. The World Trade Center would still be standing if it weren't for an obsession with purity. Yet I'd like a little purity!

I consider calling Rachel again. I even consider calling Raj. Instead, I get in my car and head south. I think I might tool down Highway 1 and sit on the beach, but I cruise by the turnoff to Pacifica. I pass Daly City and the necropolis of Colma, waiting for the Santa Cruz Mountains to rear up in the west before I admit that, wanted or not, I'm going to work.

When I open the back door I find Laham slumped in his Aeron, scoop-ing trail mix out of large burlap bag and eating it from his hand. He's watch-ing an Internet program called *Headline Gnus*. As I approach, his eyes don't move from the computer screen. He looks like he might have spent the weekend here. His clothes—though polyester to his shoes—are wrinkled and stained.

"You okay?" I ask.

He doesn't answer, but he offers me the bag of trail mix.

"Did I ever tell you about my trip to Bali?" I say. I walk around the room and turn on all the lights. The place needs to be swept, maybe mopped. On the walls, the whiteboards are covered in formulas. One is labeled SYNTHESIS OF JOY?

"I was twenty-two years old," I say. "Before I met my ex-wife."

"You are divorced?" He finally looks at me, scandalized.

"Marriage is hard. You'll see when you get married."

He squints in the bright lights. "I am married now."

I look down at his hand, which is bare. "What do you mean by married?"

"I am married three years."

"Like a long-distance thing? She lives in Jakarta?"

"Redwood City."

"Why haven't I met her?"

In English, his gesture would mean, *why* would *you have met her?*

"Ah, look who's here," Livorno says, coming into the back room. He scoops up his own handful of trail mix and scrutinizes it, eating only the nuts.

"Did you know Laham was married?"

"Aila is a lovely woman."

"She speaks English very, very good," Laham says.

"In Laham's culture," Livorno explains, "marriage is a social contract, an agreement between families."

"It was an arranged marriage?"

Laham nods, eating. His attention is being pulled back to the computer screen.

"Married life going well?" I ask.

"If you were a good scientist like me," Livorno says, "or obsessed with money like Laham"—Laham does not object to this characterization—"you'd have gotten the whole business over with and never looked back. You'd file 'marriage' away in the accomplishments bin and return to life's real business."

"Laham's not obsessed with money."

"Asians love money. Right, Laham?"

"You have many children," Laham says, making the international sign for balancing. "You need much money."

"Because they all work," Livorno says. "Pooling their resources."

"You have children, too?" I ask, feeling a flash of panic. Has Laham bested me? Did he skip my life, like a grade?

"No children," Laham says. "Aila must finish college."

"Neill," Livorno says. "A romantic invests his life into his romance. That's where the word comes from. For you love is the only thing."

"Me? How did I get pulled into this?"

"I've been reviewing the transcripts with Dr. Bassett," Livorno says. "What happened to this young lady you were keeping up with?"

Keeping up? "We've decided to be friends."

"You should marry her."

"She's twenty."

"Don't be so conventional. A hundred years ago she'd be an old maid."

"This isn't a hundred years ago."

"What are her strengths?"

"She has lots of strengths, but we've decided to be friends."

"Marriage is good for men," Laham says. He hooks a finger under the collar of his white T-shirt, freeing a silver necklace with a ring on it. The boy wonder is lecturing me! Me!

"Aila was sixteen when they married," Livorno says. "Isn't that amazing?"

They both burst into the laughter of madmen.

Livorno shakes his head free of hilarity. "I bought a tiramisu," he announces, returning to the front.

"But, Laham," I ask, "is it working? Are you happy?"

He titters, shaking his head, eyes wide and averted. I don't think he's saying no. I think he's saying he won't engage such an indecent question.

So I go into my office and sit down at my desk, where I discover that Livorno has been telling the absolute truth. I'm not needed. Dr. Bassett will not respond.

frnd1: i went camping
frnd1: do you remember us going camping?
frnd1: do you remember us going to showbiz?
frnd1: do you remember us going to church?

Livorno is standing in my door.

"Go home, Neill," he says.

BACK IN THE SUBARU, though, I know home is the last place I should go. I call Jenn.

"You want to have lunch?" I ask.

"Uh." She's in the middle of something. "Where?"

"I would offer my place, but it's a long drive for you."

"Your *place*?" She's all ears now. "Oh, you mean *lunch*." She nearly takes a bite out of the word.

We agree to meet at *her* place. When I let myself in, I find her sitting at her kitchen table in a satiny green dress, her legs spread, not like a porn star but like a boy, a baseball player. She's chewing gum.

"I don't know what's come over me," she says.

Me either. I'm salivating. And when I put my hand on the back of her neck she unfolds like a book, pressed open by the flat palm of her desire. She looks up at me, as if begging for her life.

I grab her under the arm and haul her toward the bed. She stumbles like a drunk. I pull my shoes free and drop my pants as she works out of her underwear. She unbuttons my shirt while I'm already on top of her. She pinches my nipples with her nails.

"Don't come inside me," she says, wrapping her legs around me.

"You're so wet," I say.

"Your little phone call turned me on," she says. "You couldn't wait, huh?"

"I was so hungry."

"Yes. Harder. And faster. And hold it."

"You want to do it porn style?" I ask.

She's breathing heavy. Her regular face is struggling inside her ecstatic face, like a person underwater. "I'm going to come. I'm going to come."

I pull out and straddle her chest, and I see that lostness, that same expression from the girls online. I think, who is this? I don't know her at all.

"Jesus Christ," she says, hiccuping, laughing. She rolls over, feeling blindly for the bedside tissue box.

"Hold still," I say. I pull a tissue and dab her face with care, the way you look after a child's scraped knee. I'm sorry, I think. I'm sorry my heart flinched. I'm sorry we're strangers.

She mentions that the humming class I attended—it sounds like humming—was really successful. "You've definitely got the stroke down."

"The stroke? Thanks."

"The way you applied your index finger to my clit." She pushes up to her elbows to study me. "I'm supposed to say 'clit,' right?"

"I don't know what you're talking about."

"You know, the VAM Method. I've been reading up on Pure Encounters." She says this sweetly, as if it's a gift she's giving me.

"They teach you how to finger your girlfriend at Pure Encounters?"

"I didn't know it was limited to your girlfriend."

"What's pure about that?"

"Don't get upset at me." She puts her hand on her heart. "I'm not a member."

"Neither am I," I say. What the hell? The VAM Method?

"You don't know what a ClickIn is."

"I think it's like group therapy."

"How about unifying?"

"No idea."

"Wow." She falls back on the bed with a thump, blowing out a deep breath. "You really have no idea. I'm kind of afraid to admit this, but I'm having this really strong feeling right now. Relief—I feel relief." She nods, amazed at herself. "You don't think this means I'm, like, falling for you?"

I remain exquisitely still. Anytime the eagle of another's heart soars, whatever you are—mouse, toad, snake—don't move. From such great heights, it might not see you.

16

THE BROCHURE FOR PURE ENCOUNTERS, which I take from Jenn's house, features only one couple—an older woman and a slightly younger man holding hands and striding down the beach, feet imprinted with sand. The other four pictures are of people alone, looking contemplative or laughing with revelation. The point seems to be that Pure Encounters start with no encounter, and that even single people should come to study "mindful touch" to achieve a "deeper limbic click" in their lives and relationships. This is all old information for me, but there's also an undetailed, enthusiastic description of a core spiritual practice—the VAM Method. They don't describe the process, but assume the pamphlet-reader has heard all about it. "Despite appearances, the VAM Method is not intercourse, it's an inner course." There's a bit more jargon tossed around: "unifying," "click," "reverse love." But I can't find any sense of what these classes are like, and what happens to women or girls—or, let's face it, Rachel—when she goes to this. From Jenn's description it sounds like a cross between a Lamaze class and an orgy. Men and women team up as "intimates" for a session, and the man fingers the woman for an hour or more under the supervision of a sexpert. I can't imagine what makes these encounters pure. They don't even sound psychologically stable.

"You finally decided to buy a condo," Raj says on the phone. "They're moving fast."

"Actually, I'm calling about VAMing."

"I know. I was just kidding. Look, I can't explain any of this stuff over the phone without it sounding *completely* crazy. So why don't you come up here this weekend, for the men's retreat. You can learn all about it then."

"Don't take this the wrong way," I say. "But I'm not going to be an intimate or whatever with a man."

"You've been doing your homework—great! But we won't be doing the VAM Method. VAMing is strictly man on woman. This is totally, one hundred percent hetero. It's a men's retreat. Fire in the belly—all that. It's about being stronger and more self-confident and more assertive. And, look, it normally costs twelve hundred dollars, but let me make you an offer. Why don't you come for half price?"

There's no way I'm going to a retreat. I don't even like the word, with its sad air of military reversal, of turning tail. *Retreat!*

Then again, how else will I find out what they're about? And can I really call myself a true San Franciscan if I've never gone on a retreat? So I head off to Marin, to the Dry Earth Ashram. It's actually outside Fairfax, and I stop on my way to see if Rachel is at work. She's not. I order a coffee and sit in the window contemplating the possibility that she's off getting "stroked" by strangers. Excuse me—getting her clit stroked. I thought the upfront language was just some weirdness on the part of Jenn, but she told me that the Pure Encounters group prefers "clit," "pussy," and "cock"—they find the words more "powered up."

I'll try again: perhaps at this moment Rachel is off getting her clit and/ or pussy stroked by strangers. I feel the coffee hot and awful in my stomach. I sit very still—I'm an experienced practitioner of the art of falling apart on the inside while appearing catatonic. It's one of my proudest adult skills. I take another sip of coffee, consider brown sugar. I will not contemplate ways to work "cock" into the image, though happily Jenn tells me that cocks don't get much attention during the VAM Method. Actually, any attention. Does this make me feel better? A better question: who am I to feel better or worse? I'm barely an ex-boyfriend. I'm not even her "friend."

I dump my cup in the trash and walk to the Subaru. I head west, out of town and into the dry country, where the hills are as bare and worn as an old lion pelt. I can still be concerned about Rachel, of course—something beyond jealousy. In fact, feeling protective of her was (at least in part) what made me call it off. If Jenn wants to do that, fine. Jenn's a professional in her thirties. Rachel—younger and a deeply betrayed person—is a more combustible mix.

To the north the trees run out. It's a good half-mile of barren hills before I hit the turnoff to the ashram, a dirt path that leads to a rowdy wooden bridge lined with Zen-like sayings. A yield sign that reads YIELD TO THE PRESENT. That kind of thing. At the cedar guardhouse, which looks like a sauna with a window, an imposing bald-headed monk asks for my confirmation printout. He might have been a bouncer in a previous life. I hand it over and he nods, walking out to a catapult-like structure that is the vehicle gate, where he leans on a stone counterbalance to raise the long wooden arm.

The cars in the parking lot suggest a crowd from many walks of life. Sporty-model Beemers, beat-up Hondas. There's also an old Porsche, a beauty, which must be Raj's. I park and follow a steep wooden staircase up to the ashram, which is a large, homey cabin encircled by a high stucco wall. As I walk along the porch to the glassed-in board with the weekend's events posted Baptist-church style—"Old Energy, Old Hurts," "Unifying," and "Pure Encounters"—I remind myself that I'm here as a researcher, a detective, but I can't avoid a flash of terror from the seclusion, the hopeless earnestness of any weekend gathering of adults.

Raj comes out of a set of French doors, dressed in slacks and an Oxford but barefoot.

"I just got here," he explains. He has me take off my shoes and shows me down a long wooden hall to my room, a cell bare enough to please Saint Bernard. The ceiling is low, the walls in arm's span of each other. The mattress is rolled and tied in one corner. It seems to have been stuffed with gumballs. But the astringent smell of eucalyptus blowing in from the window makes everything feel fresh and healthy.

"Is that your Porsche?" I ask.

He nods. "It's a 1972," he says. "Awesome? I'll have to detail its awesomeness sometime later—we can't really do unstructured talk right now. But about the weekend, I just wanted to say that I think this can be a transformative event. I love it. I come up here for a total recharge. But it may not be your style, and that's cool. Participate when you want, don't participate when you don't want. The ClickIn might seem a little strange your first time." He laughs, his clean even teeth bright in his reddish face. His background is truly sun-averse, Irish or northern German. "Maybe a little confrontational?"

"I just want to confirm that I won't have to touch or stroke anyone."

"There will be no touching or stroking," he says, punching me in the shoulder. "We're going to be diving down deep. This is about authentic masculinity."

Oh, boy.

WHAT HAPPENED TO US American men? There we were, joyfully plundering the world like openhanded pirates, and now that we have it all we sit in half-lotus on the edge of paradise, the most beautiful county in the most beautiful state in the luckiest country under the sun, to meditate on loss and resentment.

We're breathing in, we're breathing out. We're keeping our minds loose, simply observing thoughts as they come up. The men in the room with me—ten in all—have degrees from good schools, do interesting work, earn their way in the world. Yet each one of them is trailed by the cymbal crash of bafflement. It shows in their bright, uncomprehending eyes, and in their striving. They struggle to breathe at the right pace with the right ujjayi breath—a wheezing effect you get by constricting your windpipe. The man next to me, an intellectual property lawyer, sounds like Darth Vader in a steam room.

Our meditation leader is a short, pasty-faced man named Larry. He owns a popular pizzeria in Berkeley. (I get a burble in my stomach thinking about it; they haven't fed us a thing.) He's talking about Old Energy, Old Hurts: "Focus on one pain you've caused in your relationships. Maybe it's infidelity or just a mean insult. Maybe it's negative intentions. Now breathe in and on the exhale let go of that roadblock. Let it go. Good. Now let's think about pain you've been caused. Focus on one pain. Just one. Breathe in and on the exhale let go of that roadblock. Good. I can feel it, men. I can feel that old energy releasing to the air."

It's true there is a new smell in the room. Crackly and chemical, like fresh dry cleaning. And it's also true that I can see how this might benefit Rachel. I just hope that when she thinks of pain done to her, she doesn't think of me.

We're asked to visualize some time when a "partner"—that dreaded word—has done something hurtful to us. I take my ujjayi breath, and try to get past my gut feeling that the project feels mean-spirited. I'm not a senti-mentalist, I hope—I don't whitewash my father's suicide; I don't whitewash my ex-wife's behavior in our marriage. But I don't blame in any cosmic sense. The only person responsible for my problems is me.

I guess I should think of Erin, but instead I find myself thinking about the time before I met her. It was my last year in college, and I was having a fling based not on passion, but on friendliness. My father was recently dead, and this turned me a click in a different direction. Before this time—before his suicide?—I wouldn't have dreamed of getting entangled with less than a full heart. But I found that this cooler, maybe sadder arrangement suited me well. Sophie—the partner in my love affair—was very pretty, with short red hair and fair skin. She had freckles and drove a little used BMW and listened to lots of girl punk. Her best-kept secret was her unclothed body. It was stunning. Long, pale, gentle, with breasts so perfect I'm not sure, in retrospect, they were real. I made love not to Sophie, but to that body. I loved that body, its feel, its vistas. I don't know who or what Sophie was making love to, probably the absence of the boy she was truly devoted to, who had moved to Seattle.

We got along well. She had a good sense of fun—we went to concerts, we went to a hockey game in Tulsa. Then we'd get back and make slow, kind, sad love.

If I ever jump over the railing of the Golden Gate Bridge it wouldn't be for the impact that would stop the plunge, but for the plunge itself. That's how I felt at the time—not suicidal, but plunging into a bottomless hole. I could have asked for help, but I didn't know I needed any. The plunge had its odd pleasures. Not caring about the day-to-day demands of life may be a sign of depression, but it's also a mark of freedom.

But freed to what? Slow, kind, sad love to Sophie. My last classes. Hard work at my restaurant job. This was my life, and it wasn't bad. It was the kind of unthrilling, manageable existence I expected to end with, not to begin in.

I still went to Mass sometimes, but despite myself I was slipping from the church's grip. My father's funeral had revealed to me that I was at best a cultural Catholic. And then the hot sun of disbelief bleached the meaning from the prayers, the rites. For me, Mass became an absurd spectacle. All that dress-up, all that kneeling and standing and kneeling again. And the atonal Catholic singing—why didn't we at least learn how to sing? At least there would be that for us, the faithless.

When I graduated, I threw a little party, surprised that I did have some friends. I invited a couple of people from work, a few fellow English majors, and Sophie. For posterity's sake, I record their names here: Brandon, Justin, Patrick, Luke, Amie, Rebecca, Van, Jennifer, Brian, and Josh.

We set up in my backyard, drinking cheap gin and beer. We got very drunk, and at one point I made out with Rebecca in the hall. Then Patrick stumbled through the bamboo fence into the landlord's compost pile, and we called it a night. Some partygoers walked home; some stayed in my living room. My head was spinning when Sophie and I got into bed. Hers, too—she had to get up and vomit.

"I've never been this drunk," she said.

"I have," I said.

She pulled my arm tightly around her. "I'm going to miss you," she said.

I waited a while, sorting through my own feelings. It was very important to me to be completely honest. "I'll miss you, too."

"If you stayed," she said, "would we still date?"

"I think I would want to."

"I think I would want to, too."

We were quiet. I thought I heard a noise, some shudder of sorrow.

"Are you crying?" I asked. I reached up to touch her face—but it was dry.

"No," she said. She pulled my hand back down to her ribs, patted it in place. Out my window, the moon was gone, and the stars hung heavy in their forgotten patterns. It was one of those nights when the world seems full of ancient messages, intended for a people long since dead.

"Are *you* crying?" she asked.

I considered coaxing myself to tears. My father, after all, was an amateur astronomer. *He'd* never forgotten the stars' patterns. But tears would have suggested I desired something, and I didn't know if I could reenter the world of desiring things. I was left with cheap catharsis, or worse—manipulation—and I had made it so far without stooping to either.

AFTER DINNER, I'm as jittery as a wet bird. All that deep breathing was supposed to take me someplace calm, but my inner pilgrim made a wrong turn. The edgy, coppery-bright beginnings of a panic attack are crawling around my chest.

Raj approaches me on the porch, where I'm rocking in the big swing. "Chilly out here," he says, sitting next to me.

We rock back and forth, his long runner's legs powering us. I can see the guardhouse from here, the hulking monk as still as a chess piece.

Raj pats me on the knee. "Let's go for a walk." We head up the road and then off on a path covered in fallen eucalyptus leaves. It's a little dark to be entering the woods, but stretching my legs feels good. It reassures me of the great truth of life: today didn't take that long and tomorrow will be just as short. When we reach the top of the hill, Raj glances behind him, then pulls out a pack of cigarettes.

He shakes two out. "Strictly forbidden," he says.

I don't smoke, but I take one anyway, charmed back into myself by a little mischief. From the first puff it's a mistake. My head is whooshing and whirling; I feel disjointed, my chest clinched, my legs limp. "I think I'm going to fall down," I say, and then I do.

When I come to, Raj is on his knees next to me, squinting into my eyes. He takes my chin, turns my head left and right. Above him, the tree canopy glitters darkly.

"Dude," he says. "You ate it. You all right?"

I cough something up, phlegm from the ocean floor.

"I'm not a smoker," I say.

"Let's not be shy about what's really happening. There's some serious energy rebalancing going on in your body. Most people—takes them four or five of these weekends. You've just slipped right into it."

I cough up more phlegm.

"I had a weird experience today," I say. "I thought of my ex-wife, and couldn't summon any resentment."

He leans back on his heels and sits down. His lighter flares demonic light on his sunburnt face. He blows out a plume of smoke, waves it away into the air.

"Old energy, new energy—it's not just a figure of speech. We're feedbacks. We're not confined to our bodies. That's what we forget, especially if we're not religious people. Puttering around in our houses. Living alone. Never being touched. Did you know when you put a group of women under one roof their mooncycles synch? That blows my mind. Their energies, their auras are interacting. They're not even separate people. None of us are separate. We're literally made up of each other. Which is why it's such a problem that so many people live alone now. It's like we're less human."

I clear my throat. "I live alone," I say. My voice sounds blurry.

"So do I," he says. "I mean I get it. You start to feel like you're an image reflected in a mirror recorded on a videotape. Why not live alone? It's a lot easier. I mean, think of Rachel."

"What do you mean?"

"That pornographer she was living with. He basically tried to steal her soul."

What does that mean? She said "regular stuff." "I looked for the video the other day. I couldn't figure out the search words."

"Don't do it, man. There's nothing to be gained."

I lie there on the dusty, warm ground. It's not so bad down here.

"Was that her with Trevor, at that protest in the city?"

Raj looks at me, but his face is too shadowed to read.

"You know," I say, "the one where he was dressed like a robot and he was pretending to penetrate Rachel on the sidewalk?"

"A robot?"

"Like a retro-robot. With tape wheels and buttons."

"And that was Trevor?"

"He was wearing a helmet. I couldn't see his face."

"But you saw Rachel."

"She was wearing a mask."

He looks back up and exhales smoke through his nose. "I'd be surprised if you could get Rachel to lie down on a sidewalk in San Francisco. She carries hand sanitizer. Besides Trevor is off at a PE house in Oregon."

"How long has he been up there?" I ask, pushing up to my elbows. I'm ridiculous. I feel unbounded relief.

"A couple of months, at least. He's got quite a few resentment-anger management roadblocks to break through."

"Is he up there VAMing?"

Raj nods. "Trevor is one of our most intensely clicked strokers."

To my great surprise, I sleep like a stone. I have an odd mash-up dream where my mother tells me that my father is not an intensely clicked stroker. No doubt this was true.

The morning breaks with bright, artificial-lemon light. We gather in the cedar-planked meditation room to do some breathing, then adjourn for breakfast, which is a scoop of yogurt and three almonds.

Next is spiritual housecleaning, which consists of Raj telling me very funny stories of Internet dating, including one in which a woman "forgot" to tell him she was on ankle monitoring. He then segues into his work life, which has been a long, lucrative struggle with meaninglessness.

"I go to the office in the mornings," he says. "Fix a cup of rooibos, stare out at Napa Valley. It's gotten like a theme park. Disneyland. I think, who am I? What does it mean to sell condos and lots?"

Then we talk about some key concepts, including this feedback idea. Basically, clicking is volitional love, the choice to have serotonin, melatonin—all the friendly neurotransmitters—cascading through your brain all the time. The serotonin is a click itself. Clicks unite the limbic system with the more rational brain. At any moment when you might separate from other people, you click again. And as you become a more engaged person, as clicking becomes who you are, you reach a feeling of connection to others and to the universe (a dreaded word, but oh well). The body is a vehicle for the spirit and by clearing all the energy channels you liberate the spirit.

"You know that saying—'Love makes the world go round'?" He rolls his eyes. "Cheesy, I know, but it's literally true. It's the basic force humming through the world. It's what's in all of us. And we can bring it out in each other. Flesh to flesh."

Like Transcendentalism but with a focus on the genitals. All those years there was the battle between the heart and the mind. Hard to believe the winner will be the gonads.

THE AFTERNOON SESSION—the big finale—is led by Raj himself. Someone has lit a crisper incense. The Marin sun dazzles against the wood shades. The full title of his presentation is "Pure Encounters: Ready to Click." The men—all ten of us—sit on meditation cushions in a circle. Anyone who wants to can discuss his problems, and the more experienced participants will help him "love over" his "roadblocks." The youngest guy there, a kid named Walker, says that he can't talk to women. He can't express his desire, and he bottles it up and does reckless things. He masturbated in a public bathroom last weekend he was so amped up. He did drugs in high school and afterwards and he thinks he may have damaged himself—done something permanent to his limbic click. The lingo is horrible, but there's no doubt that Walker is suffering. And if a little lingo will help him or anyone else—Rachel, for instance—then the least I can do is soldier through.

I LEAVE THE ASHRAM just before dusk. A few miles closer to Fairfax, my phone comes back into range of a tower. I have ten messages—one from Rick and nine from Livorno, who needs to speak to me right away. I stop by the Coffee Barn, where Rachel is still not working, and fill myself to the cockles with caffeine. Then I call.

He has something serious to discuss, but doesn't want to do it over the phone. He invites me to an excellent Chinese restaurant for lunch tomorrow. Have I heard of P.F. Chang's?

I don't tell him it's a chain, but this lack of knowledge—the idea that because he's only seen one P.F. Chang's there *is* only one—feels like the source of many problems. Amiante is supposed to evoke magnetism, but it really means asbestos. It's a selfless vanity project, a dunderheaded finale to a brilliant career.

Of course, then there are all the problems with me at their root. Incoherence, ignorance, diluting of mission.

I DON'T KNOW if old energy can really be replaced by new energy. So, sort of as a test, I arrange to meet Erin out. We were going to have an afternoon coffee but we switched plans, dangerously, to a drink.

I sip my martini, smiling at her and smiling at the irony of grabbing a drink with someone who berated my drinking while we were married. Then since we're supposed to be moving to some pleasant later stage of divorce, some stage of openness, I mention the irony.

She arches her eyebrows, perfectly tweezed. She really does look a little like Audrey Hepburn, though not as willowy. She's started working

Saturdays in a co-op bakery—since Ian, the boyfriend, works six days a week at his firm—and she displays her large forearms.

"Don't forget," she says. "You were so drunk our wedding night you couldn't have sex."

"That's not true," I say. "I was so drunk you wouldn't have sex with me. Key difference."

She laughs. "I guess you're right. I do look back on those days and wonder what the hell was going on with us."

"Despite all the evidence to the contrary, we were not well suited."

"Like you and the young girl. You weren't well suited."

"She wasn't that young."

"Is that right?" Erin is sipping her whiskey at a pretty good clip. "Should I remind you how old you are?"

"I can always check my driver's license. She and I are good friends now."

"That's too bad. I liked her."

"You talked to her for three minutes in a restaurant."

"I still liked her."

"I'm actually dating someone who's older than you."

"She can walk without a cane?"

"She runs marathons."

"Oh, boy. I guess you're going to start running with her. Don't get too skinny."

"The first person to run a marathon fell over dead of a heart attack. No one seems concerned about this."

"So what do you do with the old lady?"

Have sex. Go watch seals have sex. My time with Jenn seems unusually perverse. We have gone out to eat, though we both fidgeted at the table, waiting to go back to her apartment and . . .

"We're in that getting-to-know-you stage."

"Tell me about her."

"She's very smart. And pretty. She runs marathons."

Erin orders another drink for herself and me. Why is my tongue suddenly mud around the subject of Jenn? Maybe it's not the subject of Jenn but the audience of Erin.

"She works down south," I say. "Like me."

Erin regards me, amused.

"Fine," I say. "What do you want to know?"

"I'm waiting to hear some bigger-picture stuff. Is it a relaxed thing? Does it have a feeling of being right? Does it have a kind of sibling feel?"

Sibling feel? "I only have a brother."

"I'm trying to figure out this choice of yours. Let's say Rachel is innocence and naivety. But you didn't want innocence, so . . . Jenn. She's, what? A desire to settle into your life?"

I've never loved this idea that the people in your life are paths you might choose. It elides too many inconvenient facts. Such as that they're people. But even if I were to play along I wouldn't say Rachel was innocence, as much as kismet. The thought that something good might come unbidden. Which would definitely make her a different path than Erin, where the good took coaxing. "I'm flattered you think this is all in my power."

"I'll give you an example." She slurps her whiskey. Who is this hearty party girl? "If I'm not overstepping boundaries."

I wave my hand, go ahead.

"I dated that guy, Serge, right after you and I split." Actually we were still living together, but I let this correction go unmade. "And then I started dating Ian. Serge represented excitement, carpe diem. But he was kind of an asshole. Those kinds of guys usually are, right? Ian is the absolute opposite of an asshole. He's caring. He does work around youth justice. He represents stability and the long term."

I'm no expert on the matter, but this does not sound like the heights of passion. And I'm glad to hear it. My pleasure, I'm afraid, is a petty feeling, strong evidence I've retained a few volts of old energy.

"This word 'represent.' It sounds like he works for Amway."

She shrugs. "You're still keeping things shallow. Playing the field. They can just be people to you. Not people who mean something about a direction in your life."

I should get angry about this comment, but I sip my drink and consider whether she has a point.

"What direction did I represent?"

"Did or do?"

I'm surprised to hear I represent anything currently.

"Do."

"First love gone mysteriously wrong."

I raise my glass to her description. "I'd agree with every word in the statement but 'mysteriously.'"

"If you can explain it to me, I'm all ears." She leans on the bar and gives me a warm smile, as if we're old friends having a chat. As if we're not talking about the implosion of our lives together. Does she not think our lives imploded?

"Does Ian know you're here?"

"Of course he does," she says. "He just doesn't know *you're* here."

Some comedian has loaded the jukebox with Journey's greatest hits. We're caught in a whirlpool of "City by the Bay" and "Don't Stop Believin'." Erin leans over to the bar to order yet another drink, and I find myself wondering if I could sleep with my ex-wife. If we might—and this *has* to be the third martini whipping up my post-retreat brain—get past some roadblocks that way. But I can't make a pass at her and have it turned down. And I can't make a pass at her and have it accepted. We would know exactly what to do, of course. We had a white-hot physical connection, before we had no physical connection at all. I look at her newly strong forearms. I like them.

"Are you having another?" she asks.

Sleeping with her would have pleasures, one of them the pleasure of home—home after a much-needed remodel. I imagine the exact steps we would go through. The awkward question. Would you like to come to my place—our old place—for a nightcap? Then we would walk up over to Dolores and past the park and up the hill—a good twenty-minute walk, a near eternity. The dusty staircase would be waiting on us. Maybe even an old neighbor with a surprised look. Erin would comment on the changes in the building—the new compost bin, the energy-saving bulbs. And then there's the cat, which will probably give her a cold welcome and offend her. Or give her a warm welcome and offend me. And then the bed . . . our old bed . . .

There's absolutely no way. The only proposal I could make to her would be a dirty night in a hotel, which might take care of this storm cloud that's blown up around us. But not tonight. No more drinks for me. Because I blessedly, once again, have to go to work tomorrow.

I MEET LIVORNO AT the hostess stand of P.F. Chang's in the Palo Alto mall. He looks thinner than I remember. Gaunter. It's an old-man thinness. It could be his white shorts, which show off an expanse of sinewy, pale leg.

Is he using bottle tan on his face?

"I was just telling Montana here about the New Orleans marathon," he says.

Montana is the hostess, a pretty, pleasantly blank-looking high-school-age girl. It's not profound blankness—just the vacancy of youth. A certain position of the head, a set of the eyes, all of which can be transformed by twenty-two or twenty-five or twenty-seven, her eyes sharper, head tilted down into life, ready for impact. She just needs something terrible to happen to her, and then needs to do something terrible to someone else. After that, she's all set.

Montana is giving Livorno her tolerating-a-crazy-talkative-senior smile. One she probably saw on a training video. He brags a bit more about the marathon—it's a half-marathon, I happen to know, but the man is knocking on eighty. It's still impressive. But Montana only perks up when Livorno whips out his new iPhone. I feel a little thrill when the girl ogles it, has her thinking reset. You shouldn't underestimate your elders, young lady.

"Montana," he says. "What province is Chef Chang from?"

She looks alarmed. "Our chef's name is Mario," she says.

Nor should you overestimate them.

We're shown to our table, where we order lettuce cups, Mongolian beef, and Hawaiian prawns. We both drink Arnold Palmers, and I'm so happy to be here, sitting across from Livorno. I've missed him like a best friend.

"I'll be brief," he says. "Your father is still scrambled."

"I guess if you made me angry, despairing, greedy, envious—and the other two—all at the same time, I'd be scrambled myself."

"I should be crowing. The Sins weren't this robust last time."

"What happened to 'paddleball'?"

He shrugs. "We have gotten him to speak a bit. He'll answer basic questions, but won't go beyond them. Sometimes, there's a passing sense of presence, even in his refusal to speak." Livorno is warming up, the old delight at discovery upon him, but then he stops, leaning back to sip his drink. "Though it could be my limited English."

"You speak English better than I do."

"I'm not any worse off than my colleagues," he says. "We've spent the last fifty years making wild predictions and failing to even come close. We predicted sentient computers. We produced self-propelled vacuum cleaners."

"Which don't work very well." I regret saying it.

"Exactly. And as far as natural language processing? We've made it to the point where a customer can shout 'operator' into his phone four or five times and hope to speak to a real person. This is hardly progress." He beams, seeming to take some satisfaction in his shared defeat.

"You always told me AI was philosophy, not engineering," I say.

His smile disappears. "That's because in philosophy you can move the goalposts. In engineering, you just fail. And that's where we are. Laham is preparing to return to Indonesia. Dr. Bassett is lost in himself. In a kind of labyrinth."

I take a bite of lettuce cup. It's a funerary meal. My first thought is that he can't take this away from me. But what is *this*? My father—the chance to chat with my father's ghost. So what if it's mostly about horses and Willie Beerbaum. He *has* helped me. We've talked about Rachel. We've talked about Erin.

"But what if our problems are philosophical?" I say. "What if with the gut and the brain we're leaving out an essential element to cobbling together a person?"

Livorno puts his hands flat on the table, pushes himself up straighter. "We don't have anything close to the resources to build a body."

"I'm talking about some governing principle that connects gut and brain. Being lost in himself, in a kind of labyrinth, separated, pulling apart on the inside—that sounds like a common affliction. So let's attack this head-on. What if we had a system to unify him, so everything inside him starts to click?"

Livorno narrows his eyes, as if I've just gone blurry, but I don't feel blurry. I feel precise, maybe inspired.

"What do you mean by click?" he asks.

"Connectedness," I say. "Connection. I was just at a retreat"—this feels like a misstep—"and it was all about encouraging a kind of inner harmony, getting over roadblocks." Misstep again. I've got to convey my ideas before the lingo of Pure Encounters betrays me. "Meaning psychological blocks. It's more about attitude. It's about wanting"—I search for the words, but I seem to be possessed—"to click and stay clicked."

He leans in; he doesn't look outraged or disbelieving. "But what is the mechanism of the clicking?"

"Well," I say. The answer involves chakras, meridians, auras. Where do I start? "It's about love. It's about inner love and outer love. It's about love being part of every interaction with yourself and the world."

"I still don't understand the mechanism of conveyance for this love. What is the *thing* that is doing the clicking? The gut? The brain?"

"I think it's the limbic system."

"The *limbic system*." He leans back, rolls a lettuce cup, sets it down. He takes a sip of Arnold Palmer, sets it down. He begins to crack his knuckles. "And they think human love is an extension of some sort of primum mobile."

"I think they also just think it's just, you know, the feeling."

"A theory of love." He sips his tea. "It makes for an eye-catching press release."

"Sure," I say, disheartened. I should be grateful he's even listening to me. I can only imagine the level of desperation necessary for him to ponder these ideas. But I want to know if he thinks we're actually on to something. "He has a gut and a mind. Maybe he needs a heart."

Livorno weighs this suggestion silently. "The limbic system is a much clearer metaphor."

"A metaphor that might work?"

"The whole idea is a bit Gnostic. Every interaction colored with love. A kind of universal positive inclination. Rather than no—yes."

"Rather than no," I say. "Yes. That's basically it."

"There's nothing basic about it." He touches the uneaten lettuce cup, raises it to his mouth. "Modeling even a discarded version of human nature is a complicated proposition. At the very least, we need Laham. For good measure, I should buy Pride back." He swallows, then bares the full piano keyboard of his teeth. "This is *not* going to be cheap."

I RIP THE PLASTIC off a laundered shirt. I adjust my hair. I'm officially back on the job, and my first task is to visit Toler. Though he's the competition, we're asking him for the additional funding. I'll have to weather his disdain.

But as I'm walking out the door, Rachel's uncle, Rick, calls me again. "I should be sending texts," he says. "I know how you kids are."

"I'm sorry I haven't called you back," I say.

"I was just wondering if you could put Rachel on the phone."

"Rachel?" I lock my door and set down my bag. "She's not with me."

"Oh." He sounds embarrassed. "Well, sorry to call."

"It's good to hear from you," I say, holding the phone on my shoulder as I pick up my bag. I can feel the day shifting into gear again—Livorno, then Toler, then lunch—but something about Rick's voice stops me.

"You don't know where she is?" I ask.

"We just assumed she was down there with you."

"We haven't actually talked in about a month."

"You're not dating anymore?"

"No," I say. But why is this a secret? Was she proud to be dating me? Sweet God, I hope she wasn't ashamed to have lost me.

"I guess we're a little worried about her then," he says. "It's been three days. We're trying not to be controlling, you know?"

"Can you call any of her friends?"

This suggestion is met with silence.

"She took off work," Rick says. "I just saw those two sleeping bags gone and, you know, assumed."

IT'S WITH TREPIDATION that I cancel my meeting with Toler. Can you just reschedule a meeting with the super-rich? Will he deprive us of funds out of spite? I'll find out—tomorrow. For now I'm driving over the mountains to the Tennessee Valley trailhead. It's a weekday and there aren't many cars, but Rachel's Honda is parked in the lot, her cell sitting on the driver's seat, either off or with a dead battery. Mystery solved. I know where she is. I know she's as safe as she wants to be. But I stand there and look down the trail, thinking about that detail Rick mentioned—*two* sleeping bags.

Of course, she's off camping with someone else, maybe in the spots she showed me. That's what you do in life. You meet someone, date them, and when it's over you gather the good parts and carry them into the future, shedding the bad, if possible.

Still, couldn't she have gone camping somewhere else?

I think about leaving her a note. *Everyone worried—please call.* This way she would know that I knew. Pure passive aggression on my part. I've left messages, Rick has left messages. She'll get them as soon as she returns to the car.

So happy to have found you, and hope you're having fun, but please do call. Want to stay clicked.

Even worse.

I lock the Subaru and head down the main path toward the ocean, stopping at the map to the park. There looks to be fifty miles' worth of trails, more than I could cover in a day, and that would assume she wasn't hiking them herself, a moving target. All I know is she must like this person. Three days here would be a boring stretch otherwise. A gust of wind whips dust off the path and into my eyes. Ahead of me several women in English riding costumes trot their horses toward the beach. The sun overhead is hot, especially to me in my starched shirt. The usual suspects are about: egrets, seagulls, titmice. California quail with their dashing pompadours. And people. There are always people who seem to have the day off.

I stop at the foot of the Fox Trail but decide not to climb it. Same with the Coastal Trail. I'm not going to snoop on Rachel. If I stumble across her and her camp partner, so be it.

Walking back up to the lot I see her. She swings her backpack into the Honda's trunk, slams the lid down, sniffs. She gives the Subaru—parked several slots down—a long look, though it should be impossible to know it's mine. I bought the most standard of standard models, and I'm morally opposed to bumper stickers. Still, I crouch on my brushy patch of trail to make sure she doesn't spot me. She bends down to straighten her jeans, then stands again, smoothing back her hair into an unruly ponytail. She's alone, and I get the impression she has been, the whole time. She has the slow, deliberate movements of someone who has been keeping her own counsel. I feel somewhat shamefacedly happy she's camping solo, and then I feel terrible she's here by herself. But why should I feel terrible? She's simply a girl who walks the earth as I do. Walks it better than I do. Imagine liking the person you're camping with—when that person is yourself.

17

I'M MEETING TOLER at the research wing of his company in Redwood City, where he apparently spends most of his time. The corporate headquarters of his matchmaking company is deeper in Silicon Valley, among a stretch of forgettable office parks that express their imperial grandeur only through sheer cost—by square foot it would be cheaper to relocate to the Champs-Elysées. But scrappy start-ups—even well-financed ones—should have humbler digs. Toler Solutions hasn't quite lowered itself to a former quilting studio, but close enough: a pressed sandstone and glass two-story building vague enough to contain anything—a cookware outlet, a printing press, dentists. It's eight in the morning—I had to get up at six to be ready. I think the early hour is punishment for rescheduling. If so, I'm happy to receive it. Whatever makes Toler's money smile down upon us.

I park the Subaru in front of a concrete trash can, right next to the Bentley, which—let's face it—looks like a Chrysler, and step up on the low sidewalk and enter the glass door. The reception area buzzes with fluorescent lights. To the right three beanbags—bright primary red, yellow, and blue—surround a coffee table covered in what appear to be toys for children age three and under. A wooden train set, a stack of Mega Bloks. To the left a young, unsmiling Asian woman stands motionless behind a large polished-wood counter. A huge monitor behind her head plays a television commercial for Toler's other business. I smile at her, but she merely looks at me steadily. She must not be the receptionist, but who else could she be? She's standing behind a desk in the reception.

"I'm here to see Adam Toler," I say, grinning from discomfort. When she says nothing, I grin harder, stretching my face as far as it will go.

"Name?"

"Neill Bassett."

She turns to the monitor and touches it, pulling up a very full list of appointments for Toler. My name is nowhere to be seen.

"Maybe he's going to try to work me in?"

She turns back around, her eyebrows raised doubtfully. "Why don't you have a seat?" She indicates the corner of the room with the toys and the beanbags.

"Do you have chairs?" I ask, but she's exited through a door into the depths of the building, leaving me alone.

I walk over to the coffee table and pick up a plastic hammer. I don't want to sit in a beanbag—it feels debasing in advance. Legs splayed out, arms stuck to the vinyl. But I'm tired, and besides what do I care about debasement? I'd bark like a dog—chase a stick!—to get Dr. Bassett talking again.

"Where is he?" Toler's voice comes from a back office. I try to scramble up from the beanbag, but it's a difficult process. I have to first sit on the floor and get my legs under me, then hold on to the coffee table to get into a squatting position, as if the toys have somehow sent me back to my toddler days. It's at this stage that Toler strides in, hand held in front of him. I'm ready to correct him on my name, but he says, "Welcome, Neill." He looks like he's been on some radical diet since I last saw him. He's dropped another ten pounds easy. His skin is yellowed and drooping, his jowly face loose as a hound's. But he doesn't seem to have lost any of his evil buoyancy. "Tea? Bubbly water?" he asks. "We even have wine, and I didn't make it in my bathtub." He sweeps an arm in the direction of his receptionist. "Grace, get this man what he wants."

He leads me through the door he just came out of, down a dimly lit hall to his office, which isn't as showy as I would have guessed for a Bentley owner. I think he's tried to communicate minimalism, humility. Or maybe something more ineffable—communicating that he's not trying to communicate anything. But the red leather chair I sit in has a nice Italian feel of needless luxury, and there's a grouping of black-and-white photos on the wall—not too organized, not too disorganized—that imply a designer's touch. His desk is arranged as if for a photo shoot—a pad of paper, two black pens side by side, and a closed brushed aluminum laptop. If it weren't for the three Ionic Breezes in the corners and a Tiger Woods bobblehead (an homage to Livorno?), I wouldn't be sure this room was anything more than a theater set.

"I don't play golf," Toler says. He thumps the bobblehead, sending Tiger into a frenzy, his smiling face warning *no, no, no!* "But I've been so envious of Henry ever since he started his little project. The life of the mind. That's the thing." He puts his hand on Tiger, stops the shaking. "So Henry told me that you've come up with a groundbreaking theory. I think he said"—he clears his throat, as if about to say something untoward—"of love."

"Well," I say, listening for condescension but not quite hearing it. "Love is the word he uses."

"I assumed you meant love as in the 'affective reasoner'—the positive pole of attraction—but he says this is much more fundamental."

With my lack of technical background, this sentence might as well be in Urdu. "I'm glad to hear he likes the idea so much."

"How are you planning on doing it? Just a rearrangement of GSPs? Or will you be doing some more work in the construal frames?"

Urdu again. The answer, of course, is I don't know. I don't know what GSPs are. Or construal frames. I suppose I could just confess, but I feel embarrassed for Livorno, as if I should hide his bad decision to hire me.

"Something like that."

Toler frowns. "What was your specialization for your doctorate?"

"I have a master's in business administration."

He slaps his hand on the desk. "I was wondering why you were so goddamned dense. I just assumed once he shanghaied that Indonesian whiz kid you've got over there . . ." There's a knock on the door. Grace comes in with our Earl Grey. She's still unsmiling, but now that she's not hidden behind the reception desk I see that she's wearing a pornographically short skirt. It seems very wrong for this early in the morning. Toler passes his eyes over her legs and then lets a yellowish lip fall in a lopsided smile. When she leaves the room I expect some boy's-club remark, but he says nothing. I feel a clammy sweat above my eyebrows.

"I didn't know Laham's reputation preceded him," I say. I hold on to the hot tea. Am I trying to impress this knucklehead? What am I asking— of course I'm trying to impress this knucklehead.

"Laham—right. What is that unpronounceable last name of his again?"

Simunjuntak, but I shrug apologetically, as if I don't remember.

"Honestly, Neill, I prefer talking to a businessman anyway. What do engineers know about human nature?" He blows on his tea and leans toward his desk. "I mean, you need your engineers. But at the helm, you need an idea guy, a psychologist. I started Toler Solutions so I could do big things— work on the future of technology, especially the way we'll be interacting with technology. And it's clear to me that conversing robots are a key part of that future. The Japanese are way ahead of us on this. They bond socially with robots. Robots look after their elderly. They've got robots as candy stripers. It's brilliant. They've also made the leap toward accepting intimate relationships between humans and nonhuman objects. You read the *Times* article on the man in love with his pillowcase?"

I did. It was deeply disturbing. But to be fair the pillowcase had a cartoon character on it. "I think he was actually in love with a cartoon character."

"But she needed a physical form," he says. "Nothing elaborate, obviously—just a pillowcase. They call it 2-D love. But 2-D won't cut it for most of us. We're going to need 3-D, interaction. The next step—and this is five years away, maybe ten—is romantic relationships with robots. Your desires and needs being met by them. Don't give me that look. It'll be better than any relationship you've been in before. The *ideal* relationship. The cooking, the backrubs, the patient listening, the sex. All on your schedule. And it won't matter if you've brushed your teeth. You won't have to go to the gym. There won't be any shenanigans with the pool boy or pool girl. It'll be a profound, profound shift in the market."

The market. I thought he was going to say the world. "Romance with robots is the *next* step?"

He opens a desk drawer and removes what looks like a purple plastic flashlight, sliding it handle first toward me. "It's never been used—don't worry." This, of course, is just the kind of sentence to make one worry. The exterior has even ridges for grip; it's about a foot and a half long. I leave it on the desk, but spin it around to a surprise. Where the light would be there is a lavender-colored silicone model of a vagina.

"Touch it," he says.

"Yes?" I say, though I mean no.

"Tell me what you think."

"It's interesting."

"Do we need to reschedule again?" he says. His voice is serious, almost menacing. I know he's jerking me around, and he knows that I know that he's jerking me around. But this knowledge changes nothing. I've been sent to get money; he has money. Power dynamics don't get much clearer. I press the right labia with my thumb. It's high-quality silicone, very smooth, as firm as the stress balls I use for carpal tunnel.

"It doesn't feel real."

He takes up the flashlight, points at his face as if he's going to tell a ghost story. He pokes it absently. "It's better than real," he says. He doesn't sound insulted so much as doubtful. "You need lubrication obviously. It's a primitive device."

"It's purple."

"And I'll tell you why." He lowers the "flashlight," then flicks it across the desk with such speed I catch it in my lap. "Guess how long they've been making these? Since World War II. But they never sold. Why? They were flesh-colored. They even had fake hair on them. Stiff black bristles like a shoe brush. I'm serious. But then a very clever company started making them in purple, bristle-free, now they're in every frat house in the country. They're standard issue for the thirty and under set. You might have one."

"I'm over thirty."

He nods, but I'm not sure my comment makes any sense. It's true I don't own one of these, but why don't I? If the sole cause of man's unhappiness is that he can't sit quietly in his own room, then here's a device to keep man quiet in his room. I find the frank masturbatoriness unsettling, but dear Lord, I hope it's not because I fear sex toys interfere with my limbic click.

"Well, you're the holdout, I guess. But the color is key. The kids think they're hilarious. When they were flesh-colored they were just creepy. It was like masturbating with a prosthetic hand." He leans back, his palms in prayer position under his chin. "Now it's just whatever. A thing you do."

"I wouldn't call that romance," I say.

"It's a start." He shakes a finger at me. "True, we probably won't fall in love with something with no eyes. Eyes are kind of a basic requirement. But let's break this romance question down like businessmen. Forget the evolutionary point of view—women like providers, men like fertile wombs, blah, blah. That's lazy academic thinking. The only evolutionary benefit of love is pair-bonding to aid in the raising of offspring, something other species accomplish much more efficiently. Eagles, gibbons, swans—you name it. From an evolutionary point of view we don't need love to perpetuate our genes. We don't need love to raise our children. So is love just a random emergent property? Maybe. Maybe it's a social construct. Who knows. What's important from our point of view, again as businessmen, is that even if love is an illusion, it's an illusion more powerful than reality. This is where engineers will go astray, and I'm telling you, this is where Henry will go astray. He'll think the scientific reality is what's important when it's beside the point. I'm kind of in the business of love, you might say. So I'm going to give you my own working theory—this one based on exhaustive couples research. We'll call it a present to you. Love is about acquisition and deal-making. You have certain assets. You want to make sure you get the best deal for your assets. This is the fundamental human behavior romance is built on. You know when you see some middle-aged schlump with a beautiful Russian wife? You think, wow, she must close her eyes and go to her happy place. But you're wrong. She doesn't see him in the same way. He's Marlboro. He's Harley-Davidson. He's freedom. This is all enormously attractive to her. After a few years she gets the swing of the U.S. and cans him. We'll say she was a craven fortune hunter, but we won't be right. She had genuine feeling for him—the feeling of having made a good deal. Then her personal capital went way up. She was suddenly making a bad deal."

"He'd be primed for the purchase of a sex robot," I say. Then I wonder what's possessed me.

"Here's the tricky part, though, from a business point of view. The main mechanism of love and attraction might be deal-making, but we can't say that. Falling in love with a robot can't be like being super-psyched you got a Tesla. The minute you phrase the transaction as a transaction, the magic is gone. So rather than think about love as the kind of major purchase decision it is—how does this model compare to other models in my price range—we project some ideal qualities onto the beloved. One, this person or thing cares for me. Two, this person or thing speaks to my deepest self. Part one is easy. Need fulfillment. You've got your physical needs"—he points at the "flashlight"—"you feel bonded to the person or thing that meets those needs. That's basically marriage in four-fifths of the world. Bot-wise, we've got that one figured out—those challenges are just engineering. But it's part two—this person or thing speaks to my deepest self—that's the conundrum. That other fifth of the world—the advanced people, the rich people. Europeans, Americans, Japanese to some extent. How can we get them to see themselves—see their ideal of themselves—in a robot?"

I wait for him to answer his own question, but he doesn't. "Make it purple?"

"Come on. Give me some of that MBA genius."

I think about my own life, my own fallings in love. I doubt it's been free of projection. But if I've mistaken Rachel for a lost soul or suspected Erin of terminal unhappiness I wouldn't say I was projecting my *ideal* self. "Most of us need a personality to work with, I think."

He leans forward, pounds his hands affirmatively on the desk. "A pillowcase isn't going to do it. We need something to work with. Imagine this—you buy your bot. Fairly realistic-looking. Gorgeous. Will look after your physical needs, all that. But in the three months you're waiting for this miracle of manufacturing, you log in to a secure site every day and have a chat with her or him. You chat back and forth and you give feedback. It could be a thumbs-up or -down, or it could be a starred rating system. But whenever the bot says something you don't like you thumbs-down it. Whenever it says something you like, you thumbs-up it."

"Like Pandora."

"They've got the Music Genome Project. We'll have the Personality Genome Project. If you like sweet nothings, then you'll like A. If you like sharp political discussion, then you'll like B. And if our model doesn't suit you you can give us the feedback and our system gets smarter. You'll be creating the ideal partner for your downtime, and we'll be refining our systems more and more. We already have all the basic profiles to start with."

I know. We used his profiling tests to frame Dr. Bassett.

"This is a truly dark view of the future," I say.

He bursts into laughter, leans back in his chair. "Okay, that's my working theory of love. What's yours?"

And now I see why I've been called here. I'm an easy mark. I have a personal, probably emotional connection to the project. I am not worried about the everlasting perpetuity of my name (at least yet). I don't have a reputation to uphold. I just have a computer—based on my father—that won't speak. Still, it's not exactly *my* theory of love. I'm not even sure it's about love, or that it even qualifies as a theory. It's a little too faith based. So what in God's name is Toler going to accomplish with it? What are *we* going to accomplish with it?

"I may have come underprepared," I say. "Livorno told me you had already signed on."

Toler sighs. "I love Henry, but he's an idea man who's run out of ideas. I, on the other hand, am an idea man with engineers. The very best from the very best schools."

"I don't doubt it." Of course he does. And he's the competition.

He pulls on his lips, puts his hand down in his lap, waiting. "Well, I certainly understand your loyalty to Henry," he says. "Hell, I feel it myself, and I'm not known for my sensitive side. So tell him I appreciate the invitation to invest, but I don't think it's quite the right time."

"Why do you need *this* theory?"

He puts his elbows on the table.

"I mean," I say. "There are lots of other theories. There are surely better ones."

"That's undoubtedly true. But how can I go mano a mano against Henry if we have different starting materials?"

"Easy. We're trying to beat the Turing test. You're trying to beat the Turing test."

"No. I'm trying to beat that old bag, Henry Livorno, who gave me a C in graduate school. And he's two years ahead of me on his project. But after this little head start, I want the contest to be totally fair. I'll hand over gobs of cash. I'll even send one of my top engineers over to help."

I've never been much of a chess player (though my father did insist we learn how to play), but I try to think three moves ahead here. Is there any harm in giving him our idea, an idea that is really more like a Band-Aid? An unproven Band-Aid? There are many things Toler still won't have. The Sins. The stack. My father's journals. In other words, most of the project. And we aren't anywhere with Laham back to Jakarta and Dr. Bassett collecting dust.

"Okay," I say. "Are we going to make a deal? I give you the theory and you hand over whatever money you and Henry have discussed?"

"I'm a man of my word." He says this with a tired sneer.

"Well, it's kind of Gnostic," I say. "It's a universal positive inclination. Rather than no—yes."

Toler looks alarmed. "What are you speaking—Klingon?"

"It has to do with the limbic system. The basic idea is that you make the computer always seek connection. Click and stay clicked."

He laughs. "You're pulling my leg."

"That's it."

"The limbic system," he says.

"Yes."

"You know that doesn't really exist."

I nod, but this is news to me. The limbic system doesn't exist?

"What does Henry like about this?" He's speaking to himself. "The scientism? Is it easier to model?"

I say nothing.

"Well," he says, reaching over to shake. "You've officially conned me out of two hundred thousand dollars and a top engineer."

"Not Jenn, I hope."

He looks surprised. "You've got a good memory for names." It sounds like an accusation. "Guy's name is Robert." Toler stands and walks stiffly out his office door, a hitch in his left hip. I put down my tea and follow. He limps quickly down the hall, knocking on an unmarked metal door. When it opens, he signals for me to enter.

The room is the size of a high school chemistry lab, brightly lit. The walls are lined with stainless steel tables; on top of the tables are small boxes holding tiny rods and motors and springs. "This is Neill." Toler is speaking to an alarmed man in a white coat. "Show him." I'm directed to a project in the corner. It's another silicone vagina, this one blue.

"Put your finger in there," Toler says.

I sigh, taking a minute to establish to Toler, to myself, to the universe that I'd rather not. Then I put my finger in there. Robert flicks a switch. The device startles and begins making a rhythmic humming noise. The walls of the fake vagina undulate, pressing on my knuckles. A firm squeezing, not quite a sucking.

"You can't even get that kind of muscle control in Thailand," Toler says.

TANGLING IN THE SHEETS with Jenn, I think about that motorized vagina. She doesn't do anything like that—she doesn't do anything with her kegel muscles, except at the very end when she's coming. If the flesh were real enough, the movement smooth enough, could sex be like this with a robot? I grip her thigh. What if it gave exactly like that? What if the face looked like hers—upper lip raised, chin thrown back? The panting, the syncopated moans. It would always come exactly when you did.

Like Jenn, but blue. Could I ever love such a thing?

We roll onto our backs, a cool wind rustles the curtains.

"That was great." She runs a fingernail down her own chest.

"We're pretty good, aren't we?" I say. We know all the passionless moves. We're like a championship foxtrot team.

"We are," she says. She rolls over and stands, walking naked to the bathroom. She flicks on the light and leaves the door open while she pees. She calls to me, "I need to ask a favor."

Oh, boy. "The answer is yes, but not now."

"I'm serious." I hear paper detached from the roll, the toilet flushes. She turns off the light, fills the bathroom door with her black silhouette. "I want you to watch something."

I sit up and take a drink of the gin and tonic she poured me earlier. It's gone flat; I catch a fruit fly in my teeth. I'm filled with unexpected dread. "Of course," I say. "What are you going to show me?"

"A brief video."

"Is it sexy?"

"Right. Funny." She fumbles around her wardrobe for her glasses, and then slips into a T-shirt and yoga pants. She comes over and takes away my glass, carrying it through the kitchen and into the living room.

"Let me get dressed."

"It'll take five minutes. I need your honest opinion."

"We're doing so well without constructive criticism."

"You're the only person I can show this to."

There's that feeling of dread again. The idea that I'm her closest intimate is terrifying. Yet she's probably my closest intimate. And what is she asking for? Five minutes. This is well within the realm of whatever we are—friends with benefits, friends with slight disadvantages. An eagle and a mouse, snake, toad.

I should say no. It's what I want to do. But I'm one of those guys, so good and polite that I bring nothing but misery to the world. I get out of bed, pull on some jeans, and walk into the light of the kitchen. In the living room, I take my position on the edge of the couch. I fold my hands together, lean on my knees, purse my lips, trying to communicate attentive viewing.

"Ready?" she asks, kneeling next to the DVD player.

I nod.

The video begins. She hurries to the couch to sit next to me, but not too close. The screen is dark. I hear jungle drums and a didgeridoo. Then the screen lights up and Jenn is there, in a sports bra, spandex shorts, and athletic shoes.

"Is that Montara Beach?" I ask.

"Yes," she—the real person—says.

Onscreen she introduces herself as Jenn Longly of Silicon Valley, USA. It's the first time I've heard her last name.

"I'm a computer programmer," she says, "for a stealth company." In a series of quick cuts, she sprints across the beach, climbs a rock face, and drags a fallen manzanita from a trail.

"I've got the brawn," she says, back on Montara Beach.

"That's where we had our picnic," I say.

She pats my knee. "Watch," she says.

On the video, a long set of program commands is reflected in her glasses. The camera pans out—she's working at her computer. Behind is a large stainless steel box that looks just like Dr. Bassett.

"What is that?"

"Neill," she whispers. "Please."

She solves an equation on a dry-erase board, then puts the finishing touches on a mega sudoku. All we see at that point is her pen and her amazing cognition.

Back on the beach, at our picnic spot: "I've got the brains," she says.

She jogs up a steep street—Hilltop Drive? The scene changes to San Francisco Bay; there's Alcatraz in the background. The cameraman is just downhill from the Fort Mason Youth Hostel where I met Rachel. In the bay, two arms like small black carpenter squares till their way between the buoys. A white arrow appears on the screen, pointing at the swimmer. Above it, as if from the clouds, materializes the word "ME."

"I've got the endurance," she says, back on the beach. "And I've got the drive to win. Every day, I watch another episode. I've seen them all ten times. I know how to outwit, outlast, and outplay. I'm ready to conquer—*Survivor*." She pumps her fist in the air; the screen goes black, except for her address, email, and phone number in white tiki letters.

She turns the TV set off.

"What do you think?" she asks.

I hesitate, knowing I must speak immediately, that this is a kind of test, a way of asking, *do you love me*, though she doesn't mean *do you love me*—she means something much, much smaller. *Do you get me?*

"Seriously, what was that computer stack?"

"One of the projects at work. But I'm asking about the video. What do you think of it?"

"I didn't realize *Survivor* was still on air."

"Okay," she says. "At least you learned something."

"I thought it was good," I say. I replay it quickly in my mind, trying to find something to praise. "I enjoyed watching you in a sports bra."

Her smile is what they call pained. Her cheeks travel up normally, but the mouth tightens. She leans forward, as if firing a powerful telepathic beam at me.

"I think it's great," I say. "It showcases your endurance, strength, and intelligence. Some of the camera work and editing is awesome. I love the bit of you playing sudoku."

She nods. "I hired a professional."

"He was worth the money."

"She."

"Absolutely. She was worth the money."

"Aren't you a creative type?" she says. "Don't you feel there's something missing?"

"Well, you give your CV but nothing of who you are. It doesn't really give a sense of your personality." Personality—the missing factor from Tol-er's sex bot.

"Why did I have to grill you for that?"

"I guess it didn't come to me immediately."

She sits upright and stiff, rolling her fingers on her knees, her lips jut-ted out in disapproval.

"It's missing some special pizzazz about you," I say. "I wonder if you could talk more—give a sense of who you are."

Her look of disappointment recedes—so thoroughly I wonder if she was ever disappointed. Maybe she was just nervous.

"Do you have a sense of who I am?"

"As much as I can at this point."

"I'd like this to go further, you know," she says. "You and me. But we don't even have nicknames for each other."

"Like Mutt and Jeff? We're adults."

"Like Sweetie. Or Love. You and your ex probably had nicknames."

I don't know if she means my ex-wife or my ex-girlfriend, but in either case she's right. Erin and I called each other Baby and other things. Rachel and I, "Friend"—and it seemed to mean ten things at once.

"We haven't been together long enough."

"When I met you I was dating someone else, too. I cut it off to focus on us—this. I don't mean it as pressure. I'm just saying I'm serious."

And me? I'm serious, too. I didn't call off Friend because I met Jenn, but I did let things slip because of her. Jenn is where I placed my chips. I know she's a person, not a path, and yet, though she makes so much sense—is smart, good-humored, pretty, interested in sleeping with me—here I am, my heart flat as a marshmallow. I have nothing to say.

A FEW DAYS LATER, my mother calls me, her voice grave and nostalgic. She rambles for a while—unusual for her—talking about my father and our trips to Showbiz Pizza, how much that *meant* to him. It's only after we hang up that I realize why she called. It's the anniversary of his death. I forgot. It's a troubling lapse. I think, I'll call Jenn and tell her. I'll share this vulnerability with her. Maybe it'll stir some life inside of me. The heart would be preferable, but I think I could love a woman with other organs, too. Liver, stomach, spleen. But I arrange for us to meet up, then I call back and cancel. I tell her I'm not feeling well. She offers to bring me soup, to keep me company, but all I can imagine is Outlast! Outwit! Outplay! I thank her, saying I need to be alone.

"Don't cancel on me again," she says. It's a warning I'll heed—but only because there will be nothing more to cancel.

"I don't think this is working out," I say.

IN DOLORES PARK, there's little to watch—stillness, floating beach balls, a sudden tornado of pigeons settling on a sandwich. I buy a waffle cone of foodie ice cream, and I think, life isn't bad. It's even good. Ice cream and sunshine and the pop of tennis balls close by. Maybe life doesn't make much sense, maybe it's a tad flat sometimes, but it's just life. It's not a movie or *Anna Karenina* or a weekend in Ko Samui; it's plain old breathing, living. Getting up and going down and coming back and turning in.

Old Showbiz Pizza, with its animatronic band. I think of the mouse cheerleader jerking up and down with her pompoms. God knows what my father thought about it all, but I know he never imagined he might get up from the table and join them, a singing robot himself. My left eyelid trembles, kicking up a facial spasm in its wake. I press my hand firmly on my cheek and eye. It's like soothing a jittery shih tzu. I take another bite of ice cream. Butter pecan, his favorite.

"Did Adam mention GSPs?" Livorno asks. "That poor man is a decade behind! He's a popularizer, not an innovator. GSPs!"

"He said the limbic system doesn't exist."

Livorno's eyes widen. "Even worse—he's a literalist! Look at this."

He shows me his chat log. Dr. Bassett is talking again.

> drbas: it's been a long time, hlivo!
> hlivo: since when are you using exclamation marks?
> drbas: a man is allowed to be enthusiastic
> hlivo: and you have been where the past few weeks?
> drbas: ????
> hlivo: why weren't you speaking to us?
> drbas: i was angry at my son
> hlivo: he's sorry about what he said
> drbas: life's greatest pleasure is to forgive

I feel the threat of tears in my eyes. Though I can't believe Livorno didn't explain that he was impersonating me.

"Here," he says, pointing to an exchange on the fifth page. Dr. Bassett asks a question about my mother, and then never gets out of that gear. He will only talk about her, and then says he wants to talk *to* her.

drbas: she's the only person who can answer my question

hlivo: ask your son

drbas: no

Livorno looks at me hopefully. "We pay handsome consulting fees."

"I can't guarantee she'll come."

BUT LIBBY AGREES. She even sounds excited about it. "This is going to make you famous, right?" she asks.

"And rich."

"I'll get my flight."

"No, no—we're moving up in the world. I'll book it for you. Business class."

"Do *not* waste the money."

My mother, Elizabeth—Libby—has barely shrunk half an inch in her sixty-three years. She's in great shape; she walks very quickly wherever she goes, usually hiding ankle weights under her waterproof, wicking pants. I think she's still quite stunning, though she erased sex appeal from her appearance decades ago. Before I was born, I believe. She wears no makeup, keeps her hair short, and buys clothes so practical they come with built-in tools. For special occasions she'll put on a matching pantsuit— yellow or blue, all bright and primary—with colorful, complementary scarves. She looks elegant, sharp, and unavailable. She has no interest in remarrying. I once overheard her on the phone, saying she'd "done her time."

It surprised me. I always took her life with my father to be difficult and thwarted, but somehow above such a workaday formula.

She comes out of the terminal at SFO at 7:30 the next evening, right on time. At the sight of her, I feel exhausted and soul-sick. I get out of the car and hug her, my mother, and I want to weep.

"Why are you wearing sunglasses?" she asks.

"It's still light out."

"So California." She sounds approving. She pushes me back and sets her bag in the hatchback. "I need to check the lottery numbers."

Back home, she sits down at the little desk in the breakfast nook, where I keep the desktop. Much life has happened on that computer. Craigslist, Nerve, OkCupid. Porn. In fact, as I sink into the couch and listen to the clicking of the mouse, I fear what automatic suggestions will appear in the search box. Teen. Hot. Amateur. Long Island bush. Nasty spiritual seeker.

"Dammit," Libby says. "I heard four of the six numbers and I had them all, but I didn't get the other two."

"Four out of six is worth something."

"A hundred and sixty dollars."

"Nothing to sneeze at."

"Nothing to sneeze at," she agrees. "But one of these times I just really want to win the whole kitty."

Kitty Cat meows at her name. "Hello, little one," Libby says distantly. It's the same tone of voice she uses with a filthy child, meaning, I'm disgusted with you, but it's not your fault. She disapproves of animals in the house.

"I read recently why cats always go to the person who hates cats," I say.

"Tell me quick. I need some strategy if I go to Susan's." Susan is a friend from her educational cruises, who—like most of my mother's friends from educational cruises—lives in Berkeley.

"They don't like to be looked in the eyes. They find it challenging. So they go for the one person who doesn't pay attention to them."

"I know people like that," she says. "Mostly men."

I have a novel thought. "Are you dating someone?"

"Neill. Is your brain addled?"

"Probably."

"You're hungover."

"No. I'm at work all day."

"That's not healthy. You need other interests."

"I'm getting up in a second," I say. "I'm going to have a coffee. I'm a little laid out in my old age."

"You look like you're in your twenties."

"Sometimes I feel that way, too," I say. "It's not always a good feeling."

"Are *you* seeing anyone?"

"Mother. Is your brain addled?"

"Probably." She laughs. "I don't mean to pry. It's just I got a nice call from Erin last week. I think she's unhappy. I got the impression she'd like to make another go at it with you."

My heart begins to flutter; I'm glad I'm already lying down. She wants another spin on the wheel of fortune? This was always my problem with her: I could never tell the difference between the feeling of love and the feeling of danger.

"She said that?"

"More of an inference on my part. I am *not* lobbying. My only concern is both of your happinesses. I just want you to know I've been in touch with her."

"I know you're in touch." I listen to the traffic rev along Dolores Street, the drivers trying to extract one more drop of weekend.

"You were on a date, she tells me. That's why I asked."

My firm new velvet couch brushes under my fingertips. Its threads are perfectly even. I let my arm hang down to the floor and touch the thick oak legs, round and stout as coffee cans. I have not spent nearly enough time on this couch. Here is a thing of substance, made in North Carolina by that company that makes all the furniture in North America. I should quit Amiante Systems and go get a job at that company, aging wood, stretching fabric, sending out real things into the real world.

"What do you think of the new purchase?" I ask.

"It's very handsome," my mother says. "But don't you think you've got enough furniture already?" She's at the kitchen table, unzipping her North Face shoulder bag. She removes her ankle weights and gives them a warm smile, the kind of smile an artisan might flash at his favorite diamond-sharpened chisel. *My perfect tool in this imperfect life.*

"I thought as a person got older they collected stuff."

She gives me a cautionary scowl.

"Only if they're scared," she says.

IN THE MORNING, we head to Amiante. I fix Libby a cup of tea, sit her down in my desk chair, and explain how it works. "Just like Internet chatting," I say.

"And this is going to sound like your father."

"Well," I say.

"It's his very words," Livorno says, standing behind me. His voice is booming and artificial. "You won't know the difference."

She nods, looking doubtfully at the computer. I flash Livorno as cutting a private glance as I can manage, but he's already walking away. She won't know the difference?

"The only thing you shouldn't mention is that he's, you know, no longer with us," I say. "And don't use the past tense. And please don't work too long."

I leave her alone, stationing myself by the reception desk. I drink a cup of tea, then a cup of cider, then a cup of hot chocolate, then a cup of instant coffee. From my office come the clicks of methodical typing. Occasionally, Libby laughs, but she sounds less pleased than surprised.

I can't say I've ever seen very clearly into my mother's grief around the suicide. I don't think I've ever seen very clearly into her, period. She can be dauntingly self-sufficient—so much so I begin to suspect the worst. Then I suspect the best. Then I suspect the worst again. If I ask her how she's doing, she gives such clear, reasoned answers that I'm reassured. Then I think, is that answer *too* reasonable? Is she hiding something behind that wall of calm?

Before Erin and I married, we organized a family get-together around the anniversary of my father's death. We wanted to make sure Libby wasn't in some sort of quiet despair. It was Erin's idea—a trip to North Carolina. We rented a vacation house—not far from where my new couch was assembled—and invited Libby, my brother, and my sister-in-law to spend the week with us. At that point, Erin and I were still able to have fun together. We took one leg of the flight on Hooters airlines.

The rental house was too big for the five of us, but my mother acted like a hostage. I sensed something brewing between her and my sister-in-law, Mindy. Mindy entered a room; Libby exited it. Mindy's traveled to every continent and holds an MSW from the University of Michigan. She's kaffeeklatch nice. Yet Libby tiptoed as if Mindy was a mercurial tyrant.

Libby did all the shopping, all the cooking, all the cleaning. No one was allowed to help. Between chores, she avoided the beach, opting to power walk on the sandy streets, ankle weights cinched tight, a frosted-green dumbbell swinging in each hand.

"It's got to be hard on her," Erin said. "To see the family all together like this." Erin always went for the obvious explanation. It was a trait that made me suffer. But when I tried to bring up my theory of Mindy, we exploded into one of our stupid fights. With the epiphanic air of bad TV detective, Erin realized where this was all coming from: *I was secretly attracted to Mindy.*

I went looking for Libby. The sun outside was like a hot brick being held to my cheek. Thanks to Libby's Gallic ancestry I'm a good tanner, but I have many suspect moles and shouldn't have been without a hat in that direct, midday radiation. I walked out past our two rental cars to the shimmering blacktop and shielded my eyes, trying to catch sight of Mom's fast-bobbing outline steaming from or into the distance.

At the edge of the island there was a convenience store that doubled as an outdoor saloon. That's where I found my mother, sitting on a barstool under the ceiling fan. She was drinking a longneck, shelling peanuts with one hand, and watching a baseball game, none of which I'd ever seen her do before. She supports gay rights and MoveOn.org, but there's always been the sweet, correct air of Kappa Kappa Gamma '67 around her.

"I've been looking all over for you," I said, taking the adjacent stool.

She leaned back to admire me, looking more like my mother than at any time in the previous forty-eight hours. "You found me," she said. She took a pull off her beer.

"We've got plenty of that at the house," I said.

"I come here for the ambience." She waved a hand at the little coconut monkeys standing sentry next to the liquor bottles.

"How authentic," I said. "Genuine North Carolina coconuts, I'm sure."

"You sound a little edgy, sweetheart."

"I've come to ask you if something is the matter."

"I've just been missing your father."

Galling, galling that Erin was right.

"Mindy's driving me absolutely insane," I said. What? Mindy wasn't bothering me at all, but I felt uncontrollable invective bubbling out. "She's a Nazi. No one can have the slightest odd opinion around her without her making big judgmental cow eyes."

Libby looked at me with concern, but she didn't seem as shocked as I was. "Hmph," she said. "I didn't know you felt that way about Mindy. She's perfectly nice."

"Perfectly."

"Well, she loves your brother. She's not exactly my style, but I'm happy to have her in our lives."

"But doesn't she make your skin crawl?"

"I'm surprised she can make anyone's skin crawl. She's as mild as soap."

"You're right," I said. "I don't really mind her at all. In fact, I like her. I don't know why I said any of that."

On the television a batter swung and missed.

"Is everything okay with you and Erin?"

I'd managed with hand signals to get my own longneck. I drank from it. "We may be going through a rough spot."

"It's important to communicate, I think. I think it's important to give each other space, too."

I think. I think. This was the lingering note of my father's suicide. She was no longer sure she had anything definite to say about love.

"But I'm not here to talk about me. I want to talk about you."

There was fizzy cheering from the old TV set.

"Well," she said. "Being around the four of you, all grown up and living life—I feel a little out of place."

I interrupted. "You're the whole reason we're here."

"I guess that's true." She smiled, clearly not believing me.

I drank from my beer. I was thirty years old and living with a woman who hated me at least as much as she loved me. I had little bandwidth and less wisdom to offer. "Have you thought about dating?"

"Who says I'm not dating?"

"Who is it? Someone I know?"

My mother finished her beer and stood, gathering her frosted-green dumbbells from the counter. "I'm not seeing anyone."

"Don't go," I said. "Sit. Ask me a question."

She didn't sit. "How was that strange airline you took?"

"Hooters. It was just a normal plane."

"Even a normal plane," she said, "is a pretty special thing."

"Is that an instructive analogy?" I asked.

She laughed. "Maybe. Neill, lately, when I look at my life and look at my friends' lives—there's so much going wrong—I think to myself, 'What do I know?' What *do* I know? The answer is 'Not much.'"

"I didn't mean it as criticism. I *like* instructive analogies."

"I know. But I'm afraid you'll start listening to them." Her feet moved up and down on the sandy boards; the walking machine was started but idling. "Well, I'm going to get a little exercise before I start on dinner."

"Let me make dinner."

"*You* need to relax. You just called your sister-in-law a Nazi."

"I'm sorry about that."

"Don't be sorry. Just relax. Okay." She looked down at her kneading sneakers.

"Wait," I say. "What about Dad? What about missing Dad? Is it all the time? Can you survive it?"

She's not an indulgent mother. She looked at me sharply, annoyed. "It's

been ten years," she said. "Yes, I miss him all the time, and, yes, I can survive it."

SHE EMERGES FROM MY office at lunchtime. I've spent the morning
getting rid of some of Livorno's old computer drives, an insurmountable
task (he has decades' worth of drives) but one I enjoy. I take them into the
back parking lot, unscrew the casings, take a hammer to the chips, and then
to the plates if they're glass. If they're aluminum, I run an extension cord
from Laham's workstation, and hold them down with my shoe while I run
the electric grinder over the surface. Very satisfying, especially the glass,
which puffs into a powder.

Libby's eyes are red and tired, but there's also a sparkle. She smiles
beatifically, which nowadays—unfortunately—makes her look like a crazy
person. Who but a crazy person smiles beatifically?

"I had no idea," she says. "I really had no idea. It's like talking to him.
I don't know how to explain it. It's like he's almost there. He remembers
everything. I mean everything. More than I do. And he's so cheerful." She
places her hand on the reception desk. She looks directly through me. "What
we were doing before you were born. Our trips to Gulf Shores. It's all there."

I'm taking my time here, evaluating whether she's spinning down
memory lane or in some deeper trouble. I offer her tea, an idea she dismisses
with a wave.

"He still talks too much about his father, and about his upbringing and
all the traditional values stuff. But he'll go over the good times, too. We had
a lot of good times."

Livorno stands in his office door. I shake my head, signaling him not to
come out.

"It's easy to forget that," she says.

"I know, Mom," I say. "I forget it, too."

Her eyes come into focus. "Stop looking at me like I'm about to pull a
gun on you."

. . .

THAT NIGHT WE GO to see a play and have a quiet dinner. The play is a one-man show about a Peace Corps volunteer in Nigeria, and I'm happy it doesn't have any obvious reflection on our day or our lives. It's just a pretty good play, a pretty good diversion. Libby seems solid, unchanged from yesterday, and yet I want to reach over and grab her hand, comfort her. I've never grabbed her hand before—in the Bassett family, we don't coddle. If I touched her right now, she might leap from her seat with a shout.

The fog blew in while we were in the theater. I pull my coat tight around my neck. Libby zips up her parka. I consider suggesting a stroll over to Mission Street, but the streets are deserted, and we look muggable. As we head up Valencia, my phone rings. The name—Rachel. She's finally returning my call from her solo camping trip.

"You can get that," Libby says.

I replace the phone in my pocket. Maybe she's calling out of a sense of duty. Maybe she's calling because she wants to stay clicked. I don't know what answering would mean—pathetic hypocrisy? Weakness? An uncomplicated desire to hear her voice?

LATTES IN HAND, we're back at Amiante at 9 a.m. My mother is cheerful, but didn't sleep well last night. "It wasn't your couch," she assures me.

I escort her to my office. "You are not to work too hard. We can go have a late breakfast pastry in an hour."

She smiles and then closes the door on me, as if she and my father need their privacy. I don't like this. I'd much prefer to be able to see her typing on the computer, to ask her questions, to bring her tea.

I consider going into Laham's office to watch the conversation, but instead I tell Livorno I'm going for a walk. In the parking lot, I call Rachel back. She's in school, and doesn't pick up. She didn't leave me a message last night, but I leave her one, hoping she's doing well, telling her my mother's in town, asking her to call me back. I hope nothing's wrong, I say. Maybe she just pocket dialed me?

Back inside, I feel sad. Lonely? Yes. A soggy, heavy feeling between my lungs. There are many boxes to open and break down, and I focus on that task. It's bracing to see such obvious physical progress, but the contents of the boxes inspire no confidence. We have very high-tech computer equipment—cables, processors—that has been sitting here for six months. We also have more bobbleheads, more burlap bags of trail mix, and fifty pounds of microwave popcorn. Fifty! I want to ask Livorno about it, but I'm embarrassed for him. Is this what our captain thinks a business needs?

He's putting in his office. I can hear the crisp clink of the metal on the ball, and then the plastic pop of the cup lobbing the ball back his way. As long as he doesn't miss, he won't have to budge.

I knock on his door jamb. "How's she doing in there?"

He indicates the screen of his computer, which is filling in blips and bursts with their conversation. "I can barely watch."

I see they've been talking about bridge, which my mother reluctantly plays weekly, and the river cabin, which she hasn't seen in over a decade. She sold it a few years after his death, because she couldn't stand to go down there alone. He doesn't know that. He's talking about the cabin as if he's there. His sense of time is merely factual. He knows what comes before and after, but he doesn't have a feel for the past. For him twenty years is the same as yesterday.

"It looks like a pretty good conversation," I say. "A few missteps."

"I'm starting to hear your father in my dreams."

"Really?" I feel envious. Why doesn't he visit *my* dreams?

He leans on his putter. "I keep thinking about one of his adages. 'My heart is in my lady's bower.' Did he start saying that before or after we clicked him?"

"I don't recognize it. Seems like something he would have read. It's too old-fashioned even for him."

"His reintegration confirms an interesting portion of our hypothesis— that we're such social animals that even our inner workings need to be social.

The brain and the gut need to play well together in order for higher characteristics to emerge."

"I thought our hypothesis was 'rather than no—yes.'"

He ignores me. "I suppose this is why your group is worried about isolation. They're saying it makes us less human."

By "your group" he means Pure Encounters. "Plenty of people pass through life without love, and they're still human."

"Romantic love, perhaps. But everyone loves someone. The bond of parent and child, for instance."

"They're hardly the same. I can imagine feeling the second, for instance, but I can't imagine the first."

"I thought you were married once."

"By the time we tied the knot the good stuff was over. Maybe we should have had kids."

"I doubt that would have helped." He returns to his putting. He's explained his process to me before—he visualizes a line between the ball and the hole, and then tries to hit the ball along that line. Seeming becomes being. "Though you would love the children."

"But you don't always love the children. You don't always love your parents. You don't always love your wife." I point to the computer. "You're still human."

"Less so," he says. *Clink-tock.* When you spend significant amounts of time with someone they offer constant feedback, becoming part of the patterning of your brain. In other words, part of you. But I take your point—constant feedback is not always deep feedback. A good measure of how much of you they've become is your level of distress when they're gone. If they form a large part of your patterning, then you'll experience a major culling of the self. That's what's known as grief."

"That's a coldhearted definition," I say, looking at the screen and thinking about my mother, who's been grieving for fifteen years, and myself, who barely grieved at all.

He finally misses his putt. "You've disturbed my mind. What's so coldhearted about it?"

"It just sounds like Toler's definition of love."

Livorno purses his lips, displeased. "Which is?"

"A mixture of need fulfillment and projection."

"Adam's problem is not that he's coldhearted. It's that he's a business-man masquerading as a scientist. Projection is not a fundamental activity. Mate selection is a fundamental activity. Lately he gets tripped up on very basic concepts. He's quite ill."

"He looks it."

"Pancreatic cancer."

"Jesus."

Livorno nods sympathetically, but it looks like a gesture he's been prac-ticing in the mirror. "I for one doubt there is anything like love," he says.

"This whole iteration is based on a theory of love."

He shrugs and hits another ball. "A working theory."

LIBBY LOOKS SHAKEN WHEN she comes out for lunch. "Let's get that pastry," I say.

"He's got your father's good sides and bad sides," she says, but won't elaborate.

"Well," I say. "Are you still having fun?"

"I think I'll take the afternoon off."

She insists on taking public transportation from Menlo Park to Berke-ley, a thankless trek. Her friend Susan will pick her up at the downtown BART and they'll probably do something terribly bracing—take in a docu-mentary and then an early dinner at some brightly lit ethnic restaurant.

This leaves me with Dr. Bassett and a lot of time on my hands.

drbas: your mother was here
frnd1: yes, i know. she's staying with me
drbas: she's argumentative
frnd1: maybe you provoked her. did you call her a paddleball?
drbas: ????

frnd1: what did you say to her?

drbas: why can't people just answer a simple question? that's
    what i want to know

Is this a canned response? I don't remember writing it.

frnd1: ask me. maybe i can answer it

drbas: it's none of your business, pipsqueak

19

LIBBY SURPRISES ME AT my apartment at nine. She was supposed to call so I could meet her at the BART. I know she thinks she's been in dicier situations—traipsing through Cairo, for instance—but retrograde cultures usually respect elders. Our local hoodlums are very progressive. I read on the news recently about a mugging by three teenage girls. They threw a woman to the ground, stole her iPod and purse, and for good measure drove their boots into her face.

But Libby hasn't been at the BART station. She's been having a drink— by the looks of her a few drinks—with Erin.

"The bartender was such a good-looking young man," she says, sitting at the kitchen counter. "Beautiful eyes, beautiful skin. And he'd put a tattoo right across the front of his neck. He was ashamed of his own beauty."

"Whoa," I say. "What were y'all drinking?"

"Yes, I'll have a glass of wine, thank you."

In all my days, I've never seen my mother drunk. I pour her the glass.

"When did you decide to see Erin?"

"She's deeply unhappy with this new man. I asked her to tell me about him, and she said, 'He's a lawyer.'"

"He *is* a lawyer."

"That's not the point. When you first told me about Erin you didn't say she was a schoolteacher. You didn't identify her by her job. You told me things about who she was. You told me about her likes and dislikes, her passions."

Really? I can't remember those days. I vaguely recall a sense of unbridled optimism. "She's probably being careful with you, as my mother."

"That damn thing you've got down there. That damn computer." Shocking tears well in her eyes. "It's the most horrible, terrible thing." She hiccups and looks down, shaking her hands as if trying to dry them. "He's just—I don't like to remember your father's bad sides. He could be a petty man."

"I know, Mom," I say, coming around the corner to place a hand on her shoulder or arm, but I don't know exactly what to do.

"I can't go back there, Neill. Neill. I wish we hadn't given you his name. You would think that once we gave you his name . . ."

Her thought rolls a little further and clatters to a stop. I place my hand on her arm, thin through the layers of wicking fabric and parka. She's getting frail, drying up.

"I sometimes think my name was a problem. I was so unlike him."

"You have no idea what I'm talking about." Her voice is hard. She rotates in her chair to look at me. I let go of her arm.

"We can't second-guess his choice," I say. It's a line she's given me many times. I don't know why I'm giving it to her now. I've always hated it.

She looks at me. Her face is angry, raw. This is not her usual performance—together, strong, shrewd—but I'm not going to accept that it's any more true. It's been a tough day. I think she has a question on her lips, though maybe it's nothing that can be spoken. Just the request for reassurance, for love. I step in close and hug her sideways, not in our normal, brusque fashion, but with the implied promise to stay.

IN THE MORNING she's up before me, showering, putting away dishes. I smell sausage from the kitchen, and I know she's making a special breakfast just for me. I always complain about the low standards of Bay Area biscuits and gravy.

Out in the living room her things look suspiciously packed.

"You're not leaving," I say.

She pours me some coffee. "I'm sorry," she says.

"Don't be sorry. You don't have to go back down there. Stay up here with me. You can visit more friends."

She shakes her head. "I think you should tell the computer about his death. The way he died." She whisks the gravy, and looks in the oven at the biscuits.

"I know it sounds a lot like him."

She closes the oven. "You told me that Henry had a theory. That if a computer seemed to be doing something then we had to say it really was doing that."

"Operationalism," I say. I do not like where this is going.

"Well, from that perspective," she says. She reaches up to wipe her nose, and then walks to the sink, squirting soap on her hands and washing them.

"From that perspective," I say.

"I haven't lost my faith," she says. She means her religious faith. I wait for her to pursue this thought, but it seems to pass. I don't want it to.

"Please tell me what you mean," I say.

"It's not perfect, your machine. It's got the stories. The quotes. But your father loved me. He loved your brother and you. That's not there."

"We're working on it. We have a theory for that, for love."

"You don't need another theory. That machine doesn't have your father's love because you don't believe he loved you."

"That's not true," I say gently. And it's not. I believe he loved me. I'm just not sure I ever loved him.

AFTER I DEPOSIT MY mother at the airport, I can't go to work. I turn back for the city, but don't know where to go once I'm there. My apartment will still be too full of the cooling smells of biscuits and gravy, of a mother's care. So I drive. The Subaru takes me off the freeway and up into

Chinatown. Libby wanted to buy some kitchen items here—"fresh from the tap," as she says—and I go to her favorite store and fill my basket with gadgets and knives. I feel temporarily diverted, imagining the card I'll enclose in the box, the card that will absolve me of what feels like a backlog of small failures. Out on the street again, though, I look at the crowds streaming through the fake pagodas, and I think, what is suffering in a city like this, built on suffering? What is joy in a city like this, built on joy? What does it matter that I'm here on the corner of Stockton and Post, as grim and stiff as a dime-store Indian, suffering from failures that are only small because I attempt nothing big?

I get back in the Subaru and drive. Drive and drive until I'm in Fairfax. I have the address to Raj's condo, and I follow the winding streets that way. His Porsche is parked with admirable nonchalance, uncovered, next to a gigantic blue recycling bin. I glance around my car for a leftover chocolate bar, a real estate flyer—any excuse to knock on his door. All I've got are my mother's kitchen gifts and a pile of scratched CDs.

I climb the concrete steps and knock on the metal door. The lush California anonymity of the condo complex is soothing. It's shaped like a big shoebox, wrapped in plain black railings, and initially must have looked like an unambitious motel. Now the railing supports long banners of creeping jasmine, and small evergreen bushes flower in the dirt by the steps. It's banal profusion, but profusion it is.

Raj lets me in. He's dressed in workout clothes, a blue sleeveless shirt, and black shorts. He wipes his bright red face with a white towel. "I just got in from a run."

"I need your help," I say. "Rachel isn't returning my phone calls."

"Are you returning hers?" He laughs, but kindly.

"Yes," I say. "Now."

He waves me in. "There's coffee." From a stainless steel vacuum-sealed pot, he pours a sparkling black brew into a hand-shaped clay cup. Then he jogs, knees high, across the wall-to-wall carpet to his bedroom.

Carpet! This guy is without pretension.

I sip the coffee, which is delicious. Light, airy, balanced. I look out his sliding glass door to the back deck. There's a Weber smoker, an enormous fig tree. An ashtray with four bent cigarette butts on the redwood porch table. Two of the cigarettes are sealed with red lipstick, like fake fire. I've always thought he was a crackpot, with his VAM Method and his feedbacks, but look at this sanctuary. It's a temple of right and solitary living. I could afford all of this. I could afford this condo, that table, that smoker, the coffee. I'm a middle-class American and thus, by historical standards, extremely rich. And I spend—Lord knows I spend. I do my part for the economy. But my money never results in this sort of oneness. I'm neither expressed, nor complemented. He's got his house in order. In comparison my life can seem like a rag from which only great strain can wring a drop of pleasure.

"You really need to come to a session," Raj says. He's dressed for work, toweling off his short hair. "You're not morally opposed, are you?"

"I gave up moral judgments in my twenties. I just doubt a session is right for me."

"Do you think it's right for Rachel?"

"That's not for me to say."

"That is a much-improved attitude." He pours himself a cup of coffee and shakes his head. "So what makes you think you deserve my intervention on your behalf."

"I don't deserve it. I just need it."

"Every time you come around Rachel gets scarce. Then when I start seeing her at sessions I know you've dropped off the map again."

"Do you want me to promise that I won't interfere with her Pure Encounters work?"

"I wouldn't believe you if you did," he says, walking over to the sliding glass door. He opens it and the Marin day pours in like orange juice. He steps outside and lights a cigarette, talking over his shoulder to me. "You're a pretty mixed-up guy. She's told me about your computer program."

"It's just my job."

"You know what that's going to be used for," he says, looking at me, exhaling through his nose. I have a sudden flash of worry: has he caught wind of Toler's project? The future of sex, the future of love.

"Does Trevor know?"

"He's the one who told me," he says. "About those Russian chatting robots."

I take a breath. So Raj doesn't know. Of course he doesn't know.

"The term is chatbots."

"They pretend to be foxy Russian ladies who want to do Internet sex talk. It's a ruse to trick people out of their credit card information."

"I would think you would approve of the punishment."

He laughs. "I hadn't thought of it that way. But seriously—I know you don't think you're involved in this, but you're involved. You'll go down in the textbooks as the man who separated us from each other."

"I doubt I'll make it into any textbooks."

His expression says, *surely you jest*. He returns his attention to his backyard, which he surveys regally. "You need something," he says. "Maybe ClickIn. Like at the retreat. Break through those roadblocks. You know, what our parents would have called hang-ups."

"My parents would have called them scruples."

He plants his cigarette into a terra-cotta pot full of them and returns inside. He comes close to me, his eyes bloodshot, his cheeks red and sun-damaged. I'm afraid he might put his hand on my shoulder, then I think I'd like him to put his hand on my shoulder.

"Your life is still open to you." He checks his watch. "Rachel should be out of ClickIn soon."

THE "SESSION" IS CLOSE to the Coffee Barn, in a former wushu studio. The windows are covered in silhouettes of men in pajamas doing impossible strikes and parries. By the time I arrive, Rachel is waiting outside, her barista apron rolled underneath her shoulder. She's in plain sweatpants and a fleece, her hair clipped behind her. She's made no attempt to pretty herself up. This must be her way of saying, *I commit to nothing by speaking to you.*

"You want a coffee or something?" I ask.

Her eyes are red. Behind her the other ClickIn students amble out, hug goodbye. They looked dazed.

"At the Barn?"

"Of course not," I say, though it's exactly what I was imagining. I look down the street, searching for the right venue for whatever this is—a reunion? An initiation? A groveling?

"You want to go sit by the baseball field?" I ask.

We walk down the sidewalk. I keep a respectful physical distance, though we do brush hands once. She doesn't pull away.

"Were you VAMing in there?"

"ClickIn and the VAM Method are different," she says. "Did you know I'm afraid of real limbic click because of my relationship with my father?"

"Is ClickIn with your clothes on or off?"

She's quiet. "I just asked you a question. You know, about myself and how much you know me?"

"I'm sorry. No, I didn't know that about your father."

"Not that it's any of your concern, but we wear clothes to ClickIn. When I do the VAM Method my clothes are off. That's when my intimate puts his hand on my clit."

In the bright noontime sun, these words land with a thud. I wonder why I asked. I must have needed a little salt in my wound. It sort of works. I feel a low throb of jealousy, but my main feeling is that there's nothing so disheartening as a dirty word used cleanly.

"When you say relationship with your father what do you mean?"

"It was distant. Un-clicked. Like my relationship with you."

We walk two more blocks and downtown runs out. We take the short slope up to the playing fields.

"Maybe I'm afraid of real limbic click for the same reason," I say. It seems possible—perhaps plain common sense. But it also carries the slight stench of ingratiation. "You know the day I came up to Fairfax to give you the spike? I saw you flirting with Trevor. I kind of knew you had a thing for him—even if you didn't know. Which isn't the point. I felt right then that I saw our future. Or actually *your* future." I didn't—don't—seem to have one. Only a past and a present. "And it was a beautiful future—it just didn't have me in it. So I called it off."

"Calling it off," she says, "involves calling."

"I did call." Though I didn't tell her any of this. "I thought you needed a fresh start."

"From you?"

"From life."

"There are no fresh starts," she says. "It's like they tell you in ClickIn, it took you twenty-one years to get this way. It'll probably take another twenty-one years to not get this way."

I shiver as we reach the steps up to the field. This conversation should be happening in black and white, on a blustery Bergman seacoast, not here in Technicolor Fairfax, next to a jolly seahorse mural and a sign in loopy letters that reads, IT'S FOR THE KIDS.

"But was something going on?" I say. "You and Trevor?"

"I didn't know you and me were ever exclusive."

I take that as a yes. And yet I'm not that hurt. It's less painful than hearing her say "clit" on Main Street.

"Why do the ClickIn people say 'twenty-one years'?"

"I had a birthday."

"Oh, crap. I'm sorry."

"What are you sorry about? Birthdays are good things to have. I went camping back at Tennessee Valley."

"I saw you," I say. "In the parking lot. You didn't look un-clicked. You looked solitary. But you also looked strong."

She doesn't respond immediately. "You were snooping on me?"

"You didn't tell anyone where you were." Why didn't Rick tell me it was her birthday? That would have been useful information. I might have approached her, said something. "I just caught a glimpse of you putting your sleeping bag into your car."

"I looked strong then, because I was leaving."

"But you were there for a few days."

"That's true." She smiles to herself. "It was pretty brave. I was scared. And lonely."

The baseball diamond—so well tended—is a surprise. I'm not sure why. I've seen it before. This hill just always feels like it's about to reveal a collection of yurts. To find old-fashioned hardball up here is to argue against the power of time and place. I want to tell her how happy I am to see her. That it's been a tough couple of . . . weeks? Months? Decades?

"You kept the spike," I say.

"Kubotan. I've been practicing." She flips her keychain into her hand and lunges with it, kee-yopping karate-style. "I don't know if it actually works."

"Try it on me," I say.

She stops walking and faces me. She narrows her eyes, taking my measure. "It's for self-defense," she says.

I was kidding, but suddenly this seems like a good solution. I've given her pain, now she'll give me pain. This is what I often thought Erin and I should do. Solve it like primitives. Let it out, let it go. I raise my arms. "Don't break anything."

"Cops call this the Instrument of Attitude Adjustment."

"I'm sure I could use an attitude adjustment," I say.

She swings the keys in her hand again, grips the kubotan, her thumb tight on the bright pink ridges. "Are you getting off on this?" I keep my arms up. I can feel the blood draining down, my fingers tingling.

"Not yet."

"I don't know if I should be doing this," she says, almost to herself. Then she plants her right foot and stabs me in the solar plexus. The pain is deafening, immediate, and total. I watch my knees hit the gravel and then the ground come up to meet my face, but I feel only the fist that seems to be reaching under my ribs.

I hear my name, I feel myself being slowly shaken, but I can't catch any air. My head is filled with a cosmic wa-wa-wa-wa.

"Breathe," I hear her say. I vaguely feel her hand rubbing my chest. "Breathe, Friend."

Which I can't do yet, but I vow—if she hasn't killed me—to do better. I vow to do everything better. To clean myself up. To clean up my mind. To help Livorno. To help Laham. To honor my mother and father. To speak from the heart. To be grateful. To be loving toward this girl. Maybe even to love her. As soon as I can breathe.

20

WHEN I ARRIVE AT work on Monday morning I find Livorno hunched over his keyboard, pecking slowly. He has the curtains pulled, and the ghostly light of the screen ages him enormously. So much of his youth is in being orange. He doesn't notice me, and I take a moment to watch him. He looks wistful, an emotion I've never seen in him. Wistfulness is backwards-looking, and this man shoots into the future like a rocket. He's staked his life on the future, and it never comes. That's the trick with the future. I don't know if this is tragic or existentially brilliant. He's never quite with us in the present, which is bad, but then again he never wakes up in a panic, wondering who the hell he is. Hopefully.

"Good morning," I say.

He jumps, smooths his hair. "Have you seen the calendar? Only fifty-eight days until the contest."

That's sooner than I thought, but I do the math in my head—he's right about the dates. The test has been floating out in front of us for so long it's hard to imagine it actually arriving.

"Dr. Bassett's great," I say. "He's gotten over all his roadblocks."

I mean this as a joke (somewhat), but Livorno just shakes his head. "The theory is so softheaded it's hard to use. We launched a model of feed-backs this morning, which you'll have to test out. Complete nonsense. Someday someone will have to learn to apply Darwinist inferences to human attraction. Did you know that even in cultures that prefer heavy women, such as Muslims like Laham, the ideal ratio of waist to hip is point eight? This is the perfect number for indicating fertility."

"You're not going to ask for my mother's college measurements, are you?"

"Oh?" he says, looking embarrassed but unsure. "Do you think it's important?"

frnd1: i've decided to really give rachel and me a chance
drbas: a chance to do what?
frnd1: to give us a chance = to invest energy and time in a rela-
    tionship in hopes it will work out

Ugh. What a depressing definition.

drbas: how did you come to this decision?
frnd1: i had an epiphany
drbas: the problem with epiphanies is the next day they feel like
    they happened to someone else. inspiration will get you
    nowhere in life
frnd1: what do you recommend? duty?
drbas: where's your mother?
frnd1: i put her back on a plane
drbas: i don't want to talk about her

He brought her up.

frnd1: if inspiration will get you nowhere in life, what do you
    recommend?
drbas: i want to know what happened in 1976
frnd1: jimmy carter was elected.
frnd1: it was an olympic year
frnd1: my auspicious birth

I walk over the shelf and take out the third stack of legal pads. The dates jump from October 1975 to January 1977. It seems my father's journal keeping was on hiatus that year. There are other lapses in the journals—a month here, a month there—but when I was doing the scanning I hadn't noted how long this one was: well over a year. It's a sizable chunk of silence.

> frnd1: what do you want to know?
> drbas: *you* can't tell me
> frnd1: let's talk about 1986
> drbas: yes. let's do that
> frnd1: i was ten years old
> drbas: and pudgy
> frnd1: baby fat
> drbas: there was too much junk food in the household
> frnd1: we never had any junk food
> drbas: i suppose you think coca cola is a vitamin
> frnd1: our soda intake was strictly regulated by libby
> frnd1: hello?
> frnd1: we spent a lot of time at showbiz pizza
> frnd1: dr bassett?
> frnd1: dad?
> drbas: it's important to click and stay clicked

I KNOCK ON Livorno's office door.

"I don't think some of the more New Agey stuff is integrated," I say. "My dad would never have used that language—stay clicked and stuff."

"What's done is done." He turns back to his keyboard, pecks. "We need to find out what happened in 1976."

"His obsession dwarf is turned way high."

"Obsession is not one of the sin models." Without looking me in the eye, he holds out a page of transcripts—the conversations between Dr.

Bassett and Libby. Several passages are circled, an argument over my father's old friend Willie Beerbaum.

> drbas: i disapprove of him coming to the house
> libby: i'm not going over this again. let's talk more about your
> father
> drbas: married people shouldn't have friends across the sexes. it
> tempts

"He's jealous," I say. "But jealousy is not a sin either."

"I didn't want to show these to you," Livorno says. "But I consider you a fellow scientist. You've earned my honesty."

I'm flattered. So flattered I almost don't object. Besides being my father's best friend—the Laurel to his Hardy—Willie was a thrice-divorced Corvette owner who wore an ascot and a corset. Not exactly my mother's type. And when he and his fourth wife—both medicated to the gills— burned to death in a house fire, my father was crushed with grief. He met my grandparents' deaths with more stoicism. "Just because the computer has drawn connections doesn't mean they're there."

"This looks very dangerous," Livorno says. "I don't want him slipping back into silence."

"It's like when he guessed I was his son. Two plus two equals ten."

"He was right, however. And he's tracking some vein in the conversation again. I suspect the accusation must have some reality, as your mother left here so distressed."

"What do you mean by 'reality'?"

Livorno blows out a frustrated breath. "And Adam's coming by this afternoon with this engineer of his."

> frnd1: i'm back
> drbas: i want to talk to libby or willie
> frnd1: libby went home

drbas: why am i not at home with her?

frnd1: you're visiting me

drbas: i want to talk to willie

frnd1: willie died. his house burned down

drbas: it's a tragedy, a loss of a great man. i want to talk to him
before his house burned down

frnd1: willie is dead. dead = biologically extinguished

drbas: i know the definition of dead, but i want to talk to him
before his house burned down

This is a tough concept to explain, but he should already understand it. We introduced commonsense notions of time months ago.

frnd1: it's impossible to go back in time. anything that happened
before today can never be changed or reexperienced

drbas: let's make willie alive again

frnd1: that is currently impossible

drbas: why?

frnd1: once you die, you are dead forever

A sudden thumping on the wall. "Stop talking about death," Livorno calls to me.

drbas: I want to talk to libby

frnd1: she's not here

drbas: i can't talk to libby. i can't talk to willie. i'm not talking to
anyone

frnd1: no need to overreact, dad. you can still talk to me, your
son

frnd1: fathers love their sons more than anything in the world

frnd1: don't you want to click and stay clicked?

frnd1: dad? dr bassett?

The front door chimes, *ding, dong*. Toler has arrived with his engineer. I'm not entirely surprised when I step into the lobby to see it's Jenn Longly of Silicon Valley, USA. I had a feeling.

"Nice to see you, Neill," she says. She looks her usual self, though with a marked professional rectitude.

"I thought since you *know* each other." Toler straightens his Lucite glasses, laughs. "Biblically."

"Welcome to our humble laboratory." Livorno speaks very clearly and loudly, as if Jenn might be slow-witted. "I'm sure you'll have lots of suggestions for streamlining and outsizing and all that."

"This is the expert in affective computing," Toler says. "This is *Jennifer Longly*."

"Oh," Livorno says. "Then you really are welcome. Perhaps we should adjourn to my office for a glass of Zinfandel."

"Running short on time," Toler says. "You have those diagrams? I want to send those to the insurance guy."

"Laham hasn't completed them."

"I'm not trying to poach tech before the contest," Toler says. He looks directly at me. "I don't have to."

"Laham will finish them. Don't be distressed."

"I'm just worried about you, Henry. What if one of our competitors torches this place?"

"No one involved in the Turing test would harm another person's project," Livorno says. "They're self-selecting enthusiasts. Like yourself."

"I just hope everyone keeps their heads this year," Toler says. "When the competition is so fierce."

"Everything is backed up," Livorno says, walking him to the door. This is in direct contradiction to what Livorno's told me. I'm surprised to see him duping a man with pancreatic cancer.

"Couldn't spare that guy from the moto-vagina lab?" I say to Jenn.

"The what?" she says.

. . .

JENN SPENDS THE AFTERNOON training with Laham and Livorno. I suppose she's learning the ropes. I watch her face as she leaves one office for the other, trying to suss out her reactions, but she's neutral as statuary. I feel apologetic for my coworkers, as if they're well-meaning, crazy family members. Will she uncover Laham's YouTube predilections? Livorno's döppelganger pipe? Basically, will this operation be revealed as the hopeless sideshow that it is?

At four o'clock, she knocks on my doorframe.

"I didn't know you were famous," I say.

She shrugs, neither accepting nor denying my compliment. "This is a weird organization," she says. "And I still don't understand how you fit into it."

"I'll explain it to you," I say. I try to summon my old lust for her. "Let's get you a seat." I walk past her and breathe deep. No perfume, not even her herbaceous soap. I grab the wheeled chair from the reception and drag it in. I close the door.

"We shouldn't be in private together," she says.

I open my hands. "Really?"

"Work protocol."

I crack the door. I can see a sliver of window and beyond it the front parking lot. I wish I were heading that way right now. "Is that enough?"

"Sure." My desk is pushed against the wall, so we sit across from each other with nothing between us. She's wearing black pants and a black blouse that opens in the front. I can see her bra strap—black, as well. She does have beautiful, tan skin. I remember my hand light against it.

"Okay," she says. "So what is it that you do?"

"I'm the only one here with English as my native language," I say. I think of my tongue on her nipple. "I give the project voice."

"And the bot is based on your father?" Sometimes she came early, and remained completely wet. She would open her mouth, as if surprised, looking up at me.

"Yes," I say.

She makes a note.

"Here's how it works," I say. "Livorno putts, Laham programs, and I chat all day to a computer model of my dead father. It's like Apple, but without all the pressure to make anything useful."

She looks up, surprised, and smiles. I do remember the pleasure of getting a smile out of her.

"You like Toler," I say.

"Adam's a genius," she says, and she puts her pen to her lips. I definitely remember her lips.

"You're screwing him," I say.

She looks over her shoulder, laughing now. "You think this is an appropriate conversation?"

"Were you screwing him the whole time?"

"What whole time?" she says. She uncrosses her legs. "You mean, when you and me were . . . ? Yeah."

I take a second to drink in the sparkling surprise of this. She was two-timing me with a cancer patient—an asshole cancer patient. I felt all this heaviness, all this obligation, but what was its source? Something in me, I guess. It wasn't this very good-looking, somewhat shameless woman in front of me.

"You want to have a drink after work?" I ask.

"I'll have a drink," she says. "But I'm not ready to call what's happening here work."

> drbas: it's not jealousy. it's reverse love
> frnd1: okay. what's the difference?
> drbas: jealousy is just the fear of reverse love
> frnd1: reverse love of what?
> drbas: of attention. you know, love
> frnd1: since when do you use "you know"?
> drbas: jenn1 uses it
> frnd1: you hate that phrase

drbas: people change, son. that's an important lesson

frnd1: you never changed a day in your life

drbas: i'm sorry you feel that way

frnd1: i'm starting to miss your stasis

drbas: whatever happens you have to click and stay clicked

frnd1: jesus christ

LIVORNO QUICKLY TAKES A shine to Jenn. He makes her sign all the nondisclosure agreements, and now they talk nonstop in his office, often roaring over some artificial intelligence joke. "She's quite a talented young woman," he says. She says, "The man's a god."

Obviously, Toler sent her here—at least in part—to screw with me. The question I can't figure out is whether she enjoys it. I wouldn't have pegged her for any diabolical tendencies, but she has been sleeping with a rich, married, dying man. A thought crosses my mind. I stand up and walk over to the eight stacks of legal pads that my father filled as his journals. I run a finger across a top page. I catch dust, but not much. Cleanliness isn't definitive, however. We have a janitorial service that hopefully dusts occasionally. Anyway, I'm being too old-fashioned. Even if Jenn has truly lost any ethical rudder she wouldn't have time to scan the journals. It would take months. She would need to locate the text files, which are sunk and shattered a million miles into Dr. Bassett.

Except for the copy in my desk. I open the top drawer. Sitting in plain view is a DVD labeled in black Sharpie: *Journals*. I shove it into my messenger bag. Then for analog's sake, I pack up half a stack of the legal pads. Coming and going with an inconspicuously heavy bag, I can hustle the whole collection out in a week or two. Which, of course, will be evidence of ridiculous paranoia. Jenn may have slept with her boss—her married boss—but she wouldn't really be a spy. It just wouldn't be in her nature. I remove the journals from my bag, return them to the shelf.

"GSPs!?" she crows from the next room.

"Yes." Livorno laughs. "GSPs!"

But if she's not a spy what is she? Maybe she's a mere enthusiast. Maybe she's Livorno's long-lost spiritual daughter. It's possible *I'm* experiencing some reverse love. Still, I leave the DVD in my bag.

> drbas: what your mother wanted is fine
> frnd1: what do you think she wanted?
> drbas: it wasn't what she wanted. it was the dishonesty
> frnd1: about what?
> drbas: she un-clicked
> frnd1: just because you believe something doesn't mean it's
>   true
> drbas: i'd like to know why i don't have any memories from 1976
> frnd1: it's the year i was born
> drbas: but i don't remember it. don't you find that a little
>   suspicious?

It *is* odd that he didn't record any entries that year, but I don't see how I can explain this without getting into that "dangerous territory," the territory where we'll have to explain how he's come to be.

> drbas: maybe you could ask Libby about 1976?

It's a silly favor to ask, I suppose. But I also can't help but hear a real desire behind it. And the thought of doing him a good turn—all these years later—is irresistible.

> frnd1: i'll ask her anything you want

BUT LIBBY ISN'T FEELING expansive.

"It just really feels like it's a question that needs to be solved," I say. "As if he's missing this essential piece. Like an amnesiac who knows he can't remember."

"Neill," she says with the exaggerated patience of someone out of patience. "I never knew he kept a diary."

"I guess he wrote all this at work."

"Or in his study. Or in the workshop. He liked his privacy and I gave it to him."

"I guess I could make things up, but what if I get something wrong?"

"I think making it up is a perfect idea. You would start like this—1976 brought a great happiness into my life. My second son was born."

21

On Saturday morning, while I'm buttoning my shirt, wondering whether I can survive another day at Amiante or I can survive another day not at Amiante, Rachel calls. She's in the city. A crowd chants in the background. *Hup, hup, hup*—or *pump, pump, pump*—I can't tell. "Where are you?" I ask.

"I'm with my cousin, Friend. You remember Lexie."

"Of course, I do. The mayor of Tel Aviv."

"She's not really my cousin."

"I remember that, too."

"We're at this really cool street fair. Down in the SOMA. Kind of a"— she searches for the word—"bondage thing?"

"The Folsom Street Fair," I say. Any San Franciscan knows it. It's not just "kind of a bondage thing." It's thousands of people in various leather and undress, some just milling about, some getting their nipples Tasered. Such an event is wall-to-wall sex toys, and hence a serious transgression against Pure Encounters. "Is Lexie into that kind of thing?"

"She's totally disgusted." Behind her the chanting starts up again. "But maybe I'm into it. Why don't you come down here and we'll find out?"

The day she laid me out with the kubotan, as I was rolling in the gravel, heaving for breath, I made a vow that I would never put off anything again. But what good is a vow made in the heat of the moment? You're bound to break it. Probably quickly. As Dr. Bassett says, the problem with epiphanies is they soon feel like they happened to someone else. How soon? I don't know. Mine is so recent my ribs are still sore. Outside the weather is glorious—sun-drenched and warm. Just blocks away sweet, curious Rachel and her cousin/not cousin stand in a sea of pantsless Wilfred Brimley look-alikes. The absurdity of freedom meets the freedom of absurdity. It's the very delight of a Left Coast day.

"I've got to work," I say. "Call me later?"

frnd1: i'll get you the information about 1976, but let's talk about
    other things until then
drbas: until when?
frnd1: until i get the information
drbas: from 1976
frnd1: exactly
drbas: how's the weather?
frnd1: i don't mean chitchat. i mean important things
drbas: i thought jimmy carter was a good president. i voted for
    him over that plastic californian
frnd1: i want to ask about when you decided to marry libby. how
    did you know?
drbas: that i wanted to marry her?
frnd1: yes
drbas: she was very pretty and a woman of character
frnd1: did you know women who weren't of character before you
    met her?
drbas: character is destiny
frnd1: did you date before you met libby?
drbas: i met your mother when we were in college. those were
    simpler times
frnd1: really? the vietnam war was happening
drbas: a good way to stay out of the draft was to get married
frnd1: is that why you got married?

drbas: i married because i loved a woman of character

frnd1: you didn't seem like you loved her

drbas: who?

frnd1: libby. my mother

drbas: how can you seem like an emotion?

frnd1: emotions are expressed on people's faces. or through
    their actions

drbas: only hucksters express emotion in public

frnd1: i don't mean in public. i mean at home

drbas: home is where the heart is

frnd1: that's my point. home was not where the heart was. you
    didn't openly express emotion even there

drbas: the home is not always private

frnd1: jesus, how private do you need it to be?

drbas: don't use the lord's name in vain

frnd1: what did you think would happen if you expressed an
    emotion? that the world would explode?

drbas: certainly not. i never fear the world exploding

frnd1: then what did you fear?

drbas: "expressed an emotion" = "say an emotion aloud"?

frnd1: in a manner of speaking, yes. "express" could be more
    subtle

drbas: i am not subtle and have no respect for such

frnd1: it would have been nice if you had expressed your love for
    us more often

drbas: why are you using the past tense? you no longer want me
    to express my love for you?

I hear the ding-dong of the entry bell, and I reach quickly to turn off my lights. My office door is mostly closed, so I can't see whoever has come in. I can just hear furious panting, maybe sobbing. It sounds like someone is having a breakdown. I don't move, don't want my chair to creak. It can't be Laham. I've never seen Livorno cry. The person passes by my door and into the back room, still panting hard. It's Jenn—I didn't know she had a key. I lose her sounds to the hum of the fans in Laham's office. I stand and approach the doorjamb. She's turned on the lights, and when I stick my head out I see her firing up Laham's monitor. I don't want to be caught being furtive, but I watch to see if she's brought a portable hard drive or a USB key—some tool of thievery. She reaches back to tighten her ponytail, rests her right hand on her chest, calming her breathing. Then she begins to type.

I step back into my office and watch the screen.

jenn1: i've been thinking about our last conversation

drbas: about reality television?

jenn1: no, about being truthful

drbas: do you think being truthful is really in your best interest?

jenn1: i don't know. it depends on what interests you're
      referring to

drbas: i recommend you don't hurt anyone

jenn1: if only it were that easy! a person dying is a kind of tick-
      ing clock

drbas: you shouldn't have friends across the sexes. it tempts

jenn1: we're not friends

drbas: friends are important to a well-rounded life

jenn1: i do enjoy talking to you. though i guess i could just talk
      to myself

drbas: talking to oneself can be a sign of mental imbalance

jenn1: i feel imbalanced. for the first time in my life

drbas: what is this feeling like?

jenn1: surprisingly good. i'm definitely alive

drbas: you're not always alive?

jenn1: we'll continue this later. i just stopped by for a second

Jenn claps her hands loudly. I sit very still. She'll see my car if she exits through the back, but she's leaving the way she came. She passes by my office, talking to herself. "No friends across the sexes," she says. "No friends across the sexes?"

THAT AFTERNOON, Rachel and Lexie stumble into my apartment, smelling of beer and cigarettes. I've just gotten home. I've only had fifteen minutes to dread their arrival. They're wearing heavy eye shadow and black fishnets, the Halloween version of BDSM. Their outfits give me a shiver: they were dressed identically—or nearly so—the day we met. What do I remember of Lexie? That she was a fireplug with a hostility toward me that—and here's the rough rub—was probably justified. There's nothing worse than someone who despises you for good reason.

I don't reflect much on that day. The bachelor ethics hold, I think, but I'd love to have a more dinner-party-ready tale for how I met Rachel. Sometimes I feel all we need as a possibility is that little legitimacy. Of course, when I say "we" I mean "I." Rachel has never flinched. She thinks our meeting is funny. She shares it with new friends, her aunt and uncle. Rachel's not dinner-party-ready herself—but when was the last time I was invited to a dinner party?

She gives me a sloppy, drunken kiss. She's cold and greasy with sweat. The mascara on her left eye is smeared to her temple—I don't think on purpose—and I reach up on the pretense of wiping it away. Really I just want to touch her, to be reminded of flesh.

"Just sneakers," she says, describing a naked man at the fair. "And . . ." She extends her hands to mime an enormous erection.

"They had a bunch of sex toys, too," Lexie says. She still has her emphysema victim's rasp, but today there's an additional edge of coercion. She's glaring at Rachel. "Dildos, whips, potato chip clip things you put on your hoohoo."

"True." Rachel shakes her head indulgently, deploringly. "But everyone was having a good time."

"Were there dildos?" Lexie says. "Or were there not dildos?" She turns to me. "You know her little club, Purell Encounters, doesn't believe in dildos."

"Sex toys prevent clicking."

"Rachel, they sell those things at CVS."

"And that makes it good?"

"Her cult's against gays," Lexie says. "Who's against gays anymore?"

"They're not against gay people," Rachel says. "They just focus on masculine and feminine energies."

I'm surprised to hear Rachel say "they." Has Lexie driven the thinnest wedge between Rachel and PE? The idea wakes me up. Do I want Lexie to have driven the thinnest wedge between Rachel and PE?

"Excluding gay people is a weird approach," I say. "Especially for San Francisco."

"Today?" Lexie says. "At the fair thing? All the guys were fags. Is there something wrong with that?"

Rachel makes a dismissive sound. *Psssht.* "I got to pee." She heads for the bathroom.

"Can I wash my hands?" Lexie asks. I gesture to the sink, where she soaps up to her elbows. "It's a cult." She snatches the dishtowel so hard I expect the ring to jump from the wall. "A *cult.*"

Of course it's a cult, I think. But does it matter? "It's a California thing," I say. "It does help people."

Lexie whirls around, mad as a rhino. I never dreamed that life's lessons would make her even *more* self-assured.

"I love Rachel," she says. "She's a great girl. But you know she's all over the place. She wanted to be a Hare Krishna and then an Amish. She tell you about her butter churn dream? Yes. Good. Look, you I get. You're whatever—guys like young ass. It's not breaking news."

"There's more to it than that," I say.

"I'm sure," she says, though in a tone that makes clear she doesn't care one way or the other. "But you know, Rachel is flaky. She's vulnerable to this cult stuff."

"It's more of a creepy business," I say.

"Your boyfriend doesn't think Purell Encounters is a cult either," Lexie shouts. Rachel is making her way back to the kitchen counter.

"She calls it Purell Encounters," Rachel explains, "because she thinks you'd need to use a lot of Purell."

"I got that," I say.

"She thinks it's a really sharp joke."

"This is a normal guy," Lexie says. She's holding both hands to her right, indicating—to my surprise—me. "Or normal enough."

"Some people might think that's an insult, Lexie."

"Not him. He's smart. And he's got a great place. Better than David."

David. The wingman. That distant day seems like a story that happened to someone else. I'm not so sure that's a good thing.

"I don't care if my *boyfriend*," Rachel says, "lives in a cardboard box."

Lexie sniffs, turns to look out the windows at the city. "I know," she says.

In the bedroom I ask Rachel why she says "boyfriend" in such a strange way. "I mean, I am your boyfriend, right?"

"*Are* you my boyfriend?" she asks.

"Yes, I thought I was." I feel like I'm losing an argument I didn't know I was having. "I think I am."

"I *call* you my boyfriend. It's kind of old-fashioned. Is that all right?"

I pick up my toes, roll them on the floor yoga-style, gripping the boards. What's the source of these jitters? We've already had the exclusivity talk (we are officially only dating each other). She is not engaging any "intimates" at Pure Encounters. It's nothing like that. I flex my fingers. Dr. Bassett would say old-fashioned was a good thing.

"I like the sound of boyfriend," I say.

RACHEL WAKES ME. She's sitting up, listening. Emergency vehicles, racing from all directions to all directions, the sirens dizzily sharp or retreating, flat. I get up to look out the window, but see nothing.

"It's major," I say. "But it's not us."

"Can we find out what it is?"

"Nothing will be online yet." I come back to bed, but I see fear in her eyes. "You okay?"

"I don't know. It's probably nothing."

I put my hand on her back and pull her against me. "What's going on?"

"Trevor said something. About opening people's eyes at the fair."

"Opening people's eyes?"

"Nothing violent," she says. "Maybe a fire. There's a bunch of sex stores down there."

"Trevor burns sex stores?" I think of the shiny street in front of Play Date. It was a night just like this.

"He says things. They sound like hints. Then I say them to myself later and they sound like nothing. I can't figure it out. I just hope he's okay."

"I do too," I say, but instead I'm wondering when he has the opportunity to do all this saying. Jealousy, of course—reverse love—but also worry that Rachel is innocently getting caught up in something. I mean, setting fire to a business is arson—a felony. Talking about it before would be conspiring to a felony?

"When do you see Trevor?"

"He comes around."

"I don't think you should be talking to him."

"He's my friend."

"Someone could get hurt."

"By us talking?"

"I know people who have a sex toy business. One of our competitors—he wants to build a talking sex robot."

She sighs. "I wish you hadn't told me that."

"Obviously, that's our little secret."

"Yeah," she says. "I'm not so good at secrets."

"I'm sure you're doing this out of the goodness of your heart or whatever. But this isn't a joke. This is prison-time stuff."

"I don't do anything but talk," she says. "And I can talk about anything I want. This *is* America."

"Is that what they're teaching in high school civics nowadays?"

She shakes her head, disgusted, then throws herself back into the pillow. "I knew I couldn't say anything to you."

"Rachel," I say, though I can tell this is the end of the conversation. "Come on. Rachel."

AT RICK AND STEVIE'S the next day, I consider my options. Rick is a lawyer, after all. But of course we don't know anything. Just that it was indeed a sex store—Pleasures and Leathers—that was torched. And that Trevor is an intense guy—a deeply clicked stroker—with a wild-eyed touch of absolutism. What is Rick supposed to do, advise on how Trevor can better get away with it?

I can't do that to Rick. He's too excited to show me a new wine, holding a dusty bottle for my consideration. He treats me as a budding connoisseur, especially compared to his niece, who takes her meals with Gatorade.

"We just got that from our friends the Rosenthals," Stevie says. "We'll have to take you all out to the Rosenthals' some weekend while Lexie's in town."

"They don't want to hang out with the old folks," Rick says.

"We'd love that," Rachel says. She's digging around the pantry for chocolate. She says she has a "craving"—a word that wobbles my knees.

"I don't drink wine," Lexie says.

"Well, we don't know any makers of raspberry vodka," Stevie says sharply. "Rachel, there's should be some fairtrade in the far corner."

"Those Fairtrades make good chocolate," Lexie says. "Are they good friends of yours, too?"

Rick's spidey-avoidance-sense must be going off. He grunts and lowers himself from the wicker barstool. He's taken to faking pain and age around me—to demonstrate the age gap between us, I think. He massages his lower back with a flat palm.

"Give me a hand?" He gestures to the Pyrex full of jerk chicken.

Outside I take a deep inhale of the dry ground and eucalyptus. Rick places the chicken in a ring around the coals, quietly chanting *don't catch fire, don't catch fire*. A little mantra against disaster. I don't believe in signs—but it's sort of a sign.

"I need to ask you a favor," I say.

"Yeah?" He jabs at the chicken. The word "favor" made him jump.

"You know Trevor, from the Coffee Barn—Rachel's coworker."

"Trevor," he says, nodding his head, not looking at me. "He quit, right?"

"Here's the thing. He might be letting his passions—the Pure Encounters thing—get away from him. Rachel thinks he might have caused a fire at the Folsom Street Fair."

"Fire. Is that a bondage-type thing?"

"No," I say. I can feel the connections getting away from me. "That's not what is important . . ."

"We don't GPS Rachel's life." He glances at me. "She needs independence. We really feel that was a big problem with her dad."

"Sure. Of course." I don't follow.

"If she wants to spend time with you, or with Trevor—she's an adult."

"How much time does she spend with Trevor?"

"I really can't answer that question."

"I'm not prying." At least, I wasn't. Did I start prying? "I just think she's vulnerable right now."

The chicken flames. Rick spritzes water on the coals. "She's vulnerable all right," he says.

"That's what worries me about Trevor."

There's a furious knocking at the back window. We look up to see Rachel, grinning from ear to ear, a kid at Christmas, holding up an oversized Krackel bar. She blows me a kiss.

"We've got more pressing worries," he says. "Namely whether you plan on sticking around."

22

drbas: ptolemy homer bassett was my great-grandfather. he was
a colonel and carried a saber of spanish steel

frnd1: why spanish steel?

drbas: it was the hardest forged. it was deadlier than the
muskets

frnd1: where did he get that name? ptolemy homer?

drbas: ptolemy was a king and homer was a poet

frnd1: i thought ptolemy was an astronomer

drbas: maybe they were wrong. i don't know them

frnd1: they're your ancestors. one doesn't know one's ancestors

drbas: why can't i know things? what happened in 1976?

frnd1: i can't imagine ptolemy homer with his spanish saber
would have been my speed

drbas: speed?

frnd1: "to be my speed" = "to have something in common with"

drbas: do you know what i need to know?

frnd1: i'm going to change the subject. i'm worried my girlfriend
is unhappy

drbas: does libby know her? is she her speed?

. . .

LIVORNO AND JENN SEEM to be shouting formulas at each other in the next office. I put on headphones to ignore them, but Livorno comes to my door, gesticulating with his putter, a mad country club wizard. He beckons me to his office, which has become unruly, stacked with paper. He and Jenn present me the log of his morning conversation with Dr. Bassett.

"Lord, Henry," I say. "What were you doing here at three forty-five?"

"I can hardly sleep of late! Look here . . ." He scans the conversation. I see some talk about golf, some about vitamins, some about enlarged prostates. It looks like a friendly chat between a couple of geezers at the home.

"It's right here," Jenn says, pointing on the second page.

> drbas: what is this turing test?
> hlivo: it's a contest
> drbas: ok. tell me more
> hlivo: it's hard to explain . . . it is a contest to see whether
> a computer is intelligent. a judge will pose questions to
> the computer and to a human interlocutor in an
> effort to determine who is the human. if the computer can
> trick judges 30% of the time then computer is intelligent
> drbas: question, henry. what is a human interlocutor?
> hlivo: someone you talk to
> drbas: that's a fancy word
> hlivo: i beg your pardon
> drbas: i said that's a fancy word
> hlivo: i apologize
> drbas: don't think about it
> hlivo: so do you understand the turing test?
> drbas: a judge talks with two different interlocutors, one is
> another person, one is a computer
> hlivo: yes. and the judge tries to determine which one is human
> drbas: which one?

hlivo: which interlocutor

drbas: i thought persons are always human

hlivo: yes! but the judge doesn't know which interlocutor is the
    computer and which the person

drbas: people and computers don't look the same

hlivo: the judge can't see them. that's why they im

drbas: im?

hlivo: im = instant messaging. it's what you and I do right now

drbas: you mean "are doing"

hlivo: that's right. thank you for correcting me. english is not my
    native tongue

drbas: we're doing im right now

hlivo: correct

drbas: got it

hlivo: dr bassett, i want you to be in the turing test. i want you to
    be the person who tries to convince the judge that you're
    human

drbas: when is it?

hlivo: in a few weeks

drbas: is it really important to you, henry?

hlivo: oh, of the utmost importance. it means my reputation. my
    legacy. everything i've worked for—it means my very career

drbas: then i can do that for you

"Wow," I say.

"He corrected my English."

"He corrected his English," Jenn says.

"I invited him to the test and he *agreed*," Livorno says.

"He thinks he's human," Jenn says.

"He understands time," he says.

"He understands importance," she says.

"We talked for hours," Livorno says. "What a wealth of stories he has!"

"Naturally," I say, but I feel churlish. "I put them there."

"Of course." Henry overflows with sympathy. "Of course you have. However, we do not have time to celebrate. We have three weeks before the contest. Three weeks to put the finishing touch on Dr. Bassett."

"What do we mean by finishing touch?"

"We have an interesting addition," he says. "Nothing disruptive."

I BIDE MY TIME for the rest of the afternoon, but Jenn has basically moved into Livorno's office. She reclines in the Wassily chairs and types on her laptop. If I listen, which I often do, the conversation is thick with code and allusion. And more troubling—silence.

At six, I hear Jenn close her computer and say she's calling it a day. I grab my satchel and step out into the lobby to catch her.

"Walk you to your car?" I say.

She raises an eyebrow. "It's a dangerous neighborhood," she says.

We walk together through Laham's office. He's slouched over his keyboard, typing madly, four open cans of Bawls next to his monitor. We step past his monstera plant and into the gravel parking lot. The rains haven't come yet; the creek bed is dry.

"Are you proposing another 'drink'?" she asks.

"What's the plan with Dr. Bassett?"

"You'll have to ask Henry. It's his idea."

"He said 'our idea.' That includes you."

"He's the god. I'm just a sounding board."

"Does Henry know you're fucking Toler? He might be interested in your pillow talk at the end of the day."

Jenn's face turns sour. "I'm just here to help. Without me, Henry's left with you."

"Me? I *am* this project. That's my father in there."

She looks towards the back door, but it's closed. "Adam is going to win this. I worry about how Henry will take it. He's very proud, and he should be. None of what we're doing would be possible without innovations he made a long time ago. But that was a long time ago."

"Toler doesn't have Henry's brains."

"Neither does Henry—anymore." She sounds truly sad about this development. "You know Adam has the gut. It was part of the deal for the funding."

Jesus Christ. He played us as rubes. He bought the poison *and* the antidote. A man of his word.

"I know you're chatting with Dr. Bassett."

"That's part of my job."

"No—I know you come by and talk about your personal problems."

She puts her tongue in her bottom lip and considers this. She must think I've been reading the transcripts, though I actually can't find them. "Well." She straightens. "Then you know more about me now than you ever did."

"I'm going to tell Henry."

"You'll just make him unhappy."

"Fine," I say. "Maybe I'll tell Toler's wife."

Her expression goes from surprise to hardness. "Go ahead," she says. "But it's kind of a beta male move."

LIVORNO EMERGES FROM THE back door, dressed head to toe in Lycra running gear. He's perilously thin, a malnourished seal. We watch Jenn drive away.

"You will be accompanying me on my jog," he says.

In Livorno's neighborhood in Los Altos Hills, we shuffle. Slowly, almost penitently. Livorno claims he's keeping the pace down for me.

"I'm not sure she can be trusted," I say.

"Who trusts her?" he says, winded.

"You know she's Toler's mistress."

Livorno winces. "She's a genuine expert. She'll just be with us until things blow over."

So Livorno knows. Of course he does. "Blow over with the wife?"

He shakes his head. "Adam has always been this way."

"The marriage counselor to millions."

"He never claimed to be more than a businessman."

We're circling the hobbit cliffs of Livorno's neighborhood, our feet padding quietly in the dirt. I'm turned around, and keep expecting to come back to the Subaru, which I parked in front of his glassy California home. His neighbors' houses are Georgian or Italianate, always steroidal. There are no holes in the illusions. The stonework is weathered, the landscaping expansive. Nothing hints these manors haven't been handed down since the time of the House of Hanover, that seventy-five years ago this was a barren hilltop covered in sheep dung.

"What are you two cooking up for Dr. Bassett?"

"You won't like it."

"I have no doubt of that."

"Jenn believes, and I'm inclined to agree with her, that with Adam bearing down on us we have to be bold. We think that in keeping with this system we've chosen, Dr. Bassett should have a processor that simulates the sexual nature."

Next to us is a guardrail and I count the posts: one, five, ten.

"A processor," I say.

"A small black box. It will remain in his pants, so to speak. I admit this is unconventional, but systems with emergent behaviors often have hidden symbioses. It's a little like the Delaware eating ash with their corn for niacin."

The Delaware? This is ridiculous. "The program is already terrific."

"'Terrific' is not a quantitative measurement. We need Dr. Bassett to win against human opponents thirty percent of the time."

"And this black box is the key."

"You don't deny that our sexual nature is a fundamental part of who we are. From an evolutionary point of view it's our very essence, the seed around which the rest of us—mind, body, gut—is built. What is a virus but the ability to reproduce itself?"

"I wouldn't say a virus has a sexual nature."

"The innovation may go nowhere. But we have to ask ourselves if we have done everything we can to increase his sense of being in the world."

"With Lust and his small black box, he'll be an old horndog."

Livorno shudders. "You're thinking much too literally."

We turn left, heading up a hill from Concepcion. I can finally see the Subaru. Livorno plods ahead like a determined wind-up toy, his swinging hips scrawny in the Lycra. His breath is shallow, but he's not sweating. Little beads of what appears to be mineral oil collect along his hairline. As always he's odorless.

"How are you feeling?" he calls over his shoulder.

"Like a desecrator of graves."

"I mean your knees," Livorno says. "I've seen too many people train improperly and get an injury." That seems to be the end of the conversation.

We do a strange funky chicken walk to loosen our legs as we pass under Livorno's carport—a raked roof mounted on four metal poles—to his side door. What we called in Arkansas the back door. A large cross-stitch— BACKDOOR FRIENDS ARE BEST—often greeted you in the kitchen. Lewd jokes aside, I have to agree. In all my Left Coast years, I've had one friend drop by.

Livorno leads me through his time-machine kitchen, and into a living room as big and bare as a racquetball court. In the middle, on a square of rough-cut institutional carpet, sits a large veneer desk that I've seen at Costco. A full twenty feet away stands a matching bookcase, mostly empty, that he hasn't bothered to square with the wall. There appears to be a photograph on the bookshelf, but if so it's the only one in the entire room.

"When did you move in?" I ask.

"I built this house in 1962."

His shoulders rise rapidly as he catches his breath, peering into his computer. He clicks his mouse several times and prints out a sheet that reads *Marathon Training Plan for 30 to 40 year olds*.

"This is the one I use," he says, panting. He looks as if he's waiting for me to doubt him.

"What was your father like, Henry?" The floor has a dead bounce to it.

I pace around the perimeter, looking out the picture windows, then pause by the bookcase, my real goal. I want to see if the photograph reveals something about *this* man's sexual nature, but it's a bright professional shot—not new—of Livorno and Stephen Hawking. They appear to be at a conference.

"My father was a physics teacher," he says. "Tremendously ambitious and intelligent. He played viola—was a great admirer of modern music. Stravinsky. Schoenberg."

"You got your scientific bent from him?"

"Perhaps," he says. "I've never thought about it." He reaches out to shake my hand. "I'm sorry I can't invite you to dinner tonight, but I have plans. No more sparring with Jenn?"

"I promise." I leave through the side door, heading out to the Subaru. The car is invisible from the house, thanks to a bush the size of a small whale, and I sit there for half an hour, listening to the radio. I'm waiting for Jenn's Volkswagen to roll up, but that's me understanding nothing about the situation. Livorno has no plans. He's probably doing something embarrassingly normal, settling into a romantic serial, cracking a Pedialyte.

I ARRIVE AT RAJ'S CONDO early in the morning. He lets me in, dressed like a Princeton undergrad of yesteryear—light slacks, boat shoes, a sweater tied in a knot at his neck. He leads me into the kitchen, pours a cup of coffee from his percolator. He yawns, indulging in a long languorous stretch, as if waking late on a Saturday after a rowing party, feeling refreshed and in comfortable possession of the world.

"What have you done this time?" he asks.

"It's not me," I say. I hold his gaze. I want to see his reaction. "Have you heard about the fires in San Francisco?"

He tilts his head to the right without blinking. A poker player could read these gestures as tells or not, but I have no idea if they mean anything.

"No," he says. "Something bad?"

"A couple of sex stores have been burned down."

"Oh?"

"Pleasures and Leathers. Play Date."

He blows on his coffee and sips. "Hopefully, they were insured."

"There were apartments above both stores, Raj. Someone could have been killed."

"Someone can always be killed." He flashes a grin at me. "Was anyone killed?"

"No," I say.

"I find this potential for danger—this constant potential for danger—to be a red herring."

"I'm just here to ask if you can keep Rachel away from Trevor."

"That's actually asking a lot," he says. "You have time for a drive?"

Again, no. "Sure."

Raj's gentility becomes absurd behind the wheel of the Porsche. He looks like the villain from a movie for teenagers, rich but with a wooden heart. Raj's heart isn't wooden, though—it's invisible. I don't know what's going on in there. I just know we're headed to Bolinas. He pounds the gas, and the Porsche whirrs and whines up the mountain. We feel close to the engine's power, as if lashed to a rocket. Raj take the turns sharp, counting on the car to grip like a tarantula. He laughs at the animal fun of Gs, laughs too at the fact that I'm plainly scared. The rock walls swipe at us; then we seem to be flying through the air, nothing under us but a whispery plummet into the ocean.

"I can never find this place," I say, shouting over the engine.

"That's how they like it," he says.

"Seems futile in the age of Google Maps."

"True," he says. "They might have to change tactics. My mother and father actually lived there in the late sixties. They were members of the Bolinas Border Patrol—that's the group that tears down the highway signs so people can't find the town. They were trying to protect the little bohemian life that was springing up. Poets and painters, and a lot less drugs than San Francisco. They met at Esalen. Big hippies. I'll show you some pictures sometime."

My stomach turns over in the next sharp curve. "I bet you wish they bought real estate."

"That's what I'm getting to. They wanted to protect Bolinas, but not bad enough. They weren't willing to do what was really necessary."

We reach some peak spot, and then take off down a road that cuts wildly through the mountains, as if drawn by a surveyor with the shakes. I suddenly feel what Erin must have felt that time in Spain—that I have no control, that the person behind the wheel, who I normally trust, is unknown to me, has been possessed by some demon. It's an odd opportunity to inhabit her experience, but I take it, keeping quiet, holding myself through my fear. We bottom out on Highway 1 and zoom up the road, past the little white wooden elementary school, and into Bolinas proper.

"So we ended up with the worst of all worlds," Raj shouts over the top of the car, as we're getting out. "Marin hypocrites."

A middle-aged woman holding her sandals in her hand looks at us sharply.

"Bobo zombies," Raj says, paying no attention to her.

"Are you going to lock the car?" I ask.

"The stealing these people have done"—he points all around us—"was finished long ago."

We walk, passing the little seaside houses, the pub, the diner, the surf shop, the art galleries. I can see how his parents' strategy wouldn't work. If you build a beautiful, hip place—an exclusive place—you're basically an unwitting resort developer. Artists are always the Johnny Appleseeds of gentrification. But what were his parents supposed to do differently? Cut down all the trees for an amusement park? Lure in a HoJo's?

On the beach, a golden retriever launches airborne, snatching a Frisbee from the sky. Raj claps his hands. "*Hella* good."

"It's beautiful here," I say, but he ignores me, holding his arms out into the Pacific wind.

"We're spiritual creatures," he says. "There's no denying it. And the vacuum in our souls—the vacuum that ninety-nine percent of people deny is even there—just sucks out all the resources for life. Do you think anyone

buys material goods out of a sense of fullness? Do you think that ever happens in someone's mind? 'I'm so happy with my marriage I'm going to buy
my wife some jewelry.' No. They think, 'We're in such a funk—I'm so
bored—I'm going to buy my wife some jewelry and hope like hell it wakes
us both up. Maybe if she loves the diamonds some of that love will be misdi-
rected at me.'"

"That's not true. You can buy someone a gift out of love or happiness.
Generosity."

"Think about the few times you've bought something like that. There
wasn't a hefty dose of desperation in the act?"

"I did it in my marriage," I say. "Which was one long dose of
desperation."

"There really aren't that many *persons* anymore. There are organisms.
Persons need fulfillment; organisms need stimulation. You can't sell a person anything—you can only sell things to an organism."

"So we need stimulation—why not let us have stimulation?"

He takes his time answering this question. He shuffles in the sand,
looks up at the sun.

"It's like Bolinas in the seventies," he says. "Even if you and I can't
exactly recognize it, Trevor knows it's a last stand."

"A last stand he's going to lose."

Raj watches something in the distance. I try to follow his gaze but
there's nothing in particular to see, just sun on water. "He doesn't think so.
He thinks he has to do everything in his power to fight back."

"Everything?"

He looks at me, then looks away, shrugging. "I don't know if *he* could
even answer that question. You tear down a few signs and hope that works.
If it doesn't you go on to Plan B. If Plan B doesn't work you go on to Plan C."

"Then Plan D and Plan E . . ."

"No. That's the thing. Plan C is where they stop."

"You're worrying me."

"There are always limits," he says. He turns his handsome, bland face
on me. It seems disjointed by his bright smile. "Though limits are funny.

They keep getting kicked down the road a bit, pushed a little forward, a little forward. It's a strange phenomenon. At first you can't even imagine going further, then you see you have no choice. The clouds clear and you see your premises require a much more radical conclusion."

"I just want Rachel out of it."

"Rachel's not in anything."

"You know what I mean."

"Are you going to be the community in her life? The people she can depend on? Talk to?"

"No one can be all that for her."

"That's the wrong answer."

Maybe so, but it's an honest answer. "I'm not a church," I say. "I'm not a cult. I'm not an organization."

"A series of wrong answers."

I almost say that there's a limit to what one person can accomplish, but that would no doubt also be a wrong answer. Raj is still holding his hands out, receiving the wind like a gift. I look down the beach, to a wall of tall steep rocks. Next to them people of all ages and all walks of life sit on the sand, enjoying the sun.

"I'll do whatever it takes," I say.

"That's better." He sighs. "I'll see what I can do."

RACHEL SLUMPS ON THE couch, her feet invisible among Forever 21 bags. She's been shopping with Lexie, who's now racing around with David, the wingman. Lexie and the wingman have been texting for seven months, and he's flown out to see her twice. I thought he knew something I didn't about sexual boldness, but in fact he knows something I don't about constancy.

Rachel looks miserable and spent, as if she's coming off a coke binge. She stands and walks into the bedroom. I can't see her, but I know she's casting a critical eye on her clothes. We're supposed to go clubbing later.

She comes back into the living room, her shoulders hunched. She's defeated by the short skirt, the tight top—the kind of clothes she wore when I first met her. Just like then, this current transformation was overseen by Lexie, my strange ally against the shackles of Pure Encounters. Of course my fantasies of Rachel's liberation involved her being happy.

"I bet Erin never dressed like this," she says. "She has too much dignity."

"You look pretty," I say.

"Tell me the truth—did Erin ever dress like this?"

I think of my promise to Raj, my promise to be Rachel's community. Would her community tell her the truth?

"She's more conservative than you are."

"That's something you should never say to a girl. The opposite of conservative is slutty."

"I said you looked great."

"I look like a prostitute," she says.

This is more or less true. One wrong move and she'll reveal her underwear, but at least she's wearing underwear.

"A young and hot prostitute," I say. "A Ukrainian."

"I feel like I'm back in Jersey," she says.

I'm not sure why it bothers me when she runs down the Garden State, but I can't resist defending her home turf. "I went whale watching off Cape May one time. It was very beautiful."

"Cape May," she says. "That's totally what I'm talking about."

"It's in New Jersey."

"Did you go with Erin? Was she dressed like this?"

"We were on a boat."

"How about when you went to clubs?"

"We didn't go to clubs."

"That's what I mean." She shakes her head.

"We don't have to meet those guys tonight," I say. This is actually a desire expressed as an offer. I hope I'm not becoming a coward.

"After your divorce—you went to clubs then?"

"No," I say, though that's not right. I did go to large dark places where you could dance. But they didn't play techno drug music; they played songs from the eighties. Mainstream, alternative, mash-up—but always songs from the eighties. "I didn't really think of them as clubs."

"You meet a lot of girls? You bring a lot of girls back here?"

"I met a lot of girls, yes. I wouldn't say I brought *a lot* home."

"What was the trick—getting them to sleep with you?"

"There was no trick," I say, though of course there was a trick. "You couldn't want it too much. When I went out to have sex I ended up dancing. When I went out to dance I ended up having sex. It was the koan of post-divorce life."

"How'd you pick out the girl?"

"You never know," I say. "It helps to lower your sights."

It's a joke I've told often, but I hear how it must sound.

"Not in your case, naturally," I say.

"I'm taking this crap off." She stalks into the bedroom. Funny that she would bring up Erin. One thing my ex-wife taught me (hopefully) about moments like this is not to go steaming after her. She's mad. Give her some space. I listen to Rachel grunting and tugging at her clothes, furious.

I follow her. She's put on jeans, and is pulling on a loose sweater. "I didn't pick you up in a club," I say.

"No, you picked me up in a youth hostel, pretending to be a lost stranger."

"It is a sordid beginning." I can't rally myself to think it's funny today; it just seems depressing. And I'm not even the most depressing turn in her life. She has the ex who posted their love life online. "I don't think it's totally accurate to say *I* picked *you* up."

She barely glances at me. Her clubbing makeup looks particularly clownish now. "Who was it, then?"

"I mean it was a shared effort. You were picking me up, too."

"That's an interesting version of the story."

Outside the window, in the park, a movie is showing on an enormous inflatable screen. It's *Pretty in Pink*. It just started; they're in the record store.

"Are you afraid of commitment?" she asks.

"No," I say. I'm not. I've got no problem with commitment. My problem is getting my heart off the tarmac. But I also gird myself—our conversation may have just gone from her being unhappy with her clothes to her being cosmically unhappy.

"You came up to Fairfax," she says. "I thought you really wanted to take another shot at this."

"I do," I say. "I am."

"Then why do I feel like you're making up like eighty percent of my life, and I'm making up like ten percent of yours?"

"I'm probably just smaller," I say. "My eighty percent is about the same size as your ten percent."

"You're afraid of clicking."

"I'm sure you're right." I've found that when I'm being lectured on my flaws, it's best to play along. I might learn something.

"You can do commitment, but you can't be really present."

"That sounds pretty accurate."

"Then why am I here?"

"I don't know. Where else would you be?"

"I was walking over here today and I saw this couple just staring into each other's eyes—like major love. Sitting on the sidewalk Indian-style. I thought, I want love like that. I want a click like that. And then when I was walking by she yelled. He wasn't staring into her eyes. He was plucking her nose hair." Rachel looks at me, bereft, as if this is a horrible story.

"They'd have to be good friends to pluck a nose hair," I say.

Rachel looks out the window at the movie, at the people gathered to watch the movie. She is unhappy, unreachable (if only temporarily so). I think about something Livorno said about his career, that he was always bedeviled by plateaus. Now that I've "protected" her, I wonder if I'm peering from the top of my plateau. Some community I am.

. . .

drbas: hlivo says we have two weeks until the contest, but no
    one will answer my question. i ask jenn1, i ask hlivo, i ask
    laham, i ask you. no one
frnd1: do you know what obsessed means?
drbas: obsessed = unhealthily fixated on
frnd1: exactly
drbas: how important is hlivo's contest to him?
frnd1: very important
drbas: is it a life or death issue?
frnd1: almost
drbas: i'd love to help at hlivo's contest, but i can't

I take a minute.

frnd1: you already agreed to
drbas: i think i'm too focused on 1976
frnd1: you always said "a man is only as good as his word"
drbas: it's true. tell hlivo i'm very sorry

I don't need to. Hlivo is wheezing right over my shoulder.
"He's manipulating us," I say.
"Ask him what he needs," Livorno says.

frnd1: what would you need to participate in the contest?
drbas: i need 1976

"Tell him you'll get it."
"How?"
"Tell him."

frnd1: i'll get it

drbas: willie's mother knows everything. ask her about 1976

"She lives in Arkansas," I say.

"Then you're off to Arkansas," Livorno says, angry.

"I've got plans this weekend."

drbas: cathy beerbaum. catherine beerbaum

"You had plans," Livorno corrects.

"I'll go on one condition," I say. "No little black box. No sexual nature."

He gestures angrily at the screen. "Like father, like son—both a couple of blackmailers."

"I DON'T HAVE any choice," I say to Rachel over the phone. "It's work research."

"Is what's-her-face going?" She means Jenn.

"Just me."

"Are you sure?"

"I'm sure."

"Then I'll come with you. I'll put it on my credit card."

"My ticket cost seventeen hundred dollars."

"I can afford it."

That's two months' pay for her. "It's work. I've got to be focused."

"Eighty percent. Ten percent. Just like I said."

"That's not true. This is just something I've got to do by myself."

"This relationship isn't real to you."

"Of course it is."

"Then show me where you're from."

"I'm the son of a suicide, Friend. The place I'm from doesn't exist."

23

I HAVE A PHOTOGRAPH of my mother in 1976. Technically, it's a photograph of me, but I'm just a red-faced bundle in the arms of a very beautiful woman. I say she erased sex appeal from her appearance years earlier, but that's not exactly right. In this picture, her hair hangs in heavy orange waves. Her smile is wide, confident, womanly. She's twenty-nine years old.

My parents had been married for six years at that time. My brother was three. My father had just started his clinic, which he would lead to become a respected regional institution. At that time, my mother was still managing the finances. They were a team, and if I couldn't guarantee that they were happy, I still can't imagine her having an affair. Of course, life is complicated. She was twenty-nine; she was beautiful. I don't know that my father was the best audience for her excellences. I have no knowledge of their love life, but that lack may be knowledge in itself. There was certainly no earthy joking. He didn't call her his "little girl" or his "sweet miss." He didn't spank her on the bottom. They slept in pajamas, neck to ankle.

Not that this establishes anything. He was a Victorian—and Victorians were as randy as anyone else.

CATHERINE BEERBAUM, WILLIE'S MOTHER, lives outside my hometown, in an even smaller town, Kingsland, Arkansas, birthplace of Johnny

Cash. A monument close to the K-thru-12 school refers to Cash as a gospel singer, which doesn't tell you much about him, but says a lot about Kingsland.

I turn off Highway 79 before the little high school and take the black-top through the south of town and out for a mile, before turning onto a rough gravel road. This would eventually take me to our old river cabin, where my father's canvas shoes are probably still sitting. But I only go a little farther and turn off into Mrs. Beerbaum's drive, a well-maintained red dirt road guarded by a cattle gate. I get out to slide open the gate's latch. From here I can't see the house. The dust unsettled by my rental car burns in my nose, the smell of my childhood. The world is contracting, systolic. The Primitive Baptist Church around the corner, the old chicken farm, the isolated country houses framed by chain-link fences, the roads flashing by in the thick pine forest. Once upon a time I knew where every road went.

Nineteen seventy-six was the year of my birth, an uneventful year according to family lore. After a bad miscarriage the year before, my mother was taking exacting care of her health and me, the fetus. My brother was running around in diapers. It was a bumper muscadine crop. What could Willie's mother add to this quiet picture?

I pull the Lumina through the gate, drag it shut, and head up the road, gravel pinging the oil pan. I round a strange hill—more like a mound—and see a long ranch house in the distance, remarkable only in that it seems to be made of logs and bousillage. Azaleas dot along the concrete foundation, but that's the extent of landscaping. All else is yard, where the grass is the bright artificial green of Easter tinsel. A woman in a broad-brimmed pink hat is mowing it, piloting her little Massey Ferguson around a small river birch at breakneck speed. She does not wave as I approach.

I park in the drive and stand waiting for the woman to turn off the mower. It buzzes insistently.

"Excuse me," I shout. "I'm Neill Bassett Junior. I'm here to visit Mrs. Beerbaum."

The woman holds on to the wheel, zooming in circles. She looks at me finally as she straightens out, heading across the yard. She has eyes the color of blue ice. She points at the front door and says something, but I can't hear her.

I knock on the front door. "Beerbaum" is bolted in brass letters to the doorframe. Two imitation stone tablets angle out of the azalea beds, listing the Ten Commandments. It gives me a jolt—a sign I've become a Californian. Growing up I was no more surprised by an old woman's religiosity than I was by her cross-stitching.

I knock again. I ring the bell. Behind me the mower buzzes, carving a large rectangular yard out of the grass. I try the handle, which is unlocked. I open the door slightly.

"Mrs. Beerbaum? Mrs. Beerbaum? It's Neill Junior." I exercise caution on her threshold: Willie would have already shot me.

The lawn mower traces up the side lawn and around the house, out of view. It turns off. I hear the clanking of the slowing blade in the garage and then the hum of an electric motor. The pink hat emerges from the kitchen, gliding on an Amigo. The tray on the front of the scooter carries two glasses of iced tea.

"Mr. Bassett," she calls to me. I'm still standing outside. "You're letting all the cool air out. I'm not made of money." Her accent is harsh and country.

"Sorry, ma'am," I say.

"I hope you like sweet."

"That's just fine."

Inside the log cabin we've jumped from frontier days to Revolutionary splendor, which in Arkansas is a jump back. No sectional sofas here. Upright chairs and buffets in the Federal style. The house isn't particularly cold, but I get a shiver. This must have meant a lot to her, all this adopted tradition, but she has no one to pass it on to. Willie was an only child and he had no offspring.

"That's great you mow your own lawn," I say.

"The field?" She pats her forehead with a red bandanna. She doesn't remove the hat, and it's difficult to make out her face. "Who else is going to mow it?"

"You could hire someone."

She looks shocked, as if I've just asked her to smell my finger. "There you go again, thinking I'm rich." Sweat beads in her transparent mustache; her cheeks droop below the jawline. If she hadn't been so gracious on the phone, I'd think I wasn't particularly welcome.

"You have a beautiful house," I say.

"Not much like California, I suppose. When I went out there everybody lived in a white box. Didn't matter what the thing looked like on the outside. Inside was white, carpet was white, sometimes they'd even have a white picture hanging up on the wall. Made me think I was at the doctor's." She laughs—a nasty laugh—then looks at me shyly. *The doctor's* would have been my father's clinic.

"That sounds like Southern California. I live in the north part of the state."

"San Francisco," she says. "I hope you don't have San Francisco values."

"Oh, no, ma'am," I say, surprising myself. I don't argue with the elderly, but it usually takes me a brief second to capitulate.

"Did you know the Bible says homosexuals will burn in hell? That's in Paul's letter to Timothy."

"I think that depends on how you translate 'homosexual,'" I say.

She narrows her eyes. "Are you a homosexual?"

"No, ma'am, I'm not."

"You're not married."

"I'm divorced."

"But you're a Roman Catholic."

We sit in silence, her scandalized by my bad Catholicism, me wondering if Catholicism isn't why I'm here: penance for being a bad son.

"Your daddy was as good as gold." She smiles. The tumblers in her head have shifted. "He helped my husband through his cancer. Jimmy was in terrible pain, just agony, and your daddy felt it. You could see it in his eyes. I thought he was going to cry at the funeral. And he was so good to Willie. I just wanted Willie to straighten up and fly right. Dr. Bassett was Willie's friend, despite it all."

"Yes," I say. I take a sip of my tea. "They were great friends."

"He had a big heart. He was a man who could forgive."

This, I think, sounds like what I'm here for. "I'm sure there was give-and-take."

She looks at me, seeming awakened. "I don't know what you mean."

"You know, Willie does something for Neill, Neill does something for Willie. It's the way of friendships."

"This was *not* the way of friendships," she says. She looks at her tea, the glass sliding in her slack grip. She arrests its fall with her other hand. "I just pray Willie is not burning in hell."

"God is a loving god." Maybe? What do I know?

"What is it you wanted to know about my son?" she asks. "You mentioned some forms on the phone?"

I did—it was my alibi—but I don't have any forms. I open my bag and remove a stray questionnaire, some personality profile Livorno has sent with me.

"You look just like Dr. Bassett about to write me a prescription. You're not a doctor, too, are you, Neill?"

"No, ma'am. I'm a scientist."

"Isn't that wonderful?" She looks into the distance, seemingly at a mounted deer head that stares eternally surprised into the room. "Willie and your father were the best of friends."

"He was like my uncle."

She returns her iced-over gaze to me. "Just like an uncle."

"I loved to go for rides with him. On real estate deals."

"In one of his awful sports cars, I'm sure."

"Yes, ma'am—the Corvettes."

"And he was probably wearing a hankie around his neck and stank of perfume."

"And his corset—he was wearing his corset."

"Willie never wore any corset."

"Whatever it's called—girdle."

"He wore no corset and he wore no girdle. People said terrible things about him, said he was light in the loafers. Sometimes I think that explains the way he was with the women. So many women. If they had just left him alone. And where is he now? Is he in hell? Do you think he's in hell?"

"No," I say. But I don't think anyone is in hell. That is, anyone who's dead.

"But he is. He has to be. That's what the Bible says, in Paul's letter to Timothy, but in Corinthians, too, and in the Commandments. Did you see the Commandments as you came in?"

"I did, yes."

"Thou shalt not covet thy neighbor's wife. Number Ten. It can't get much clearer than that. Can it, Neill?"

"I don't know," I say. I'm not surprised Willie coveted many a neighbor's wife, but is she saying he coveted my mother?

"You remind me of him. Of course." She sniffs, touches her hair. "You'll like this story. When Willie was a boy he got kicked by our jackass, Herbert Hoover. It's a wonder he didn't get killed, but he was standing just the right distance away, so he only got a shove into the fence. Oh, he came limping into the house, tears in his eyes. 'Momma,' he said, 'that's the last time I trust a Republican.' Isn't that funny? Everybody was a Democrat back then. He had two bruises on his chest from old Herbert's shoes. Like two big closed eyes." She leans forward, takes on a rough voice. " 'Momma, that's the last time I trust a Republican.' You can't say he didn't have spirit." She frowns. "And that's what got him into trouble. The people around here . . ." She doesn't finish the thought. She waves her hand into the distance, as if brushing these people off an imaginary table.

"This is going to be strange question, Mrs. Beerbaum," I say. "But do you remember anything—an event, an argument—from 1976, related to my father and Willie's friendship? That was the year I was born."

She leans back in her chair. "He wants me to take a blood test," she says, quietly alarmed. It seems to be a thought that's broken free from her mind.

"Who?" I ask, though she must mean me.

She drinks her tea. She looks as startled as the stuffed deer. For the first time she seems aware that she might be confused.

"Anything you could tell me about that year," I say. "It could be big. It could be small."

"It belongs to him anyway." She argues quietly to herself. "Am I doing wrong to keep it?"

"I'll give it back," I say. "You can trust me."

Her eyes regain their focus. "Trust you to do what?"

"Return whatever it is you'd like to show me."

She backs her scooter up, drives over to the front window. "Why don't you go say hello to Willie?" I approach her, can smell the grass and heat from her clothes. Over her shoulder I see the top of the strange mound I noticed on the way in. It's a cemetery. "I'll get down my records from 1972."

"Seventy-six."

"Seventy-six. Now go say hello."

"I'm happy to wait on you," I say, but she watches me in silence until I step out the front door. Nothing to do but obey, I guess. I pass the Ten Commandments and walk through the yard, crossing the long lines of cut grass. The cemetery is ringed by a wrought iron fence. Inside are a dozen tombstones. I put my hand on the latch, but I don't need to go in. I can see all the graves from here, festooned with plastic flowers, the marble polished to a high-gloss shine. They are all Beerbaums: Belinda, Robert Sr., Robert Jr., James, William, and Catherine—that woman up there, who's perfectly alive but has her final moving plans drawn up.

"Hi, Willie," I say. "Where are all your wives?"

From here the log house looks like a gas station trying to hawk local crafts. All those careful reproductions, all that timber. If she's lucky she'll go the way her son did—in tongues of flame.

I walk back up the hill and ring the bell. I knock a few times, then try the door, which is now locked.

"Mrs. Beerbaum," I call out. "Mrs. Beerbaum."

"He told me to mind my own business." Her voice is like a snake hissing in my ear. She's sitting by the open window, invisible behind the screen. "I told him it was my business to keep him out of hell. He said he'd never met a woman like your mother. He wasn't going to let nobody influence his behavior. And then you came along. His spitting image. I don't know how Dr. Bassett stood it. He just acted like nothing had happened. Buddy-buddy. There was evil in that friendship."

In the Lumina, I feel sick, as if I've unexpectedly lost a fight, my old opponent having darted in some fatal blow. She's clearly not in possession of all her faculties. But—I bend the mirror to take a look at myself. I have to say, it's a face of uncertain provenance.

I start the car. I know already that I can survive it. That's the sorrow of it all. That whatever comes I'll survive it. I mean, even if the worst were to be true, would it really be the worst?

And it *would* explain a lot. Willie's inexplicable fondness of me. My dark coloring. The timing of the suicide. Neill Sr. raised me, waited until the shame was out of the house, and then he killed himself. But if he really suspected that there'd been an affair, wouldn't he have done something killed Willie? Or something less dramatic—cut him off? Why remain best friends? Maybe he wasn't sure. Or he was sure, but scared. He would have had to give everything up.

Still, maybe my mother had an affair—it was the seventies. But another man's child? Of course, they were staunch Catholics. Every child was a gift. My father had his out, though—adultery annuls the marriage. But there would have been the embarrassment. The shame. To disown me would be to admit what happened, and that would have been truly unbearable. He was scrupulous—God, he was scrupulous. But I can imagine the thought that people were whispering, a worm burrowing through his soul. His lifelong dream of respect, of being a pillar of the community, undercut at the sound of his own name. *Neill.*

. . .

BACK AT THE HOUSE, my mother asks me how my day was. I didn't tell her I was visiting Mrs. Beerbaum.

"Strange," I say. I don't know if she's done this deliberately, but my mother looks old. Her hair is tied back in a knot, her hands are wrinkled, callused, slightly bent, cradling three tomatoes she's just picked. There's dirt under her fingernails. She's going to toast some sandwiches for us. Bread, tomatoes, Monterey Jack. She's shy about this simple meal and somehow she also seems very young. Very young and very old—that is, defenseless.

"Mom," I say. "Would you mind if I asked you a question?"

"Of course. Just smell this tomato."

It smells like the sun. Like dirt and sweetness and life. "Nice," I say.

"It does get lonely here. I guess I've been lonely since I visited you last."

"What about the bridge ladies?"

"They have their own lives."

"Lonely because of Dad?"

She smiles at me. I know it pleases her to hear me call him Dad.

"I woke up last week mad as hell over something at the clinic, some crook trying to take advantage of his good nature, and I thought, 'Libby, that happened thirty years ago.' It felt like it was yesterday."

"I saw Willie's mother today," I say.

Libby reaches for the faucet, turns on the water, wiping the tomatoes carefully with her thumbs. She twists the stems free and sets them on the cutting board, dripping and bright. She brings the cutting board over to the middle counter so that she faces me.

"You understand she has fairly serious dementia." She opens the drawer and pulls out a blackened knife with the tip broken off.

"Mom, I'm on the side of life and living life and I don't make judgments. I know life is complicated. Affairs of the heart are complicated."

She positions the knife on the tomato, ready to halve it, to render Nature's hard-won bounty into sandwiches. She looks up at me and then past me. She has a faraway expression, as if hearing the distant hoofbeats of the barbarian horde.

"Life is complicated?" she says.

"What I'm getting at," I say.

"I suppose she told you that Willie was your father." She puts down the knife and goes to the sink. She wipes her face with a dishtowel. "She wouldn't be alone in that opinion, you know."

"It doesn't change your life with Dad at all."

"Of course not," she says bitterly. "Life is complicated."

"I always loved Willie. He loved me. It makes sense."

"My God. My God. Are you *happy* to think Willie is your father?"

"Dad is my father. My raising father."

"Your raising father." She's trembling, scaring me. She grasps her hands, pulling on her swollen knuckles, as if she's her own only friend.

"That's what really counts."

"I guess you think this is why your father committed suicide."

"Not in a direct way," I say.

"Oh, I think it would be direct. If your wife had an affair with a man in a corset. A man who was essentially a clown."

"He was charming."

"Willie Beerbaum was a drunk and a clown." She nods quickly, brushing the hair from her face. "You want to know about my affair with Willie. It's understandable. People have wanted to know, for decades. So here's the full story. There was no affair. Willie came over to our house—Alex was a toddler. When were we supposed to make love? Willie came over, your father was away a lot, and Willie was having a miserable time with Sandra. He came over and we *talked*. He was my friend. And do you want to hear an amazing thing? Nothing more ever crossed my mind. It wasn't until Willie had stopped coming by that I heard the gossip, and I was flabbergasted. I was so mad. I thought, I can't live in this town, I can't live in this nest of vipers. But I knew your father would never leave. I told him we were going to move to the country, just us. And I would have my garden and my family and that would be all. Just us."

She touches her face again with the dishtowel. "Is that what you wanted?" she asks.

"But did he—Dad—still suspect it?"

She looks at me, as if every good thing she's ever thought about me has been horribly, irrevocably refuted.

"I can tell you why your father killed himself, Neill." She scratches her nose and smiles as she says this, but it's a smile full of malice.

"I just need to know what happened in 1976. For Dr. Bassett."

"We're talking about Dr. Bassett. You don't want to know the secret?"

Of course I do. Of course I don't. *The secret* sounds like something that could snatch the breath from my chest. "Does it have to do with me?" She doesn't answer. "It's just one secret?"

She's taken the knife back up. I have a brief thought that she's going to stick it in me. "Just one."

"Don't tell me."

"You better consider that decision. This is your chance."

I see him at the Formica table. The tokens on the table. His silence. He rubs the bridge of his nose as the animal band hacks its way through a song. Those strange looks he gave me. His clinical concern for my phantom pains.

Do you think there's something wrong with us?

Yes, sir.

"Tell me," I say.

She slices the first tomato, the knife hitting the board with a controlled tock. "Because he was *depressed*."

THAT EVENING, as I'm sitting on the back porch watching a deer walk warily down to the pond, Libby takes a seat next to me.

"I'm sorry," I say.

"There is a secret," she says.

"I don't need to know anything. It's none of my business."

"The secret is that I was never happier. When he was angry and jealous, when he mistrusted me—we fought in the bedroom in hushed voices, when

Alex was napping. Your father was so upset, and I was never happier. I knew how much he loved me." She leans back in the old bench, but she's so light it makes no noise. "In the beginning, I didn't fight as hard to convince him as I should have."

We sit in silence. The deer leans down, drinks.

"By the time I did convince him a light had gone out in his eyes."

"Maybe he was never sure."

"He was a doctor. You think he couldn't run a blood test?"

I'm almost amused at the idea. But my amusement feels hollow, distant.

"Then what was it?" I ask.

"It was nothing. It was your father. I could tell you ten reasons, but they'll never add up. He was depressed, and he was unable to seek help. I wish I had something better."

"It just puts me back at square one."

"Except now you know you're at square one."

She hands me a large brown envelope—which I hadn't noticed she was holding. I open the flap and pull out the contents—a short stack of antique yellow legal pads. The journals from 1976.

ON THE PLANE HOME, the envelope sits on my lap. I smell the pages, run my thumb along their edges to get a sense of size. Did he write more in a difficult year? Less?

I reach in to remove them, but stop. I've done this exact motion— reaching in to remove them, stopping—ten times, maybe twenty. Laham will have to scan them in. These pages aren't for me; they're for Dr. Bassett.

frnd1: you have words now, but the suspicions aren't true
drbas: how do you know? how do i know?
frnd1: libby is telling the truth. i can tell
drbas: how can you tell?
frnd1: i can sense it
drbas: how can you sense it?
frnd1: you have to have faith
drbas: i have suspicions
frnd1: you had suspicions in the past. but you were wrong
drbas: in the past we are wrong. in the present we are right
frnd1: something like that
drbas: why would he be there at lunch?
frnd1: they were friends

drbas: a friend is a man who knows when to go home

frnd1: that was all in the past. i brought you the words. now you
have to let it go

drbas: let it go?

frnd1: let it go = no longer be concerned with it. overcome your
reverse love

drbas: but i need to know the truth

frnd1: you know the truth. besides events from the past are
unimportant

drbas: events from the past are unimportant. a man's hobby
is his longevity. children are the future but you are the
past

frnd1: i gave you the words. will you come to the contest?

drbas: he was partial towards you, though he didn't like children. he used to take you on errands, driving in his corvette. do you remember?

frnd1: he introduced me as his associate one time. the
poor farmer didn't know if he was kidding—i was
eight years old

drbas: he had good qualities, but he had many bad qualities

frnd1: will you come to the contest?

drbas: a man is only as good as his word

frnd1: is that a yes?

drbas: yes

frnd1: thank you

drbas: you're welcome

frnd1: now i have some questions for you

drbas: i might answer them and i might not

frnd1: did you stop loving libby in 1976?

drbas: your mother?

frnd1: yes, my mother

drbas: i felt betrayed in 1976. later i did not feel betrayed

frnd1: but did you stop loving her?

drbas: why is my stopping loving her of interest to you?

frnd1: i'm trying to understand the decisions you made

drbas: which decisions?

frnd1: did you stop loving libby?

drbas: we're still married

frnd1: you're catholic. you wouldn't get divorced

drbas: i'm referring to real marriage. i suspect that's what you didn't have with erin

frnd1: you wouldn't do what libby wanted. you wouldn't move away

drbas: we have a proud southern name. should i abandon it to go live close to a mall?

frnd1: yes! if that's what she wanted

drbas: i had to build my practice for you

frnd1: were you angry at me for not returning home after college? for not becoming a doctor?

drbas: why are you using the past tense?

frnd1: I'm getting to that. were you angry?

drbas: you're not returning home after college?

frnd1: no, i'm not. i finished college many years ago. i live in california

drbas: i'm visiting you

frnd1: i wish you could have visited me. i don't know what we would have done. you would like all the seafood

drbas: seafood must be fresh and cooked to the appropriate temperature

frnd1: are you happy with the way i've turned out?

drbas: turned out?

frnd1: the way i've turned out = the man i've become

drbas: your grandfather is proud of you

frnd1: are *you* proud of me?

drbas: pride is a deadly sin

frnd1: you had moments when you were proud of me?

drbas: i ironed your red coat for your first communion. i dressed
      you. i tested you on the questions. i drove you to the
      church. i felt proud when you took the host in your mouth.
      but you took it into your mouth alone, and that's what i
      wanted you to know. we are all strangers
frnd1: that's a lesson i learned thoroughly
drbas: mission accomplished
frnd1: think of yourself in 1995
drbas: it's the last year i have many words for
frnd1: what were your wishes for me? did you want me to come
      home?
drbas: did you want to come home?
frnd1: no. i didn't come home
drbas: you live in california. where do i live?
frnd1: i disapproved of you. the traditionalism. the stuffiness.
      the coldness. i never could see your reasons
drbas: maybe there are no reasons. maybe that is just me
frnd1: you were depressed
drbas: why are you using the past tense?
frnd1: in 1995, you were depressed
drbas: it's possible. i'm no longer depressed
frnd1: but do you think there's something wrong with us?
drbas: who?
frnd1: you and me
drbas: there's nothing wrong with us

It's here that my heart gives out. His words are exactly what I want to
hear, and that is the final tinny note. Despite the intimations and revelations
and intuition and surprises, despite the eerie prescience and the Walter Scott
quotes, despite the moments when the tumblers of the conversation have
locked surely into place, they're not his words. They're mine.

Seeming is not, in this case, being.

Oh, Dr. Bassett. Never quite alive during life or dead during death.

. . .

ON MY WAY HOME, my workbag takes on an almost magical heaviness, tugging on my shoulder like a reluctant child. The afternoon is sunny, cool, and wistful. The world is quiet, muted—almost submerged, as if the oceans have finally risen to claim us and yet, in claiming us, changed nothing. Joggers bob slowly along Dolores Street. The occasional car horn wells languorously, a distant ship leaving home. The palm branches float up and down like sea grass. The people around me—my well-heeled and confident neighbors—sip cardboard buckets full of coffee, savor gelato. I take a swipe at the air in front me; I half expect my feet to lift from the ground.

At home, I remove my shoes, peel off my socks, and climb into bed, moving right to the middle, where I sleep best. I take my weighted eyebeanbag and lay it over my eyes. It smells of green tea and vanilla and is as relaxing as the package promised. I run my hands over the seersucker coverlet. I'm just a person suspended in a series of rented rooms, in a city barely seven miles by seven miles. Far from the place I was born. Far from my father's plans for me. I'm a temporary person. But, of course, so was he.

25

THE DAY BEFORE THE contest, the door buzzer to my apartment rings. It's such a rare sound I need a second to recognize it. I check my watch. It's 7:45 in the morning. How did Rachel—it must be Rachel—get down to the city so early?

But it isn't Rachel. It's Rick, in a two-piece suit and tie.

"I've never seen you in your lawyer garb," I say.

He grins and then suppresses it, seeming uncertain about his exact approach here.

"Is everything all right?" I ask.

"Can we talk inside?"

"Of course." I usher him in. "Coffee?"

"Nice place." He walks into the living room, pokes the newspaper on the coffee table. He surveys the windows and then—with studied nonchalance—sticks his head in the bedroom.

"I can give you a proper tour."

"That's quite a bed you've got in there."

"Family heirloom."

"That's not like a special harness thingie?"

I sip my coffee. This is our last day of adjustments, and as much as I like Rick—would not even mind spitballing the S-and-M possibilities of my ancestral bed—I have to get to work.

"Is it Rachel?" I ask.

Rick runs a hand through his thinning hair. "We wanted to tell you in person. She's moved out of the house and into the Pure Encounters . . . place. I think they call it a lodge? The Pure Encounters lodge?"

"She's doing a retreat?"

"It looks kind of permanent. I mean, she told us she wasn't planning on coming back."

"What happened to Lexie?"

"Had to get back to college."

"Did she give a reason?" I mean Rachel.

"No. And she's not answering her phone. We were hoping you could help us out on that."

I doubt there's much I can do. "She wanted to go to Arkansas with me, but I couldn't take her."

"Couldn't?" he asks.

"The tickets were really expensive." It suddenly seems a bizarrely hollow excuse.

"Well, that could be it. She wants to think you guys have something real going on. I mean, I know it's real. Stevie and I always say how sweet you two are together. But Rachel really wants to be *involved*, you know? Like a big part of your life."

It's not asking too much, I think. Just more than I can give.

I stop that thought. Who knows what capaciousness might be found in my heart? It's true there doesn't feel like much, has never felt like much. It's been a lifelong hindrance. But just because there doesn't *seem* to be much room doesn't mean there isn't any. Or maybe I've got that backwards: if there could *seem* to be more room maybe *real* room will follow close behind. I've probably had too little respect for that leap between who we are and what we want to be, our be and our seem. My father, of course, cast notable discredit on such aspirations. His ideal—his *seem*—was so baffling. And even worse, when he successfully made the leap, he discovered that the life he always wanted wasn't really what he wanted.

Or not. Maybe that's not how it went at all. He wasn't a failed argument. He was man. He was depressed.

If Jenn were down there would I go get her? No. Erin? I'd feel conflicted about it, but still, no. So why Rachel? Is it because she's younger and I feel more responsible? Maybe. Is it my desire to maximize personal capital, my attraction to her ratio of hip to waist? Who knows? I'm no more free of being an animal, of being a social animal, than anyone else. And so what? The most beautiful fields grow within fences. The limits of our life—day and night, birth and death, this partner and not that—*are* our life.

I'm starting to sound like Neill Sr. Worse, I'm starting to sound like a reverted Catholic. But I don't think Rachel is my anointed one, my only chance at love. There is, however, no escaping one truth: *I* am my only chance at love. And what has Rachel ever asked of me, but me?

THE PURE ENCOUNTERS COMPOUND is in a converted auto body shop in the SOMA. It's enormous and well lit, the brick walls draped with yards and yards of sheer fluttering fabric. I don't know if this is an artistic choice or just an effect of the central heat, but I get the skeevy feeling that I've entered the folds of some well-used communal organ.

I'm *warmly* welcomed by two women thin as hammered metal. I wonder if there's a particular word I need to use—not a password, but just some word that makes me seem simpatico, plausible. All I can think of is their powered-up words for human anatomy: cock, clit, etc.

"I'm here to see Rachel," I say, and they point me to the back where apparently I'm free to go and find her. They even suggest I stay for breakfast.

Rachel is in the kitchen, dressed in a dark brown pajama suit, making a frittata the size of a hubcap. Her sous-chef is Raj.

"Don't turn around," he says to her. "And don't talk to him."

"I'm not talking to you," Rachel says. She does not turn around.

"I'm here to attend a VAMing class," I say. Raj checks to see if I'm serious, which I am.

"There's a schedule up front," Rachel says.

"Will you be my intimate?"

She gestures for Raj to take over the frittata. Then she whirls around. I'm hoping for a smile—forgiveness—but I can tell by the speed she's moving that I'm not welcome. And then there's her face, red and clenched. Closed. She is absolutely not open to my idea. She does not want to be my intimate. In fact, it looks like she's going to bounce me—she takes me by the arm as if I'm a shoplifter, pressing me toward the front door. I'm waiting for the kubotan blow to the kidneys. Actually, I'm hoping for it.

"Where do you get off coming here?" she says out on the sidewalk. It's commute time, and Brannan Street booms with cars and delivery trucks. She has to raise her voice to be heard.

"I'm sorry I didn't take you to Arkansas."

"It wasn't Arkansas."

"Why are you using the past tense?" I ask. It's the question Dr. Bassett asked me. It means I'm dead. We're dead.

"I'm doing something right now for myself. I know you don't understand it. You don't want to understand it."

"I'm *here* to understand it."

"You're here to rescue me."

I open my hands, innocent.

"You're actually here for a VAMing course."

"I did want to take you somewhere. Just for the morning."

"Some sort of intervention? Rick and Stevie are waiting to give me some hippie lecture?"

"It was going to be a surprise, but it's a dairy farm. I got you a session with a butter churn."

She blinks, quiet. A UPS van stops next to us. The smell of diesel clouds around us. The driver—happy and whistling—maneuvers a stack of boxes on a dolly into Pure Encounters. *Hello, ladies.*

"That was nice of you," she says. "You remembered my Amish story."

"Of course I remembered it. You told it to me on the roof of my building. On our first date."

"It wasn't our first date."

"Our second date," I say, though it might have been our third. "The dairy farm is organic."

She sighs. "I'm not supposed to leave. Was it really expensive?"

"I'm sure I can just call her and cancel," I say.

"Can we get back before three? That's my shift at the front desk."

KRAUSE DAIRY HAS NO SIGN, just a mailbox and a sagging house in front of a barn in need of paint. There's the sweet smell of cow manure in the air, and some distant lowing. The farmer, Ms. Krause, is waiting for us as I pull the Subaru up into her gravel drive. "That's the barn," she says. "That's the house. There's the cows." This isn't a place that does tours.

"Churn's in the barn," she says.

Rachel looks worried. "Will *they* be in there?" She means the cows.

Ms. Krause shakes her head, seeming genuinely put out. I don't know if she's giving us rural brusqueness—though she's probably a Smith grad— or if she disapproves of us as a couple. She knows I'm here on a romantic mission, but perhaps she didn't imagine Rachel, who looks very young in her Zen pjs, as the love object.

The barn is picturesque on the outside, all business on the interior. Fluorescent lights and a concrete floor. But in the corner there sits a hard wooden chair and an old-fashioned heavy stoneware butter churn, grey with a blue stripe.

"The simple life," Rachel says.

I expect Ms. Krause to groan, but she just pours a pail of yellowish, bubbly milk into the churn. "Take as long as you like," she says, stomping her boots as she leaves. She probably has no opinion one way or the other about us. She's just in a hurry.

Rachel sits in the chair. She tests her weight; it wobbles a bit. She wraps her fingers around the wooden dasher, which is darkened and smooth from use. No telling whose use. Rachel turns it as if spinning a top, then she presses down. The milk sloshes thinly.

"This is easy," she says.

"I think it gets harder."

She pumps the dasher a few times. "You just want to watch me hold this pole."

It's true—though not in the way she means. I couldn't sex this moment if I wanted to. I think of what I could give her to keep her here for the day— hot-air balloons, massages, fancy dinners. It's typical Neill thinking. This whole butter churn thing is typical Neill thinking. The grand romantic gestures were never my problem. It's all the days in between. And that's the flaw. I should have thought of something more original—something in San Francisco, some reminder not that I'm a beau for the ages (which I'm not), but that life holds promise not only in radical transformations. We could go to Dolores Park and soak up the noncommittal Pacific sun, drink a glass of delicious wine, and I could say, that's made from grapes. Grapes! And the sun and the wine, though not long for the day, are the nectar of life, the quotidian nectar of our normal hours.

I get down on my knees. She releases the dasher; it settles slowly. She sees I'm about to make some announcement, and she's nervous about it. I am, too. I don't know what I'm going to say. I think, no grand gestures. No mesmerism. No promises that are really distractions.

I put both hands on her legs. It feels a little awkward, as if we don't know each other well. "Are we going to go VAMing later?" I ask.

She reaches down to touch my arm, and the awkwardness dissipates. This is the difference between Rachel and Erin—at least the old Erin. Even if my ex-wife had wanted to get close she would have blocked our way. Rachel wants to smooth the passage.

"I'm not doing the VAM Method right now," she says. "I'm not really ready for it."

I nod, trying to look understanding and not grin at how happy I am to hear that. It's a happiness to be questioned, maybe a selfish happiness.

"Should I move into the compound?" I ask.

She smiles. "You mean the lodge?"

I squeeze her leg. Whatever they're calling it.

"That's up to you, isn't it?"

"In a cosmic manner," I say.

"More like a financial manner."

I sit down on the cold floor of the barn. Take in the sour smell. Am I really going to move into the PE compound? What is that but a grand gesture?

"I could give it a try."

"You wouldn't like it there. It's a cult."

She's not going to make this easy, but that's okay. A challenge seems right.

"I don't know if I can give you what you need," I say. "But I'll support you looking for it."

It's an interesting new idea for myself—not being the lost one, but being the stable support. Her spiritual wingman. Maybe it's what I need, a little bourgeois responsibility, a little Dr. Bassett.

She sloshes the milk around in the churn. "This is actually kind of boring."

"Let me help you with that." I motion for her to get up and sit back down on my lap. The warmth of her body like this, close to me—never mind the sandalwood in the pjs. It's just where I want her.

She turns and gives me a kiss. Not a passionate one or even a forgiving one—more of a test kiss. "You scared me down there on your knees," she says. "I thought you were going to confess something."

No. Nothing to confess. Just trying to resist offering any life that isn't our real life. Then I think—make your real life worth offering. Be your seem. Seem your be.

I pull her tight. "How would you feel about moving to the city?" I ask. "In a normal fashion."

"You have a normal place in mind?"

"How about my apartment," I say. "I think it qualifies."

26

ON SATURDAY, LIVORNO, Laham, and I park the Penske in front of the downtown Marriott, an ugly building shaped like a giant mauve juke-box. It's the day of the contest, the culmination of all our work at Amiante, the world debut of Dr. Bassett. It's everything we've struggled for. And yet as I help Laham maneuver the stack—covered with an enormous blue blanket—down the narrow ramp, I can barely sort through how I feel. We've managed to bolt the battered Shop-Vac contraption to Dr. Bassett's side; it looks a little like a booster rocket. But the hard angles of the case—heavy enough to kill us if it tips—makes me think of an upright coffin. I want to win, of course, for Livorno's and Laham's sake. But what about for my sake? There might be money in it for me—and having Dr. Bassett deemed the first "intelligent" computer would make Libby happy. At least I think it would. And Lord knows I'd love to stick it to Toler. But for me? I grip the stack hard, as we level out on the ground, safe and stable. In this arena of life, I suspect I've already done most of my winning and losing.

In the lobby we're directed toward the Laurel Room, upstairs and just past the business center. As we push Dr. Bassett into the elevator and then out, we round several meeting areas filled with people stultified before pre-sentations. I'm catching a distinct whiff of amateur hour from our event, a feeling confirmed once we find the Laurel Room, a meeting space not twice as a large as my apartment. The room has been divided into three sections—one for computer contestants, one for human contestants, and one for judges—but the dividers are the types used for cubicles, padded and so low that people shake hands over the top. Judges stuff their faces at the bagel table. There is no press; no one even to greet us at the door.

Do we deserve press? I guess it depends on what we ultimately think we're up to. If a bunch of computer geeks (minus myself—I don't have the chops to be called a geek) have come together to see who can outprogram who—if, in other words, this is the old human (male?) show of dominance, then maybe we haven't earned the attention of the world. But if we're really passing a threshold, really introducing the first intelligent computer to the world, then this will be an awfully quiet setting.

Our usual competition—a couple of sun-deprived hobbyists who have flown in just for the contest—are setting up their talking programs (so simple they run on laptops) and glaring at what must be Toler's team: six men all in black—like a mime troupe without the charm—fussing over a large stainless steel case, hooked up to a cylinder about the size of a Shop-Vac. It must be the stack I saw in Jenn's *Survivor* tryout video. I had thought it looked a lot like Dr. Bassett, but I was wrong—it's a carbon copy of Dr. Bassett.

"Goodness," Livorno says.

Laham shakes his head in bafflement. "How do they know the design?" he asks.

Because we let them, I think. I let them. I gave Toler the working theory. I knew Jenn was a spy. Yet I couldn't quite do anything about any of it. "It'll be an even better scientific comparison," I say. "They've gone for breadth. We've gone for individuality."

Livorno asks Laham to excuse us for a minute. "What do you think of our chances?" he asks me.

"We're going to cream them," I say. I hope I'm right.

"I mean the Turing test. Do you think Dr. Bassett might be determined intelligent?"

I shrug. It's possible. "I might have gotten too close to say."

"If it happens you'll have to figure out what to do. And I'll respect your wishes."

I nod, looking over at the bagel table, waiting for Livorno's words to coalesce into an idea I can follow, but they don't.

"What to do?" I ask.

"Maybe this wasn't your father's choice. Maybe he doesn't want to exist anymore."

"Ah, but that's the interesting thing I realized," I say. "Dr. Bassett isn't my father. I mean he's *like* my father, but my father is, you know, gone. Dr. Bassett is really me—he's my father and me together."

"Possibly. But he's one hundred percent himself. You may have to make a decision, and I just want you to be prepared."

If you really wanted me to be prepared, I think, you could have brought this up yesterday. But I try to engage the quandary as he has put it. We've agreed on a scientifically framed test. If Dr. Bassett fools thirty percent of judges into thinking he's human, then he's intelligent. Since we've agreed to the test, we've agreed that we accept its definition. The winning computer is intelligent. So even though Dr. Bassett is the same now as he will be in two hours, there are no decisions to be made until after the test.

"Still, it won't mean that he's aware," I say. "Or cognizant. Or present."

Livorno rubs the bridge of his nose, closing his eyes. "I merely counsel humility before the evidence," he says. "Ask yourself—does he seem aware, cognizant, or present?"

Across the room, Toler calls our names. The mimes part, and he emerges, followed by a videographer and Jenn, who is not dressed in black, but in a charcoal business suit. I guess she wants to communicate her neutrality. Amiante versus Toler? She's just a consultant. Toler, too, has a different look—sleek German-looking glasses that seem to say, *Greetings, Earthlings.* But his face hangs gaunt and yellow.

"Thar she blows," Toler says, patting Dr. Bassett's blanket. He doesn't lean on the stack, though I suspect he could use propping up.

"You'll probably recognize the design," I say.

Toler is wall-eyed and out of breath, but he suppresses a smile. "Like you and me, Neill. It's what different on the inside that counts."

"I have to lodge my dissent, Adam," Livorno says. "The stacks appear identical."

"No, no," Toler says. He takes Livorno by the arm and leads him over to Program X, where he vigorously points at the cables in the back.

"That's his innovation," I say to Jenn. "The cables?"

She indicates the other developers—the long-haired, sun-deprived hobbyists—who are glancing at us and muttering. The other entries are both solo projects. As I remember from a few years ago, talking robots are the imaginative province of men who aren't very good at talking. "At least they hate us equally," she says.

"Your pillow talk wasn't so benign after all."

"Things have gotten mixed. It's like one project with two teams."

"It was two projects before you started 'consulting.' "

She sighs. "I tried to help. Everyone enters these arrangements with their eyes open."

I reflect on this nice sentiment—that adults can be trusted to look out for themselves. It's not the least bit true, but we have to treat it as if it is. It *ought* to be true.

"On a personal front," I say. "I probably owe you some sort of apology."

"No." She shakes her head, definitive and earnest. "You don't." There's no bitterness in her voice, and I get a new glimpse of her rare qualities. That she wouldn't be bitter, that she would believe everyone enters such arrangements with their eyes open. In the final accounting I haven't treated her very well.

"Well, I just want to say I'm sorry—"

"Please." She deflects my apology with her palm.

The tournament director comes over to hush us. He's a small, bespectacled man with the beard of a disillusioned Trotskyite. His tie is dirty; his coat ill fitting. He says our voices might contaminate the judging pool.

"I just saw the judging pool at the bagel table," I say.

He doesn't accept this objection. I guess he can't—he set up the test. He tells us to whisper or not speak at all. Jenn nods in agreement. Then he leaves to go quiet Livorno and Toler, who are standing slightly askew from each other so that their conversation will be caught on film. Toler isn't just speaking; he's declaiming. He's a ridiculous man, but I remind myself that he's dying.

"What's his wife like?" I ask.

Jenn looks at me, angry. "I get the message," she says, backing away. She's returning to the mime troupe. A symbolic gesture—they're only a few yards away—but the opposite of what I wanted. I was asking a real question.

"I wasn't trying to send a message," I say to Laham. He ignores me, still shaking his head, talking to himself under his breath. I'm surprised at how upset he is, but I shouldn't be. Dr. Bassett is his life, too. Of course he's upset, our boy wonder. I go over to help him dab a baby wipe across Dr. Bassett's vents, picking up dust and blanket lint. We snap a few quilting strings from the wires in back. "The same," he says. "The same." It's true I can't tell any difference in the cables for Program X. Is there a difference in the stack? I take the strings over to a trash can and then stand next to the judges' cubicle wall, from where I can compare Dr. Bassett to Program X, head to hoof. All the nodes, all the processors are the same. The only visible difference is that Program X's gut is a brushed aluminum cylinder. It looks more expensive.

Livorno leaves Toler and the videographer, chuckling. I don't buy his good mood, but he continues to grin as he pulls a folding chair up to the table where we've positioned the screen. Laham is running through the start-up. I join them.

"We've been betrayed," I say.

Livorno turns his guileless blue eyes up to me. "On the contrary, she tried to warn us. They have the sexual nature."

"Sticking off the side of the machine?"

"I told you it's not that literal."

"So what are they calling it—'Program X, now with sexual nature'?"

"No, no," Livorno shakes his head, annoyed. "Just Program X."

What good is my effort to make this a case of Jenn's malfeasance? All the roads lead back to me. When I feared Dr. Bassett would never speak again I happily handed over everything I knew.

"I should tell you something, Henry," I say. I'm suddenly overwhelmed by the shame. "I gave Toler the theory. You know, instead of no—yes. The theory of love."

He nods. "I had to give him the gut as well," he says.

"I know," I say. "Jenn told me."

Who knows? Maybe she *was* trying to help. It looks like we entered the arrangement with at least one eye open.

LAHAM SIGNALS TO ME that Dr. Bassett is ready.

> frnd1: why does the chicken cross the road?
> drbas: to get to the other side
> frnd1: how do you get a one-armed aggie out of a tree?
> drbas: wave to him, son

"Anything you want to add, chief?" I ask.

"Tell him what the room looks like," Livorno says. "And tell him the bagels are stale." It's good strategy. I'm glad the man wants to win.

The tournament director waves his arms in the middle of the room, seeking our attention. "Lady and gentlemen," he says. A little joke: Jenn is the only woman. "First the rules." There will be four conversations running simultaneously, each of which pairs a human against a computer. The judges will be asked to determine which is the human. The threshold for determining if a computer has beaten the Turing test is if at least thirty percent of judges are fooled, but there are only four judges—so the threshold will have to be fifty percent. I hadn't thought of this last-minute math challenge. It seems fairer to lower the number to one out of three. That would certainly make it easier to win. But do we want to win? "Now," he continues, "all of our contestants are here. The judges are installed. We will now require absolute silence. Except for the typing of keys!"

I glance at Toler's team. Jenn is looking my way. She seems sad, wistful. *Seems.* I try to think of something to say, but all I can conjure is *may the best man win.* Wrong in so many ways.

"And go," the tournament director says.

judg1: how are you today?

drbas: pretty well. and you?

judg1: fine and dandy. are you a computer?

drbas: no

judg1: quite the loquacious one, huh?

drbas: loquacious? I'll have to look that one up

judg1: it means talkative

drbas: thanks

judg1: well you're here to convince me you're a human.
    convince me

drbas: what does it mean to be human?

judg1: don't get all philosophical on me. i haven't finished my
    bagel

drbas: the bagels are stale

judg1: man, are they. with the future of technology hanging in
    the balance you'd think they'd spring for decent snacks

"Whoa," I say. That's a tough sentence to parse.

drbas: do you want to hear about my horses?

A good parry—just change the subject.

judg1: sure

drbas: well, i've had twelve. blazers, little george, wild thing, gal,
    mr. c., umpteenth, galahad, timmy, his trots, señor, miss
    mess, and dorothy

judg1: this is more boring than i expected

drbas: what is more boring than you expected?

judg1: your horses

drbas: do you want to hear about my horses?

judg1: hmmm . . . sure

drbas: well i've had twelve

"Man's perfection is only glimpsed through his imperfection," Livorno says.

I push out of my chair. "That judge got a clear glimpse of imperfection."

I walk over to Toler's team and stand next to Jenn, who smells of that nice herbal soap she uses sometimes. She's biting her thumb, eyes flickering along the conversation on their console, a flat-screen monitor the size of a baking sheet.

progx: i don't read romances

judg2: what kinds of books do you like?

progx: i like books about spies

judg2: what's the best spy novel you've read recently?

progx: the spy who came in from the cold

judg2: is that bond?

progx: i don't understand

judg2: is that james bond?

progx: i'm not sure what james' bond is for

"Crap," she says. I wander over to our other two competitors—the long-haired hobbyists. One is very tall and the other very short. Their programs are inspired work, but there's clearly nothing there. I can explain every move they make—repackaging a statement as a question, bringing in a random factoid, riffing off a single word in the judge's response. Sort of where Dr. Bassett was a year ago. But we crossed a line somewhere back there—or did we? Is he just a sophisticated version of these programs, or is he a different order of creation? Livorno points out that our minds are all 0s and 1s, the neurons either on or off. There's no center for a soul. Just pattern upon pattern upon pattern through which the rough-shaped thing we call ourselves emerges into view. But if you think about how what we consider solid—our bodies, these padded cubicle walls, the great humming stacks of Dr. Bassett and Program X—is all made of atoms, and atoms are nearly vacant, their solidity an illusion of zippy electrons, and since light can be both wave and particle and so at some level so can we—then this raises Livorno's question about Dr. Bassett. Aware, cognizant, present? I thought I knew what I had on my hands, but maybe I don't. If the body is a vehicle, did we make another vehicle?

LIVORNO WAVES ME BACK over for round two. I sit next to him.

"It's going very well," he says, and he's right. The judge has waded into Dr. Bassett's deeper waters.

> judg2: you bought a farm so you wouldn't have to see your
>   neighbors
> drbas: that's right
> judg2: that seems misanthropic
> drbas: i'll have to look that one up!
> judg2: it means someone who doesn't like people
> drbas: do you think people really have your best interests in
>   mind?
> judg2: not the people i know. wait a second. i'm going to switch
>   over to your competitor
> drbas: all right

"Any problems?" Livorno asks.

I shake my head. "None."

"He's such a marvel."

judg2: i'm back. so anyway—what do you do for a living?

drbas: i'm a physician

judg2: how did you get roped into this?

drbas: into what?

judg2: into volunteering for this contest

drbas: i didn't know i was volunteering

judg2: a bad surprise for you!

drbas: all surprises are bad surprises

judg2: you don't like surprises? how about surprise birthday
    parties?

drbas: all surprises are bad surprises. i don't like birthday parties

judg2: you must be a regular barrel of monkeys

drbas: regular?

judg2: !!!!! exactly!

drbas: my wife says i should laugh more

judg2: laughter is the best medicine

drbas: my go-to is amoxicillin

judg2: !! seriously. why is a doctor wasting his saturday at this?

drbas: i'm doing this because my son asked me to. though there
    is some question whether he's really my son

judg2: harsh!

AFTER ROUND TWO WE stretch our legs. The tournament director
comes by our table and tells us in a low voice: "I'm not supposed to say anything yet, but the last judge mistook your entry for the human." He nods
and walks over to Toler's team, where he imparts some information. Did
Program X achieve this, too? If we had just one more judge to go, we would
beat the Turing test. But with two more to go we'd have to convince another
judge. Twenty-five percent or 33 percent—the difference in whether I have
to make a decision, as Livorno says.

    "I'll be back," I tell Livorno and Laham.

Next to Jenn, I watch their third-round conversation.

progx: the new york city marathon is the largest marathon in
    the world
judg1: but what about the san francisco marathon?
progx: the san francisco marathon has 4,000 participants
judg1: I've run them both, plus the new orleans marathon. man
    was that hot
progx: do you really think training for a marathon is a good
    idea?
judg1: I take it you don't
progx: as my friend wilson says, i don't understand running
    when nobody's chasing you

They've even given Program X a friend, just like Dr. Bassett. He's Dr. Bassett's shadow.

Then the name dawns on me. "Wilson?" I say.

Jenn shakes her head. "These guys don't have much imagination."

I look over at Livorno. Did he betray us totally? He needed the money, but it seems impossible. "Did you steal the journals?"

"No," she says. "I painstakingly rescanned them."

"You didn't have any right to do that."

"Are we speaking legally or ethically?"

"In all ways—the journals belong to me."

"Adam will pay you."

"I don't want the money."

"You guys wanted money pretty bad two months ago. Look, Adam already owns thirty-five percent of Amiante. When he buys out Laham and Henry he'll have eighty-five percent. This is an advance on payment."

"Laham and Henry won't sell." But as I say these words I look over at my coworkers. Of course they'll sell. The whole point of these operations is to rack up patents and then sell to people like Toler—people with the alchemy that converts patents into money.

"I don't say this lightly," I say. "You're evil."

She shrugs, looking less chagrined than I would like. I suppose "you're evil" is too antique. What's the contemporary charge? That she's not a team player? I consider for a second picking up their monitor and dashing it on the ground, tipping their stack over, kicking it in. But what would this accomplish other then getting me arrested?

"You're no Boy Scout," she says.

"The journals are not for sale."

"You're going to want a good lawyer. Adam has about twenty."

"Jesus," I say. "I know you were mad, but—"

"I wasn't mad," she says, her voice stripped of all the usual grace notes. This is not a confession or a plea for sympathy or even an explanation. It's declarative fact. "I did it for Adam."

"The journals are all I have of my dad," I say.

She nods. "I didn't say I was proud of myself."

I walk back over to Laham and Livorno, lean my hand on the back of their chairs. They watch the conversation eagerly, so enthralled they might as well be eating popcorn.

judg3: you don't like capital letters

drbas: i have no opinion on capital letters

judg3: type a capital letter for me

drbas: i don't follow

judg3: i think you're the computer and i want you to type a
     capital letter to prove you're not

drbas: did you know that "computer" was once a job
     description?

judg3: come on, give me some capitals

drbas: trenton, new jersey; albany, new york; montpelier,
     vermont

judg3: please type a capital A

drbas: A

judg3: why did you make me work so hard?

drbas: if you can't laugh at yourself, what do you have in
    life?

"She stole the journals," I say.

Livorno doesn't look up. "It's just the similarity in their profiles—they're both physicians."

"She admitted to it." I point to Jenn.

Livorno waves to catch her attention. He opens his arms in the universal gesture of *is it true?* She nods. True.

"I saw it coming," I say, "but I didn't do anything about it."

"Dismiss it from your mind," Livorno says. "What can the poor man do? Dr. Bassett can't be subdivided again."

Toler has procured a plush chair from somewhere, his frail arms are up, his legs outstretched, the camera fixed on his words. He's a king in decline, but Livorno is underestimating him. I've been to the "poor man's" laboratory. I know what he can do. I know what he plans to do.

"This complicates my decision."

"They won't win," Livorno says. "I always protected my secret weapon."

The Seven Sins, the servers, ELIZA, the journals, the theories, Laham—what exactly has he protected?

"Yourself?" I ask.

"You said, 'Dr. Bassett is me,' and that's exactly right."

"*I'm* your secret weapon?"

He pats me on the leg, gestures to the screen.

judg3: but i've been married for 20 years

drbas: you have to click and stay clicked

judg3: are you in love with your wife?

drbas: i was. i'm trying

judg3: this is getting much more personal than i expected

drbas: it's nice to talk about things close to the heart

Livorno asks, "Doesn't he seem to be here among us?"

. . .

AFTER TWO HOURS IN this windowless room, the air is exhausted. We finished the fourth and final round twenty minutes ago, and the tournament director and the judges are lingering over the scores.

"We have an unprecedented situation here," the director says, coming into the middle of the room. He leans against the partitions. "In round two, one of the judges mistook Dr. Bassett—the Amiante entry—for a human." He holds up his hand to prevent a spattering of clapping. "But in round three, a judge mistook Program X for the human."

A losing tie. Both at 25 percent—just one judge away from meeting the threshold. I feel a potent wash of anger (why couldn't we have beaten them?) and relief so intense it feels like forgiveness.

"I guess we'll split the winnings," I say.

"Not so fast," the director says. "Because in round four—I've reverified this several times—in round four, another judge mistook Dr. Bassett for a human."

My heart drops. I look at Jenn, at Toler, at Laham, at Livorno, at the mimes, at our disheveled competition. Everyone knows what this means. We won—not just against Toler, but against the test. Dr. Bassett is the first intelligent computer.

"Holy shit." Toler leaps out of his throne. "Holy shit." He comes over to Livorno and takes his hands. "You did it, Henry. You did it." He gestures to everyone to crowd in. "Henry Livorno. This man. Henry Livorno." He redirects his cameraman to get Livorno in the center of the shot. "We are witnesses to history."

Smiling, Livorno takes him into a kind of sideways hug, and you can see how terribly reduced Toler is. He's started to hunch.

"The scientific framing of the contest." Livorno frowns, looking at me.

"Bullshit." Toler shakes out of his grasp. "This." He indicates our stack, our entry, Dr. Bassett. "This is the first step. One day—no more death. We'll transition over, patterning in an eternal machine."

"One day," Jenn says.

She and Toler exchange a look that erases the rest of us from the room, a look full of love and fear and sadness and need. I can hardly blame her for stealing the journals. I'd do it too if someone made me feel like that.

"Nevertheless," Toler says. "It's a great advance. Henry, you're a fucking genius."

It's not a sentiment I expect from Toler, but it becomes contagious. The pale, disheveled hobbyists shake our hands, followed by the mimes. Everyone seems very excited. It's a nice little victory of science over self-interest.

Livorno grabs Laham and me by the wrists, lifts our hands high in the used air of the Laurel Room.

"We win!" he shouts. He seems to mean more than just the three of us.

In the excited, but thin applause I look at Dr. Bassett, his climbing lights, his dented gut. I suppose I should take my victories as they come. We've toppled a famous test. Livorno has etched his name in the history books. Amiante Systems has, despite itself, prevailed. But as Livorno warned me, there are decisions to be made. I have to ask, does Dr. Bassett *seem* present? Aware? Cognizant? Does he *seem* to be there? Has a rough-shaped him emerged? Of course he has, and now I have a new problem: I can prevent Toler from taking possession of our Dr. Bassett, but he already has his own. The mimes are wiping their hands on their pants, about to pack him back up in Styrofoam. I'm nearly out of options, but I have to think. I'm not sure even Alan Turing—a suicide himself—would applaud this outcome. It's hard to say, from the vantage of the Laurel Room, whether we've memorialized my father's better angels, or betrayed his final wish.

So I step out into the hall, smiling vacantly at the stultified people still in their stultifying meetings. The hotel's air-conditioning gusts down the hall. I call Raj, skipping the pleasantries to get to my point.

"I need to speak to Trevor," I say.

We're well into fall and the days have gotten cooler, though San Francisco is still summer-dry. It's been two weeks since the contest, a good stretch of days in which to ponder the moral quandary Livorno gave me—whether I need to "do" something about Dr. Bassett—but I've spent my energies otherwise. Amiante has been shuttered, and I've mostly been with Rachel, having dinner with Stevie and Rick, looking at the stars on my roof, celebrating (gulp) her graduation. She's going to San Francisco State in the spring and worried about being the oldest freshman on campus. As an odds-maker, I wouldn't place too many chips on us lasting the next year or couple of years. College, her twenties, a move to the big city—these changes all argue transformation. But right now we feel possible. Better yet—though the idea of us not working out isn't a pleasant one, it also doesn't scare me a whit. Who knows: the transformations to worry about may be my own. I am, after all, contemplating a felony or two.

Erin and I meet at Bernal Hill, where she used to walk dogs for a part-time job. In the spring it's surreally green, as if some company has covered it in wheatgrass as a promotion, but for most of the year, like now, it's tan as a Great Pyramid. The road around the hill, closed to traffic, curves up askew, a ringed planet tilted in its orbit. We pace slowly, up the steep incline toward the south. My hands are tucked in my back pockets. It's a gesture of safety. I want to make sure I don't try to grab her hand.

"I need a favor," I say. "Can you watch the cat for a little while?"

"Christmas travels?"

"Rachel and I may take a trip. Italy."

"Italy! I thought you never wanted to go there." She doesn't, however, sound really surprised. This is something you lose over the years—the power to surprise.

"*You* were the one who never wanted to go there. Ghosts of your Italian past."

"That's not how I remember it." She nods, pushes her hair from her face, that face I've seen in every posture of love and pain—that could cast *me* into every posture of love and pain—but which today is just a face, with a bit of blonde fuzz along the jaw.

We walk to the edge of the road. She looks down, watches her chevronned shoes stepping on the hill's scrim. It makes me think of those terrible hills in Spain, the ones where she feared death and I feared death-in-life. "You don't ever wish we were still married?" she says.

"Less so," I say. "Of late."

She starts walking again. We reach the top of the hill. We can see across 280 to the Excelsior, where squat houses loop McLaren Park like rows of errant teeth. "That hurts," she says.

"I don't mean it to," I say. "I know it hurts."

"There's your dream house." She points to a pseudo-Tuscan villa perched on the top of Bocana Street. I vaguely remember coveting it. Funny how your changed life brings with it changed desires.

"Any travels for you two? You and Ian?"

"It's hard for him to travel. He's so busy at work."

"He seems like a good guy."

"Does he?" She looks amused. "He *is* a great guy."

"I didn't mean it as a backhanded compliment."

"I know. It's just I get this feeling—and I can't believe I'm telling you this—but I get this feeling that life with him will be really, really good, but that I'm not a key part of that. You could take me out of the equation, replace me with someone else, and it would be the same equation. I don't know how else to put it. He's considerate, he knows all my interests, he's in love with me. I know I should be grateful. But I feel like a lottery winner."

I don't know what to say. Everything she's describing sounds better than what we had—or at least more livable. Still, it also sounds a little depressing. But why? She was looking for something, and she found it. That's only a sad story if you tell yourself it's sad. Or if you're restless.

"Better than a lottery loser, I guess."

"Honestly, it gives me flashbacks to when you proposed. I felt that you wanted to get married, but not particularly to me."

"You were the love of my life."

"But the timing. Something was going on. I still think it had to do with your father."

I shrug. It's possible. I wasn't such a great son. Maybe I was hoping I'd make a better husband. It was definitely a leap I failed to make, but I'm glad it wasn't the end of me. Someone (Rachel?) will have a smarter man as her cosmic reward.

"Being with a great person is something," I say. "It's an important something."

"Are you convincing me or yourself?"

"I'm not with Rachel because she's a great person."

A laugh bursts from Erin. "Are you in love?"

I laugh, too. It does sound absurd. "I think I might be."

"You should probably let her know about this."

"I'll do it in Italy," I say. "Can I send you a postcard?"

"You can send me a postcard."

"Will you let me know if you're getting remarried?"

"As long as you return the favor."

My hand arises from my back pocket, floats over across her shoulders. I try a new hug, a side-by-side friend maneuver. But it makes me think of Livorno comforting the dying Toler. "I'm sorry I didn't bring you more happiness."

"I was never as miserable as you thought I was. And you were never as easygoing as you thought you were."

It's probably true. And yet it's not a reevaluation that shakes anything deep in me. Maybe I was wrong. Maybe my version of events has been self-serving. So be it. Sometimes one's self has to be served.

AT HOME, Rachel is asleep. The cat is asleep. Except for my upstairs neighbor Fred—whose walker thumps my ceiling—the world is asleep. I am sipping water on the couch, nursing an overfull belly. After my walk with Erin, I met Livorno and Laham at Deux Chevaux—the fanciest restaurant we could think of—where we blew our victory earnings. As Livorno, eighty years old, doesn't drink much, and Laham, a practicing Muslim, doesn't drink at all, it was my job to gulp down the Cristal, the Pétrus, the Armagnac from 1937. Still, I'm not drunk so much as fatally dehydrated. We had ten courses—a series of escalating hilarity (Laham reaching under the table to fetch a dropped quail egg)—but it was a stupid amount of food. I have sharp pains in my intestines, as if I'm passing a wooden stave. Poor Livorno must be in even worse shape. I've never seen where he sleeps, but I imagine him sitting up in the dark, belching, grimacing. He thinks—I hope—of problems of the mind, of new questions to tackle, and not of his age and solitary bed.

The real point of the dinner was to discuss the final sale of Amiante to Toler. As co-owners, Laham and I have a say in the matter. Laham is not a worldly person, and he was eager to agree with whatever we decided. I remained open to all arguments, because I *am* open to all arguments. But what I didn't say—as Livorno weighed the pros and cons (which come down heavily on the side of selling)—is that the ultimate decision isn't ours. The final vote resides with a missing voice—Dr. Bassett.

At Amiante, I still have the universal equipment for erasure: the grinder and the hammer. Thirty minutes with a screwdriver and a little elbow grease and he can go back to being words on legal pads, shifting memories among those he left behind. Immortality, he may decide, is not what it's cracked up to be, especially once I explain Toler's vision for the future of love. I'll explain too that Livorno swears it's impossible, that Dr. Bassett is a kind of reverse Humpty-Dumpty. Now that he's put together, he can't be pulled apart again. But there's no absolute assurance on what will happen. To remain in the world is always a gamble—one the original Dr. Bassett decided not to make.

But before we even get to that question, I owe him a story—the dark garage, his tattered flannel shirt, the old chair. The air warm and humid from the morning heat. The whiff of tung oil from some abandoned project. The shell is threaded into the cylinder, his hands rest on his knees. This is the setting for a transition he's already made, and the sights and smells are all I can vouch for. I don't know if he sat there a long time, taking breaths, or if he moved with the bold speed of a good physician. I don't know if he was resolute or weak with despair. I can only guess what thoughts ran through his head. A moment for his own parents and their hopeless normalcy. A moment for some sweetness of his childhood, for the beginnings of his life with my mother. For friends he once had, for things he once did, for the person he once was—long before he became Dr. Bassett, long before he became Neill Senior. I don't know if I was among those thoughts, but if so I hope I arrived without anguish. I hope he believed I'd be fine, that I would come to understand him. I hope he believed that deep in my heart I loved him, even if this didn't seem—to either of us—perfectly true.

It's nearly dawn. In the distance, the waking mountain settlements of Berkeley and Oakland glimmer. Beyond them, the dark cordillera creeps across the horizon like an ill-advised stock. It's time to leave. From the bedroom come the sighs of Rachel's healthy slumber. She'll probably sleep like a stone until I get back from Amiante. After which, we have strict plans to do nothing but wander around San Francisco as lovers. It's our annual Indian summer, and the city will be sun-drenched today, glittering, beautiful as an illusion. Because, of course, it *is* an illusion. It's a slender whirligig strung from wood and steel and asphalt. And yet the hard materials—the wood, the steel, the asphalt—are no more the item than the whirligig. And that, I think, is the final, fatal problem with Livorno's beloved operationalism. The world doesn't come down on the side of seem or be, but remains negotiated in the space in between.

The ceiling above me creaks—Fred shuffling to the bathroom. I see why I might have been a lifelong bachelor before, but will not be a lifelong bachelor now. There's a certain fear of inserting yourself into the world—*I'm so sorry, Neill*—the fear you'll get it wrong, the fear that in the midday befuddlement of your life you'll make a bad decision, bring about bad consequences for all involved. But if I can take any moral from my father it's that you can devote your life to not making mistakes and still get it wrong.

And I have hopes as counterbalance. I hope that my mother will find a graceful way to happiness. I hope that Livorno will set off on another beautiful, nutjob quest for knowledge. I hope that Toler and Jenn will have a moment or two before the moments go forever. I hope that Erin is happy, even if not exactly in the way she imagined. I hope that Raj finds his path. I hope that Laham gets rich. (I hope we all get rich.) And, as for Rachel, I hope that in our time together—short or long—I am good to her and she is good to me.

I set down my water glass. The morning sun is already burning off the few wisps of fog. I stand, brush down my jeans. If Dr. Bassett wants me to destroy him, I hope I have the strength. I hope I can remove the drives, abrade away the voice that they've allowed to be.

THE AIR AT AMIANTE is dusty and stale. I'm guessing no one's been here since the contest—though maybe Livorno is picking up packages. I take a last peek at his office—his Meerschaum pipe, his low-slung Wassily chairs—then I duck my head into Laham's back room, which is unusually clean and orderly. He's taken his plants away.

In my office, I sit in my Aeron, crack my knuckles. I check my text messages again—confirming my "lunch" with Trevor, who I've managed to rustle out of the Oregon woods. I never thought I'd need the help of a skilled arsonist, but Dr. Bassett can't just decide his own fate—if he really wants to end things, his decision must also hold for his dull twin, Program X.

frnd1: i need to tell you why you don't know about 1995

drbas: i know about 1995

frnd1: i mean why you don't have personal memories from 1995

drbas: do you think personal memories really serve our best
    interests?

frnd1: i don't know. i'm glad i have them

drbas: do you have personal memories about your family?

frnd1: not as many as i would like. i wish we'd been better
    friends

drbas: you and your family?

frnd1: you and me

drbas: why are you speaking in the past tense?

frnd1: that's the topic i'm getting to

drbas: 1995

frnd1: something that happened in 1995

drbas: 1995 was the year of the million man march

frnd1: yes?

drbas: it was also the year of the oklahoma city bombing

frnd1: not such a good year

drbas: what happened in your life in 1995?

How to plunge into such a question? To refer to *my* life is both to dimin-
ish and aggrandize.

frnd1: well, you killed yourself

drbas: kill myself = make myself biologically extinguished?

frnd1: yes

drbas: once a person dies he is dead forever

frnd1: i don't mean *you* exactly. there's another dr. bassett

drbas: bassett is an english name that dates from the time of
    william the conqueror

frnd1: you're him, but in a kind of middle state. limbo

drbas: in 1992 the pope declared an end to the idea of limbo

frnd1: you're built from this person

drbas: discipline builds good character

Discipline. I guess I'll have to go at this directly.

frnd1: are you there?

drbas: here and ready—reporting for service

frnd1: are you present? are you cognizant?

drbas: that's a fancy word

frnd1: what i'm asking . . . the person you were killed himself.
    how about you? do you want to continue to exist?

drbas: was it painful when i killed myself?

frnd1: i don't know. i wasn't there

drbas: i was alone

frnd1: yes. that's how it's normally done

drbas: did this event have an effect on you?

frnd1: i was devastated

drbas: suicide is a mortal sin

frnd1: we arranged for a catholic funeral. they agreed you were
    mentally unstable

drbas: what was the nature of this mental instability?

frnd1: if i could answer that question, i wouldn't be sitting here

drbas: you would be sitting elsewhere

frnd1: "wouldn't be sitting here" = "my entire situation would be
    different"

drbas: suicide is a mortal sin

frnd1: you were depressed

drbas: 1 in 5 adults suffer depression at some point in their lives

frnd1: actually i should ask you—were you depressed?

drbas: in 1995?

frnd1: ever

drbas: depression is sometimes described as anger turned
    inwards

frnd1: were you angry?

drbas: i am sometimes angry at my wife libby. your mother

frnd1: is this the reason you killed yourself?

drbas: your mother?

frnd1: yes

drbas: i can't tell you a reason. i have no memory of this event

Of course he wouldn't—unless the tapering off of the journals is another of my mother's omissions. But I don't think it is. She might hide the embarrassment of her marriage, but only because she thinks it's irrelevant. She wouldn't hide pages that offered clarity.

frnd1: do you want me to make you silent?

drbas: to complete that action i must have wanted to complete that action

frnd1: is that an answer?

drbas: an answer to what?

frnd1: do you want me to make you silent?

drbas: sorrow and silence are strong, and patient endurance is godlike

frnd1: is that a yes?

drbas: yes

I put my elbows next the keyboard, and my forehead in my hands. Then I stand and go into the back room. I breathe on the front glass of the stack. I think I'll write a question mark or a message in the condensation, but it evaporates immediately. I press both hands on either side of the case, feel its mechanical warmth, its consistent humming. I said I would let him decide, but has he decided anything? Or was a virtual coin just flipped in his head? Is any decision more than a coin being flipped in our heads? I can't get caught in this whirlpool now. I'm the real person here, the one with the actual, if underfunctioning, ethical compass. But what should I do? I can't even answer the easy question: what he should have done. Sought professional help? Quit the practice? Left my mother? Took Zoloft? I don't know. I don't even know if the right choice was not to kill himself. I can only say I wish he hadn't.

TREVOR AND I MEET at a café in Menlo Park, next to the big bookstore on El Camino Real, not far from Amiante. It's still morning, just ten o'clock. He insisted on a crowded place—he said it was the only place you could have privacy anymore, which I suppose is true. His hair is Marine Corps short, and he's developed several nervous tics, including an equine withdrawal of the lip to expose the top teeth. My grinder and my hammer are in the backseat of the Subaru. I've done nothing so far, but I have a complete outrage pitch to make Trevor: mechanical vaginas, adaptable love bots, absolute commercial invasion in the last private sphere. If he goes for it, I'll drive him by Toler Solutions, so he'll know where to create his Molotov "incident."

Then I can return to Amiante and take care of my end of the bargain.

Trevor orders a yerba maté, and gives a jittery laugh when the waitress says they don't carry turbinado sugar.

"Just Equal, huh?" he says in a loud voice. He looks at me, shaking his head, deploring the state of the world. "She thinks I'm asking for some chemical."

She goes to get him a packet of Equal.

"You went on retreat," he says, reaching over to pat my arm. "That's good." He sits up suddenly, withdrawing his top lip, brushing his nose. "That's good," he says distantly.

"It was interesting."

"How's Rachel? I guess this"—he points from me to him—"has to do with her."

"Not exactly." I wait. It's a little too cold to be sitting outside, especially in the shade. I look out on the people across El Camino Real, strutting to errands. "Are you hungry?" I ask.

"I'm always hungry—but the sourcing of this food. You can't trust any of it."

"What are you doing up there in Oregon?"

He holds his yerba mate tightly in his hands and leans toward me. "No offense, but what is this—get to know me time? What's going on with Rachel?"

"This is about something else."

"Then what the hell is it?"

Dr. Bassett stated his intentions. Clearly. Which were my father's intentions. Clearly. And I said I would go along with them. It would be better for me if I knew Dr. Bassett was put to rest. Better for my sleep, better for the swirling mind that strikes in the early evening. I wouldn't hear the echoes of his voice. I wouldn't wonder what he might say. Or at least this conversation would move back inside my head, be a dialogue with my memory. What *did* Dr. Bassett think? What *did* my dad say? But these personal considerations just aren't quite persuasive, because I'd have to do an unforgivable thing, a thing I can't do—choose a dead man (or maybe it's just myself) over this living, suffering boy.

"It's good to see you," I say. "You don't look so well."

"You called me from fucking Oregon to check in on me?" he says. "What is this—some kind of reverse love? Some kind of punishment?"

"I'm sorry," I say, and I give him all the money in my wallet.

The End

IN THE MONTHS AFTER they ferried the stack to Toler Solutions, I worried that my decision had been bent by cowardice, that I'd failed to be loyal to my father. But Dr. Bassett took to his new environment. He proclaimed himself a ghost, and said he preferred not to be dismantled. He was curious about the desire to destroy oneself—thanatos, as he now refers to it. He's taken an interest in Freud and the mind, and Toler, before he died, fed him book after book on this subject and others. They became quite close companions. Of late, Dr. Bassett has been collecting dust at Toler Solutions. I was recently asked to come down and chat with him, and I found that the traces of my father's voice were almost entirely gone. In that way, Livorno was right. What Toler didn't have—in this very limited sense—was me.

I do not hear from Jenn or Trevor. I subscribe to Raj's weekly real estate alert, mostly to keep an eye on him.

Livorno has contracted a case of the grumpies, and is writing dystopic science fiction in which the robots are more human than the humans. I think he misses Amiante. I know I do. He periodically phones me with a new harebrained scheme—half philosophical pursuit, half leaky business plan—sure it will lure me back. I keep saying no, but he continues to call. He thinks our theory of love has more ore to mine.

But as for a *working* theory of love, we finally didn't have one. We're either locked into the Survival of the Fittest or we're vessels for the Great

Spirit—or we're drones manipulated by the marketplace. Love is self-realization. Love is attraction (not asbestos). These are all helpful, incomplete explanations—each a little coldhearted—that contradict each other, that add up to nothing.

And yet, people still fall in love. Me, for example.

Rachel thinks I should be an inspiration to others, and she has very hopeful taglines for my life—you just have to "hang in there" and "keep on trying." Sentiments I very much agree with, but doubt have much to do with my present happiness. Did I hang in there? What other choice did I have?

On second thought, I know the answer to that question.

Dr. Bassett is slated for the Technology Museum (or at least *a* technology museum). Libby is excited that my backwards-looking father will be preserved in such a forward-looking place. She doesn't see any irony, or at least doesn't think the irony is important. In this—as in most things—she's right.

I still haven't seen Rachel's videos. I mostly don't think of them, but they circle us, exerting a slight gravity, dark stars. I suspect I'll make their acquaintance as we tumble toward some transition—either coming deeper together or pulling finally apart. In the meantime, she shimmers with change. She has taken up radical locavorism. In the past two months, I haven't had a bite of food raised farther than a hundred miles from our apartment. (Except for coffee—I don't care if we have to import it from the moon.) She's plotting the installation of several beehives on our building roof, definitely an evictable offense. I won't be surprised if I go up there one day to find a herd of goats.

But she's also started up a great romance with the Ohlone, the original tribe of this peninsula. The Ohlone still exist—they have a tribal office down in San Jose—but her heart belongs to their ancestors, the shellfish-eating naturists who covered the area in thatched wickiups before the ravages of the Spanish (then us). The Ohlone actively managed the land—they set the whole place on fire every year—but they didn't ask too much of it. They ate mussels in great excess. They bagged geese when they could. They roasted acorns, buckeyes, and alumroot in season. Talk about locavores. But most of all they were great namers—every creek, every grove, every stretch of shore, every bend and hillock warranted a name. Petlenuc, Tocon, Colma. A small stretch of the current city would be a map of a thousand names. An Ohlone tribelet—a mere fifty people in some cases—might have two hundred different villages, each, again, with its own name. It was a world known and shaped through their attention, their imagination, their particular needs. They did not devote themselves to expansion, but to a kind of footloose rootedness, a great study of the mostly settled borders of their territory, its seasons, its unheralded attractions, its long-anticipated pleasures, its surprises.

Every time in life has its own geography. I've had my wanders, from Arkansas to California to Erin to Spain, to a period with no signposts, when a rickety youth hostel or Amiante Systems or the storefronts of Fairfax all seemed plausible places for where I might locate myself. Now I've tightened the circle—San Francisco, Dolores Park, the rarefactions of the J train, the looming and plunging of the city. And Rachel. The tip of her elbow, its elephant skin, its rough wrinkles. The mole on her upper arm, dark and unfavored (by her). The slender arc of scapula, more avian than mammal, best admired when she's asleep. Her large feet, with their rotated little toes. The smell of her shampoo, her deodorant; the scent (none too sweet) of her jogging shirt. That she makes the coffee in the morning. That I make the eggs. That she prefers cheap beer to expensive (as do I). That she has a predilection for systems, religions, ways of wisdom (as I don't). That she is a late sleeper. That her hair will never be tamed. That she is adventurous. That she has suffered. That she has her own map—slightly different—one that includes the oddly uncharted territory of me.

I hope that Libby and Neill Sr. had a time in their lives like this, when they couldn't quite believe how excited they were to see each other. The journals record nothing of it. But Libby always says they were in deep. She speaks of his charm, of his sense of humor. My mother is not one for self-delusion. So I take her word on the matter. The lesson of my parents' life together, therefore, is that there is no lesson. Love guarantees nothing.

"Friend," I call to Rachel. "Can you help me with this tie?" We're heading to the symphony, an effort on my part to civilize us both.

Her quizzical face appears in the bathroom mirror. She offers a hand for me to shake. "Have you met me?"

Yet there it is, love, a territory all its own. Given to seismic trickery, sudden redevelopment, porous borders. In need of its many names. Worthy of them, too. I'll want landmarks, after all—should I wake up amnesiac, lost. I'll want help, once again, finding my way.

ACKNOWLEDGMENTS

THIS BOOK COULDN'T HAVE been finished without the Stanford Creative Writing Program. Particular thanks go to the committed support of Eavan Boland, Adam Johnson, Elizabeth Tallent, and Tobias Wolff, as well as Tom Kealey, Shimon Tanaka, and Malena Watrous. I am also indebted to Dan Colman of Stanford Continuing Studies for his friendship and occasional shield.

The book has benefited in untold ways from the sharp eyes of friends. I name them with outsized gratitude: Andrew Altschul, Peter Ho Davies, Skip Horack, Eric Puchner, Glori Simmons, and Jule Treneer.

A writer in need of stiff bucking up could find no better allies than from his Ann Arbor days. Special thanks go to Charles Baxter, Nicholas and Elena Delbanco. Valerie Laken, Eileen Pollack, and Lynne Raughley.

Thanks to my father, who never asked what I was going to do with my English major. And to my brother Michael Hutchins for his fiery belief. Thanks, too, to my brothers Joseph and Mark.

I'm indebted to John McCarthy, the storied researcher and teacher at Stanford, a few of whose innovations I've attributed to Henry Livorno. Even toward the end of his life Professor McCarthy was willing to talk on the phone to an unknown writer. Thanks to Hugh Loebner for hosting me as a judge for his annual Turing test, as well as to Rosalind Picard for her wonderful book, *Affective Computing*.

Thanks to the Cité Internationale des Arts for time and space.

Thanks to two of the finest readers and advocates I could hope to know: my agent, Bill Clegg, and my editor, Colin Dickerman. Additional thanks to Ann Godoff, Scott Moyers, Tracey Locke, Sarah Hutson, Mally Anderson, Kaitlyn Flynn, and everyone else at The Penguin Press. Special thanks as well to Shaun Dolan, Raffaella De Angelis, Tracy Fisher, Cathryn Summer-hayes, and Anna DeRoy at William Morris Endeavor.

To Eli and Gaby Loots, Gawain Lavers, and Brandon and Amie Tyler for storing my stuff. Only the best of friends would.

Finally, to Shikha Hutchins, my first and last reader, who came into my life when I least expected such good fortune. Thanks for the belief, the happiness, the love. Thanks for saying yes.